Do You See Me Now?

Do You See Me Now?

EZEKIEL MURPHY

RESOURCE *Publications* · Eugene, Oregon

DO YOU SEE ME NOW?

Resource Publications
An Imprint of Wipf and Stock Publishers
199 W. 8th Ave., Suite 3
Eugene, OR 97401

www.wipfandstock.com

PAPERBACK ISBN: 978-1-6667-5346-2
HARDCOVER ISBN: 978-1-6667-5347-9
EBOOK ISBN: 978-1-6667-5348-6

09/23/22

For my mum and dad, who have supported my writing and been my parents. Thank you to my mum for reading through my manuscript in-amongst her tight schedule. For my teachers, lecturers, and mentors who have taught me and educated me. To my friends for encouraging me and welcoming me in. Much love to you all.

A special mention to Kyle at Wipf and Stock Publishers for creating such an amazing cover.

PREFACE

<small>HELLO READER.</small>

My name is Ezekiel. I am the author of the simple-to-follow and illustrative story you're holding in your hands. It is most lovely to make your acquaintance. I also go by Zeke if that's easier to say. It brings a smile knowing that you endeavour to read the story that follows (you wouldn't be reading this otherwise), and it is on my heart that you are blessed by the story that finds itself on the pages to follow. This story was gently constructed over eighteen months, in the quiet times after dinner, the breaks from university study, and as a way to pass the time. In those eighteen months, I found myself connecting with and presenting small parts of myself within the characters I wrote. I feel happy when they are happy, sad when they cry, tense when they are tense, and at peace when they are at peace. It has been a delight to incrementally put the following story together, and it is my greatest joy to share it with you. Should you want to hear, I'd like to share the story of how this story was born. You will find that this tale had its birth in year seven NAPLAN.

In Australia, where I call home, we have a National Assessment Program for Literacy and Numeracy (NAPLAN). It starts in year three and concludes in year nine. The objective of this program is to gauge the general aptitude of the next generation of Australians, determining their general strengths and shortcomings. In year seven, we were asked to write a practice short story. I did, though I struggled to keep it within the two or three pages we had to write on. Afterwards, I found myself enjoying the story that I had written. Being in year seven, we were also tasked to do touch-typing practice. So, I thought, "why not do both?" I got about three or four chapters in when it found itself lost to the background of school and life.

In year twelve in 2020, I rediscovered the computer I used to write my story when I couldn't use my school laptop. Originally, I was excited and curious.

That didn't last long.

The plot didn't make sense, the writing was over-the-top, and I didn't know how I enjoyed writing any of it. It was then that I determined, "I can't leave it like this. I can do better than this."

18 months and 96-thousand-and-something words later, I had written a full-length novel.

I remember when I was going through the third chapter, I found myself doubting whether I should complete the story or not. I had done barely any planning besides some thoughts for the first few chapters, half of which I ended up discarding. What kept me going?

My mum.

My mum is legendary with food. It is almost a guarantee that a person will enjoy whatever my mum has chosen to cook (there is only one meal in my entire life that I remember not enjoying). When she was about my age, she and my father were living in Western Australia (where I was born), and my father was a volunteer firefighter. I believe her gift in cooking and food preparation started then, when she started bringing small things to the small get-togethers my dad had with his firefighter friends and their partners.

My mum was nervous then; now she's infamous in her spheres of influence.

She cooked for my brother and my youth group for church, has fed the homeless, cooks enough food to last a family a week when they are sick or grieving, and promises any of her guests that they will not walk away hungry after she feeds them. It's a promise she has yet to fail.

And with that, I kept with my writing. I didn't know what would happen, but I knew that anything was better than not trying at all.

As I wrote, there were two themes I wanted to keep in mind. Firstly, and without question, it had to be engaging. I kept in mind that the modern person has a terribly short attention span. You'll find that the story to follow is written to be simple to understand and follow, with action sequences described succinctly and effectively to assist you, the reader, with being enthralled in the fight scenes.

Next, I wanted it to teach something.

I won't limit you by stating explicitly what I wanted to teach, but I encourage you to learn something from this story. I write from my learnings as a disciple of Christ, but the story doesn't do this overtly. There are concepts that I have applied from Biblical principles, but I have not done this explicitly.

With this said, it is a delight to know that you are reading one of my stories.

Much love,
Ezekiel 'Zeke' Murphy

P.S. it would be incredible to hear from you! I invite you to send an email to authorezekielmurphy@gmail.com; introduce yourself, share your thoughts, and say hi. If you believe I should write a sequel, please say so! I'm excited to hear from you!

PROLOGUE

IT WAS A LOVELY day; the breeze was a little strong, and the temperature a little hot, but it was delightful all the same. It was an excellent time to be outside, but no-one chose to. Paths showed only concrete. Roads showed only tarmac. Everyone was inside. There were no people. No footsteps. No running children. No laughing adults.

It was bare.

It was empty.

Raktaar appreciated the emptiness.

It left no opposition.

It would make for a clean and quick day. He could target the two children he needed to target and have energy to affect the next one. He appreciated days where it was this simple. They were generally intense and demanding. Today was going to be especially draining.

He had to get everything exactly right.

He could imagine what would happen if these children lived unaffected lives; lives unphased by his hands.

It did not go well for him.

He had experienced children *like* this in the past. They were powerful foes.

He wanted to avoid it.

He needed to avoid it.

His only course of action was to ruin these kids. He was left with no other option.

He approached the house on his four pointy legs, each a large arm with a spear-like appendage where a hand would be. Solid, black bone tapped rhythmically on the footpaths. His long torso towered over the mortals he strategically destroyed. His general form looked like a normal human being: midsection with arms, neck, and head. He was once a man with an incredible gift. He was able to do marvelous things with this gift . . . long ago.

He had the opportunity to live a wonderful life, but he chose another way filled with predatory anger. He never regretted it, for he thought little of his disfigured and traumatized soul.

He was always in pain though.

He loathed and delighted in every day; he loved and cried in every moment.

Coming across the house he needed to enter, he smiled, quietly chuckling to himself a little. His grin showed a set of curved, pointed teeth, teeth that were arranged neatly on his top and bottom gums, slobbering with a viscous spit, deep red in color; nothing like human saliva. He glared at the house with his white and red eyes. The white of his eyes showed his undying humanity. The red came from his vile, wicked blood that flowed through him and drove him to do all that he did. He made his approach to the house and climbed over the fence. Breaking it down would not be a dilemma for someone of his strength, but it would raise unwanted attention.

Seeing a neighbor's fence fall on its own accord caused more problems than he wanted to handle.

He made his approach and thought as he walked. He needed to find a large way through. He could make his own entrance, but interacting with the world in any way other than his bone-spear feet allowed others to see him. He had to be subtle. He looked. He waited. *It had to be right,* he thought. He looked some more, wanting something large and already open.

He found it.

A human mortal was walking out the front of the house. The oldest of the two children he was targeting was walking out the front door. *Perfect.* He began moving forward. *She really is an ignoramus, isn't she? I love it when they're ignorant and stupid,* he thought. He quietly chuckled to himself. "Let's have some fun." His voice was deep and menacing. He made haste for the door. He glanced at the girl. She was taking her rubbish to the street; *very colorful rubbish,* Raktaar realized. *She's a creative one. She'll die with fight and life in her. This will be good.* His feet were going through the front door. He crouched as he entered. He was able to squeeze through.

He was in, but–

A creak.

Loud and sudden.

Was that me?

He ceased all motion. There was a boy sitting to his left; his second target. He had heard something. He was looking at where he heard the creak. *Has he seen me?* Raktaar wondered. *No. He would go wild if he could see me. He's currently curious.* His hands tensed into fists. He moved them violently through the air, releasing his anger without hitting anything. Hitting something would make noise. Noise would prove his own sloppiness.

He couldn't have that.

How could I be so stupid! It could only get worse if the boy touched him; if the boy inspected the noise and went to touch him.

Even the slightest touch would cause chaos.

He had watched these children for some time now. They weren't like his other targets. The moment they see him . . . he didn't want to focus on that.

He kept observing the boy. He could see how the boy was looking closely at where he heard the noise. He was staring, squinting, concentrating. *He's seen me. I'm dead.* He put his head in his hands, letting it hang. *One mistake and you . . .* he looked up to be sure.

The young boy shrugged.

He thought nothing of the noise.

Raktaar relaxed.

He breathed out in complete silence, letting his arms hang and relax. He moved his feet slowly, being sure not to make any more noise. He made his approach to the boy, noticing how the young boy was working on a great number of small robots.

He was intrigued.

He moved closer, realizing that he had to be more careful than normal. There were randomly scattered patches where he could put his feet, but the floor was smothered in these tiny machines.

His knees were near his chest to get so low, bending forward to get lower still.

The robots were incredibly small.

The boy required magnifying glasses to see them, his eyes as big as Raktaar's hands.

The glasses were not the finest quality. He realized the boy had made them. *Scratched edges. Scrap parts. He is only young . . . he made glasses specifically for this project. Such care for his work.* Raktaar smiled to himself. *I like this kid.* It reminded him of when he was younger; the passion for his gift. He was able to remember some fragments of his youth. There was some good . . . he didn't think much on it. His youth had brought him to where he was; a lord and a slave to himself.

He quietly sighed.

He thought to investigate the boy's work. The boy could fit a small squad of these small robots on his fingertip. Four legs on each robot. A square body. *They look like my legs,* he realized. He couldn't make out anything else, but he admired it nonetheless. He enjoyed watching the boy work. *Such focus. Such commitment. Such craftsmanship. He really is bright, isn't he?* His mind went back to the girl with the colorful rubbish. *I knew these children weren't normal. I had no knowledge that they were so incredible in their gifts. They glow so brightly.*

After many years of vile, wicked blood flowing through his body, his eyes earned the sight of a light that came from certain human mortals. This light only came from highly capable individuals; individuals that change the world so wonderfully. It glowed strongest from what made them special. The boy glowed a soft yellow all over, his head and hands shining particularly nicely. He remembered the girl's light glowed the same way, her heart and chest also glowing brightly. It had a depth in her chest unlike anything he'd seen before, as if from her shoulders to her midback was somehow a gift in itself.

He always enjoyed watching human mortals with this glow make use of what made them special, for it was wonderful to watch them work. They spent most of their lives harnessing what made them so incredible. Always sharpening. Always training. Always practicing.

Raktaar was like that long ago.

He had a gift that was so wonderfully unique. He remembered how much he enjoyed his gift. He did so many amazing things with his gift.

That had died with his human body.

He connected with these two children. *They're both like younger versions of myself.* He smiled at first, then frowned. He breathed out slowly and deeply. *I can't have that.* He knew they would threaten all he had done. *They are an issue.* He sighed a quiet sigh. *I'm beginning to like these kids. It's a shame I need to horrify them.*

He sighed a quiet sigh.

He smiled.

I'll enjoy killing them though.

He took a deep breath.

I need their blood to live.

He began his extraction.

He envisioned all the horrible things this boy could do with these robots, something that took very little time. The boy could overpower another human mortal without even trying. He could fulfill so many ravenous fantasies—a weakness he could exploit in all male human mortals. He directed these thoughts into his left arm. It glowed an intimidating red, beginning at his shoulder and flowing down; down to his bone-spear fingertips.

His joints had flesh and ligaments, but everywhere else was terribly wrong. His fingers were almost bone, their tips like his feet. His arms had patched skin exposing grey flesh, brought about by many centuries of lone-liness; a life struck dead with neglect.

He intensely venged against all that he did. He had done so many things; so many hurtful things . . .

But he laughed a quiet laugh, and he smiled a little smile, and he en-joyed all of it.

He delighted in everything that he did. He basked in the screams and the blood and the near-immortal life. He could live forever and feel alive with every day . . . so he tells himself.

He went back to the boy.

He always started subtle with his introduction of despair when ru-ining someone. Ideas brought fear and disorientation. They were exposed. Vulnerable. Open. Truly themselves. He knew they were ripe for harvesting when the slightest noise brought overwhelming terror. It all started with in-jecting these concepts, the collection of which grew closer to his fingertips.

He put them very close to the boy's head. Thought planting only worked with near touch. *Too far and it won't work. Too close and I'll touch the boy.* He breathed deeply. *Careful now. Slowly. Gently. Steady now.* The glow released from his arm into the boy, the red smeared through the yel-low and made a dark orange. He had removed the yellow. It would never be so bright as before. There would always be a stream of red through his thoughts. *No matter what happens today, there's a cap on how great you can be.* The boy would never see the infecting glow, but he felt it.

His face first showed shock.

Then it twisted into disgust.

He's an older kid, Raktaar thought. *He's years away from being a young man. He can feel the pain in these visions but he won't understand half of it.* He smiled. *Children will always feel pain even when they don't understand it.*

The boy began to scream. The more the thoughts seeped through, the more he saw what was happening, the louder his cries were. He put his hands on his forehead. He wanted these images and sounds to stop. Raktaar could see the pain on his small face. *It's working.*

The boy's older sister came to comfort him.

Raktaar knew that she had come in from getting rid of her artistic remains a while ago and went to her room; he always kept a visual on where everyone was. He had learned to be careful of that.

He watched how the sister comforted her brother. She was much older than the brother; she was becoming a young woman. She would fully ma-ture in a few years, but she wasn't very skilled at caring for her brother in the way that he needed it. "What's the matter Boris?"

He kept on screaming and crying, really sensing the fear and horror in these visions.

She asked again, "What's the matter Boris? You're not talking with me." She paused. She was getting frustrated. "Talk to me Boris!"

He didn't respond.

She had no idea what was going through Boris' head.

Raktaar observed the interaction between the siblings. *She would react with much more severity. She would understand more of what he was thinking.*

She then had an idea.

She didn't know how else to help her brother, but she knew this would work. It always worked. "Hey Boris. You wanna show me your little robots–" He aggressively scooped and threw the little critters by the handful into the wall. Tanya was confused. *He's never like this with his machines.* "Boris! What are you doing! You've put so much work into them!"

He wasn't listening.

Tanya wasn't liking this. *This is not Boris.* She had no idea what was happening. "Stop it Boris! You're scaring me."

The boy looked up.

He heard that he was scaring his older sister.

That couldn't have been better timed, Raktaar thought. He smiled

Just at that moment, Boris was realizing that he was the one doing all the atrocities he'd been experiencing.

He controlled the robots tearing men apart.

He was hurting wonderful women like his sister.

He was the man in his head doing everything he wanted to stop.

He was the monster.

Only monsters scare their sisters, Boris thought.

Raktaar smiled to himself yet again.

The boy realized he was a monster because of his creation.

The boy lost it.

He pushed his sister with a solid shove. She landed on her back. She breathed quickly. She was scared. Boris wanted to be left alone. He wanted it all to stop. He wanted to be free. "Boris! Stop! That hurt!"

He'd hurt his sister.

He was becoming the madman in his visions. He began to rock. He hit his head with his hands.

Yes, Raktaar told himself. *It makes no sense does it? How could something so dark be within you?*

He laughed to himself.

He chuckled and enjoyed the fury the boy was holding back. It was a deep laugh, from the belly, despicable in tone. He laughed some more. He always enjoyed this stage. It was so easy for him, and it reminded him of his pleasures. *I can see the life I can get from you–*

He stopped.

Something's not right. Something's out of place. I've done something. He enjoyed the red smeared over the beautiful yellow, but he was tolling an idea in his head.

He was in danger.

He hadn't the knowledge how, but he had made a terrible mistake.

What have I done? he wondered. The back of his head grew warmer.

He didn't like that feeling.

It spread to his left shoulder.

It meant he had done something wrong. He concentrated on that feeling.

It was on his left.

He felt compelled to turn his head. *Whatever's wrong is on my left.* He turned slowly. *What could I have possibly done wrong–*

The girl.

She was looking his way.

She was looking at him.

She was looking into his eyes.

He could feel the little girl looking *into* him. No-one had ever looked into his eyes so deeply. She couldn't process what she saw. It made no sense to her. She could only stare with a pale face; she didn't breathe, she didn't move. She had no idea who or what he was; she was terrified. Everything crashed together in his head. *My laugh.* He hit his forehead with his hands. *She could see me because of my laugh! Why did I laugh!*

His face dropped.

He breathed out.

He closed his eyes.

It was years since anyone had seen him.

It royally disturbed everything he needed to do.

Human mortals found power when they could see him. They could see what was wrong with them. They could always see him after then. They knew that it wasn't them that was infected with immorality; they were victims.

Of him.

A great part of his strength was his secrecy. They were weak when he wasn't seen; critical when his existence wasn't even heard of.

The rest of his strength came from sheer muscle, strengthened, hardened, and powered by all he did. Centuries of ruin give a mighty fuel to the body at a hefty cost. Speed and strength were vital in this line of work.

He had to be fast.

She began to scream. She didn't know how to react to this thing in her home.

He did.

His face bore the face of one ready to slay.

He knew what he had to do.

He noted the girl's height. She was much shorter than him. *I can use that.* He rose slowly with his legs, straightened his back, and prepared himself. He towered over the girl, making himself terrifyingly tall and so much bigger than her, knowing he had to be ready for any circumstance. *These children won't die without defending themselves.* He had learned never to underestimate children who glowed as strongly as these two. Everything he did needed to be precise and deliberate. *Chest out. Arms out. Fingers curled. Stance open. Back hunched towards her. Teeth and tongue out. Eyes wide open.* The little girl's lungs had never worked so hard. Her little heart was about to quit on her. He could feel it.

Her eyes started to water. He was so close to scaring her to death.

He paused.

He relaxed a little.

She's so small and sweet.

He closed his eyes.

He breathed in, his nose feeling the air flow through.

He breathed out; the air navigated through the gaps in his teeth.

His eyes opened.

They were redder than normal.

I have to do it. I have to get her blood.

He began his approach.

He lowered himself down, getting his eyeline down to the girl's. He let his tongue hang floppily. He maintained a fixed distance. The trick was to *intensely* scare them. He got the most sludge that way. That was what he needed. *Beautiful red sludge.* He needed that sludge to live.

She decided to move slowly from this thing.

He slowly moved with her.

She moved quickly.

He did the same.

Sudden move to her right.

He followed.

The other way.

He maintained his distance.

She got the message that she couldn't outrun him. He was faster than her. She had no idea what she could do. She screamed louder. His ears were mellowing in it. He had not heard a greater sound.

He wouldn't enjoy it for long.

She had grown tired of the intimidation.

She was not one to easily submit to something greater than herself. She kept a solid stare but was thinking only through impulses. She was crawling back, wanting to find something to hurt this thing scaring her. She could feel the wall getting close.

She couldn't go much further.

She could do nothing but keep her distance. Her feet moved her along, her hands helping. She hoped and waited that something hard would get in reach.

She reached the wall.

It was cold on her back.

She pushed into it.

It didn't move.

It reminded her that she couldn't escape.

She couldn't go anywhere.

Raktaar slowly approached.

He wanted to drag the fear as long as he could; he had one chance to get the sludge from her.

Her hands were feeling around, keeping eye contact as best she could. Her hands were frantically feeling around for something to use. Anything would do. She had no idea what else to do.

She could see this thing get closer. She knew this would be it. This thing was going to kill her. She turned away. It was too hard to look into such horrible eyes so close.

Wait!

She felt something.

It was solid.

Firm.

Throwable.

She liked it.

She reached for it, trying to be as subtle as possible. She grabbed a handful of this solid rescuer and threw it to his face.

She realized it was one of Boris' screwdrivers.

The handle was heading directly to the thing's eye.

He hadn't been observant enough to his surroundings to realize; he was so focused on terrifying the little girl.

The handle connected with his eye. He reeled backwards, lost his footing, and collapsed onto a nearby chair.

His weight forced the chair to crumble under him. Boris immediately looked up out of instincts to see what was happening; his ears heard danger.

Raktaar had ruined his entire mission.

He was off his solid spear feet, his rotting torso on the ground. *They can both see me!*

Boris also didn't know how to react with this creature in their living room. He had a similar reaction to his sister, but something clicked.

He knew that those visions he was experiencing weren't his. Everything that he'd been living in his own mind came from the creature lying on the floor; how else could those ideas so persistently stain his head? *That . . . thing . . . is the only one here that could do that.* He grew angry.

Furious.

Enraged.

He was tortured from the inside, and that monster was the one that did it.

He knew what he needed to do.

He flicked a switch on his glasses. He could see much clearer, his eyes were his regular size, and lines and numbers surrounded the edges.

His eyes grew narrow.

His courage surged.

His mind cleared.

His fists tensed.

Let's go! he thought.

Raktaar was finding his footing again. He knew what he needed to do. He had to kill them both.

Now.

I won't get as much red sludge, but I won't die by . . . children. He began to regain himself. His left eye couldn't open, but his right worked well enough. He saw the little girl on his left.

She stood up.

She saw how this thing was collecting itself, readying itself, and wanting to hurt her; to do what he was trying to do before. She made haste for her bedroom, the safest place she knew. She tried to make a wide sweep around him, keeping as much space from him but moving with great energy. She ran with a large stride.

She was almost past him.

She was going, nearing the hallway.

So close–

She wasn't wide enough.

Raktaar was on his feet and jumped, his unusual legs launching him far and hard. He dived towards the girl, arms out, his face twisted with fury.

He grabbed her shoulders, jumped over her, landed into the wall to the girl's right, and forced the girl to fly up and over him.

She was down.

She couldn't think clearly; her head had met the wall unpleasantly. He was on his side, also collecting himself. *Walls are harder than I remember.*

She tried to get up.

He pulled her leg from under her.

She fell.

Dazed, she didn't have the alertness to react.

He used this.

He crawled over to her. His fingers were sharp; he saw her shoulders begin to bleed from where he gripped. Losing blood was what allowed him to get his sludge.

When under fear, any warm-blooded creature would give this sludge in their blood. He could reduce it and refine it, leaving a tar that he used to continue his work.

He needed more blood; her midsection was a sack of it.

He prepared his fingers. He needed as much blood from as little effort, though he wasn't safe enough to extract it now. *The kill stroke: down the chest.* He got his hands near her shoulders. He extended his pointer fingers and pressed harder than the rest of his fingers. His other fingers made smaller scratches on her small chest with a large, deep cut down her center.

He finished the slice. The slightest move and her organs would make an appearance.

He had found they could feel this and they would not move. It also made his extraction easier.

I'm so close! Almost there–

He was abruptly interrupted. His skin howled with pain.

He had never felt so mortally afflicted.

He looked down.

Those things!

The boy's small grey machines covered his body. They started with his legs and worked up; his feet were held in place by these electronic vermin. He could not move; he could not escape.

Boris had found his own bravery.

His chest.

His steel.

He could control all the robots he made and see how best to use them. *Mech-Ants,* he called them. Powerful in numbers, they congregated over the creature's body, their tiny claws ripping his skin.

Boris was saving his sister.

He did it with a smile. He had never wanted to destroy something so violently, yet his sister needed her protection.

I'm her guardian.

Goosebumps covered his skin, his jaw was tight, his muscles were tensed, his breathing was fast, and his eyes were narrowed.

He was enraged.

"Enough!" he shouted.

Raktaar failed his mission.

These children glowed too strongly for secrecy not to be his primary weapon. He did all he could to flee this burning, searing pain. He lifted his legs by any means he could, but the little machines pinned his feet to the floor. He swept them away from his arms, but more filled its place. *I'm drowning in a molasses of little machines!*

He swept some more.

More robots filled their place.

They were on his hands now, spreading up his arms. *I'm running out of options.*

There was one left.

He had to eliminate these pests, and he now knew exactly how. He remembered how the red glow he used to infect the young boy could also be directed out. It was a strong field that shoved anything away. It would make him safe. He could blast them away from his feet and make for an escape.

He harnessed his pain, his anger, and his helplessness into his feet, the red glow brewing in his trapped limbs. The glow was brightening. His skin was still being torn from him, his hands were still clenched, his roar was still heard. He felt how close these things were to getting him; he didn't have much more to give. He felt all his apathy and despair brew at his feet.

He was ready.

He pushed the red glow into the ground.

The blast shot outwards.

The Mech-Ants flew everywhere, a shockwave of little metal shards.

Boris' glasses saw this coming: a collection of energy always meant something was about to happen. He dropped behind the couch and found a shield for the blast. It wasn't strong structurally, but the Mech-Ants were flying blades to the skin at that speed—nothing more. The couch took all the shrapnel.

He was safe.

Tanya had no cover.

She couldn't protect herself from the cyclone of metal.

She saw that something was about to happen. She saw the thing's legs glow. She felt that she needed to move, but the cool on her back reminded her again that there was no escape. She tried to get up, but stopped the moment she felt the weirdest sensation she ever felt. She didn't like it, and her body was telling her to stay where she was. She knew she needed to move, but she physically couldn't find the strength to get up. She covered her face with her hands and brought her legs up.

She braced and prepared.

She squealed.

She knew this would hurt.

THE BLAST PHASED THEM both. It was a red explosion. No smoke. No other colors. A field of anger large enough to get the Mech-Ants away from Raktaar. It took some force to remove these strong things, but he was safe. He saw how they were both stunned. He thought it best to make this the time to get out. Walking through the door, he stopped to make sure no-one else would see him. *Those other children will be for another day. I need to rest . . .* he made his way down the empty pathway and alongside the empty road. He left Boris to care for Tanya.

Boris . . . what a name. What a kid.

He stopped.

He looked back.

I'll remember him.

BORIS WAS ABLE TO get to his feet. He could see how his Mech-Ants were all over the floor and walls, his wonderful creation splattered everywhere—it was like it meant nothing. He didn't appreciate it. He had put so much effort into these things.

Now it was nothing.

Then he saw his sister.

"Tanya? Tanya!" He stepped up and over the couch, ran to his sister, wanting to see what was wrong with her. Her skin was barely being held together. Her face was in almost good shape, but the rest of her body flaked apart. He had no idea what to do. He had never seen such a frenzy of red.

His Mech-Ants couldn't help him.

His parents couldn't help him.

I have to save her. By myself.

He had no idea how to help her.

Then. An idea.

He bolted to the first aid pack in his room. "There's a lot of long bandages in there. I can wrap them around her. It's the only thing I can do . . . it's the only thing I know to do." He got all the bandages he could.

He sprinted back.

Starting at her arms, he held the bandage and wrapped as tight as he could. He wasn't sure how the skin was still holding on. The bandage would keep her from falling apart. "This will hold you together Tanya." He continued to wrap. He had both of her arms done.

Two bandages down.

Two left.

Legs next.

He wrapped her legs. At this point, his hands and forearms were covered in her blood. He had never seen his sister so vulnerable, nor had he ever been so dirty. He needed someone to help him, to teach him.

He was only a boy.

He did his best to ignore the mess on his arms.

His breathing quickened.

His eyes watered.

What am I supposed to do? Am I doing this right? He did his best to slow his breathing. He knew he had to focus. This was all he could do.

This is what he knew he needed to do

Her legs were almost done and the fear in his veins started to lower. He moved back to see all of Tanya. *Both arms and legs covered in white . . . red . . . bandage. Midsection–*

He thought.

He wondered.

He needed to wrap her in something.

An idea.

He jumped up to get two towels. There were two in particular that would help him: his parents' towels. They were large and wide, perfect for wrapping her midsection. He raced back, a towel in both hands. On his knees, he continued to help his sister. *Almost done. You'll make it Tanya. You have to make it.* He laid both towels down, one on the other. He grabbed as high as he could on the bandage on her arms, lifting her forward and up enough to get her entire back off the wall. He dragged her on her feet, laying her back down on the towels on the far-left edge. He began to swaddle her, wrapping the towels over then under. Over then under again. He made sure it was tight; tight meant she was being held together the best she could. The final round of towel wrapping didn't reach to get under her, so he rested it on top. She was going to survive. *You're going to be okay Tanya.*

She was going to live.

He knew it.

He couldn't feel calm though.

It was a really weird morning. He had no idea what that beast was. He didn't know how it could make his robots do *this* to his sister.

He needed his sister.

He needed someone.

Anyone.

He needed to be held, to be told that he had done well. All he had was his sister.

He realized he could still hold her. He lifted her up, sitting her in his lap.

Then the arm bandages began to unravel.

Boris freaked.

He threw his arms to the bandages, stretching them and tightening them as much as he could without hurting his sister.

His breathing rose dramatically; his chest rising and falling rapidly.

He then felt calm.

Trying again to hold his sister, he lifted her up, slower than last time. He was gentle; he didn't want everything to unravel. He held her, arms around her; his right cheek against her left. He held her tight. Tears began to stream down his nose and cheeks. He wanted his sister to be okay. He needed her to be okay. He couldn't live without her. He loved her. "Please be okay Tanya. Please be okay."

HE WAS LIKE THIS for some time. He was waiting for someone to come and help. *Surely someone would have heard the blast,* he thought. It was morning when this all happened. Morning slowly became midday. The sands in the hourglass of time didn't want to run with gravity as hastily today. They knew that falling to the next chamber would mean helping Boris. It would mean comfort to him.

They didn't want that.

They grasped as long as they could before falling.

The sun had a different treatment towards him as well.

Generally, it rose with merriment. It rejoiced upon arising from the ground, a soft-edge disk blasting a wonderful 'good morning' to anyone that could see.

It knew it was mighty, but it also knew its place beneath the falling sand. The sand did not fall with haste; the sun did not rise with haste.

Boris had felt both of this. He felt how nobody knew what had happened. He felt how excruciatingly long it took for the day to go by. He then realized he would have to try and explain to another set of ears what had happened that morning.

Tanya had it easier: she could visually express her pain and hurt.

Boris wasn't gifted in such ways. He would have a harder time expressing what he saw and felt.

To Tanya and Boris, that day was to be remembered as 'The Day'.

'The Day' saw something else happen.

A white flower with large petals and a small stem found itself growing behind Boris on the outside of the wall. It was in the cool of the house's shade, and the grass around it nearly hid the small item of flora.

This helped to hide how the flower wasn't rooted in the ground.

Being behind the house, its glow was also hidden.

The flower sensed that Tanya required medical assistance. It too sensed Boris' stress.

The bandages worked, but it would only delay the incredible bleeding that Tanya was experiencing.

It sent a pulse, then resumed its normal glow.

It slowed Tanya's bleeding and started healing her skin, knowing such a blast with such nasty shrapnel is lethal. It started to reconnect what skin was left, and most importantly healed the large cut down her midsection, keeping her organs inside.

Having started to heal Tanya, knowing her body could now fight its way to recovery, it knew what it needed to do next.

It unclicked its petals from its stem and started flying up, spinning the petals around its stem. It caught itself in the breeze, and rode the wind. As it flew, it could see Raktaar walking away on the footpaths.

The flower pulsed.

It spoke to itself in a deep man's voice.

"It has begun."

CHAPTER 1

SWORD IN THE RIGHT, left hand free, Boris fell to his knees.

He could no longer see his shirt through the blood and dirt. His hot breath couldn't feed the savage beasts his lungs had become.

HE MOUNTED HIS DEFENSE at dusk, well-aware that the night had awaited numerous methods of thwarting his strength. He had prepared himself for a long night, unaware that it would drain his drive to fight as much as it did.

He remembered when the sun lay to rest at dusk. Darkness seeped through the plains; an attack was mounting. He had found that the land's simplicity and calmness was free of the urban black, grey, and white. It was pure, untouched wilderness. So, when the vivacious green before him fell victim to the sun's descent into the ground, he stopped. He had to prepare himself. He closed his eyes.

He breathed.

One long breath in.

One.

One long breath out.

Two.

Another long breath in.

Three.

Another long breath out.

Four.

His eyes opened.

Creatures ascended from the sun's slumbering place.

Winged beasts made their flight, their wrinkled wings flapping violently. Vile faces with black eyes. Bare ribs breaking the skin. What kept their bodies together peeled from its host, giving up on concealing the rotting flesh beneath. Legs much like a human's with the feet ripped from their ankles; sad, unhealed stubs screaming hurt up the creature's legs with every pace. The farewell the sun projected to the awed audience of the world shrouded behind the enormity of the onslaught. The horizon spanned with these abominations. Their ferocity bred the closer they got to Boris. He could feel the wind from their wings pressing against him. They were charging with ravage haste. Boris' heartbeat grew faster; the drum within gaining rhythm, sounding him, calling him for action.

It was not the horn of fear that blew.

It was the siren of anger.

He had bonded with these hills. He didn't know why, but he loved this place. He yearned for any moment to stay in communion with this place.

He was going to protect this place with everything he had.

His ears were shrieking with the wild passion that ran through him. His eyes focused on the closest creature, ready to slay it. It grew larger the closer it got. Hairy wings beating on a broken back, a snarl let loose a flapping tongue dripping with red sludge. His right hand held fast his weapon; the white of his knuckles fueled by the visible veins in his wrist.

He was ready.

He caught the stare of the closest creature. Its black eyes dripped with fear and hatred. Its mouth opened as it got closer: wide, large, and black. Its teeth were ripped from animals born to devour flesh and driven into its gums.

Its face wasn't human anymore.

These creatures were broken and darkened, twisted and without recognition; they weren't part of mankind anymore.

It was getting closer. It tilted his head. It wanted to maul him, to ruin him, to devour him.

Boris raised his sword.

Let's go.

The creature made a dive to his head.

Boris had parried it just before it could even think about evading. It flew into the sword, sliced between its jaws. The whole creature split in two, crash landing behind him.

Boris felt almost nothing. His sword was sharpened by magma rocks and compressed by the depths of the deepest waters. He knew that it could handle the armada that flew towards him.

He relied on the creature's weight to drive their jaws onto his sword, leaving them in half and him fueled for battle. When they came in greater numbers, he would slash them in half such that he had time to react to the next winged creature that came at him. Over and over, he did this. Creature after creature flying into his sword, corpse after corpse lying behind him. Over and over this happened.

The other winged post-humans flew around Boris, creating as much commotion and distraction as they could. They wanted to extend his suffering to tire their target.

Then they would go for the kill.

He started strong.

He could perfectly maim every creature that made their attack. He knew that every creature behind him was dead, and he had faith they wouldn't decide to attack from behind him. Over and over, he did this. He could see the rotting skin, smell their filth, hear the sword cutting through the creature's bone and flesh. Over and over, he felt this.

His eyes began to die in their vision, unable to keep them at rest for more than the smallest of moments. He could feel them strain with every movement, and the frantic flying of the creatures around him. He had no idea how long it had been since the sun set, and there was a glow around him when the moon launched into the sky. It was staring into Boris, feeding the weakness in his human body. It wanted to use up whatever Boris had left in his mind. His mind did nothing but plan the path of the creature and hold firm while it killed itself on his sword, each suicide leaving some splatters of its red blood, thick and gluggy. He was drenched in what had originally kept these creatures mobile and was powdered from the storm of dust these creatures created with their flight.

The blood was getting sticky. He had to focus on moving harder with each motion. He felt how little he had left to give. He saw how many he still needed to slay.

His demise had begun.

He began to miss their jaws and shoulders and clear their wings or a side of their head, rarely able to slice a whole creature in half like before.

He felt the fatigue of battle.

The creatures howled in pain upon their forceful collision with the Earth, for they weren't dead when they contacted the ground. They regained their strength when they realized that they were still alive. They had a renewed anger for this absurdity of a human. They couldn't determine what had kept him fighting. They knew that he should have given up simply by seeing them like all their other victims. They crawled to Boris, shrieking from the fire shooting up their broken, unhealed limbs. Boris heard the roars from behind him. He felt his legs and arms telling him to stop; they could not go on.

He dropped to his knees.

His lungs were a monster wanting more air. He raised his sword when he could, but it did nothing. It only shielded the abominations.

It didn't stop them.

It didn't discourage them.

He collapsed face first and let go of his sword.

He had done his all.

He could give no more.

His spirit could not enact its will through the dying vessel of his body; yet, it had served him well and brought honor to the land he wanted to protect.

Then he saw something with real life that was not yet touched by the creatures he slayed.

He noticed a patch of grass within arm's reach. Small with jagged boundaries, he noticed how alive and green it was. He noticed how it stood strong and firm against all that wanted to bring it harm. He used what he could to extend his sore arm. He used the last of his reserves to stroke the blades of nature. He knew that these little things would always slice deeper and harder than his sword could ever reach.

He felt them.

They were soft and flexible.

Real, proper grass.

He delighted in its life.

He was satisfied with how this land still inspired him.

A creature he maimed was crawling towards him. It was the first to reach him. Boris could see it, but he could do nothing. His mind wanted to flee, but his body wouldn't follow. His brain told his muscles to get up, to ready themselves, to not be weak.

His muscles couldn't follow their orders.

They lay on the ground.

They didn't want to move.

They didn't care if they died.

They knew they had done their best. They knew they could not do any more than that.

The creature's face was in line with his. Its mouth opened. It latched onto his arm with a powerful bite.

He could feel its teeth in his muscles, each pointed pain bringer digging into his skin.

Then it bit into his bone.

He sat up with violent speed.

He drove his hands hard into his bed, breathing harder and quicker. He started to calm down after the initial scare. He felt the mattress' springs beneath him. He felt his pajamas on his skin. He felt the cool of his room and the warmth of his blankets.

He slowly gained the realization that all he had done, everything that he had been put through, was the darkest, weirdest, most frightful dream he'd ever experienced.

He rubbed his eyes with his shaking hands. His head shook at the absurdity his mind had put him through. He recognized that he was in his room. He was certain of that now. He summoned his body to leave his bed, seeing the sun coming from around his curtain. *It's okay. It's safe.* His bare feet felt the solid ground beneath him. The carpet was soft. He liked it. Reality flooded back to him. *I'm back,* he told himself. *I'm okay. I'm alive.*

When he started thinking through what he just experienced, he came to realize that he should have died well before he grew tired. A small group would have overpowered him, and any of the creatures he killed would be replaced almost instantly.

Creatures I killed, he laughed to himself. *I didn't do anything. I was dreaming a freak of a dream.*

He then saw something fly by his bedroom window outside.

A flower with large white petals and a small green stem coasted on the wind. He didn't think much of it.

After this, he remembered what the day would entail.

He stood up, turned around, and saw his desk. He side-stepped and walked sideways between his bed and his always messy desk. He then opened his door, covered in plans and important pieces of paper, and began his day.

He first saw his sister Tanya: his older sibling by a number of years, she was always taller than him and had always been stronger. Her hands, legs, and arms were littered with scars from her younger years. The worst were hidden by the school shirt she wore—the nastiest rested behind her tie.

They smiled upon seeing each other.

They were close.

What Tanya bore on her skin, Boris dragged with his heart and mind.

He remembered The Day every time he saw those scars. He had not shown his sister more care than on that day. They were almost inseparable since then.

That day changed them.

Forged them.

Inspired them to be better.

They gave each other a hug, embracing another day where they could enjoy the other's company. They always appreciated that. He gave his sister a kiss on the cheek. She gave one on his forehead. He continued to the bathroom, where much needed water could be splashed on his face and cool his warm chest. He could feel the heat leave his body. He felt cooler and calmer.

That's better. He felt ready for the day that would be. His posture straightened. His chest stuck out. Shoulders broad, smile on his face.

He was ready.

His routine was not much different than any other morning: his Mech-Ants would prepare him a bowl of cereal, his wardrobe held and prepared his uniform for him, a candy that dissolved plaque rested by his watch, and his mum passed a lunch to him on their way to school. It had taken him years to establish this setup, using whatever he could find to add to it whenever he could, and he appreciated how easy it made his morning. It helped him move on and go about each day. Walking with Tanya was particularly helpful for him.

They walked to school together. Every day. Side by side, talking and enjoying the morning. He was in a light green formal short-sleeved shirt with long black pants. She wore a grey knee-length pleated skirt and a white shirt bearing a grey tie, proclaiming the school crest—worn only by student leaders.

They had arrived at the school gates; large, black, and intricate in detail. A usual day for them both, save for one man and one movement.

Boris kept casual pace as he crossed between the sandstone brick barrier that was the school walls when he felt his right shoulder be drawn back with no-one close enough to touch him. He saw nothing touch his shoulder, but was certain something had pulled it back. He felt forced to turn his head with his shoulder. Something strange caught his eye. He saw, next to the gate hinge, a bald man who had donned a suit of dark red blazer, pants, and darker-than-the-blazer tie. His white shirt was as white as one could imagine. His forehead bore the mark of a slashed vertical line. The cut was years old but had a rough and scratchy outline to them. *After all this time?* he thought to himself. *They should have smoothed out by now.*

He felt something off about the individual.

He didn't like him.

Something isn't right.

He closed his eyes. He shook his head.

When his eyes opened, he could not find the man.

He breathed heavily out of his nose. He knew that wasn't normal, but he didn't know what else to think. He shrugged his shoulders, and went to join Tanya.

He had to look to see her. He found her some distance away. Her stance was wide. Her hands were open, showing someone that they were empty. A circle was being made around her, wedging apart the inbound students. He arrived with apprehension.

A young man who Boris knew had been tripped on the steps leading to the community of school buildings. A classmate of Tanya's lent over the young man with a stick in his left hand.

The end of this stick saw it tipped with a red sludge.

The young man was shorter than Boris. The thickest of glasses sat on bulging, disfigured skin from a house fire he lived through as an even younger boy.

He lost his right arm that day.

Both his parents too.

He was never the same since then.

Patrick was his name.

Boris always had time for Patrick.

They were good friends.

On top of Patrick was a young man of much larger build. Arms and legs ravaged with hair and muscle. The broadest of chests and shoulders joined his weapons together, the command center of which coated with red, curly hair. The command center controlled dark, sad eyes and bore a worn face. Tanya knew him as Tony; the school community knew him as Beringei. Upon tripping Patrick, a wide gap was given to Beringei. They didn't want any involvement with Beringei. Any involvement with him brought hurt. Even the teachers at the school knew that Beringei could hurt them.

Always.

Tanya knew that.

She stayed well clear of Beringei. Never talked with him. Never got close to him. Kept her guard up when he was around.

She also thought highly of Tony.

His mother died during his birth; his father was . . . somewhere. None of his extended family wanted him, and he was passed through the hands of at least eight families before his fifth year of life. None of them knew how to raise this screaming child that wanted some care and attention. He didn't know what it meant to be close to another human being—he hadn't been shown closeness himself. His childhood had accumulated to where it was now. Experience after experience compounding his broken heart into ruin, wound after wound inflicted by the people around him.

But not Tanya.

Randomly and without reason, she, one day, gave him half of her lunch when he didn't have any.

He cried himself to sleep that night. He brought so much hate, and no-one had treated him that well.

Ever.

He thought highly of Tanya after that day. He saw a good friend in Tanya.

She spoke, "Listen to me Tony." Her voice was a blend of a mother's and an experienced conflict resolver. "Remember me Tony? Tanya, you're friend. You have a friend Tony." His breath changed in pace. It grew fast then slow. Fast then slow again. Boris had felt that frantic breathing; he knew what it was like to have lungs go rogue on him. They formed a coup against his body's directions.

Tony recognized that he wasn't in control.

He knew that already.

Beringei loved the power.

He had grown in supremacy as the years passed. He was in Tony—Beringei was Tony's internalized identity. They shared control over his body, though share is a stretch of the word. Tony could feel awake and alert, feeling his environment and sensing all that he could sense, and Beringei pulled the levers of anything he wanted to use. Every day was torture for Tony. He did things at random—he sometimes felt unconscious as Beringei manned the post—and was forced to live the punishment. Tony would always suffer even though Beringei would be the one instigating the trouble. Tony wanted to stop. No-one believed him.

No-one but Tanya.

Tanya, he thought. *Good morning. It's always good to see you.*

Tony always thought highly of Tanya. She had become an amazing friend to him.

Beringei also appreciated Tanya.

He lusted over Tanya's fit form. He wanted to use her in so many disgusting fantasies. *The things I could do to you*, he thought. He laughed as he thought. He smiled as he thought.

He was very broken.

He responded to Tanya, "Why would I listen to you?"

"Because I'm your friend Tony." Tanya's heart was beginning to beat stronger for Tony. She wanted this to end well.

She really wanted this to end well.

She could see this end one of two ways: the first allowed everyone to walk away with only a bit more cortisol in their blood. No shalom, but at least they were at ease. The second . . . force. She didn't want to hurt Tony. *You won't hurt Tony*, she told herself. *You're protecting Patrick. You're standing up against Beringei. Do what you need to do. You're in charge here Tanya.*

"Tanya! Please! Help me!" Tony was pulling the stick from Patrick with his right hand, but the stick wouldn't move. The red sludge near its tip wanted to be near its target. His arms wanted the wood against Patrick's throat.

His legs positioned to assist. His chest faced Patrick, screaming intimidation and supremacy. "I don't want to hurt the guy. My leg was just there when he tripped. I didn't want him to fall."

"I know that Tony. I know you don't want to hurt anyone. I know that's all you've been shown. Talk to me Tony. You remember how good it was to talk with someone?"

"I want him out Tanya. I don't want him sharing my room. I don't want to see him in my eyes. I don't want the blood from his hatred on my hands. My hands Tanya! Not his! I got here first. I'm the captain up here!" He pointed to his heart with his right when he said that.

"You are the captain Tony. You'll always be the captain. Beringei wants to feed on power. Power over you. Every day he calls for a mutiny, but you can stop it. You can fight him trying to overturn the chain of command."

"I want to stop him! I know I can stop him Tanya. I know it."

His voice got higher in pitch. His eyes were squinting. Boris had never seen a man of such size tear up in public. He could feel how Tony had lived with this . . . thing . . . inside him for years. He didn't like it. He hated it. He wanted it all to stop. He just didn't know how.

Boris could feel his pain.

He wasn't a bad man like everyone says.

He just needed some help.

Patrick felt the same.

He could see that Tony was being sincere. He appreciated how someone of that size was showing compassion and care. Anyone of such physical fortitude almost always gave him physical torment.

It was hard for Patrick to find friends.

Looking different than everyone else does that to you.

He could also see how Tony really wanted to change.

He had the thought that he could be friends with Tony. He thought that they would make good friends. Broken souls finding a broken friend. *Yes*, he thought. *Someone that hates their life. I can relate here!*

He had an idea. He could help Tony get better. "I forgive you Tony–"

"You have nothing to say to me!"

Beringei's voice.

Deep and dripping with malice.

Darkness was at the helm. His source of despair and ruin had returned.

He was never juvenile with his tormenting. Every hateful act he did was constructed in his twisted mind to permanently scar his victims; he wanted to end them.

To destroy them.

While inexperienced, on rare occasion he was successful; he occasionally drove people to such emptiness where the candle of their life was snuffed by their own hands.

But no-one knew it was him.

Then there were times when he did the snuffing with his own hands.

They were all regarded as rumors.

"You really are pathetic, aren't you?" started Beringei. "You walk along my paths every day, and what do you add to it? You stain this concrete with your arrogant intelligence and these . . . things." He dropped the stick with the sludge tip and picked up Patrick's backpack. He opened it and dropped his calculator, pencils, and everything inside over Patrick's face, a painful rain of plastic and wood. "That's really annoying isn't it? You want me to stop, don't you?" He chuckled, amused at how Patrick was squirming. He had his eyes closed when his stationary was falling on his face, but he couldn't turn away; Beringei used his right hand to hold Patrick's face in place, cracks forming on his glasses.

He then looked Patrick square in the eyes.

Patrick opened his eyes.

All of his attention was in Beringei's hurtful eyes; everything drowned in his stare.

It was toxic.

Terribly, overpoweringly toxic.

He knew it would be all lies. Whatever Beringei was about to say was done with a vile tongue, but his heart wanted to know Beringei's opinion of him. No-one had looked into him as deeply before. He wanted to know what Beringei thought of him more than anything he knew before.

Then Beringei spoke, "You will never amount to anything. You are weak. Pathetic. Kill yourself before I do it for you."

"Beringei!"

"Tanya! How rude! I'm hungry for someone's emptiness, and you interrupt my meal?"

"You don't need to eat Beringei. There are better things to feast on." Her stomach didn't like how she had to say that. *I hate this imagery.*

"Really! You were always so naïve Tanya. The world is a horrible place. Bask in its filth. Delight in your disgust. Oh, it feels so good!"

This was a new use of language for Beringei.

The red sludge on the end of the stick also glowed gently when he said this.

"But there is good out there!" Tanya responded. "Real good! Pure good! The world was created so wonderfully. You don't need to be this. You can be better. You can be kind Beringei."

This took him back.

He hadn't been told that.

You can be kind? This was really tolling his brain. *Why would anyone be kind? It doesn't do anything. Does it? No! Shut up! It does nothing. Life is in the darkness. My chest breeds it.*

Again, the red sludge gently glowed.

He remembered how his chest also collapses in on itself when he takes over Tony. He wondered whether there was any truth in what she was saying. *The issue is, I can beat kids like this flake. It feels so good . . . yeah . . . that feels good.*

"There are better things to plan for." Tanya was digging deep here. She desperately wanted everyone to walk away alright. She had seen what Beringei could do; what Beringei had done with kids before.

She remembered vividly.

She breathed deeply.

She so wanted to avoid that ending.

"You're right . . . there are better things to plan for." Beringei had an idea.

"Yes Beringei! That's the way! You can do some really great things. I know your life will be really great. I really know it. Just walk away."

"My life will be really great?"

"Yes!" She began to walk closer. *Slowly approach. Calm now. Don't startle him.* "Let me help you Beringei."

"You want to help me?" Beringei sounded confused. That was another first.

She was really something.

"I really do, yes. I can help you Beringei. Just let me show you."

Beringei thought this through. She could help him out. He liked where this was going.

"Can you help me with something?" Tanya believed Beringei. *This was really something*, thought Tanya. *He's making progress.*

"Yes Beringei! What is it?"

"Can you pass me that really thick book please? I'll start getting this kid straightened up. He needs to look how he should."

Tanya's stomach felt uneasy about this request. *What was his game?* she wondered. She didn't want to doubt this progress. He was thinking. Contemplating. Wanting to change. She wanted to take this opportunity.

She grabbed the book, giving it to Beringei at arm's reach. She hoped this was going how she thought it would. He dropped Patrick's backpack—in the literal sense—and grabbed the book from Tanya. A thick body of paper, glowing with knowledge and academic wonder.

Beringei felt the weight in his hand.

This will hurt a lot.

"Thank you, Tanya."

He smiled.

Tanya's face dropped with shock.

He laughed.

He turned to face Patrick. Holding him down with his right, he drove the solid weapon across Patrick's face with his left. His glasses flew, bombing the nearby bricks with an explosion of glass. His neck twisted violently. He felt his jaw separate. His left cheek collided with the steps; his skull rammed into the cold slabs of hardened clay that held his body.

Patrick began believing Beringei's lies. *I'm so pathetic. I deserve to be down here.* Beringei laughed and laughed and laughed. He raised his left hand again. Another savage attack to his face. Skin started to flap; blood and spit shot from Patrick's mouth. His gum started to drip. *I won't amount to anything.* Beringei raised his left hand one more time. *I'll finish him with this one. Directly to the temple. Straight to the brain. The blood will be everywhere. He won't be getting up.* His weapon was up. He tossed his weapon gently to obtain a new grip. His torso ready to twist. He made his final blow–

His hair was pulled violently out of his scalp.

His whole body was flung backwards. Tanya had in her hands a handful of Beringei's red hair. She pivoted on the balls of her feet, pulled with her hips, used her left hand to counterbalance, and slammed his head into the ground. She turned her wrist during the maneuver, forcing his ear to collide with the ground—she didn't want to kill him.

Not if she could avoid it.

He stumbled onto his elbows and knees, groaning in pain. Tanya's eyes started to water, "I'm sorry I had to do that Tony. I know you're still in there."

He was, but Tony was on his knees in his mind.

Beringei stood over him, a giant that loomed over a small bug. Beringei was gaining control. Tony knew he needed to get bigger. He tried to make himself bigger, but Beringei was already working on destroying him. Beringei had gotten his fist and raised it high. Tony knew there was nothing he could do in time. He saw how Beringei was distracted from controlling his body. He took control of the vocal cords. He wanted to say one more thing to Tanya.

He wanted her to know how much he appreciated her.

He spoke. "Thank you for being a friend Tanya. I will never forget you. You have helped me keep going."

He breathed deeply.

"Goodbye."

Those were Tony's last words.

He had done his all against Beringei. He could do no more. He surrendered to Beringei's reign; his fist slammed into Tony.

Tony's body collapsed.

He was dead. *He's gone.* This was over. The adrenaline stopped flowing, and her breathing slowed. The shame drenched her.

I hurt him! Why?!

For Patrick and Boris. He was a threat. You neutralized the threat.

He's gone! Tony's given up! I really liked Tony. He was a good friend.

She started to sob.

What have I done?

By now, only Boris and Patrick were with them both. Everyone else wanted nothing to do with any of them. The four of them, despite their pasts, were the background. They were never the center of attention, the elites of the school in any field, or more than a classmate someone knew. If they were more popular others would have kept by, but being in company with Beringei was regularly discouraged. No-one saw what happened after Tony died.

No-one saw how Boris was still processing what had just taken place.

No-one but Boris saw how Patrick, in attempt to collect himself, put his hand on some droplets of the red sludge, noticing particularly how it spread over him slowly.

No-one but Tanya saw how Beringei's muscles became red in color and how his spit and eyes dripped with the sludge first found on the stick, his hand having landed on a small drop of sludge from the stick.

No-one but Tanya saw Beringei's . . . Tony's . . . body rise from the ground.

No-one saw any of this, save those that were left.

Tony's body was captained by Beringei now. He rose from the ground on his hands and feet, the ground collecting puddles of red sludge. His breathing was deep. His eyes were red with a black pupil, dripping in that foul slime. The pure white of his eyes had died with Tony. His spit had become the red sludge. His ears were dripping with it. He was hunched, his hands clenched fists, his smile a lustful smile. He was driven to get and do anything that made him drown the insanity swirling in his head. When he saw Tanya, he pictured all the animal things he could do to her. All those ideas swirled, conjured, manifested, conspired, and summoned themselves.

He caught Tanya's facial expression. He could see her pain and confusion.

She had no idea what he had become. *Beringei had died with Tony. How is he still alive? Or was he reborn?* She could see this sludge monopolized on and in him. *Parasitic*, she thought. A devastating thought then occurred to her. *I can't beat him. I could only catch him off guard and weaken him. He always outmuscled me. He would win.* She saw how his muscles were stretching his skin. His flesh was tearing the beige, wanting to be out and unbound. *Ew!* she thought. Reality clicked in her head. *I need to run. Work with me legs. Run!*

She made for a hasty escape.

First step.

Then the next.

She gained speed. *Yes! Moving!*

She stopped.

She wanted to bolt, but something was holding her back. *No, no, no, no, no!*

Beringei had lunged forward, held her collar, dropped to the ground, and brought Tanya with her. Her breath was slammed out of her. Her nose and forehead had made contact with the ground. She got onto her hands and knees, gaining her senses. She couldn't stop Beringei from rolling her onto her back. She couldn't summon the strength to keep him from getting on top of her, dripping the red sludge over her. Her arms were trapped by his legs.

She could do nothing.

She was defenseless against the barrage of fists, nailing her face and chest.

She screamed and cried.

She felt humiliated.

She felt the hope get pummeled out of her.

Not again! The Day. This is so like The Day. She sobbed as she suffered. *Why am I even alive?*

Boris had seen all of this.

He was much younger than Tanya and had even less courage. He started to quiver and shake. *The Day. This is the day all over again.* He could see how much pain Tanya was tolerating. He felt the urge to do something, but what? Beringei couldn't be communicated with. He couldn't be outmuscled. Any mistake would leave him . . . he didn't want to think on it.

He had an idea.

He didn't like it, but it was all he could do.

First and last chance.

No mistakes.

One attempt.

Come on Boris. Let's go.

He positioned himself such that he, Beringei, and the garden bed bricks made a straight line. He took two steps and dove over Beringei. He grabbed Beringei's collar with his right, bracing for the landing with his left. He tucked, rolled from shoulder to shoulder, and catapulted Beringei up and over him. He used his entire body weight to plant Beringei's face into the garden bed bricks with their sharp, rough, and coarse edges. Beringei's face was sliced open.

An eye had met with the bricks.

It didn't make it.

The nose had a similar confrontation.

His forehead splintered into his brain. Boris could know that it was Beringei only from having killed the guy himself. His body was red and significantly larger and uglier, and his face couldn't be called a face.

Boris felt relieved that he was put down. No-one could survive that kind of blow.

He roared from the passion flooding his body.

He felt ready to do anything.

He chuckled to himself.

I can do anything.

He could see why Beringei craved the power over another human life.

It was satisfying.

He had mustered the strength to rid another human creature of their life.

He was strong.

He was powerful.

I love this, he thought.

He held two handfuls of hair with his sweaty hands. Using his legs and core, he raised Beringei's head, and drove it into the bricks. He heard the skull crunch, felt the sudden stop at the end, and saw a bright red pool appear near his feet.

He raised and slammed the beaten head again.

And again.

And again.

And again.

And again.

The control was intoxicating. It fueled him. He craved it. He had found a new addiction.

Then reality slapped him on the face so hard that it hurt his soul.

The passion left his body at once.

He was mutilating another human being.

Yes, it was a mangled carrier of Beringei's persona, but he didn't deserve this. *What am I doing? This isn't okay. This isn't right. Why? How? No! No! Stop! Stop it!* He dropped Beringei's head. *Who am I to say when someone will die?* He fell to his knees. *What have I done–* When his knees contacted the ground, Beringei's blood splashed up and away from him. The blood was still warm. He collapsed backwards when he felt the dampness on his knees.

He had spilt that.

He had done that.

His lungs birthed the monster he knew too well.

He couldn't control it.

He had lost control of everything.

I'm not that powerful. I'm not that strong. He held his head in his hands. He grabbed his hair with his fingers. He wanted to punish himself for being an animal. *How can I be so despicable?* He started to scream into his hands.

Then he heard footsteps.

Loud and solid.

Get up! he thought.

He jumped to his feet and turned to the noise.

Solid boots.

Huge men.

Boris, and everyone else, knew them as Gollums.

Vests of peace-keeping tools, hairy arms, tall and staunch. Deepest of chests. Eyes distant and cold, solid as stones, ripped of faith in humanity. They took brutal deaths with sheer disgust and force; they wanted Boris to die for bludgeoning someone's face.

They were defects from 'Project Monster', a majorly successful attempt to weaponize the human being.

They were also the only 'humans' that could take down Beringei.

Boris saw Tanya moaning in pain on the ground.

She couldn't move.

He had to carry her.

They both had to go.

Ranger Roll, he thought. *Here we go.*

He commando rolled, slipping his left hand underneath her left leg, wrapping her body around his shoulders. He kept himself low until he was sure his right hand had his sister's shoulders. *Got her.*

He stood up and saw the Gollums approaching.

He saw an easy opening to his right: the school fields, in the same direction as his home.

He ran.

No plan in mind, he knew he could formulate something as he evaded. Fear and panic were driving him. He was still rational, but his legs were ordered to flee. He could feel the stomping feet from behind him. Booming, heavy steps. Solid boots that have squished the faces of many a perpetrator. *These guys are fast.* He noticed a sandstone wall of the school ahead of him, on the other side of the school. *That's twice my height. The only way? Really? How?* He didn't have long. He had to think. Plan. Execute.

Tanya on his shoulders. Gollums behind him. Legs frantically moving. *How can I get over that wall? I can't. I can't get over . . . disregard.*

Being someone that made things regularly, he remembered that air flows around an object however it can. It can cloak the object in any direction around it.

He had to think like air.

Left and right, he thought. Checking left, he saw another sandstone wall. He saw how it was, again, twice his height and no greater an option than the wall ahead of him.

He would have to curve his direction too.

Curving his direction would create a chord between his start and end points. On that chord, the Gollums chasing him would gain distance. *They're closer than I'd like as it is. Disregard.*

Checking right offered some hope.

The school itself was on his right. He had an idea but thought to plan it out. He disconnected from himself, sending the command to his legs to run until he told otherwise. He would curve right on the largest arc he could make. *Make that chord not much shorter than my arc,* he thought. *I'll make it to the oval first. Science building after that. Manual arts after that. A network of concrete joining them together. Flat pathways. Greater friction between shoes and ground. Greater speed . . . possible.* He imagined himself navigating through the maze of buildings. He knew that he could gain distance. He knew that there was hope. *Yes! That would work–*

Then he remembered a vital fact.

Gollums are resourceful.

Very, *very* resourceful.

They planned better than him. They thought ahead of him. They would have predicted his path through the school.

The shrieks confirmed that.

They were the shrieks of Hailers.

They were quieter than normal, suggesting they were still far away, but still a problem.

Horrifying in appearance, their arms had been ripped and replaced with mechatronic wings. Their legs were entirely metal, specifically designed to jet-propel them through flight; they didn't have feet anymore. They moved on all fours whenever they had to walk. They carried—had fused into their backs—a pack to power all that made them effective 'humans' in combat. Their eyes were replaced with 'Hailer Eyes', unique only to those that were made to fly above their enemies. The ideal fusion of a high-speed aircraft and a land-based soldier. A would-be father now the modern pterodactyl.

Boris' heart dropped when he heard their presence, a piercing scream unique to them. It was a scream literally refined to instill terror. Gollums and Hailers were unbeatable in hand-to-hand. Survival for himself and Tanya meant avoiding them both. He retreated to reality.

He could feel her body on his shoulders. His back was straining from holding her weight so unusually. His arms wanted to cheer the legs with their movement, moving with them and helping keep his body balanced, and were hurt that they were given another task. His shoulders stepped in place of his arms. He gritted his teeth from how much his body was moving and working. He needed to find a way out.

He couldn't keep this up.

His mind started to bring up some new ideas. *I could just turn myself in,* he wondered. No more running. Tanya can get treated. He would step into the light. He would become better. He could be free of the guilt he felt. *I killed Beringei. I broke his face. What's wrong with me! This is wrong. I need to stop.* He wanted to check all his options. He was getting closer to the wall. Next way out was under. *That won't work. Disregard.*

He could end this all if he stopped. *Yeah, I'm running, but they'll show mercy. They want to help me. They want to keep everyone safe. Maybe I should stop . . .* He was getting closer to the wall. All practical methods were disavowed. There was nowhere he could go. He couldn't escape the Gollums. He started to slow his stride as he mellowed on the thought. *Maybe it's for the best–*

He then remembered something.

He quickened his stride, running faster than he ever knew he could. He had found a reason to continue.

He knew his escape.

He roared as he approached the wall. He knew this was going to hurt him; this was not going to be easy.

He remembered that there was a reason he recently favored this wall during breaks. The sandstone walls measured twice his height, going into the ground almost as far. He knew that, and it wasn't something easily marveled at. Going over and under was not possible because of this—not that going under was feasible anyways.

What he remembered was that the walls were very thin, no wider than his head—'ease of construction' the school said.

Critically, he remembered that there were unusual cracks in a section of wall far from the collective of school buildings. They were not jagged like lightning strikes; they were smooth and curved. It fascinated him. Anything that was not of normal nature fascinated him.

It also made the wall weaker.

Much weaker. Every day a little bit falling away.

He could see the cracks in sight. He was close. It had to be his only option.

He couldn't get this wrong. He formulated his line of attack.

He had seen the other side of that wall for years now. Well-kept grass edge with a thick perimeter of shrubbery. Leaves, thin branches.

Soft.

Good for landing.

He would drop his left shoulder and not stop—he was right-handed but thought best not to lead with his sister's head. He would break the wall, run over the grass, leap into the greenery, and hide from the Gollums and Hailers. *It's all I got.* He squinted his eyes. *Let's do it.* He took control of his legs. They were yelling at him to stop. They had been running for half the school's width, as great a haste as he could gather.

I'm at school, he then realized.

While trivial in nature, that information was keeping him alive.

Gollums and Hailers have had previous experience with lawbreakers evading on school premises. In the process of their apprehension, there have been cases where a series of events led to another student being made collateral. After this, Gollums and Hailers had direct orders to never use ranged tools on school campuses.

Boris could have been forced to the ground as soon as he started running, but those incidents gave him the freedom to keep going.

Those incidents were the only reason the Hailers weren't immediately taking him down.

Those incidents stopped the Gollums doing their takedown.

Once he got outside the sandstone walls, he would have no options left.

His plan had to work.

When he took control conscious control of his legs, the only thing preventing collapse was the passion flooding his blood and his sister on his shoulders. He knew they could have their rest soon. They had a little more to give. They could co-operate for a little longer.

He was about to hit the wall.

It was different today. He noticed there was a flower with wide and beautifully white petals enjoying the cracks in the wall. A dark green stem held nicely in the broken sandstone edges, with a dot of yellow binding the white at one point.

He thought nothing of it.

The rationality in his head was more noticeable.

It pleaded that he stopped.

He wasn't supposed to go barging through walls. His brain was reminding him of that. He felt his body slowly side with him. They were all in agreement that running into the wall, with only a half-baked certainty, knowing the other side was more dangerous than the side he was currently on, was foolish.

He concentrated on drowning it out, having faith that the other side gave him more options.

He also had a feeling that the new flower with the white petals did something to the wall in his favor.

He psyched himself up. He lowered his left shoulder. He twisted his body. He roared. His face was twisted and warped with his heart to escape.

He had reached the wall.

Let's do this.

He felt the solid brick touch his skin. He felt it crumble as he went through. The crash of the debris echoed through the grounds. He moved through the wall with considerable ease, barely any change to his velocity, and saw the wide-spanning neighborhood ahead of him. His legs were ready to die on him. They were steps away from going rogue with his lungs. They physically did not have the ability to continue for much longer.

His heart was still pumping passion. His shoulders had only a little more to give.

The jump was next.

His final hurrah.

Please work. He was not particular with the distance of his jump; the vegetation was on a slope. He reached the edge of his refuge. His final step was with his left. He used his right foot to stomp into the ground. It gave him the upward energy he needed.

He groaned as he stomped.

That was it for his legs.

They had done their best and had done him well.

His left knee swung forward, propelling him over the edge and into the safety of the green. It joined his right leg. He groaned again. Both his legs were rogue. They could not do any more. He dived feet-first down the hill. He knew this would make him scream, but it was all he could do. He tensed during the flight. He braced for the landing.

He felt time slow when he was aloft. He could feel how nothing was below him. The oceans of sweat on his clothes cooled from the breeze. He felt relief. He recognized that everything would be okay after this. *I'm safe now.*

The ground approached him.

Stick the landing. Stick the landing!

He used his heels to slide against the vegetation.

His legs were stiff, though he felt a fierce flame scorch his muscles when he landed. He wanted to use his feet as brakes against the dirt, but the fury and outcry his legs were sending back was undeniable and near overwhelming.

He overestimated the slope's incline.

This will hurt.

His tailbone made a forceful greeting with the growth. His back directed the force down instead of into itself, banging his head against Tanya's torso. She collided harder than he would have liked. *I'm really sorry Tanya.* He slid down the hill, his pant legs tearing from the force. His feet drove away the prickles and branches, but small rocks had attached themselves to his legs. He could feel the skin starting to wear away from the friction. He closed his eyes, tensed his jaw, and groaned. He had never yelled so loudly. He started to cry. He wanted it all to stop.

It almost broke him, but it didn't.

He made it.

He stopped a considerable distance down the hill.

His lungs were still wild. They weren't pleased that dust had slipped by with the air. They retaliated. He violently coughed. He regretted trying to breathe normally, but he needed the air so bad. His chest was crushing itself, but the dust needed to get out. He breathed in again. More dust. Another cough. He banged his fists against his thighs. He scrunched his face from hitting his incredibly sore muscles. He needed to breathe. He was desperate. He used his nose to filter the dust. It almost clogged itself, but he breathed out with his nose, letting it work again.

It was a horrible smell. He smelt the moistness of the ground. His own sweat. The heat coming off his body made the air warm. With that, he smelt the vegetation. There was nothing like it. He didn't appreciate its intensity either.

His lungs wanted air; his nose filled with what the lungs didn't want. His legs had ignored any command he sent. They needed time to rest. His arms let go of Tanya, letting her flop down the hill a few rolls. She was safe. Unconscious, but safe. He could breathe normal air. He felt calm. He felt safe. He knew everything would be alright. He just had to hope that the Hailers wouldn't find him.

THE GOLLUMS HAD SEEN Boris' charge through the wall. They had seen the spectacular explosion of sandstone rubble follow him out. It morphed around Boris. It coated him in the name of honor, a cloud of his followers trailing behind him.

The Gollums had stopped when they heard the crash. Either side of the break saw some more wall crumble; the Gollums stepped back.

They were misdirected by the broken wall.

They did not see Boris jump, nor hear his cries of pain: the sound of sandstone falling, which caused some more wall to fall with it, hid all of that.

They stopped. They waited for the rubble to settle. When it did, they made haste, using hands and feet to get over it. They got to the other side, wanting to catch this guy. They needed to detain him.

They got to the hill.

They saw nothing.

The hill was a normal hill.

No-one had been there.

Hailers were flying above them and saw what the Gollums saw. They saw the well-kept grass. They saw the vegetation. They saw everything as they did when they first flew to the school.

They didn't see Boris terrified at the sight of the Hailers. They didn't see Tanya, still unconscious. The only thing that caught their attention was a white flower, floating gently down the hill. It did not sway with the wind, nor did it deviate from its path for but a moment. It flew as straight as they did.

They were confused.

Who is this freak?

They had heard how he bludgeoned a man's face repeatedly, and they had seen how fast he could run. They had witnessed the guts he had to run shoulder first through a wall.

This was someone of powerful abilities.

The two Hailers began their descent to be in company with the Gollums. The Gollums, observing the Hailers' descent, made space for their landing.

In the few moments before the Hailers joined them, the Gollums talked. Their voices were deep, and every word was enunciated. "How . . . " the first Gollum wondered.

The second Gollum found himself confused too, though he had other thoughts he was processing. He looked to the first Hailer.

The first Hailer nodded back.

The second Hailer, still unsure of what just happened, shook his head and turned back, wanting to be sure he hadn't missed anything. He kept flying, circling above the hill the young man should have been on.

The first Hailer landed next to the Gollums. "Well, that's a first," he said.

The first Gollum agreed. "That's not possible . . . "

"Yeah . . . " the second Gollum agreed. He threw a glance at the first Hailer, who received and returned the glance.

They had a thought about how this was possible.

They really, *really*, didn't like it.

Then they saw the first Gollum observe their glances and subtle communication.

"What are you both thinking?" The first Gollum asked with genuine curiosity and intrigue. *Do they know something?* he wondered.

The second Gollum answered. "Just amazed that someone could do something like this. Not even we're that good."

The first Gollum saw through it. "That's not it. You were saying something to each other. You were afraid for a second—it wasn't amazement."

The second Gollum laughed, bent forward as if to stretch his back, bent backward to stretch the other way, then let his hands rest on the back of his pants. "You're right," he replied. "That was freaky."

His face showed, for a moment, trepidation.

He then looked down the hill and found a small smile.

It was only a slight smile, but the first Gollum saw the second Gollum's right ear rise. *He's smiling?* he wondered. He drew in a deep breath, then exhaled. "You're working with 'him' aren't you?"

The second Gollum returned a look of confusion and betrayal, keeping his hands resting on the back of his pants, palms-in.

The first Gollum continued. "You act weird any time we try and detain someone who isn't like everyone else we detain–"

"Because it annoys me, dude!" the second Gollum replied.

"What's he offered you?" the first Gollum asked.

"Nothing!"

"And *that* annoys you, not *this*?" He pointed down the hill.

"What are you even saying?!"

"You know how unethical it is to work with 'him'! You know the terms you have to agree to!" He stepped forward. "I haven't seen some Gollums since they started working with 'him.'" He stepped closer, wanting to make it personal. "Do you want to be one of them–"

The first Hailer gave a quick glance. The second Gollum had but a moment to see and return it. Upon its return, the first Hailer turned and made the famous Hailer shriek. The first Gollum, trained to respond to a Hailer shriek, turned to look where the first Hailer was looking.

The moment the first Gollum did this, the second Gollum used his right thumb to press a panel that hastily opened to a Gollum Tooth. He felt the small, curved, dagger-style blade handle be pushed into his hand, where he, in one swift, full body motion, stabbed the first Gollum's neck.

The Gollum Tooth sliced through the first Gollum's brain stem and windpipe. The first Gollum couldn't breathe, make any noise, or do anything with his body. He flopped to the ground, only able to control his face.

The second Hailer, after being certain there wasn't anything he could investigate further, looked up to see a Gollum lying on the ground with a Gollum Tooth in his neck.

He noticed too late that the first Hailer had made his approach.

The first Hailer had his wing aimed directly for his head.

Contact.

The second Hailer's thrusters cut out, not receiving any commands to fire. He started to glide to the ground and finished with a painful crash landing.

The first Hailer then flew back to the second Gollum, not being the first time he has had to kill a fellow Gollum. He extended his S.M.A.R.T.— Sequential Mechatronic Articulate Retractable Tactical—rope from his pack and held firm the first Gollum. He then flew to the second Hailer's head and body and did the same thing, wanting to be as efficient with it as he could. He then flew to where he knew was an easier access to his master's throne room, knowing he would be very appreciative of the new supplies.

The second Gollum did the same. As he walked, he smiled brighter than he had ever before, then spoke to himself.

"Raktaar will be very pleased."

CHAPTER 2

IT TOOK BORIS SOME time to regain his strength. How he was able to move at all astonished him. His breathing had slowed; his lungs had decided to co-operate again. He was able to sit up, not liking how this moment of rest was earned. He too noticed the white flower from before floating down the hill. He had never seen anything so white and unblemished, apart from the shirt of the bald guy near the gate hinge. The same dark green stem was hanging under it. The smallest yellow dot he'd ever seen joining all the petals together, wide and flat and acting as the wings of the flower. *What a lovely sight,* he realized.

It was even more lovely when he saw—with complete certainty—the flower wave at him with one of its petals.

His sore body reminded him of his pain.

He realized he needed to check how he was after the fall. He moved his wrists and hands, loosening them and moving them, hoping they wouldn't grow stiff and unmovable. "They're okay," he said. His shoes had stayed strong after the mayday. Looking up, he realized it took him half the hill to slow his descent. He was surprised his shoes didn't break or rip; not so much as a tear could be seen. "That's incredible . . ."

His pants had not been so blessed.

Holes twice his hands' span splattered along the back. Rips on the sides where the stitching would generally hold strong. The skin on the back of his legs was splotched with red. Large grazes dripped with his blood; sensitive to touch and in need of rest. His back had sustained similar treatment; the rear of his head as well. To move anything took effort and pain. "That's a problem." He sat there, not moving anything, just breathing. He just sat there and rested, recovering after his escape.

He felt the gentle breeze against his skin. He felt the ground: it conformed to his shape. He rubbed his hand against the grass and leaves around him. Cool to his skin and untouched by dexterous hands. It did nothing all day but stay in place. The leaves would sometimes tag along with the wild journey the wind wanted to go on, but the grass always stayed. It liked being at home. It enjoyed the peace too much to partake in the spontaneous escapades that the wind always organized.

He gained his calmness. He was safe now. He was okay. *Was Tanya okay?*

He noticed her lying by his feet, her head uphill. She hadn't moved since he picked her up before the chase. She breathed, but nothing more. She needed a safer place to recover. The wrath Beringei had surging through him during his barrage of fists left her in a miserable condition. Her cheeks were beginning to bruise, her lips cut numerously from her own teeth, which were all in place: they had been protected by her limp neck. "A stiffer neck would have brought resistance to the strike, doing more damage," he said aloud, confirming the physics he thought through in his head. Her breathing was raspy, shallow, and slow.

She was alive, but not okay.

They both needed rest. Proper rest. Recuperation. Healing.

Their home was within sight, on the top of the neighboring hill.

Boris thought through how he would get back. "It's good exercise using that hill every day . . . I can't make it back. Gollums will see me. People will ask questions." He exhaled with sadness. "We can't go home. Not yet. Disregard." He knew he had to get out of sight. He also knew Tanya had to do the same.

The road on his left had the occasional car. People found that pathway good to walk along this time of day. There were several dog-walkers and joggers that he had seen. Only one glanced at the hill. A man on a gentle stroll just happened to look directly at Boris.

He didn't see Boris.

He acted as if he saw nothing but the hill he'd always walked past.

Boris was sure he looked directly at him. "He didn't see me . . . how?" His peripheral vision saw the flower's petals glowing in the distance. They glowed white, its yellow center a yellow hue, and a green radiance from the stem. It only did so when someone looked at the hill.

He remembered it glowed the same way when the Hailers flew above him.

Boris tried to connect the information. He didn't know how it worked, but it was the only line that tied both facts together. "The flower makes us invisible. How does that work?" He couldn't get how something so small—anything—could do that. "That doesn't make any sense. How? No. Surely not. But . . . wow."

He stopped trying to understand how it worked.

He simply admired the glowing flower.

He had never seen anything like it. It was a wonderful sight. In a better condition, he would have chased it frantically, hoping to catch it and understand what it was. He would treat it well, but he would lose his connection to time by studying and observing it. "I wish I could study it . . . "

Then he realized the insult that would be to the flower.

It was a flower that floated by itself, glowed, and made invisible what it wanted invisible. "Part of its grandeur is its mystery . . . " He simply gazed at the flower. He breathed a large breath, a smile finding its place on his face.

He shook his head. "Bring yourself back Boris. You don't know how long this will last." He needed a place nearby that he could drag himself and Tanya to without needing to walk. He took note of his surroundings. *Shrubs. Vegetation. Mostly flat. Discrete mound of natural material? Conspicuous. Disregard.* He then noticed a lonely tree some way to his right.

Ohlman's Tree.

Perfect.

The founder of the school, Dr Heineman Ohlman, had a tree planted in his memory when he died. It was well before Boris' birth, but it was legendary when he was younger. It was the greatest tree in his suburb for climbing. "So many memories in that tree . . . let's make another one . . . "

It had an incredible view of the open undulations spanning out to the North. Thick enough to hide behind and no-one would see him.

He was going to drag himself and Tanya to Ohlman's Tree.

He determined a straight line to the tree would work best: he was almost at the elevation of its roots as it was. "Getting there will be the challenge . . . " He rolled himself over onto his knees. The ground surprised him with a moist sensation. "The dirt isn't that moist." He pondered. "How could it only now be that moist–"

He looked down.

Beringei's blood.

It had infused with the sweat from his legs and now stained from the brown of the soil. A tsunami of shame and guilt collapsed on him. He caught himself. He didn't have time to cater for this line of thinking. He shook his head. He needed to move on. He needed to recognize this wasn't the time. "I'm messed up." He shook his head again with more energy. He needed to focus. "I'm so twisted!" He grabbed his hair with his hands. "Shut up! You're all wrong! But they're all so right!"

He had heard enough.

He slapped himself.

His right hand made firm contact with his right cheek.

He shook his head again. "That's better." His cheek stung enough to notice. It did not faze him.

The voyage to the tree would be worse. *This is going to really suck*, he realized.

He grew faith in his legs and put wait on his feet, mostly holding himself with his arms. He was able to balance on the balls of his feet, but had to go for the test.

He tried to stand.

"Bad idea–"

His legs couldn't lift him and felt even more sore than when he landed. "Why did I try that?" Looking to the tree again, he figured the only way he could get to the tree was on his hands.

Every time he moved along the ground his whole body would scrape.

He couldn't see any better option.

He first tested this method by going to Tanya. He needed to get her along as well. "She'll have to drag with me–"

A thought.

He remembered the rope he had in his right pocket. He made it himself, but it was terribly weak. He had melted a year's worth of milk bottles, fed it through hundreds of hair-sized holes and spun it into rope, melting the ends to keep it all together. The rope was half his finger's width and he needed three strands to support his weight, but it would drag his sister well enough. He did two bowline knots, one at either end of his rope. One end went around Tanya's shoulders, the other his waist. "I told you I'd use this one day," he said to Tanya, resting her on her back.

He had been waiting for a time to use the stuff.

He locked his eyes on to the tree. He knew he could make it. He knew that he had it in him. His arms had vigor in them.

Let's go.

His body scraped along the ground. He realized his pants weren't meant to be dragged along the ground, and he could feel them lowering from his waist. He re-did his belt, going as tight as he could pull. He did not care how much it hurt his hips. He needed something to keep the bowline up; his pants and belt were the best option. He muscled a new hole into the belt's leather with the spoke generally used to hold them in place. His arms had been used considerably to do so.

He had to be careful not to tire them too early.

He still had a journey ahead of him.

He realized Tanya would feel something similar: her skirt wasn't made to slide with the ground beneath her. He crawled back to Tanya, glad that the uniform made all the seniors to wear belts. They were thin, but it worked for his purposes. He realized he would need to add another hole to her belt.

He groaned, but now her belt was tighter than it ever was.

He didn't want to use up more of his energy, knowing his priority was getting to the tree. "I'll just need to push myself more . . . " His reserves weren't at full capacity, but he had to dig as deep has he could. "For Tanya." He used the friction his arms and hands had with the ground to slide himself and Tanya along.

It hurt his forearms: all that weight at an unusual angle was uncomfortable. He wanted to find a more ergonomic technique. He found that lifting his chest and pushing himself up and forward worked more effectively, feeling how his palms contacted the ground quite nicely. He knew that the tree wasn't within unreasonable distance, but he would almost be spent when he arrived.

He developed a rhythm to make it a mindless activity. "Thumbs out. Hands down. Push with the palms, not the fingers. Up a little. Push forward. Down. Repeat." He tried to control his breathing as he went. He wanted to make sure he stayed calm and concentrated. He couldn't allow his brain to get distracted.

He was getting closer to the tree. He could make out the breadth of its mighty roots. "Thumbs out. Hands down. Push with the palms, not the fingers. Up a little. Push forward. Down. Repeat. Thumbs out. Hands down. Push with the palms, not the fingers. Up a little. Push forward. Down. Repeat." He continued this again.

And again.

And again.

And again.

And again.

And again.

And again.

His back had started to sweat from the sun's heat, and his shirt started to stick uncomfortably. He could feel how the ground was getting warm; not uncomfortably hot, but he couldn't wait until the ground burned his skin. He kept going. "Thumbs out. Hands down. Push with the palms, not the fingers. Up a little. Push forward. Down. Repeat." His stomach began to feel irritated from being dragged across the ground. Leaves became sharp, and twigs were scratches to his soul that he tried strenuously to avoid, with his shirt slowly being stripped of its buttons. "Thumbs out. Hands down. Push with the palms, not the fingers. Up a little. Push forward. Down. Repeat." He could see the bark on the tree, thick and dark brown.

He was so close.

"I can make it. I can make it. I can make it!"

He saw the trunk curve around.

He reached the other side.

"I made it!"

He began to laugh with himself in relief and satisfaction. "I made it . . ."

He sat himself up against the trunk, loving the shade that he had found himself in. Being on the hill now would be terribly painful under the heat.

He used what he had left in his arms to haul Tanya underneath the shade. She was still breathing, and she was still bruised.

But she was still alive.

And she was still his sister.

He couldn't help but sit her up and hold her in his arms and feel her skin against his.

He held her for a while. He wanted to be near Tanya.

Ever since The Day they had always made sure the other was well. They told each other everything. The Day really brought them together.

Today would have a similar effect.

He saw her face on his shoulder. "Love you Tanya." He kissed her forehead, not liking how blue and black it was turning, holding her for a while longer.

He started to talk, not knowing what else to do. "This really hasn't been my day Tanya. I had this awful dream this morning. You've had this happen to you"–he stopped, feeling a sudden grunt of emotion change his face. He cried. He didn't want his sister like this. He wanted her full of life, to be his big sis, to open her eyes. He held her head into his chest and embraced her.

He needed that hug.

He needed someone to be near him.

His breathing slowed, and he started to feel calm. He felt Ohlman's Tree had provide some of the nicest shade he'd ever experienced. The breeze was gently cool. The grass was soft beneath him.

It was what he needed.

He felt his eyelids grow heavy. He felt ready to rest.

He was safe.

He re-adjusted his posture, letting his head lay against the trunk of Ohlman's Tree, and allowed his body to entirely relax. He closed his eyes, and he slept.

THE LAST MEMORY TANYA had was of Boris picking her up. She remembered the Gollums. She remembered Boris' amazing speed; she hadn't remembered Boris ever being that fast . . . she remembered nothing after that. She opened her eyes. She was sitting on Boris' lap, her head on his chest.

She looked around. "Where am I?" she wondered. She saw hills and dips in the land on her right, as far as she could see.

She looked up. "Ohlman's Tree. What am I doing here?" Boris had dirt and leaves on his front. His rope–"he actually used that rope," laughing as she said this–was around his waist and her shoulders. She removed the rope, placed it in his hands, and stood up.

She hadn't been to Ohlman's Tree in years. She remembered how often she came here with Boris. They would lose their sense of time as they climbed. It was such an easy tree to climb. "The height we used to get on here . . . " she reminisced.

She smiled.

She then saw how Boris was sleeping. He was at peace. He looked content. She thought to get up and look around the tree, wanting to see if it's changed since she'd been there. She put her weight on her feet, using the tree to right herself with her left hand.

She dropped onto her knees.

She winced. "Ow."

She grabbed her chest.

She winced again.

She took a deep breath.

Another wince. It hurt for her to breathe deeply.

It hurt for her to move her arms.

She took slower breaths, wanting to make the most of each breath. *It'll hurt less.*

She focused.

She was okay.

I can't move my arms. She could handle that. She stood up by moving her feet into a balanced stance, then pushed up with her legs. She was up. She was standing.

She walked around the tree. It was huge like she remembered it, the trunk thick and wide. "Strong as always." The closest branch wasn't within reach when she was younger. Now, she could almost feel it brush past her head. "I could climb it. Go to the top. See the amazing view . . ." She remembered her arms and sighed.

She smiled.

She liked this tree.

"I'll come back and climb you again. One day."

She looked down, then panned around to see what else was around. She noticed the hill and was confused at the sight of it. There was a ditch about Boris' size, and it ran for half the hill. "What has Boris done?" She noticed a trail of dirt in line with the tree, just then feeling the dirt against her own clothes. Her hair had the same sticks and leaves that Boris had on his shirt. The back of her shirt and skirt as well.

Then the belt tightness came through.

She looked down and saw a new hole be made in her belt. She loosened it and re-adjusted. She felt the tightness on her skin release.

Shen then looked around and tried to put everything together into a story. "Boris had dragged me? There must be a reason . . . " She would have to ask him.

She noticed the top of the hill. The gap in the sandstone wall caught her stare. "Boris charged through that? He did that–"

She then felt a sharp pain from her rear and the back of her thighs. She rubbed her hands gently on them to soothe it, but it didn't do anything.

She looked back up, and was now even more confused. She couldn't make sense of why Boris was so determined to escape, nor of what happened this side of the sandstone wall.

She did know that there would be a reason.

Boris was her little bro.

He took care of her when she needed it.

She smiled.

"I've got a good bro."

Then it came to her.

She remembered why she needed Boris so desperately.

"Beringei–"

Her legs fell from under her and she collapsed. She remembered what happened, and the pain came back to her.

Beringei's fists were humongous. She could feel them against her face, each blow twisting her neck sharply. She knew keeping it loose would do less damage to her, but she felt how sore her neck now was. She could feel his fists drive into her chest, and the look in his eyes was terrifying. Red with black pupils. He slobbered red sludge, and she felt the drops on her chest and neck; she couldn't feel it now . . . she remembered that sludge burning her skin then, but only going skin deep. She never remembered them going as deep as it was with Patrick.

She didn't remember much of what happened to Patrick.

She could feel her burns. It was sensitive. As she processed, she remembered the hopelessness she felt. She couldn't do anything.

She started to cry. She hated it. She wanted him to stop. She wanted to be free. She started to sob, but her chest hurt with every gasp. "Why! Why did he do that?"

It then occurred to her why she had her head in Boris' chest.

She got herself on hands and knees, wincing again at the pain in her arms. She groaned amongst the tears: it had become habit to get up with her arms. She balanced on her feet and pushed up. Now standing, she walked to Boris. He was still asleep. She sat down, snuggling into Boris' chest. She put her arms around him, keeping them below her shoulders. She needed someone to hold; to cry into.

She felt relaxed as her tears dropped down. She knew Boris could protect her. She let her moist eyes grow heavy. She really needed rest. Beringei had mentally exhausted her. She closed her eyes and slept. Boris was comfortable to sleep on.

BORIS AND TANYA BOTH opened their eyes. They breathed deeply when they woke. The air was still cool under the shade of Ohlman's Tree. The breeze was still gentle and well-received. They both rubbed their eyes, seeing the sun gently setting not long after midday.

"How are you going?" Boris hugged her as he asked. "You don't look too great." He said this with a smile, not sure how else to say it.

"Yeah . . . " she thought. She didn't want to hide anything from him. *What example would I set if I did?* She hadn't been so vulnerable with Boris since The Day . . . she never liked being vulnerable ever since. She took another long breath. *I need to do this.*

She looked at Boris.

She remembered how she felt being beaten. The emotions came back to her. The hatred. The fear. The loneliness. The helplessness. The sadness. The anger. The twisted idea that she deserved it. The violent notion that she wanted to do the same to him.

She looked into Boris' eyes, tears beginning to fall gently.

Her face contorting. Her lungs bracing for the sobbing breathes.

"I'm not okay."

Her eyelids covered the windows to her hurt soul, her cheeks guiding a stream of her despair, making a canal for all the sadness. Boris held her tighter. He cried with her. He didn't know what else to do. He remembered this helped her on The Day; he was hoping it would work again. He thought to be honest with her. *She's been honest to me . . .* "I'm not okay either." Neither of them talked. The only sound they could hear were the wails of their sibling and best friend. They cried. They wept.

And they healed.

CHAPTER 3

BORIS AND TANYA HAD let out their frustration and hurt. They did this for most of the afternoon, sometimes breaking their tears to try and piece the madness together.

They wondered what the sludge was, and they wondered how it turned Beringei into . . . *that*.

Boris did tell Tanya about how he saved her, including Beringei's demise.

She hugged him tighter.

He was relieved she wasn't angry or disturbed. She did hope that he would be able to move past it; the look in her eyes told him that.

Her eyes were powerful like that.

It also said in a gentle, quiet voice that she still loved him.

She had always loved him.

THEY BOTH WONDERED WHAT time of day it was, and, noticing the sun near the horizon, determined it was part-way through the afternoon. They had plenty of sun ahead of them, but the day was closing nonetheless. They figured that it was best they head home.

They used quiet backstreets away from the busier roads to avoid attention—explaining why they weren't at school was something they wanted to avoid. Boris' legs were working for him again, and he appreciated that he could walk, though walking was the highest setting. He hadn't successfully negotiated with his legs yet. They were still angry after being used so intensely.

They both did not talk much on their travels home. They kept mostly to silence, though a question often presented itself. They asked the other their query, wanting an answer, hoping that some sense could be made of their day.

Often it didn't.

They both realized they needed time to accept today and recognize the weirdness of it.

They made it home without alerting anyone's attention. No-one noticed them walking along the streets. No-one asked why they weren't at school. No-one thought to ask why Tanya had been so brutally beaten. No-one wondered why their uniforms were so dirty.

No-one.

As they stepped through their front door, Tanya saw a woman through the kitchen window. She was standing in the neighbor's land, was bald, wore a dark red blazer and pants, a white shirt, and a jagged vertical line scar protruding from her forehead. No tie. She closed her eyes and shook her head.

Upon looking up, she disappeared.

She squinted her eyes, rubbing them shortly after. *Not another unnatural thing. Please!*

Boris noted her squinted eyes. "What do you see? Is there something out there?"

She had his curiosity. "Yeah, I did . . . "

She breathed out. She wasn't ready for something else. She didn't want anything more to happen. "There was this bald woman," she replied, "near my height. Fit build. Red blazer and pants–"

"She didn't happen to have a jagged scar on her forehead, did she?" Boris asked

He was hoping for a no.

He was pleading for a no.

He couldn't take anything more.

His breathing quickened. *Don't be a yes. Anything but a yes.*

"Yeah, she did."

She was confused with Boris' anger. He rubbed his hands through his hair, gripping and pulling, wanting to do something with his fingers to let out his fury.

Tanya wanted to understand and help. "The line had jagged edges even–"

"Even though it looks like it was years old. It protruded from her head a little too, didn't it?"

She was hesitant to answer.

He wasn't himself.

She wasn't herself for that matter, but he looked hostile. The fear in his eyes made a strong recommendation to keep their distance.

She didn't want to be close.

She moved to the opposite corner of the living room. "Yes–"

He snapped.

He roared.

He grabbed a tiny coffee table, no regard for what was on it, and launched it into the wall. The crash was loud, and the table broke. He yelled, roared some more, and put his fists through the wall. He didn't care that his knuckles were bleeding. He didn't care that he was scaring his sister. He didn't care that the dust in between the walls was covering him. He wanted to be free of this confusion. He couldn't understand what was happening, and it made him truly mad. Nothing that was happening to them made any rational sense. He hated this weakness that he had where there were some parts of his life he would never understand.

He felt his duty to protect Tanya earlier, but he hesitated.

He had given more than his body could handle during the escape.

He couldn't process how so many things went against what was naturally possible.

"Why am I so weak!" He yelled angrily, continuing to barrage the wall with his fists.

Tanya ran for Boris. She needed to hold him down and stop him doing this to himself. She held him in her arms in a tight squeeze that told Boris he was going to get better.

He fought and struggled and squirmed and resisted. "Let go of me!"

She held tighter.

"Stop it!" he shouted.

She held him without a word coming from her mouth. He needed to be held and loved. Words couldn't express it.

She had to show it.

Boris released his frustration in words. "I want it all to stop! I want to have everything normal. I want to not have these weird dreams! I don't want to feel like I can't tell what's natural and what's strange! I want a normal day"–he wriggled in Tanya's arms when he said this.

Then he started to elbow her.

She tensed her stomach and took the hits. They were sharp and hard. He had effective elbows.

She remembered how she held the first board Boris broke when they were younger and wanted to be more in defending themselves.

They didn't want to be so inexperienced when faced with a tall man-like thing with four legs.

She remembered his first board break was with his right elbow, and it was on his second try. It had been a longer training session, and it was particularly warm that day. She was hoping that he would make it.

She remembered how she had taught Boris correct elbowing technique. *Whole body motion. Pivot on the feet. Never hit with the point of the elbow; always above or below it.*

SHE HELD THE TEARS, knowing that he was inflicting his knowledge back on his teacher. She had to be strong for Boris. She had to be solid, but she didn't know how high her dam wall could be built; there's only so much tears a human can keep in.

Then she felt the elbows slow in pace. They started to hurt less as he started to relax. He started to tear up again. He held her arms in his. He sobbed again. "I want it all to stop Tanya. I want it all to stop . . . "

"I know Boris. I know."

They sat on the floor. They knew they were safe here. They had no desire to do anything else. They wanted to sit. To process. To comprehend. To unwind.

To be them.

THE SUN HAD DESCENDED some more from its peak. It was getting later in the day, and night was approaching. Boris and Tanya were wondering how to spend the rest of the day. They thought to sit on the family couch and simply sit; nothing more than to enjoy the other's company.

Boris used that time to make networks in his head. He knew he was safe, so he retreated into his own mind. He recognized a relationship between his dream that morning and what had happened.

The red sludge appeared in them both.

What was with that stuff? He remembered that Beringei had been devoured by it like he was the victim of a parasite. "That sludge that came from Beringei . . . " His mind wondered. *I killed Beringei-*

"Yeah Boris? That sludge that we saw today?" Tanya could see his mind wondering. She needed to limit how much his mind did that. He hadn't come to terms with today yet, and his brain always wanted to find connections. His head would take any chance it could to remember today.

"That sludge was in my dream this morning"–he looked at her.

She looked confused.

He re-adjusted himself, knowing he would need to explain this. He continued. "It dripped from these flying creatures. Horrible things. They're like Hailers but so, so much worse. That sludge . . . it was a red sludge, wasn't it?" He wanted to be sure.

Tanya remembered easily. "Yeah . . . yeah it was. It was a rich red, a nice dark red sadly. Viscous consistency . . ." She noticed Boris' gaze into the distance, like he was daydreaming.

Boris' brain was trying to work for him.

He had heard that before.

Red sludge wasn't new to him; only its appearance was.

He got up and paced back and forth, wanting to think.

He knew there was something else about it that he had to remember. It was critically important. He remembered that someone's mortal existence had a connection to it.

Someone close to him.

It was written down.

It meant a lot to them.

Then it clicked.

"Patrick!" He yelled it at Tanya.

He had remembered.

"Patrick . . . " The waves of memories came back to him, and he remembered briefly what happened with Patrick. "I left him there! He died because of that sludge."

Tanya was worried he'd have another outburst.

"That red sludge got to him . . . " The gears in his mind were whirling, but they were getting back on topic. Tanya could see that he was going to be calm. She settled herself.

Boris spoke. "In case the red sludge gets to me, Patrick . . . "

Tanya didn't know what he was thinking.

Boris remembered perfectly.

He remembered Patrick being particularly weird this one day.

It was a school day like most others: thick books in hands, their classes enjoyable as always. Nothing exciting. Nothing different.

Except Patrick.

He wasn't himself.

He was nervous. Withdrawn and anxious. He had a note in his books. He wanted to give it to Boris, and he knew it would be weird. *No-one expects to read a note like this,* Patrick thought. It was an immense surplus of courage that let him give it to Boris. He had never trusted another person to this extent. He knew that it wasn't merely a token of trust. *There's so much balancing on how he reacts to this.* He gave it to Boris.

Boris didn't understand why. He didn't know why Patrick—or anyone—would think of a note with that on the front. "In case the red sludge gets to me, Patrick." He knew that Patrick was a boy unlike many—anyone really. He knew there was a reason behind the letter.

It was just weird.

He thought nothing of it.

HE COULD SEE THE confusion on Tanya's face while he was remembering. He gathered his thoughts, using his hands to help explain—it wasn't a normal message to pass. "Patrick . . . " He remembered how hurt Patrick was under Beringei. The fear in Patrick's face and eyes. He had been through so much as it was. He remembered–

"Stay with me Boris." Tanya broke the wandering thought. "Patrick?"

Boris focused. "Patrick gave me this weird note. I don't know how long ago it was. Would've been ages"–he went to his room. Tanya followed. He took large steps as he went. He had energy in him with every movement. "This was important to Patrick. It must be significant." It took a lot of rummaging through the paper on his door, but the note from Patrick was at the top, as high as he could reach.

It was old fashioned in delivery. "He did always appreciate history. I've never seen a note like it."

It was thick and rough. It felt good to hold. He remembered how Patrick wrote. "His writing was really something. I've never seen a guy work a pen this well." He remembered how much Patrick loved to write. "I always enjoyed reading it."

It was a yellowy-brown envelope, the same color as old paper. Most would seal it with their moist tongue and use the glue already on it, but Patrick had made this envelope himself. He fastened it shut with a grey wax seal. The emblem proudly showing two arrows with their heads facing up making an 'X.' A quill lay on the center of the 'X', with its ink tip between the tails of the arrows. The quill was on fire, and its flames flowed up with the quill's feather.

It showed his passion for his work.

He remembered how excited he had been when he made that emblem. "I'm going to make him a necklace with this emblem on it. Bury it with him . . . " He felt the emblem with his thumb. "I've never opened it. I always wanted to keep that seal as it was given to me." He knew he had to open it, but he admired it for a little longer. He breathed out.

His eyes caught the lettering on the front. "Look! 'In case the red sludge gets to me, Patrick'. This is it!" He got his multitool from his desk and very gently cut the seal from the paper. He grabbed the note from inside, seeing how it was the same paper as the envelope. "Patrick did always like old paper . . . "

He unfolded the note and prepared himself to read it.

He could see there were several pages folded as one—this would be a long read. "These are Patrick's last words to me . . . " He rubbed his eyes.

He thought so highly of Patrick.

They were genuine companions.

He prepared himself.

He took a deep breath.

He needed to read it, but he knew he couldn't hold his grief in. "These are Patrick's last words to me . . . " It sunk in. He closed his eyes.

Tanya could see his pain. He wasn't ready to read it. "Let me read it Boris."

He looked up, his eyes beginning to gloss with grief. He liked that idea. He nodded. He wasn't ready to read the note yet. He accepted that.

"Okay. You read it."

She received it from Boris, being sure she was gentle. Slow, planned movements. She wanted to be careful.

She deliberately read slower. Having met Patrick, she remembered how he talked slow enough to be considered wise but not be annoying.

It was unique to him.

There was something special about how he used the English language. He wanted to try and sound like him, blending herself with the speech patterns of Patrick. *I hope you like it Boris.* She read, "my valiant Boris. If thine eyes partake this penned ink, the voyage of my life hath run aground. Alas, a vessel will always find its bow dry and its sails sagged no matter the voyages it's gone on. The ocean's waves might wreck it, or it might be plucked from the waters by its captain's will, though I pray mine was put to land by the King of the seas.

"I am made disheartened by writing that my pen cannot quill as the legends of literature once did—not for long at least. I remember how eagerly you used to read my work. I wish I could write with influence like texts gone by, but those times are now no more."

Boris looked up in confusion.

She continued. "Now, I must now write how things are about to happen. There are things that—I hope—have already happened, that will show you there is more to our world than what the two white spheres in all our heads will let us see.

"We were close Boris. I would not write this to anyone else, and I know that having the bond that we had would have left you as a valued friend in a miserable mental state. I take a breath and a moment before writing more, for I know this is not the last words you wanted my pen to bring under the light of day.

"I cannot successfully explain to you in writing how vital your next actions are. The envelope writes that this is to be read only if I die—lacking any better name or description—by a red sludge. This substance has a history spanning far in time and deprived of human affection. I MUST STRESS TO YOU BORIS. THERE IS A STRONG CHANCE YOUR FUTURE WILL BE BLEAK SHOULD YOU CHOOSE NOT TO TAKE WARNING FROM THIS INK. This groggy, viscous matter is POWERFUL; nothing wielded by human hands can supersede what it does. It is a malleable substance, providing healing to its master—HE is your ONLY concern now—and refined from the fear of living creatures. I say this in the literal sense of 'refined'.

"To beat an adversary, you must first know it. To know this sludge, you must understand its origins. You'll be glad to know I have done this for you. You will find this in my room on my shelf. From a brother to a boy that changed a life, Patrick. P.S. Thank you for all that you did; for being a wonderful associate and one whose company is simply splendid. Live well. I beg of you."

Boris couldn't contain himself. His eyes were already red from the tears he shed today.

This made it worse.

"I'm going to miss him Tanya. I'm really going to miss him . . . " He cried into his hands. The wonderful memories he had with Patrick no more. "He was so like me . . . we got along so easily . . . " He sobbed again.

Tanya did her best to comfort her grieving brother. She held him. She rocked to-and-fro with him. "It'll be alright Boris. Just give yourself time."

He wanted to tell Tanya what he was feeling. "He was a really great friend–"

Then he snapped back.

He rubbed his eyes. He focused. He started to think clearly. "What am I doing?" He put his hands on his bed. He processed. "So . . . " He tried to think; his emotions clouded his head. He shook it. *I need to focus.*

"With the note . . . "

Tanya wanted to help. She tried to talk. "With the note . . . "

He talked, but no sound came out. His lips were moving but no sound was made. *He's not talking to me,* she realized. She said nothing. She kept holding her brother. She needed him as much as he needed her.

As she did this, he was beginning to piece everything together.

Now he had to gather the courage to say it. *That can't be. How? That just can't be . . .* he calmed himself and turned to face his older sister. He used his hands to help explain. He didn't know how to say what he needed to say. "Everything that happened today. Every weird event that has happened in our lives. It's all in that book." That made sense to him. He could process that well enough. "The thing is . . . " he couldn't believe he was about to speak this. "He wants us to protect ourselves and everyone else from a threat only he knows about?" He didn't understand that. "Why us? What makes us so special?"

"I have no idea Boris. I have no idea." She paused. She recognized how little she knew about this.

Any of it.

She relayed what she did get. "Patrick wants you to read a book. You can read a book simply enough."

Boris nodded in agreement. All Patrick wanted was for him to read what he wrote. "Let's read it then," getting up as he said so. He was excited. He wanted to see what his friend had written.

Tanya raised her arm and grabbed his shoulder.

She winced.

Boris turned. "What happened?" She breathed deeply, moving past the sudden pain in her joints.

"My arms. I can't raise them. It doesn't matter."

Boris sat back down. She continued. "We can't go there yet. Not like this."

He realized what she meant. They were both dirty and unpresentable. He had blood on his knees and his hands needed a wash, his clothes in need of repair. Tanya was . . . she needed time to herself. Her face bore unhuman colors, sensitive to the slightest touch. She was defenseless should they need to stand their ground. She had been focused on him and was yet to care for herself. *She needs her own time,* Boris realized. "We can't be seen. Not yet . . . not yet." He agreed.

An idea—he had a potential solution.

His face lit up. "Who says we'll be seen?" He motioned outside. There was some light left, but the sun could give only so much. "We can go when it's dark. No-one will see your bruises"–he caught himself. Tanya's reaction displayed how sensitive she was with her appearance. "I'm sorry." He paused, then continued. "No-one will see us. We won't have to deal with Patrick's aunt and uncle. They wouldn't know yet . . . " He slowed his last words. *Patrick's aunt and uncle. How could I forget.* He had to say his next words carefully. He breathed in deeply, letting it out slowly. He hated how he had to say this. "We'll have to get into Patrick's room without anyone knowing. Anyone we meet will simply slow us down. From how he writes it . . . we need to be quick." He didn't want to admit it. He didn't want to follow through. "It's not okay to go to the room of a dead person. That isn't normal. What's wrong with me?" He stood up.

"None of today has been normal Boris. You heard what I read. A lot of what we know is about to die"–she stopped.

Boris stared.

She rephrased. "Not make sense. Sorry."

He breathed out. He understood. "I know what the note said. You read it to me." His demeanor changed. "Thank you for reading that too. I wasn't ready to read too . . . "

She could see humility in his face. She wanted to support it. "I know Boris. I know."

Boris was wanting to put what he felt in words. "It's just . . . " *English is really average sometimes,* he thought. "You don't expect this from a friend. This isn't what you want your friend to tell you when he dies." He breathed out a long breath. "He's right. This isn't something you ask anyone to do." The doubt filled his mind. It was talking to him, reminding him of the insanity presented to them both. *You know this is ridiculous. You know Patrick shouldn't have asked you. What was he thinking?* He listened. He mellowed on those thoughts. He knew a lot about Patrick, and he knew a lot about himself. He knew that Patrick wouldn't ask more than what he could deliver. He was capable.

He was ready.

Are you ready? Can you really do what he wants you to do? You couldn't handle Beringei properly. You couldn't give more for Tanya. You know you'll fail Patrick. Admit it.

He began to agree. "Maybe we shouldn't follow this through . . . Patrick did have some random ideas . . . " Tanya could see something different in Boris. His face hung with gloom. His eyes grew dark.

He's looking different. Something's up. What is it? "He was your friend Boris," she told him. "You can read the book at least. It's just a book–"

Boris retaliated. "What does it matter anyway?" He felt empty and hollow. "He's dead now. So's Beringei." His hands held his face again, his hair struggling to stay in after being pulled on so much. "I'm going to get punished so hard." He spoke louder. "Why should I ever leave this room. Everything is so dangerous out there, and I add to that when I step outside, and I can't think properly, and I'm so worthless, and . . . "

Tanya could see something now.

Something on his forehead was wanting to stick out and show itself. She couldn't see it clearly, but something wanted to make itself known.

She didn't like it.

He needs to get out of here. I need to be subtle. "Why don't we go to my room Boris. My wall might help. It always does me good after a rough day." Her wall was a vast mural of a rainforest, with various animals and insects.

When focused on, one couldn't help but fall into the lushness and wonder of the rainforest, delighting in the natural spectacle.

His forehead flattened. He winced, but knew it would be for the best. He nodded. "Yeah. Your wall always helps." He walked behind Tanya to his door.

He stepped through.

He was about to leave, then his head got caught on nothing.

It was about to pass through the frame of this door, but it wouldn't go through. He staggered back. He collided with his bed and found himself on the floor, hunched over. He held his forehead in his hands. He had to gather himself. *That hurt a lot.*

Tanya saw how weirdly Boris was acting. The mark on his head was defining itself. *A vertical line.* Everything made sense.

She saw it on the random lady through the kitchen window.

It was causing this pain in Boris. *It needs to go.* She walked slowly to Boris. He was on his knees. His back was arched, and his elbows dug themselves into his thighs. Tanya thought to touch the spot with her fingers. She wondered if she could feel what was in her brother. Pointer and middle finger extended, she used any muscle she could to be gentle on the mark.

He roared.

Chest out, head back, fingers curled.

All his muscles were tense.

Tanya's peripheral saw a man in the corner of his room. *Tall. Bald. Dark red blazer and pants. Black shirt. Vertical line on his forehead.* She collapsed back. She was startled. "Boris! There's someone in your room!"

He knew.

He could see the vertical mark, thin chest and arms in his mind. It was the man he saw at the front of his school. When he felt his head collide on something, he was forced to retreat into his own head, where he saw the bald man with a sword in his left. It was long and dark. He approached on nothingness, a ground beneath his feet but no ground could be seen.

Boris was on his back.

He felt the terror as this man approached. He wanted to escape. He tried moving his hands and feet, but they were wrapped in chains. He saw how he was on top of a skinny, solitary cliff with nothing else in sight. He could not move, and the sword was growing larger and nastier with every step the bald man took. "Get him out! Get him out!" he screamed in his head.

Tanya looked up. She wanted to find the man.

He wasn't there. *Where did you go?* She touched the bump again, hoping to see the man and face him.

He appeared.

He was diving over Boris' bed, hands outstretched and bearing the face of a predator.

She had no time to react. She only saw this wild man with snarled teeth and a desolate look in his eyes.

Then he landed on her.

Her head smashed into the hard carpet floor. The wooden beams holding the carpet left Tanya's head bleeding. She kept rolling back, her neck disliking the uncomfortable and unexpected angles it found itself experiencing. The bald man had commando rolled over her, sliding on his feet until arriving at a stop; his legs were ready to pounce. His left hand held his body up. His right was drawn back and fully extended. Its fingers were curled and their tips were growing longer and darker, a dull point making themselves known.

He had successfully disturbed what he determined to be the greatest threat in the room: the girl. They were both incapacitated: the boy almost ready for picking and the girl wouldn't be a threat. *Raktaar will be delighted.*

He knew how much he used the red sludge, and he remembered his master's addiction. His hunger for the stuff . . . he shook his head.

He focused.

He saw how the girl was rolling over, getting ready to stand up. He crawled over and placed his bone-hard fingers on her head. He pushed her face into the ground. He could sense in her thoughts that she was still working on getting her bearings. He could hear how the drum of her heart was off-time to the guitar of her lungs, putting the ears through forced manual labor to make sense of the disunity. He could also hear how they were all playing at an incredibly fast pace. *She is angrier than what most experience. What else can I use?* he wondered. He gently lowered himself down and spoke.

"I am sensing much hatred in you," stroking her check as he said so.

She instinctively clenched her fist. She tried to talk, but her tongue produced illiterate sounds.

The bald man spoke. "Do you know who I am?" He stroked her hair as he continued. "I am Raktaar's myrmidon. There are many who are me, and they are all starkly different to me. Do you want to know why I'm here?" Tanya was alert enough to respond. She said what first came to her lips, unable to sustain the cognitive ability to filter her thoughts.

She replied in a quiet and firm tone. "No."

He struck the wall on his left. He twisted with his hips and pulled back with his left, slapping the wall as hard as he could with his right hand, leaving splintered timber lying to his left.

He didn't like that answer.

"No?" He shouted in disbelief. He lifted her head by her hair. She gritted her teeth and winced. "I'm going to tell you! I want your blood! That gorgeous red life that flows and weaves through you!" He smashed her head into the ground. She lost all focus again. Her mind wanted to enact and retaliate, but the orders couldn't be sent. All she could do was listen to what he said.

He breathed out. He knew he couldn't submit to his rage. He had to remain cool. Dipping his toe into the heat always led to a loss of control, and that brought him close to a mortal death. He breathed in deeply. It was always a strain to control his anger. He breathed out. He thought to help the girl understand. "Your blood is a highway of ships. It sends oxygen to the cells and trudges away with the waste, and it only stops when you die. But that highway is very important to me. See, very few know how powerful this highway is. Let the ships move too fast and the body believes its threatened. Let them slow down and the cells can't work to a schedule that allows you to live. Let their cargo take too much space and all sorts of nasty things happen." He smiled as he said this. "You can clog the highways with this disgusting fat and cause a miserable backlog of ships that can't go anywhere. You can mess with how the ships work by playing with what goes into your lanes. Importantly, these ships can also be tasked with delivering certain messages. Mass deliveries to the body." He paused. "My master needs that from your blood. Because . . . " He ran his finger gently across her neck. "There's this one message that he enjoys quite a lot. You lot call it adrenaline. We hail it as the thing that gives us our power. When your blood fills with it, you feel so afraid. Your sacks of pinkish red are being told that there is something dangerous, threatening, and fear-invoking nearby. The funny thing," he laughed before finishing with his favorite part, "is that we love it. My people scare your . . . people . . . and your blood fills with what we really want. Oh, it's really something. My master boils it and reduces it until it's a thick sludge. It slops by the handful. Gloopy, glorious stuff. Then we bathe in it. We soak in it, and it's what makes us what we are."

He saw how she was beginning to talk.

She was awake enough to consciously think and utter sounds that could be translated into words. She knew she couldn't be loud; a whisper took most of her strength. He could see that she wanted to speak.

He bent down, wanting to hear her.

She spoke. "Hideous ogre."

He laughed. "You are so right. I am a hideous ogre." He prepared his bone-hardened finger, running it across her neck. "I generally drag this out and get more from the harvest, but why waste time I say."

THE BALD MAN POINTED the sword to Boris.

Boris could do nothing. He had no muscle to raise his limbs and had no ideas that could save himself from a sword. It was almost the length of the bald man's legs and he couldn't move anything to stop it. He saw how the bald man put the point of the long blade on his chest, wanting to be sure he would hit his mark.

He loosened and re-did his grip, and he smiled. His eyes looked into Boris'.

Boris could see that the bald man was going to enjoy this. The bald man was raising his sword as high as he could reach. Boris could see the groove down the blade's center. He closed his eyes, bracing for his painful death.

His eyes opened.

The blade was being plunged.

He breathed in a short gasp, only just seeing a white flower fall with the sword. He saw how it glowed, only to then feel the blade go into his chest. He felt how it sliced his skin and tore through his flesh. He could feel the blade push apart what generally kept him together. It reached the opaque white underneath, and he awoke, hearing a large part of a wall opposite him break apart when he did.

He saw the bald man over Tanya. Boris kept breathing loudly, but he knew he needed to quieten himself. He put his hands over his mouth and nose, trying to not raise the bald man's glare.

It was safest for everyone if he regained himself first.

Then he could help his sister how she needed.

He closed his eyes. He couldn't understand how another creature could warp what his mind let him do. He stopped trying to understand, knowing with certainty that it would only make his head hurt more than it did.

He gathered his senses. He felt his bed on his back, the carpet on his rear and feet, and a warmth in the air that his skin didn't appreciate. He was calming himself, but he continued to breathe. He knew he needed to help his sister, but he knew he wasn't ready.

He needed to gather himself some more.

In doing so, something white caught his eye. Large petals. Tiny yellow center. Dark green stem. *That's the flower from earlier . . .* he remembered how it kept him and Tanya unseen from the Hailers. He remembered how it was falling down the bald man's sword—he stopped.

He felt his chest, putting his hands where he remembered feeling the sword's tip. It felt the same—no harm had been done to it. *That thing saved me?*

He couldn't understand it.

He stopped trying to.

He admired the beauty in the flower.

It was being upheld by the floor; its green stem looked like it grew from the carpet. He reached with his right and picked the flower. He felt how light it was in his hand. He felt how pure it was, how it was filled with natural, untainted life. He felt a true shalom pass through his body. He breathed a new breath. A smile planted itself on his face, his eyes were filled with a cheerful look.

He was ready.

He put the flower in his shirt pocket, letting it rest by its petals. He got to his feet and stayed low. He saw the bald man put his ear close to his sister.

It didn't sit well in his stomach.

He wanted to save his sister. He felt a renewed anger. It was stronger and deeper than anything he'd ever felt.

The flower glowed in his pocket.

He focused, feeling also a revived strength in his muscles, but not a total revival of strength.

He planned.

He first recognized that he had to catch the bald man off-guard. *I can't engage in direct hand-to-hand. I'm not strong enough for that. I could yell at him . . . he could still hurt Tanya. The smallest move and she's dead.* Boris shook his head. *Disregard.* He noticed the wall behind the bald man. Boris planned. *I could dive into his shoulders. His head would collide with the wall. That'll hurt me more than him.* He breathed out. *Disregard.* He didn't like how little ideas he had. He knew he couldn't outmuscle the bald man and was safe so long as he didn't engage. He forced himself to stay where he was. Everything was telling him to do anything, but he knew he needed to think. All his ideas were only possibilities. He had no certainty that any single idea would work.

He rubbed his thighs. He felt the frustration of not doing anything. He hated how he could do nothing. He sat back down by his bedside. He felt useless. He put his hands on the carpet, running them under the bed, flopping his head on the mattress. He wanted to think. He wanted anything that could be of help to him and his sister.

He froze.

His hands stopped.

They felt something solid.

It was cold and smooth. Long in length and wide enough that a claw-like grip was needed to grab it. He re-adjusted into a low squat, quietly flicking up the sheets of his bed. He saw that it was a metal pipe as long as his arm span, had a few switches, an aiming scope on the side, and a trigger one-quarter of the way down from his right. A strap made from a repurposed belt made for easier transportation. He remembered he made this weapon a year after The Day. He wanted something he could grab easily and that could annihilate whatever posed a threat. He knew the projectile would spin as it flew out and cause as much damage as it could.

He aimed with the scope directly at the bald man's head, who had been entirely oblivious to Boris.

Anytime the bald man looked with his peripheral at Boris, the flower pulsed a glow.

He donned the earmuffs he let rest on his weapon, preparing for how loud it would be, and pulled the trigger.

He felt his back bend backwards under the sudden force, pushing himself into his bed and forcing the bed to slide along the carpet.

It was a clean pressure release explosion, leaving no trail of gas, nor did any light come from either end of the tube.

But it was loud.

Very loud.

The sound echoed throughout the neighborhood; a strong, deep boom that broke the windows in the nearby rooms.

Opening his eyes after being pushed back, he saw how the bald man's head was no longer there. His body collapsed to the ground, landing on his side; Boris breathed out.

He was relaxed.

He and his sister were safe.

He dropped down to the carpet, loaded another projectile, tapped on the safety switch, flicked some more switches to let the pressure build, put the belt strap over his head and let it rest on his left shoulder, duffed his earmuffs, and went to Tanya, stepping around the body that was now in the hallway. She was covering her ears with her hands and curled herself up. "Tanya? Are you okay?" He shook her shoulders, hoping for a response. "Can you hear me Tanya?"

He saw red on her hands.

He looked closely.

Her ears are bleeding.

He grabbed his hair with his hands, groaning as he did. *I did this–*

He stopped.

His whole body made itself stiff. He held his breath. He couldn't see the impending horror, but he could hear it.

Hailers were circling overhead.

They heard the deep boom.

He knew he needed to escape, and he didn't like the solution that presented itself. He knew he needed to read the book Patrick wrote, and he knew Tanya should be with him when he did. He also knew she was too disoriented to walk properly. He closed his eyes and breathed out. *This is gonna hurt.* He ranger rolled Tanya onto his shoulders and stood up. He navigated through the doorway and began to run. He collapsed, groaning as he fell to the floor. He couldn't stop Tanya rolling away from him. He tried to get up, but his legs resisted. They couldn't be pushed again; they hadn't rested enough. He crawled to Tanya, the flower still in his pocket. He was within arms-reach of his sister.

He could just touch her arm with his fingers when he heard shattering glass.

He stopped any of his muscles from moving, but he kept his fingers on Tanya.

He saw the Hailer ahead of him. It was walking slowly through the house. It knew it couldn't move quickly indoors, but it knew it didn't need to.

It also knew something incredibly dangerous was within a residential house.

He looked around, his body facing Boris' left. He was a fair distance from him. He looked at his right and panned left, looking just over where Boris and Tanya were lying.

It then panned right.

The Hailer saw nothing.

It can't see me, Boris realized with confusion, forgetting that the white flower was keeping him invisible. He relaxed, resting himself on his elbows and letting go of Tanya. A scream behind him made him freeze. He turned slowly and saw another Hailer. It unfolded a crossbow from its right wing and shot a black disk at Tanya. It stuck to her, and bolts of electricity arced all over her body. It forced all her muscles to contract, and her body shook as if it was shivering. The black disk stopped, and she lay there.

Eyes closed.

No sound.

Boris got on to his hands and knees, but he stopped himself.

He wanted to be brave for Tanya, but it would do nothing for her.

To rescue her, he would need to take down two heavily armed, incredibly angry, and mightily skilled Hailers.

He remembered seeing videos of them at school, and he remembered the power these creatures had. He remembered how they could fly through buildings and clear whole rooms of hostiles with little effort.

He knew he couldn't defeat them. He got back on to his stomach and used all his self-control to not be the hero he knew he couldn't be.

The first Hailer approached Tanya. Boris could see in its man-made eyes that he was looking into and over Tanya. It could see that Tanya was a victim. It turned around and let a S.M.A.R.T. rope fall from its pack, doing Alpine Butterfly knots around her shoulders and waist where it then returned to its pack. Tanya was dragged out of her home, for the Hailers were limited in what they could pick up with their hands. Boris got up and went to the front door. He saw how Tanya was flown into the air behind the Hailer.

They flew up a fair distance, and she was let go.

She started to fall from a high height; a controlled free fall to the ground.

The Hailer looped around and caught Tanya by adjusting his movements and connecting her hands and feet with where a Gollum would hold onto, then went East with the second Hailer.

Boris knew that it was for the best. "It's not like I can do any better," he told himself. At that moment, a wave of grief and shame fell over him. It only just occurred to him that he could have held on to his sister, and she would still be with him. The smallest touch, and she would be with him still. He fought that wave with his head and his heart, knowing that she needed real help. "It would have been selfish to hold on to her." He nodded his head. "Yeah, it would have been selfish." He saw how the sun was setting and thought to make use of the dark. He went to his room and grabbed a backpack to carry Patrick's book, letting his hands be free, and navigated its straps under the crude belt strap.

When he walked out of his room and turned right, he saw a bald lady with a black shirt and dark red suit in the hallway.

Boris froze with fear.

The lady in the dark red suit then lunged at Boris as he was fumbling for the switch to fire his shoulder-strapped weapon. When she got too close, he side-stepped out of the way, making a run for his desk to get his Mech-Ant glasses—that was the invention he could rely on.

He saw the lady approach with remarkable and scary speed. He saw how she jumped high, so he ducked low. When she cleared him, he ran as hard as he could out of his room, wearing his glasses, backpack, and his strapped weapon.

His legs were suddenly motivated to work with him.

He slammed his door shut behind him, wanting to slow her down. He turned right, wanting to give himself time to think of something. He turned right into a guest bedroom, closing the door just as he heard his door be broken down. When he closed the guest bedroom door, he threw off his backpack and shoulder-strapped weapon and pressed all his weight into the door, using the door's hinge to leverage how he was holding the door closed. He wanted to contact as much of the door as he could. He donned his Mech-Ant glasses and got them ready, not yet sure what he would do with them.

He thought to listen to the hallway and check where the lady was. He deduced that he slammed the guest bedroom door when she broke down his door, so she didn't know where he was hiding. She heard the carpet make a gentle noise near Tanya's room and the bathroom next to her room.

He looked back to his glasses, seeing that most of the Mech-Ants were turned on and ready for use. He knew they were all huddled together like a giant nest of bugs under his bed frame, keeping them out of the way and well out of sight.

Those Mech-Ants saved his and his sister's life: secrecy added to what was a considerable force.

Knowing that a swarm of these little things would be hard to hide, he ordered them to hide around behind his doorframe, knowing that once they were all assembled and ready, they could be set to feather-tip mode and be barely audible even when close.

They would also slowdown in speed.

He heard footsteps approaching.

He set his Mech-Ants to feather-tip mode, and saw them, through his glasses, climbing on the ceiling in the hallway.

He then heard the footsteps be on the other side of the guest bedroom door.

She then heard her speak. "That wasn't closed when I walked by . . . "

Boris' whole body tensed, using every single muscle fiber he could use to brace for the lady's kick. He got his hand around the handle of the door, moving it so that his body was the only thing holding the door closed.

He then felt a strong kick that surged through him and into his legs. By taking some of the force of the kick, the wooden door only cracked in slightly.

Boris then pressed two buttons on his glasses with what little time he had, wanting the Mech-Ants to be on the lady as fast as they could move.

He braced for another kick.

Crack.

He had taken some of the force again, but there was now a scrap piece of wood hanging off the door.

Boris could see his Mech-Ants be nearly on top of her, but he knew he needed to hold the door a little longer, working through the ankle sprain.

Then the Mech-Ants were right above her.

He told his Mech-Ants to target the lady with a command he had been working on for this moment: 'Piranha'.

Then the Mech-Ants dropped on their target.

ON THE DAY, BORIS knew very well that he saved his sister by tearing the flesh, little bit by little bit, of the four-legged creature that invaded their home. Being young and innocent, he didn't know how best to do that to the intruder apart from making the little legs of the Mech-Ants be little needles scratching the surface.

Since then, his talents had grown.

He had put extensive time and energy into making his little Mech-Ants a better defense, and a countermeasure he added would do what he did to the man-like creature on The Day, but better.

He took his inspiration from a fish that, when in swarms, frenzies about a bit of meat, and, in a matter of seconds, is left with nothing but bones.

After many experiments with fruits and tree branches, he found the best way for his Mech-Ants to pull living creatures to pieces, including bone.

THE MOMENT HE SAW his Mech-Ants land on the lady, he closed his eyes.

This was nothing like tearing up fruits and branches.

What made it worse was the scream behind the closed door.

Not wanting to open his eyes, and knowing his glasses well enough, he set his invention on a general setting to locate noises, then attached the Piranha command with that.

Blissfully, the scream stopped.

He kept his eyes closed, keeping his fingers in his ears, so very greatly regretting the horrible setting he had added and spent so much time finessing. He then waited a little while with fingers in his ears, wanting to be sure that when he opened the door, he would be safe and wouldn't be able to hear his Mech-Ants at work.

After waiting that little while, and knowing well the layout of his glasses, he set his Mech-Ants to transport the target to behind the house.

As he pressed those buttons, he forced down a gag.

He removed his fingers from his ears, hearing the gentle scurry of his little creation do what he told them to do

He then sat there, back to the door, unsure what to do next.

He was so amazed and proud of his creation, working so efficiently and so well.

He then turned to his right and threw up, unable to shy from how well his Mech-Ants worked at pulling someone to pieces.

He threw up again, feeling utterly and disgustingly terrible, yet a pride in his chest brought a warmth to the smile on his face.

He then looked ahead half dis-engaged, tossed his glasses onto the guest bed, blew the vomit out of his nose, breathed in as best he could, and exhaled. He spat out whatever was left in his mouth and stood up with his backpack. Seeing some of his vomit get on the shoulder-strapped weapon, he thought to leave it. He navigated around the scurrying Mech-Ants, doing his best to disengage from what he just did, went to the front door, walked to the road, and made his way to Patrick's house.

He walked with a slow waddle, feeling the pain in his legs return. He also needed the time to calm himself and bring himself back to reality.

As he was walking, he looked down and saw the white flower glowing very nicely in his pocket.

The brighter it glowed, the more he felt the darkness drip away. He felt light again. He went on in his slow pace, but he took the slower speed to admire his surroundings.

He had made his way to Patrick's house without any issues. The flower glowed brightly wherever he went, and no one saw him. He was able to walk without haste, and his legs were appreciative.

He remembered Patrick's room and he could see in his head a large bookshelf that would contain Patrick's book. Boris knew he couldn't go through the window and the front door would be locked, but he knew their back door would make for a good entry.

He knew this because of how difficult it was to get to it for any stranger.

Their fence was a solid metal sheet painted a dark green that extended a little above his head. The other side of this saw a trio of dogs, birthed by the same mother and collectively a brotherhood of savage animals that worked very effectively at keeping their family safe.

They were familiar with him, however.

He would be safe from them.

"Everything will be alright when I get inside," Boris told himself. "Now, how am I going to get over . . . " he wondered. He put his hands on-top of the fence and felt a wide metal u-beam with the base of the concave on top. "Perfect." He prepared to jump with his legs, but he felt a pain shoot from them. They weren't ready to exert themselves like that. He groaned, then covered his mouth. *Keep quiet Boris!* He had found noise to ruin the effect of the flower, noticing some looks from strangers and onlookers whenever he made noises.

He didn't want to raise the attention of Patrick's aunt and uncle.

He couldn't handle talking with the aunt and uncle of his passed friend. He couldn't stomach talking to them about his death, how he died and what happened up to his death. *I can't talk to them about Beringei.*

He shook his head and thought through his options. *I can't get over this fence. I'll need another way.* He then continued in thought.

Then a voice came into his head.

"It would be good to start by keeping in mind how your legs need to restore their strength should they continue their service to you."

Boris froze.

Everything was tense.

It was a voice deeper than anything he'd ever heard, like a wise man with a long beard had just spoken to him. He replayed what he heard through his mind and recognized that it was not his ears that heard the advice. He turned around very slowly, but saw no-one.

"I'm sorry. I should have introduced myself." Again, the voice was not external.

"It's in my head . . . " Boris realized.

"Very good. Nehemiah is the name. Yours would be Boris–"

Boris cut Nehemiah short and responded in a stern and quiet voice. "I have had far too many things be in my head over the years. Get out!"

Nehemiah responded, "You need not be afraid, young Boris. I wish no harm upon you. I do wish that you will read your friend's book . . . " He faded into quietness.

Boris questioned it. "What do you get from me reading this book?" He paused and shook his head. "What am I asking? Where are you?!" All was said in a quiet voice not to attract attention.

"Before your first question is answered I must satisfy your other queries, for the first will require trust between you and I, something I only have in you and you not yet in me. To answer the second, I will first say that it is a good question to ask, for that leads into the third, where I say that I am in your left pocket. It is most strange talking to a flower I must admit–"

Boris rubbed his eyes with his hands. "I wish I could say talking to— no, having a conversation with—a flower is the weirdest thing I've been forced to experience, but it isn't," he paused for a deep breath, smearing his face with his hands as he did.

He only just noticed that he hadn't washed them since escaping the Gollums and dragging Tanya to Ohlman's Tree.

His face was now covered in dirt.

He groaned, did what he could to keep the dirt away from his eyes, and continued, "and I wish I could have a normal life." His anger surged. "I wish everything didn't talk to me in my head," he said with a fierce tone to the flower in his pocket.

Nehemiah responded, "Yes, talking in your head would cause confusion for you; though, I must say you will prefer this."

Boris, in his manly ego, countered. "Try me."

Nehemiah chuckled a little. "I appreciate your boldness–"

Boris growled to himself and put his hands through his hair violently.

Nehemiah continued. "I do believe the book you are after is one you must read. Shall I be of service?"

Boris immediately declined. "I'll remind myself to bury you when I get home. If you could keep it down up there, I'd really appreciate it."

He turned and put his hands where he had them before. He squatted and ignored how much his legs disliked it. He jumped, groaned loudly, and pulled with his arms. They were now extended with his waist resting at the top of the fence. He groaned yet again and swung each leg over the fence. He pushed forward with his arms and collapsed onto the ground, wincing dangerously loud. He rolled onto his back and sat himself up.

"That looked painful," Nehemiah said. "Are you sure you wish to decline my help?"

Boris breathed deeply. He groaned again. "No," he replied with distaste. He breathed a large breath in and clenched his fists. He continued in a grumble. "I need your help." Boris could hear Nehemiah breathe in his head. He was pleased that Boris was finally going to accept his help, but knew that Boris wasn't one to trust the abnormal, and he knew perfectly well why.

"Boris," Nehemiah started, "I am going to speak for a while, and it is my hope that you keep quiet this time, for Patrick's guardians are aware that someone is in their yard. You will also remember that canines have average eyesight and they wouldn't be able to see that you are you, something you thought to rely on. They will be too energized to smell you properly, expecting a threat more than a friend, and hence they will see you as a threat to their family. You'll remember your fourth sleepover with the young man's family?"

Boris did remember, though he tried not to.

There was an intruder that attempted to enter Patrick's house as Boris had tried too. The family's dogs were kept inside that night to keep them warm from the storm outside. When a splash was heard where Boris was currently sitting, the dogs were let out to investigate. It started quiet, then there was more splashing as the man tried to get away.

Then the man tried to attack one of the dogs with a knife. The love of keeping their masters safe was well exhibited that night by the trio of dogs.

The threat was neutralized.

He closed his eyes and stopped his memory from playing further. "I don't like to recall it. But yes, I do remember."

Nehemiah spoke, "Very good. Now, your legs aren't in good condition to evade them, so I will make us invisible for the time being. Make yourself comfortable good Boris. There is a great deal of information you must understand."

Boris reluctantly agreed. He dragged himself to a wall and let his backpack cushion the prickly concrete. It wasn't comfortable, but his back was supported well enough. "Can't they smell me?" he asked.

"No, Boris," Nehemiah explained. "I'm in control of your invisibility now. There is now much greater power in your disappearance. Before, it was not as strong."

Boris watched as the dogs came by to investigate the noise, observed how they looked around like they didn't see anything, then walked near the light that shone from the back of the house. Boris breathed out deeply, amazed at what Nehemiah just did. "Thank you," he said. He hated saying it, and his tone reflected it.

"Now you are totally safe. Nothing is going to hurt you here."

Boris appreciated such a claim, though it came with hesitation. "How can you be so sure?"

"I'm not limited by matter like you are." He said this with such confidence that it frightened Boris. Nehemiah continued. "If you'll let me talk without interruption, everything will make sense—"

"Everything will make sense?" His tone was surprised and doubtful.

"Yes. Even what happened when you were younger will make sense when I am done."

Boris breathed deeply again. Nehemiah had his attention. "Alright. I'm listening."

Nehemiah began. "Splendid. Now, to obtain this book, you are going to have to trust me. This will not be easy for either of us, and the success of what I'm about to say is dependent on your commitment to your friend. That book will save your life, your family's life, and the lives of anyone targeted by the enemy it writes about . . . " He paused, feeling how Boris was taken off-guard by this statement. "I know it doesn't make sense and I know it will be hard. You must have faith in our ability to work together. Does that exist?"

Boris held his head in his hands and hated how ludicrous it sounded. "Do you really want me to trust a talking flower?"

"You don't have many choices in terms of obtaining this book and"–he paused, then continued–"and in terms of what I know, you can do nothing."

Boris felt anger rise in him again. "I can do nothing!" Remembering how invisible he was from reality, he continued with greater volume. "Who are you to say that?!"

"Read the book good Boris. Please. There are some things you can *never* escape from."

Boris replied with exhaustion, "Do you know what you're asking of me? Do you know how much weight you're putting on me? How reading a book is the only thing I can do against what sounds like a stupid powerful foe."

Nehemiah corrected, "It is you that is oblivious to the weight I am putting on you, Boris. I have set out a plan, and this plan will only deliver its fruits should you choose to do as I am about to say. Failure to do so . . . " He exhaled in Boris' head.

"You really need my help, don't you?" Boris realized.

"It is not me that requires the service, Boris. When you finish reading this book, you will recognize how there are threats in the world *you* have no chance of surviving. Trust me, Boris, or you will die a long and painful death."

Boris breathed sharply out. He then elbowed the wall behind him, strike after strike releasing his anger. He cared not for how his skin broke and his capillaries bled. He elbowed with his left and right repeatedly, wanting the life of anyone else. He stopped. "There's no way I'm getting out of this is there?" he asked Nehemiah.

"There is actually."

Boris looked directly at the flower in his pocket.

Nehemiah continued. "Should you choose to decline, I will help you get through the fence and back to your home without harm brought upon you. Should that happen, you will find me not in your pocket and I will only be seen to you with great trouble and pain on your part. You will see glimpses of me but never me entirely, for you have chosen to reject me and I will help make that doable. You will then need to explain to your parents why your sister is with those Hailers and not with you. You will also need to explain to them how there came to be random bits of flesh behind your house and why the carpet in front of the guest bedroom's door is moist with something it shouldn't be moist with. You will then be made forever vulnerable to this enemy which has attacked you, those that are dear to you, and many, many others. Or . . . " He paused, then went on. "You can do as I am about to say, no matter the difficulty or troubles you experience in doing so, and save everyone around you from things the human brain will never comprehend properly. The choice is in your head."

Boris punched the ground furiously and pressed his head firmly against the wall he rested on. "This threat you keep talking about. You sure I can't face him alone?"

"You can't face what you can't see. That's where I come in."

Boris breathed in deeply. In, then out. In, then out again. He hated this idea, and he hated how little he knew about Nehemiah, who interrupted his thoughts. "I mean not to hasten you, but the sands of time till these threats strike their hardest are falling."

Boris heard and understood. "That book will help me understand threats I have no way of defending by myself?"

"Correct," Nehemiah replied. "That's where I come in and where the book answers your questions."

Boris nodded his head. "Okay. What do you want me to do?"

Chapter 4

Raktaar was in a pool of his red sludge when the second Gollum and the first Hailer approached him.

The second Gollum got onto his stomach, lying flat on the dark red hard rock floor. The first Hailer delivered the new-found materials for his master and did the same, though getting that low required considerable effort.

The second Gollum spoke. "Master?"

Raktaar didn't move.

It was hard for him to hear anything when his entire body rested underneath the surface of the red sludge.

"Master. I wish to speak with you," the Gollum repeated.

Again, Raktaar remained motionless.

The Hailer yelled, having greater volume with a voice that wasn't as deep as a Gollums. "Master!"

Raktaar began to rise from the sludge, wiping his face when he did. He heard someone calling him. "Yes . . ." he said with apathy.

"We have found a young man that will serve your needs most well," the Gollum said.

A pause.

Raktaar spoke with authority. "What is so special about the young man Gollum?" His tone suggested a superiority that assumed an inferiority on the Gollum's part.

"Forgive me master." He rested himself on both his knees, wide and solid, covered in what was made to look like a black fabric but was a literal thick skin. "The young man was able to outrun us, and run through walls, and"–he got closer to Raktaar. "He can disappear."

Raktaar was impressed by this. "How did you find him Gollum?"

"On my usual patrols master."

"So"–Raktaar laughed–"you didn't actually find him? You stumbled across an incredible human mortal and believe that's your required collection for the day? You have been slacking on that recently . . . "

The Gollum clarified. "I didn't find him breaking through walls and outrunning us master. I found him colliding another human mortal's head into some sharp bricks."

Raktaar breathed out. "Very well." He was impressed. "A dark human mortal with impressive abilities." He looked into the Gollum's eyes. "Were you able to capture him for me?"

The Gollum hung his head. "He . . . he escaped master"

Raktaar clarified with a mocking tone "He disappeared." He followed this with a riotous laugh, utterly mocking the answer.

When he caught the fear in the Hailer's face, he stopped.

Now he was concerned.

He darted his eyes quickly at the Hailer's thrusters, noting the scratch just above the bottom of the thruster. This was one of his most valuable Hailers.

This Hailer rarely got scared.

"Speak," Raktaar commanded.

The Hailer held the stare from Raktaar, then closed his eyes, looked down, brought himself onto his wings, and found the bravery to speak. "There . . . there was a flower." He let his head hang as he said this.

Raktaar looked at him with a stare that broke into the Hailer's soul. "A flower?" He clarified in a gentle tone.

The Hailer returned a somber nod.

Raktaar removed himself from the sludge by climbing out on what was, for him, the right side of his pool. The dark red cave floor held the falling drips of sludge as he did so. His footsteps echoed through the cave with the high walls of the throne room adding to this. He spoke to the Gollum. "Can you agree?"

The Gollum looked up. "I can master."

Raktaar exhaled deeply.

This was bad news.

He then spoke. "I will manage him. You need not be afraid."

The Hailer looked up and responded. "The stories master–"

Raktaar answered. "All true. But I will take control of him."

The Hailer looked down, feeling a little easier.

The stories he had heard from Raktaar were frightening.

Then Raktaar changed his tone. "You haven't given me anything for some time Gollum . . . you remember the terms?"

The Gollum looked up fearfully, regretting how he didn't listen to the Gollum he killed earlier that day. "Master! Please! I will bring you something–"

Raktaar grabbed the Gollum by the shoulders and threw the brute into the sludge. The Gollum yelled at Raktaar, feeling the pain of the sludge begin its work. "I'm sorry master. Please save me!"

Raktaar cared not for the Gollum's pain. "I gave you a simple task. You knew what the conditions of doing business with me were. Fail me and you'll become a Scream." He extended one of his legs and pushed the Gollum into the sludge.

Before the Gollum could speak, he was enveloped by the red sludge. Bubbles slowly came to the surface, his howls of pain trying to find a listening ear.

Raktaar noticed the supplies brought by the Hailer. "You did all of this?"

The Hailer gave a large smile. "Yes master. I killed them both."

Raktaar smiled. "You did well, as always." He motioned to have access to the Hailer's back. The Hailer understood and turned to show his master his back.

"More speed master?" the Hailer hoped.

"Faster than any Hailer before." Raktaar smiled.

The better he made his Hailers and Gollums, the more resources he acquired.

Raktaar then let the Hailer walk out of the cave and commanded some sludge to go to the new-found materials and collect them. The sludge followed their command, branching out to the dead Hailer and Gollum.

Raktaar then held his hand to the ground and tapped his fingers, hoping to talk to Maargalla through the rock.

It was a call to her, telling her to make herself known.

She approached from his front, with the entrance to his throne room behind him. To his left and right were walls of fire to light up his throne room, also allowing him to see Maargalla enter.

Maargalla was a large creature.

Her arms and legs were exactly like an octopus' legs, but they were as long as a person is tall. They were also proportionately wide to give strength. Along the sides of her torso where limbs the same as her arms and legs, four on either side in-between her arm and leg sockets. She had skin and flesh the same as Raktaar, but she had no head. Her eyes were on the end of tentacles that were much shorter than the rest of her tentacles and a smaller tentacle with four hard independent points coming from her neck. She 'talked' through these hard points into the ground.

Maargalla was Raktaar's first, and only, attempt to construct a living being.

They talked with each other through tapping and sliding their hard points along a solid substance. Maargalla listened by feeling the vibrations of what was tapped.

Maargalla gave a reply. "You called Raktaar?" She was the only one that could refer to him by his self-given name.

"Yes Maargalla. I have some more bodies for you to work with. You'll know what to do with them."

"Yes Raktaar." She reached into the pool of sludge with her tentacles, felt two more bodies and a head to collect, and used her arm and leg tentacles to support herself while her other tentacles went for the extraction. She had them around the second Gollum's shoulder and waist and used her whole body to pull her newfound resources from the sludge, feeling the resistance of the gloopy substance. She continued to talk with Raktaar while she pulled. "How are my Screams going?"

Raktaar smiled. "They are working wonderfully Maargalla. I used them against a young man in a dream I gave him. He was terribly frightened. They are simply brilliant."

"I'm delighted that you appreciate them."

She retrieved the first Gollum from the pool of red sludge and wrapped her tentacles around her newly retrieved materials. She made her way to her section in the throne room, hidden by a door of darkness and seen only if one was looking for it.

"Maargalla . . . I must speak with you about something very important."

She turned. "Yes Raktaar?"

He breathed out. "The young man who received one of my nightmares this morning. He is one of two that I spoke with you about some time ago. The ones that defended themselves against me?"

"Yes, I remember."

"I fear that our reckoning is soon to be brought to us by this young man and his sister. They glow with more strength than I have ever seen in a human mortal, and their bravery compliments it."

"These two bring much worry to you. Have you sent your agents after them?"

"I have sent two, yes . . . ." He was hesitant to continue. "We both know how powerful my agents are. You know that when those I do business long for real power, they become one of my agents and prove remarkably beneficial. I'm yet to hear of any significant failure from them . . . " He drifted and closed his eyes before continuing. "Two of my agents were killed today."

Maargalla was confused by this. "That's never happened before."

"I know it hasn't. I would expect to lose an agent through capturing a rogue Hailer or Gollum, but to lose two at the hands of a human mortal . . . I cannot underestimate them. The second died so painfully too . . ."

"Do you know where they are? The siblings?"

"A Hailer informed me today that one was sent to their Facility. He tells me it was the older sister. I know not of the young man besides what I saw through the eyes of my agents."

"She would be incredibly vulnerable then. How did he know that it was the older sister you are after?"

"When I was . . . hurt . . . by the two I told you about, I informed my more experienced and better Hailers and Gollums. I wish not to waste resources when it does nothing for me, but to have individuals of such power be observant of two devastating threats was something I wanted. Not many of my resources know that they exist."

"You are discerning as always Raktaar. What is the closest network point there?"

"I will need to walk a fair distance, but it is relatively close."

"It is the Facility though. Wouldn't you have an exit at the Facility?"

"I would. I would much prefer that as well, but Nehemiah . . . "

They both shivered.

Raktaar continued. "He would expect that Maargalla. I've told you stories about his cunning."

Maargalla tapped. "Understood . . . Raktaar, how will you handle these two you speak of?"

"I know not how. They've been able to evade my Gollums and Hailers, and when they are granted supplies, they are able to defend themselves against my agents." He rubbed his bald head with his hands. "I *might* be able to capture them, but they've *seen* me! I won't be a secret to them! You know how powerful secrecy is to me." He breathed out. "These two will not be defeated easily."

"You are the strongest foe they have. I fear the only way you will capture these two is by doing so yourself. I can create something that will be of service as well . . . "

"You believe so, Maargalla?"

"Yes, Raktaar. It is far more powerful than anything I've currently created. You brought me a Gollum some time ago, and I've been experimenting with him. I have a feeling he will serve you quite well."

"That will be dearly appreciated Maargalla . . . ." He paused, then spoke. "I fear we will need it soon."

Maargalla responded with a stare.

He continued. "There was a Hailer just here that spoke of a white flower gently gliding down a hill . . . ."

An awkward silence was held between them both.

Only conversations about Nehemiah would make them this quiet.

Raktaar broke the silence. "I will leave you to your work."

Maargalla expressed her thanks, then walked with greater haste to her section of the throne room.

She had a new reason to work quickly.

RAKTAAR NEVER KNEW WHAT exactly she did with what he gave her. All he knew was that whatever he gave her came out with flesh like his, removed feet, wings on their backs, and the ability to do anything that was asked of them until they could not physically continue further.

He made his way to the exit of his throne room and made his way to the older sister. His throne room and Maargalla's workspace were the only two places in his cave. He had no need for anything larger. He walked through the exit and began walking through his network.

HIS NETWORK WAS AN extensive labyrinth of cave tunnels he constructed to make movement around the Earth easier. He once considered attaching a Scream's wings onto his back, but he remembers vividly a flight he once took on a Hailer's back and how vulnerable he felt. Every side of him was exposed, and he needed an overhaul of weapons if he were to undertake such an endeavor.

He had developed these tunnels so that it would only take an hour to traverse one side of the planet to the other, faster than any Hailer would ever be able to fly. He exited these networks through hidden trapdoors that only he and those that were under his service could see.

No-one with regular, blanketed, human eyes could see these trapdoors.

He started to go through the network channel that brought him as close to the Gollum and Hailer Facility as it would take him.

He began to walk, but his walking started to slow. He saw a network channel with a bright white shining from it.

His breathing quickened.

He had seen such brightness only once before.

Nehemiah.

He made haste for that tunnel, running as fast as he could, only to stop suddenly. He realized how he needed to obtain the older sister *and* investigate this brightness. He looked back and forth, attempting to determine which was more important.

He stopped.

"I can do both," he told himself.

He sprinted back to his throne room and scraped his bone fingers along the sides of the hallway, seeing a fine powder come from the walls. He went to his reserve of sludge and scooped up a sizable chunk of the stuff, noticing that it was an abnormal clump that didn't happen often. He sprinted back to the hallway and dropped the sludge at the hallway entrance, commanding it to collect the fallen rock powder. He went ahead of the sludge, hoping to give the sludge more rock to work with. When he got to the hallway's end, he controlled the sludge to form two wings with four legs at its base, hoping that the rock he gave it would provide the strength it required, acting as a thick outline for the wings and leg-tips. He thought about what his little mindless minion would be tasked with doing and how it should go about it. He channeled those thoughts into his arm and forced the glow through his little critter.

Its wings started to flap and its legs started to move. It began its flight to the older sister, knowing that it would impersonate its master and capture another target. It would care not for what was around it or what it meant to undertake its task.

Raktaar could see his small creature fly to the older sister through his network. He turned and went towards the bright white light, hoping to destroy Nehemiah and whatever he was after.

CHAPTER 5

"You'll need to listen closely for this to work and have faith in what I can do. *You* are going to get into your friend's house from *here*, as your legs deny your orders, yes?"

"Wait. I'm getting into Patrick's room from *here*?" He looked around. No windows. No doors. Nothing of interest.

A blank wall.

"How?"

"My good Boris, you would never understand how. What you *will* understand is what you're about to do. Before I can continue, do I have your trust?"

Boris breathed, then spoke. "Yeah . . . yeah you do. What do you want me to do Nehemiah?"

"Lean back Boris. Push into the wall you're resting on."

Boris' face showed confusion. *Really?* he thought.

"Yes Boris. Lean back and push into the wall behind you."

"That's really easy though," Boris replied in more confusion.

Nehemiah chuckled. "It is."

Boris nodded in acceptance. He corrected his posture, brought his knees to his chest, and let his hands push on his knees for more shove. He smiled, not understanding why Nehemiah made the task sound so complicated. He pushed into the wall.

He was instantly frightened.

The wall was no longer solid.

It let his body sink into it.

He could feel himself going through the wall. It felt like a cold slime resting on his back, and the further he pushed, the more his body felt the cool. He had never felt like this and tried to pull himself out. He grabbed his thighs and pulled, though it was with great resistance. "What did you do!" Boris yelled at Nehemiah.

"Again, that is something you'll never understand. You must trust me Boris. Do you trust me?"

Boris replied, "I trust you, but . . . can't we walk in like a normal person?"

Nehemiah was hasty in his reply. "A normal person doesn't have defiant legs. A normal person doesn't know what you know." He then spoke slowly and deliberately. "You were never born to be normal, Boris. A normal person doesn't hold conversations with talking flowers that make them invisible, nor have their childhoods wrecked by four legged creatures that tower over men of any height."

Boris was taken back by Nehemiah's last point, "You mean . . . on The Day . . . that thing . . . you know it? You know the thing that . . . " His breathing quickened. "You know?!"

Nehemiah breathed, then responded. "Yes Boris, I do know of Raktaar. I fear I know him more closely than you do and have been hurt more so by him than you. Do what I ask, and he will not hurt any others."

Boris snapped when he heard Nehemiah's response. He realized how he had a chance to face what had made his life what it was. He realized this was what he had wanted for years. Anger and fury surged through him, both of which were sirens of action calling him to rise to the task given to him. His face screamed with wrath, and passion lit fires of energy in him. He leaned forward, letting his chest rest on his knees. He looked to the flower in his pocket.

"I'll do what you say. I can't let anyone else get hurt." He pushed hard, driving himself into the wall.

He felt the wall flow around him. He used his core to push through the wall faster, now having a stronger desire to get this book of Patrick's. He closed his eyes and tried to ignore how he was going through what was a solid wall.

He felt how soft the solid wall had now become. He could feel his head appear through the other side, and he opened his eyes when they were out. He pushed a breath out, then drew another in—he couldn't breathe when going through the wall. He looked, though his head couldn't move, and saw how he was in Patrick's room. He felt his chin leave the wall and he looked around some more.

He could see the bookshelf behind him. It was tall and wide, filled with all manner of books. He could feel his back getting close to the floor, a cold carpet that hadn't been stepped on all day. He saw how there was lots of scrunched paper on the floor with plenty of pencil shavings. He saw how his walls were scattered with posters of great writers of the past and how they had snippets of their work surrounding them. He pushed along the floor with his arms, pulling his legs through the wall. Nehemiah stayed in his pocket, and kept silent while Boris was going through. It took less effort to get his legs through, though the inability to use them posed a challenge.

"Alright Nehemiah. I did what you asked. What's next?"

Nehemiah replied, though it was unusual. "Boris, you had trust in me before and I will ask of it again, for this is where my instructions must be followed with particular detail. Shall we continue?"

Boris breathed a deep breath, not liking the severity of Nehemiah's words. "Yeah, let's keep going."

"You choose well Boris. If you could sit yourself on the wall such to see the bookshelf behind you, for you are not yet capable of standing on your own strength. I'll show you your good friend's book when you've done so."

Boris followed the request and dragged himself onto the wall, feeling how much smoother it was. "Alright. I see the shelf. Which one is Patrick's book?"

The flower glowed brightly in his pocket, then spoke in his mind. "I will show you. Throw me to the shelves and I will land on your friend's work."

Boris chuckled. "You're a random little thing, aren't you?"

"This proves much more effective than to attempt a description of the text's outer, and it is always pleasant to delight in the freedom of floating through the air."

Boris smiled as he tossed Nehemiah up and to the shelf. When the flower reached its highest, it curved its petals and glided to the shelf. It was a slow flight, and it swayed side to side as it descended to Patrick's book. It landed on a leather book with its stem balancing on the book's spine, a little thinner than one of Boris' fingers.

"Now, Boris, we must take this book."

There was a pause before Boris replied, "How?"

Nehemiah chuckled. "If I must explain, you take your weight onto your hands rather than your rear, and position your legs to push yourself up–"

"Yes, thank you for helping my two-year-old me take his first steps. Remember how my legs don't work?"

Nehemiah chuckled again. "Yes, I do remember. You said you would trust me, remember?"

Boris hanged his head and rubbed his eyes. "I'm telling you; I can't get this book. My legs are dead from today. I can't get up, and I can't simply walk over . . . " As he was saying this, he rose to his feet and made his way to the shelf. He had no knowledge that he was standing easily and walking without strain, for he was too distracted by wanting to prove Nehemiah wrong. Nehemiah was laughing with himself when the light of confusion and realization dawned in Boris' head, who looked to the flower and asked in a tone of confusion. "How?"

Nehemiah continued to laugh a deep belly laugh that boomed in Boris' head. "I am certain you would take mountable pleasure in receiving that knowledge, but that is not what you should remember. See, it was me that allowed you to walk again. I can power you to do many wonderful things, but it is through me that such things are done. You do not undertake these tasks on your own strength. Will you be able to learn this?"

Boris breathed and rubbed his shoulders. "Nothing you say is ever done simply is it? Everything a chance to teach me something?"

"Yes, Boris. We are then capable of discussion, a reciprocating system of ideas that allows for a connection to be assembled. There is more that we are yet to do, however, and there are times you are going to doubt me more than you have ever conceived the idea of doubt. It is also in my nature to ensure what I say and do is correctly understood."

Boris laughed to himself. "You're an unusual character, Nehemiah." He went to remove the book from the confines of its neighbors. "Though your manner is truly kind–"

Boris stopped talking when he saw Nehemiah slide down to where he was about to grab the book.

"It is well heard Boris, though . . . " He paused. "This book is unlike any other book. A standard text allows ideas to transmit into your mind and brain through physical extraction of the information yourself. This text . . . is not standard. Should you simply contact this text through sensory touch, you will have a lens removed from your mind so long as this contact is maintained. You are not ready for such sight. No person truly is."

Boris sighed, "So the weirdness begins."

"The weirdness does begin yes, though we are not yet close to the apex of weirdness you are yet to experience."

Boris breathed out. "I don't like the sound of that."

"You need not fear, Boris. That is some time away. Now, we must take this book and properly read it somewhere else. If you can remove your back-pack from your shoulders and undo the zip"–Boris did so while Nehemiah continued–"I will remove the book and help drop it into your backpack. Acknowledged?"

"Acknowledged. How will you drop it?" A light of excitement flew through him. "Will you change into your real form?"

Nehemiah laughed with joy at such ideas and to how he really was going to drop the book. "I do feel that you will enjoy how I will undertake this task. You are ready to catch, yes?"

"Good to go."

"Let us then obtain this book."

Nehemiah extended his flower's stem such that it was perpendicular to the book's spine. The petals extended themselves away from each other and set themselves collectively to the same angle. Then, with a little 'pop' coming from the flower bud, the petals began to spin at great speed. Boris could feel the pull of air towards the flower, and the book started to move. It was slow and gradual, and Boris could see that Nehemiah couldn't hold the book in flight. He brought his backpack close to the shelf, positioning it such that the book would fall directly into the backpack. Nehemiah continued to spin with great speed, pulling the book from the shelf. He let go as the book fell from the shelf and corrected his petal's angles such that he was flying upright. Boris felt the gentle weight of the book through the backpack.

Nehemiah stopped spinning and began to glide to Boris, who knew that he was to catch Nehemiah and put him in his shirt pocket. "Now we have the book. It is best you read it."

"Very well." Boris zipped his backpack and let the straps rest on his shoulders, doing them tight such to keep the book as close to himself as he could achieve. "Where am I going to read this?"

"You will need a place to yourself, without human distraction that is. I must be there to answer your questions, and this place must be less accessible to the threats that the book lays plainly open. They are vulnerable through that book, and they are not pleased with humans, like you, to read about it. I believe Dr Heineman Ohlman has left such a place."

Boris instantly knew. "Ohlman's tree!"

"Fine thinking Boris. Shall we depart?"

"Gladly." He took a step, then stopped. "How are we going to depart?"

"Through the wall."

"Of course we're going to walk through the wall," said with a tone like there was nothing weird at all about such an activity. Boris had a thought. "We could just walk through the house unseen?"

"We could, though there is more enjoyment to be had in walking through a wall. We could walk through a house entirely undetectable, but something assures me walking through a wall sparks your interest more?"

Boris breathed out and smiled. "Yeah, you're not wrong." He made his way to the wall he leaned through earlier. He pushed his chest out and straightened his back before taking his left foot and placing it through the slimy wall. He let his whole leg follow through, and he went through the wall sideways. It took more effort to get more of his body through the slimy wall, though it was easier now that his legs worked. He made his way through and looked around as he did. It was exactly how it was before he went through the wall, though it was entirely dark now. The moon was full, though the trees blocked the light and covered some of the ground in total darkness. He took some steps forward away from the wall, leaving him open to go anywhere Nehemiah thought to go.

He smiled. "That was enjoyable," he said. "Are we going through the fence the same way?"

A voice on his right answered that.

"No Boris. You won't be."

Boris froze when he heard that voice.

He had felt that it was not new to him, but he knew he hadn't heard it with such clarity. It was too dark for anything to be distinguishable by sight, though he felt much fear in what he heard.

"Make yourself known," he shouted, not knowing where specifically he should shout, though he knew that Nehemiah would protect him.

"I don't need to do that. You already know who I am."

"Then let me see you."

"Are you sure you want that?"

"I have no fear. Do you have the chest to face me?"

"I do. I've been waiting years for this Boris."

A deep and horrible laugh came from Boris' right.

A violent and evil red glowed to his right. It permeated equally from its source: 4 spear-like legs, an incredibly tall torso, and a bald head controlling a mouth of many sharp teeth. His hands had spear-like fingers that were curled and prepared to rip flesh. His eyes were open, a mix of red and white, and furious.

"Hello Boris. Remember me?"

CHAPTER 6

TANYA LAY AWAKE ON a bed.

It wasn't hers.

She knew not whose it was, and she knew not where she was.

The room she was in was clean and bright. She was just waking up, but she could feel that something wasn't right. Her surroundings were blurry and she couldn't hear well, but she could feel how her face hurt less. She adjusted herself, sat herself up, and rubbed her eyes. She felt more alert, though she didn't appreciate what she heard and saw.

The screams of Hailers and the grunts of Gollums were around her. She knew she was at a place of treatment, but she knew it wasn't a normal hospital. She hadn't been to a normal hospital since she was a little girl. They still existed, but everything changed after Project Monster.

PROJECT MONSTER WAS AN initiative that came about when it was realized how untapped the human body was in terms of potential. Some saw how effective it would be for peace-keeping purposes if the capabilities of man and machine were joined together. Those that weren't as effective in their designated operations, under Project Monster, were tasked with protecting their fellow, however far a stretch it was, 'humans' on a 'homier' level. This was amazingly successful, and the initiative was dubbed 'Project Solace'. Societies had never felt so safe, nor had they ever felt so cautious about doing serious wrong.

Safety was at a high, with everyone knowing how well protected they were by the Gollums and Hailers that worked under Project Solace.

With the Gollums and Hailers being overall better than the unmodified human at peacekeeping, it also opened itself to a dark reality: the greater something is, the more corrupt it can become.

The things that kept homes and families removed of crime and violent malice soon reconciled with their inherent, untreated human nature.

They had so much power over the people they protected, and some desired for more.

When this desire spread among other operatives, talk grew of a creature that could offer this power.

It started in a small group, but word spread among the Gollums and Hailers. The conditions were simple for those that were interested: report, and bring back humans that were exceptionally brilliant, and they would be granted abilities not even machines could give. Foresight that could change the course of missions, strength that could only be found in mountains, and anything the Gollum or Hailer required to make them greater than their peers. Many heard these conditions and thought very little of them, though they knew not what the creature did with these exceptional humans.

That creature is Raktaar, and those that are doomed with knowing what he does with the exceptional humans become enslaved to him, assisting him with his continual harvest. Some are horrified at what they now know; they become Screams. Some are fascinated by the power that they see before them; they become agents.

All of them delightfully and fearfully serve under Raktaar.

Tanya knew not of Raktaar, his name at least, nor his connection with the Hailers and Gollums. She did know that she was in a place where they worked, for she knew that if anyone had anything to do Project Solace, including being rescued by either a Hailer or a Gollum, they had some involvement with their unique Facility.

She was in the medical area of this Facility—in her town's Facility at least. The rooms were small and held space only for one other patient, such to keep each other company and the Facility's numbers manageable.

She could see how there was a young woman on her right. She had short yellowy-green hair, light skin, freckles, and long arms and legs. Tanya could see the shoulders of what was a light green skin-tight shirt.

"Hey," she paused while she thought. Her head was clouded with pain relief. "My name's Tanya. What's yours?"

She didn't respond.

She was looking at the ceiling when Tanya first noticed her, and she hadn't stopped looking.

Tanya assumed that her other eye was a normal eye, though all she could see was her left eye.

A Hailer's eye.

It was designed like a normal eye—they didn't want it to be too creepy—but the white of the eye were many silvery metallic-grey panels that came from the center of the eye and worked around the eye, back into the socket. The panels overlapped, and the center of the eye was as black as a human's.

Tanya kept talking. "I really like your hair. It looks really cool."

The other girl said nothing.

Her face remained motionless. There were patches of skin, but there were lots of scars. One across her machine eye, another across her mouth. Many smaller scars across her face. Her whole body was covered in marks and imperfections.

Tanya could see these.

She looked on her arms and felt down the center of her body

She connected with them.

"I know what it's like to have scars like those. To have a past you want to ignore. To know things that you dream about forgetting–"

"I don't want to talk with you." The other girl spoke.

"I'm sorry." Tanya paused. There was an awkward silence between them. Then Tanya attempted conversation again. "I know what it's like to feel pain like that." She nodded to the other girl's scars, a clarity returning to her. "I just thought to express that–"

"You don't know pain. You don't know what it looks like. You don't know how hard it hits." She turned her head. "You'll never know." Her entire face could be seen now. Only her left eye was from a Hailer. The other was a human eye, its iris blue. She had long scars on her face. Thick scars. Her face was young and attractive, despite the pain it showed.

Tanya mellowed on this response. She breathed, knowing each reply she could give. She could stay silent, though it offered her or her 'roommate' nothing. She could be emotional and let her frustration and anger talk, though hostility did nothing for either of them.

She let out a long breath, closed her eyes, and dropped her guard.

She knew vulnerability would be the only way something good could come out of this. She talked to the other girl, letting her know her past. "I know what it feels like to lose all control. Twice actually. The first time I saw a tall . . . thing . . . that wanted nothing but to destroy me, to walk around and know I will never be me again–"

"Why do you talk to me?" She sat up but stayed on her bed. Tanya noticed how long the girl's arms were. They were unnaturally long and easily showed her veins, marked with a vibrant blue only seen in a cloudless sky. There was muscle to her arms too. "We both need treatment. We're getting that. Then we . . . you . . . can go home. Clear?"

Tanya's heart was beating strong, and she felt her stomach hurt, for she felt pain for the young woman across from her.

Tanya turned, letting her legs hang off the bed, and looked the young woman in her Hailer eye. "My name is Tanya. When I was thirteen, I was attacked by a creature I can't bring myself to describe. Today I was beaten by a friend I held close to me–" She paused, let her head hang, and composed herself. Her eyes started to water. "There were times I hated my life. My brother and my parents kept me to Earth. I let my art direct the hatred from me into something else. I could then literally *burn* that hate. It was no more. It was gone to the fiery depths, never to be seen again. I was shown grace and love by my family and by artistic expression. Something tells me you could use that too." She was crying now. Gentle tears, but still sadness and a deep passion.

Her eyes hurt from how much they had cried recently, but this wasn't something she could keep in.

The other girl saw this pain. She swung her legs off the bed to her left. She was facing Tanya—she never stopped looking away—and her entire form could be seen. Her legs were abnormally long—also muscular—with the same vibrant blue marking every major blood vessel in her body, glowing just like her arm veins behind dark green skin-tight pants that were the same texture as her shirt. Her bare-feet were proportional to the rest of her, though Tanya could now see what the other girl really looked like. Her sheets were down, and her midsection was shown. Tanya could see the young girl and all that was wrong with her. Patches of grey splotched her body. She *looked* like she once was young and really sweet, but her body was ravaged by circuitry and metal. Tanya had no clue as to what part of her was hers and which was installed into her.

What was even more troubling was that the shirt neatly stopped around the edges of the metal and circuitry.

The other girl talked with heart. "Why do you want to talk with me?"

Tanya drew a deep breath in then out. She closed her eyes while she did this, then opened them and spoke. "Because I can see the hurt you have. I've always been able to see when someone is really hurting. I always call it a gift. Plus . . . " She paused. "You seem like you're really cool. I don't know. I just thought to be a friend."

"I don't have friends. I have teammates. I have colleagues. I have connections. I was born into this wretched career. I don't have 'friends'. You make friends, you get close. You get close, you can be *betrayed* and *hurt*. I've been hurt before." She let her head hang and withdrew what emotion she could control.

There was a long pause before she continued, and Tanya saw that the other girl was working through something.

She just sat there and got ready to listen.

The other girl spoke, "I was friends with a Gollum. He and I were really good friends. I've never had a family, but I've seen how they act. We were, what you would call, siblings. His name"–she paused with emotion–"was Boaz." She hit the bed she rested in with her palm. "He was strong. He lifted trees like they were twigs and boulders like they were stones. He saved so many lives with that strength."

Her eyes began to water.

"He did some business with this thing. He was bald—I think he was a dude. He was something. He had these reddish eyes . . . " She wiped her eyes. "I don't have friends for a reason." She breathed out. "But . . . my name is Ariel."

"It's nice to meet you Ariel." Tanya said while she cried.

"I don't want to talk Tanya."

"I'm beginning to feel that." She paused. "You do look like a really sweet girl though–"

"I'm not sweet." Her tone was harsh and stern, as deep as she could go.

"You're not sweet?"

"I've killed people. I've destroyed about everything you can think of destroying. I've seen things. I've done things." She lay back on the bed she rested on. "I don't know why I'm telling you all of this."

"Because you still want a friend. You hate being alone. You hate how no-one can look at you normally, as if–"

"As if you're no longer human. You're something else that they want nothing to do with. The distance."

"The stares."

"The awkwardness."

"The weirdness."

"The hatred."

"The rejection."

"The loneliness."

"The darkness," they said together. There was an agreed silence between them, then Tanya continued. "We would be good friends for each other."

Ariel breathed, then shook her head. "I can't have any more friends. It hurts." She lay on her bed without any movement, though her hands now rested on her stomach.

The other girl was becoming more relaxed.

Tanya had a thought.

She knew not where it came from, but it was there.

She got up, now feeling much healthier after her treatment, and walked to Ariel. She didn't know how this would be received, nor what Ariel would think. She summed the courage not to care, knowing this is what the young woman in front of her needed. She found herself next to Ariel, who had not moved since she last spoke.

Ariel looked suspiciously at her.

Tanya bent over, wrapped her arms around Ariel, and embraced her in a hug.

Ariel instinctively saw this as an immobilizing enemy, and felt how restricted her arms were, though she also felt how she could still move them. She squirmed, delivering powerful blows to Tanya's ribs as she did. Tanya winced after every blow, though it only made her hug stronger. Her hands had reached around Ariel's body, and she could feel what was happening inside Ariel's body through her skin.

She could also feel that Ariel's shirt *was* her skin, assuming the same would be for her legs.

Ariel had whirring fans, buzzing circuits, and binding gears, and it felt unnaturally cold. There were warm spots, though everything else was cool. Her back was particularly startling: there were clamps and gears and screw holes. She expected to feel skin and bone, but it was designed to hold something *in* her skin, and it wasn't supposed to be removed easily. Tanya cried when she felt this. She knew not how to feel about knowing a young girl, who would have lived a wonderful life, have everything she loved, and should have loved, removed from her.

She thought to say something; anything to fill the silence.

She thought against it.

There was nothing she could say, so she spoke with her actions.

Ariel was confused. "Why are you doing this?"

"Because you need a friend, and I'm here to be one."

Ariel heard this, and she processed it.

She knew of various ways she could remove Tanya—some gentle, others lethal. She had thought each idea through at least four times now. She had been captured before and knew what it meant to be restrained. Some by human hands. Other by objects designed to hold her back.

She knew of a multitude of ways to remove Tanya from her.

She could do them swiftly.

She could do them effectively.

She could escape without any issues.

But she didn't.

She hadn't felt like this since her friendship with Boaz.

She had never felt this warmth since him. She never had a parent to love her or others to show such unrelenting kindness.

Her childhood had been filled with solidarity, formality, and violence. She didn't know how she could escape these confining walls of her life, though her siblinghood with Boaz certainly helped. Since his loss, she grew colder and more distant from the world.

Tanya's embrace, even after initial countermeasures to her ribs, was still there. She had used those countermeasures against Gollums that got too personal, but Tanya kept holding on.

She fought, but Tanya held her.

She resisted, but Tanya put a hand behind her head and let it rest on her human right shoulder.

She didn't know how to respond to this, but she felt, from another set of instincts, that she was to put her arms around Tanya.

"I haven't hugged anyone since Boaz," Ariel said in a sad tone. She had no-one that could appreciate her for her.

In her career, a person's occupation was their life. They wanted something more satisfying, but they didn't know what that something was. Ariel had found it once before, and she knew she found it again with Tanya.

"That's why I'm here" Tanya replied.

"Thank you." Ariel was in tears, sobbing and pressing herself into Tanya. She felt a warmth on her skin and a wave of relief flood her and wash over her, cleaning the darkest parts of herself. She couldn't feel the Brasher Blood flow through her like she always could, which was what made her cold to touch.

It was what made her who she was in combat, and it was what made her skin and blood the color it was. It made her one-part Gollum and the other part next level operative.

Tanya brought a warmth that the hottest deserts couldn't bring.

She couldn't hear the machines whirring in her body, which she used to survive what couldn't be survived.

She could only feel Tanya's warmth from her human skin, sense her human heartbeat through her hand, and feel the rise and fall of her human lungs.

She tapped Tanya to signal that she could let go now. It was received. Ariel sat herself up and Tanya stood straight, having now shown Ariel the kindness she had always yearned for.

They both wiped their eyes and laughed.

"I'm such a mess," she said as she removed the tears. "Look at me. Crying! I haven't cried since Boaz . . . "

"It's just the hatred falling out. It's quite okay."

They both smiled and laughed, having now closed the gap that existed only a short time ago.

Then Ariel froze.

Tanya's face morphed from happiness to confusion. "Ariel . . . " She looked at Ariel's face. It was looking down, though her ears suddenly glowed the same vibrant blue that was everywhere else in her body. "Ariel?"

Ariel was hearing something.

She had heard this sound before, and she liked it now as much as she did when she first knew what it was. "Four legs. They're in a rhythm I've heard once before. I know that gait. It sounds a little different though. The timing is . . . off." Her eyes opened wide, wider than Tanya ever saw them open. Her breathing quickened, and her face dropped into horror. She made haste out of her bed and looked under the bed, hoping to find something. She pulled out a pack not unlike those worn by Hailers. She let it rest on her back and allowed it to clamp to her.

She looked to the window, knowing that it was not easily broken through.

She breathed out in frustration, knowing that everything was contained in the one ginormous building and the glass was a layer of protection for those inside.

She then looked the wall next to the window and knew how weak it would be from the inside. *Who thinks to go through walls from the inside?* she thought.

"Ariel? Is everything okay?" Tanya wondered.

"Do you trust me?" Ariel replied.

Tanya was taken back by this.

"Tanya! Do you trust me?"

"Yeah, I trust you."

"Good. We need to go." She let some S.M.A.R.T. rope come out of her pack and had it tie itself into a harness knot around Tanya. The rope tightened to keep Tanya secure, though it wasn't constricting. Ariel turned to Tanya. "Let's go. Run through the wall. I'll catch you."

Tanya was confused at this. "Run *through* the wall?"

"Yes! We're only four stories high. I'll run through first to break it, then you'll jump out after me–"

Tanya could now hear the rhythmic tapping of four hard legs, though her hearing warned her too late. She turned to the entry door and found a tall creature with peeling skin and decaying flesh. Its torso was a little shorter than she last remembered, but a mouth full of sharp teeth bore a hideous smile. It spoke first to Tanya. "Hello Tanya. Remember me?"

Ariel turned and saw, knowing well that Boaz was lost to him.

Flashbacks of her final rescue attempt for Boaz haunted her resurging anger.

The cuts.

The hits.

The beating.

The hopelessness.

She knew it was best if she and Tanya ran.

It helped that Ariel knew how to fly.

She yelled at Tanya. "Let's move!" Fear inspired them both to run. Ariel ran first through the wall. It had some strength in it, but it stood no chance against her Brawler Blood. She jumped, feeling the awe and excitement of free falling, and relaxed her arms to help feel the rush of air through her fingers.

There were many parts of her life she hated, but she loved how she could fly.

Her pack thrusters activated, and with it her pack unfurled into two wings that almost matched her arm span. She had done extractions like this in past and knew how to make this not terribly uncomfortable for her casualty, remembering the timing required for each maneuver.

Tanya followed Ariel's jump. She had never jumped off something so high. She felt some of the dust of the wall fall on her, then felt it fall off as he flew behind Ariel. Tanya could feel Ariel's experience, swaying a lot less than she expected to. Ariel looked down and tried to see her new friend. Her eyes couldn't see in the dark of night, and flying above the lights of the world made it harder. She winked with her left eye, and her Hailer Eye allowed her to see heat rather than visible light. She could see a form of red, yellow, and orange, and how it was holding tight to the rope harness around it. One couldn't tell that this form was Tanya's based on the red, yellow, and orange. But Ariel knew that this blob of colors hanging to her by a thick strand was *her* friend.

She smiled, though her eye focused shortly after. There was a form behind her that she had recognized many times before in thermal. The bottom of the form was as white as her thermal could show. Distinct wings on either side. A soft red in-between.

A Hailer.

Hailers have their packs infused into their spines, allowing the operator to 'think' through them. The trailing Hailer talked to Ariel by doing so. "You have defied my master Raktaar–"

"I've seen what your master can do. I've seen the power he gives and I've seen the hurt he leaves." She rolled left and pitched up, preparing to fly behind the trailing Hailer. "I'll try and make this painless." She kept in mind Tanya hanging from her pack. Her turn wasn't as tight as she normally would perform it.

The trailing Hailer saw Ariel turn through his thermal sights and turned left himself. He wanted to stay behind Ariel and make the most of the turrets on his wings.

He had experience in eliminating rogue Hailers, and he delighted in destroying those that wanted to run away from the fear they found themselves amongst.

He set his Hailer Eyes on Ariel and focused on her pack. She couldn't do anything if it wasn't working, particularly being so high from solid ground. With his wings locked to his body, as a Hailer always does in flight, two plates of dark grey metal slid down from his shoulders to his wing's tips. They exposed two long and thin cylinders on both shoulders that fired what was known as 'Hailer Hail': long, thin cylinders with a dome top and a raindrop-style base. Designed to make each shot matter, they were explosive and blew up whenever the Hailer commanded to do so; either on contact or near their target.

His Hailer Eyes allowed him to see Ariel through what was a very dark night. He could see how he was closing the distance, and he caught sight of his target's pack. He commanded his shoulders to fire their Hailer Hail onto the enemy's pack. They adjusted.

He was close.

His guns were ready.

He was about to shoot and bring down his target.

Then Ariel dived down, almost an instant drop, out of the Hailer's sights.

She circled around the Hailer from underneath. The Hailer was still confused by the sudden disappearance of his target and couldn't see Ariel behind him. She established her Hailer Hail turrets to fire on the center of the Hailer's pack, hers being shot from her wing's tips.

He looked behind him, as best he could, to see Ariel trailing him.

She fired.

The Hailer stood no chance.

He couldn't react fast enough. The Hail rained on the pack with a focus on power and not fire rate.

It took three shots before the pack failed.

The Hailer could only glide. Ariel continued to fire on the Hailer, unleashing more hail to make sure the Hailer could do no more harm. The legs began to explode, noticing just briefly in the moonlight that the Hailer had a single scratch on his thruster.

Then the Hailer became a fireball. She breathed, hating how she had taken another life.

She had lost count of deaths that could be attributed to her.

She flew through the fireball, smiling as she went through the hot air. It was such a strong change from the cool air she felt from flying so quickly, and it was so sharp that Ariel could never get bored with the sensation. There were parts of her life she enjoyed.

Small parts.

Very small parts.

SHE WAS CONFUSED THOUGH.

Only the best Hailers could match her speed—or get close to it. She deduced that, under that thing's enslavement, the Hailer she just destroyed was granted better speed. What confused her was the training he didn't follow as he went about his pursuit. The better Hailers would have seen how Ariel dived and followed hastily after her. They would have cut their thrusters, kicked their legs to change direction, and re-engaged their thrusters for a sharp turn to see their six.

But this Hailer didn't.

He expected to get Ariel as if she was like any other target.

Like an arrogance clouded his thinking.

She shook her head, removing the Hailer's arrogance from her mind. She had more important matters to concern herself with.

She saw a large mountain range on her right and thought to land on its peak. She descended to the peak's altitude.

When she got closer to the mountains, she pitched up and undid the S.M.A.R.T. rope around her friend, letting her begin a controlled free-fall to the ground. She dived down and caught Tanya with her arms, kicked her legs to change pitch, then engaged her thrusters for a controlled descent to the peak's surface.

She could feel Tanya shivering and see how pale her face had become.

Ariel landed, lay her friend on the ground, and got to work. She found what flammable materials she could find and made the beginnings of a small fire. She activated her thrusters to light a stick and placed it on her gathered materials.

She had lit a fire and kept her friend warm: this brought a smile of satisfaction.

She then heard footsteps coming from her right.

She froze.

She looked to her right, forgetting that she couldn't see well at night. She switched to her thermal vision.

She saw an invading armada of creatures she had never encountered before. They flapped their wings, but she couldn't see much else.

"Of everything I have to use, they are one of my greatest tools."

Ariel shot herself to the skies, wings still deployed, keeping herself from the ground, and hovered while she determined who spoke.

She didn't need thermal vision to confirm who was there.

Four legs.

Decaying skin.

Rotting flesh.

All glowing an intimidating red.

"Hello, Ariel," the creature said.

Ariel's anger surged through her.

She set her Hailer Hail to fire on the thing that brought so much darkness into her life. The cylinders pushed out from her wings and pivoted down, angling themselves inward to fire at the thing's head.

She didn't fire yet. "What is wrong with you?!" She asked.

"Many things honestly."

"How-how did you get from the Facility to here? You can't fly."

"I don't need to fly. If I need something done precisely and properly, I use my corrupt Hailers. If I need something done with unformidable strength . . . " He looked to the horizon, "I use my Screams."

She spoke in a fierce tone. "How did you get here?"

"I simply appear. I need no method of moving myself apart from my mind. I can simply think myself to be somewhere, and I'm there. See, I could think that I'm on your pack–"

Ariel spun around, anticipating Raktaar to be on his pack.

He wasn't there.

The thing laughed. "You really are afraid, aren't you?" He couldn't control his laughter. It was a horrible laugh, not one of true happiness. It was a dark and disgusting sound.

It gathered itself. "Now, I really need to ask. What's stopping you from killing me now?"

"Honestly? Nothing." She opened fire on Raktaar, unleashing a storm of fiery bombs onto her enemy. She fired for as long as she was angry, letting loose every bit of hate she's ever held against the thing that showed her the meaning of pain.

She stopped when she realized the explosions weren't exploding where she wanted them to happen.

She just made a large crater on top of the mountain-peak.

She ceased fire and saw a tall creature with four legs with spear-like tips laugh again. His laugh was louder and deeper this time. He spoke, "I am vulnerable to whatever means you devise to eliminate me, but that doesn't mean I need to fall servant to them. You aren't bound by the natural when you're supernatural."

Ariel screamed in anger. She never knew an opponent she couldn't beat. She never knew someone that could find her weaknesses so finely and press it until it broke her.

She looked and felt the danger that was imminent, a multitude of enemies larger than she'd ever versed.

She looked ahead and saw an opponent she was unable to defend against.

She thought to fly away, and she knew she could, but she then looked to the fire.

She saw her friend.

Tanya was on the ground, close to the fire, trying to stay warm. She had been attacked by him before and was likely to finish his task.

She was also asleep: her body was retaining what warmth it could.

Ariel closed her eyes. She breathed a large breath in, summoning her courage to push herself further than she'd ever pushed. She breathed a large breath out, attempting to remove all her fear and concentrate on what she needed to do.

She would fight to save herself and Tanya.

Whatever was required of her.

As far as her body could take her.

Even to her last breath.

CHAPTER 7

"You!" Boris exclaimed at the glowing creature to his right. "Do you know what you have done to me and my sister?! The pain you brought to us both?!"

"Do you know the pain you brought me?!" Raktaar responded. "I need you and your miserable kind to live!"

Nehemiah spoke. "There was a time when you didn't need such things Adam–"

Raktaar saw the glowing flower in Boris' pocket.

"Leave me!" He side-threw with both his arms a circular pulse of bright and fast-moving red, hoping to destroy the current vessel Nehemiah chose for himself.

The pulses connected with Boris' chest and forced him through the fence he jumped over not long ago. He felt his back collide with the ground and grip the grass. He felt his neck stretch as he rolled back. He felt his knees collide with the hard ground, his ankles stretch, and his arms unsuccessfully cushion his fall.

"We must depart, Boris," Nehemiah said quietly.

Boris was groaning and gaining his composure. "Aren't we still invisible?"

He talked at a fast pace. "You are correct. No-one but us three know the real condition of the fence or yourself. Note the powerful creature in-front of you and note *your* inability to successfully defend yourself against it."

"Can't you fight him?"

"I could, and in due time I must. Such a creature as powerful as Raktaar is not easily defeated. Remember the plan I have, Boris. Trust me, and that four-legged horror you see will be no more."

Raktaar had waited to see what condition Boris was in after the forceful shove of his pulse. When he saw that Boris was coming to, he made a quick approach.

Boris saw the terrifying sight make its way to him, and a powerful surge of fear flooded his body.

Nehemiah spoke. "Sprint, Boris! Sprint!"

Boris got to his feet and ran the way he first walked, not knowing where else to run. Nehemiah still glowed strongly in his pocket, and Boris felt a speed unlike anything he'd experienced before. He felt the strength of the wind on his body and the power he had in his legs.

RAKTAAR WAS CHASING FURIOUSLY behind.

His legs were moving faster than he'd ever felt them move.

When he saw Boris gaining distance from him, he roared loudly and forced his legs to grow. He felt his midsection shorten and his height increase as his internal reservoir of sludge was used to make his legs longer.

He was now gaining distance.

Nehemiah spoke to Boris. "Young Boris, this is where your faith in my abilities is dearly required. Does this faith exist?"

Boris replied as he was breathing quickly. "Yes . . . what do . . . you . . . have in mind?"

"Begin to arc right as I request so, then jump as high as you can in the air and bring your knees to your chest. Hold them there with your hands. You can move when I say you can move, and you will need to hold your breath. Is this doable Boris?"

Boris closed his eyes and focused. "Yeah . . . that's . . . doable . . . how close . . . is the . . . arc?"

"Within two houses from . . . now."

Boris continued to run while Raktaar continued to chase. Most of Boris had the strongest urge to fight, but a small part of him recognized that it would mean nothing. He recognized that Nehemiah had a plan, and he could not formulate anything better on his own mental faculties.

Raktaar had only felt so enraged once before.

"I will kill you Nehemiah! I will drown you in my sludge and use you to make more Screams!" He yelled. He roared a powerful roar and pushed himself to run as hard as he could.

"Arc right . . . now!" Nehemiah shouted in Boris's head.

Boris began to run in an arc to his right. He was running between two fences that had a thin walkway between them; a simple concrete path that cut through the block of houses. He ran along the pathway for a little while, feeling the secrecy he had in-between the tall trees on his left and right.

"Jump now!" Nehemiah whispered with energy.

Boris jumped as he did after breaking through the school wall: he stomped with his right foot and used his left knee to gain more momentum up. He raised his knees into his chest and held them tight with his hands. He instinctively pressed his face into his knees and fought every desire to prepare his legs for a painful landing. He took a big breath in.

He felt the ground through his rear and feet.

He then felt the ground through his ankles and thighs.

He then felt the ground through his chest.

He felt the cool as he went through the ground into the dirt underneath. It felt exactly like when he went through the wall at Patrick's house. He felt the cushioning effect of the ground as he fell through it.

Then he felt the sudden stop.

He had never fully understood the terror of claustrophobia.

Now he had.

He felt the ground go solid around him, and he felt the inability to move anything. He felt the dirt press against his mouth and nose.

He had faith that Nehemiah would tell him when it was safe to move.

He hoped with every nerve that it would be soon.

RAKTAAR SAW BORIS CHANGE his direction. He saw him arc to his right and disappear behind trees of considerable height. He stopped where he saw Boris disappear and looked down the path.

He couldn't see anything.

He continued to glow to help himself see and shortened his legs to their usual height, returning to something he was familiar with. He walked slowly along the path, not knowing how he and Nehemiah could vanish into nothingness. He looked closely at the ground, checked behind trees, looked up into the branches.

He couldn't see anything.

He roared.

It was a fierce roar, shouting hate and anger. "I will find you Nehemiah! I will kill you! I will burn you! I will let my Screams tear you apart!" He laughed as loud as he could laugh, hoping they would hear.

BORIS AND NEHEMIAH WERE able to hear Raktaar. Boris was doing his best to hold his breath, but he felt the strong urge to take a breath in. He could feel the solid dirt block his nose, and he knew he could only breath in the brown dust.

He wanted to move, but he couldn't.

He wanted to open his eyes, but he couldn't.

He felt the air leave his lungs and be replaced by what his body wanted out. He could feel the beginnings of a riot form in his chest, as his body wanted the supplies it needed to live.

He tensed, knowing that he wouldn't be able to satisfy their demand.

Raktaar, still confused and angry, pushed his hands slowly outwards and sent a field of red around him. He wanted it to be a field that expanded slowly so that he could see what it would reveal. He saw the insides of trees and the other side of fences. He could see rats scurrying around in the darkness and people asleep in their beds, as if there was nothing stopping his sight. When he did his scan of the ground beneath him, knowing that Nehemiah was crafty in his escapes, he saw small chunks of dead plants. He saw lots of leaves and concrete chunks from decades ago.

He saw a flower and a body.

He raced to the flower and body . . .

But then he stopped.

He had an idea.

He tapped above where he saw the body and the flower.

He would wait until Boris choked to death.

He would die a claustrophobic, frightening death, without any light to see anything, and his skin feeling only the weight of the dirt above and around him.

He would die a very terrible death of being buried alive.

At this, Raktaar laughed to himself.

Nehemiah and Boris felt the taps. They heard the dull thuds of the dull point of a foot against the dirt.

Boris did not appreciate this.

Boris felt his body riot against him. He could feel his legs yell their concern about not moving, his arms shaking in fear, and the weight of the dirt above him. The strongest of all the unbearable voices was his lungs, who were screaming as loud as they could.

They wanted to supply what the body needed to live, but they couldn't.

They were furious with Boris, wanting him to better care for his body.

The monster in his chest had never howled so loudly.

Nehemiah sensed that Raktaar was above them.

He knew he could burst through the dirt and throw Raktaar away to be dealt with later . . .

But doing so would kill Boris.

He was limited to his flower form.

But this still had use for him.

He sensed, through the dirt, where Raktaar had placed his feet. Knowing his back two were out of sight, he thought to mess with them.

He told the ground beneath his back left foot to go soft like the ground Boris jumped into.

RAKTAAR FOUND HIMSELF TERRIBLY off balance.

He felt his entire body angle down towards where his foot was sinking into the dirt, and he found difficulty in resisting the mush.

Then he roared in pain as the bone he used as his back left foot snapped in half.

He could feel the bone puncture what was left of his skin and muscle, and he felt the exposed bone against the weirdly sloppy mud.

He felt the mud mercifully push the broken foot out of the ground, forcing Raktaar to adjust his entire body over three legs. It wasn't something he was used to, and he felt a gentle pain rise from his spine and back right leg as his body learned to adjust.

He used his reserve of sludge within his midsection to heal his back left leg, but healing was a resource intensive job. For such a break, his sludge reserve would reduce it only to a slight break. It wasn't a pain he was unfamiliar with, but it wasn't helpful to have either. And it hurt to stand on and put pressure directly on. He couldn't safely stay and watch Boris suffocate to death.

He'd have to bathe in his bath of sludge longer tonight.

In his anger, he roared at the ground, then began to walk away. Around the corner. Along the path.

Back to a network entrance to heal.

BORIS COULD HEAR THE roar.

Boris could hear the snap of Raktaar's foot.

Boris heard the groan as Raktaar learned to balance again.

He could feel his brain slowly lose control and slip into a darkness it couldn't be saved from.

Then he heard the most amazing words of his life. "You can get up now, faithful Boris."

Boris fought his way furiously to the surface.

He pulled with his arms and pushed with his legs, feeling his surrounds go soft again. He scrambled to feed the monster in his chest. He felt his head go light and his arms and legs lose their strength. He felt his head peak through the surface, but he didn't know if his nose would make it. He could feel his heart thunder in his chest, his stomach muscles tensed to hold his diaphragm in place, and he started losing conscious control of his body.

Then his nose broke the surface.

It breathed out and let a new supply of materials flood through.

Boris could feel conscious control of his body return.

His shoulders relaxed, and a shiver went over his arms and legs. The monster in his chest was appeased, and he had a strength that he was used to. He was able to pull himself out, feeling how the ground became solid under his hands. He did his best to control his breathing, but it was a challenge. When he pulled his feet from the ground, he collapsed onto his back, relishing in the freedom his limbs now had. He now had an appreciation for something he never knew he could lose.

"We're . . . safe . . . now?" Boris asked Nehemiah through the gasps for breath.

"Yes, Boris. We are safe. Very well done."

Boris kept breathing heavily, feeling now a turbulence of emotions in his chest. "That . . . was . . . hard."

Nehemiah breathed out. "I know. I know that was hard, and I know that made you reach a level of uncomfortable that you have not reached in some time." A pause. "I must ask though. Do you still trust me?"

Boris began to sob. "I trust you . . . it's just that . . . " He began to cry. "This is . . . really hard." He sat up, resting on his arms. He was able to speak in longer sentences now. "You keep asking a lot of me Nehemiah," he sobbed, "and I don't know if I can do everything you ask of me."

"Young Boris, I know this will not be easy. You wish to bring a halt to his tyranny, yes?"

"Yes, I do," he sniffed. "I just never knew it would be this difficult."

"I'm afraid the plane of existence he and I live on is the birth of difficulty. We think higher than your kind and are faced with problems that are entirely unknown to you, with your solutions to those problems being entirely ineffective. If you were to attempt his demise on a plan of your devising, you will find yourself in the leagues of his Screams. Should you trust me, no matter how ridiculous I sound or how challenging the task that I present is, I assure you that you will make it through. Now, shall we rest, then go and read that book?"

Boris sniffed again and rubbed his eyes, but paused before doing so. He remembered the dirt on his hands from when he dragged Tanya and himself to Ohlman's Tree. He got the inside of his shirt and used that instead. He appreciated how Nehemiah could keep himself clean otherwise.

He then nodded his head. "Yeah . . . let's read this book."

Boris got to his feet and began walking to his house.

From there, he would be able to find his way to Ohlman's Tree.

CHAPTER 8

ARIEL COULD SEE THAT the 'Screams' were a fair distance away.

She had some time before they would reach her and Tanya, though she knew it wouldn't be long.

She saw how the creature with four legs was the more imminent threat. She fired her Hailer Hail as much as she could, directing it to the creature's head. She could see that the creature had a red field around it that stopped anything from hitting it. She knew she wouldn't be able to hit it directly.

She also knew that anything was only as strong as its supports.

The field was impenetrable, but the creature could be put off balance.

She blasted the creature with more Hailer Hail, knowing she had plenty of rounds that she could use. She knew each explosion created a small fireball, with each blast leaving a little cloud of black smoke. She had lost count of the shots she fired, but she knew that there was a cloak of black now surrounding the creature. The crater she created, having now blown away the loose dirt, stopped growing. She sent some more rounds, then ceased fire.

Instantly after, she kicked her right leg up, then her left, letting herself roll backwards. As she rolled, she commanded the panels in her palms to open, letting two double-edged blades with simple handles slide into her hands. The panels closed, and she now held in both her hands sharp weapons that were two-thirds the length of her long fore-arms. She cut power to her thrusters for a small moment, then activated them at full power.

She flew at full speed, aiming directly at the creature's chest.

She angled the blades such that their tips overlapped. She brought her arms close, hoping to spear herself through the creature. She squinted her eyes and focused on where exactly she wanted to stab it.

She flew through the black cloud and saw her blades contact its red field.

She saw the abomination topple over onto its back. Her blades had not pierced the field, but she knew the creature before her was taken off-guard. She kept her thrusters on as it fell to the ground.

Startled by Ariel's anger, it dropped its shield.

Ariel flew closer to its chest, driving her blades into it. She saw how the skin tore apart, and felt how it stabbed the ground. She cut power to her thrusters, knowing she didn't need to dig herself deeper. It yelled in pain, and Ariel tried to slow her breathing down. She knew that she had killed the creature that removed Boaz from her life, and knew how satisfied she felt knowing she wouldn't do any more harm.

Then, as her breathing slowed, she had a thought that changed her perspective.

She realized that this had been too easy.

She remembered how hard this thing fought the last time she saw it, and she remembered how close to death she was. She used up every reserve of strength she could find to merely weaken such an abomination when they last versed.

This time it wasn't such a challenge.

Her breathing had returned to normal, and she wanted to know what this creature really was. Its midsection was slightly shorter, it was more scared of her than it should have been, and it shouldn't lie there with her swords in its chest and not attempt to retaliate.

She asked the creature. "Who are you?"

It didn't respond.

Ariel removed one of her swords, repositioning then slamming it into its chest, wanting to keep whatever was in front of her still. She removed the other sword, then moved it around its body.

She had found every creature has a spot that they hate being touched, and they felt terrified when her sword found it.

She began with its head, letting the point rest on its forehead.

It continued to be afraid like before.

She started to slide her sword down its body. She was kneeling over it and could only go as far as her knees.

It didn't change.

She got up and crouched beside it, continuing down its midsection.

She reached its waist; the join between the main body and its legs.

It froze with fear, locked its eyes onto hers, and breathed very quickly but very quietly.

Its eyes looked at her with desperation. "Don't press any harder," they were saying, hoping they would receive mercy.

She pressed gently against its waist and spoke slow and deeply. "Who are you really?"

In a male voice similar to that of a teenage boy's, it spoke. "I'm a drone of my master. I'm only doing what I'm told."

She began to cut his skin gently. "What were you told?"

He spoke very quickly. "To imitate my master and capture the young girl. To do whatever was required of me to complete this task. If I die, so be it. Please, don't kill me!"

She stopped cutting its skin. "I won't kill you . . . but I command that you stop your horde of 'Screams.'"

"There isn't anything to stop. They're real because you let them be real–"

She looked to the horizon and saw what she originally saw as a problematic threat. She processed the idea that they weren't real.

She blinked.

She couldn't see a single Scream.

"And I'm the same," it continued. "All of this is real only if you let it be. The only real part of me is hidden where you just had your sword."

She exhaled and pulled the sword from the its chest.

She blinked, and its entire body vanished.

All she saw was a small critter with two wings with a thick outline of rock powder and four legs with rock-powder tips. She saw how most of it glowed the same red as before. She picked up the critter with both her hands and felt its stone feet on her palms.

She commented on its small wings. "How did you follow me?"

It answered in Ariel's head. "I rode on the back of the Hailer that chased you and flew away when you blew him up."

She nodded in understanding.

She thought to ask another question. "Why is your master so determined to ruin my friend?" She looked to Tanya, then back to the critter in her hands.

It answered in her head. "I don't know. All I know is that I was created to take your friend. The finer details of my task would suggest I should have killed you by now."

"Why didn't you?" she asked.

"I had every intent to. My master isn't one to let his subordinates to go about failing him, and my existence comes from the death of your kind, but . . . that girl you call your friend . . . " A long pause. Then, "she isn't like every other human mortal. When I took a closer look at her, I realized it wasn't the fire that lit the ground so well. I've heard stories about her. The Hailers and Gollums that keep check on her." It turned to face Tanya. "I'm made from fear and refined into a thick sludge to serve my master. I felt myself collect into what I used to be before I was turned into this, then he scooped me up and made me into this. When my master gave a red glow over me, I could see attributes to your kind that you only see the fruits of. Your friend . . . has . . . a white glow about her. My master wants to stain that white as deeply as possible. Your kind pose a very strong threat when human mortals like her are not turned into sludge like me. Their white glow is contagious." It turned to Ariel. "I see it on you as well. Not as brightly, but it's there. That's why I didn't fight when you stabbed me with your swords. That glow saved you from me."

She was taken back by its answer, though appreciative that she now knew. She put away her swords. "Why is this white glow so powerful?"

"This white glow can kill me. Your friend"–it turned to face Tanya–"is immune to my master's greatest weapon. So long as the glow inside of her glows as brightly as it does, brighter than my master has *ever* seen, we, as the red sludge, can't do anything against her. Really . . . I'm petrified of her."

Ariel laughed. "You're petrified of her?" She moved her hands closer to Tanya.

The little critter shivered and cowered into her hands.

Ariel realized, now being serious. "You're really scared of her."

The little critter nodded with its body.

Ariel breathed out, realizing that this couldn't be right. "So, if I brought you really close to Tanya, and she laid a hand on where your red and gloopy, you'd die?"

"From what I've been told," he said in a shaky voice. "The sludge talks when it isn't told to do anything."

Tanya called to Ariel.

"Hey Ariel, you okay?"

Ariel looked up. She hadn't realized that Tanya had warmed herself up from the fire. "Yeah, I'm okay." She paused. "I'm going to bring something over, and I have a feeling you won't like it."

Tanya replied with confusion. "Okay?"

Ariel got up with the little critter still in her hands and brought it closer to the fire. The little critter tried to fly away. Ariel grabbed its wings and held them together, still walking to Tanya and talking as she did. She was oblivious to how the sludge could spread over her hands.

The little critter forgot he could do that too.

Ariel spoke, "So, this is what was scaring us at the Facility. It was mimicking its master whom you and I have met before. This little thing also tells me that it's scared of you–"

"Please don't kill me!" the critter yelled.

Tanya was startled, but smiled and laughed shortly after. "Why would I kill you?"

The critter spoke quickly. "You have a white glow that not many have and you're not vulnerable to us sludge and you're able to breed that white glow in others and the moment you touch me you'll kill me and–"

Tanya looked closely at the critter. "I can do that?"

"Yes! My existence is based on hate and fear, and you're able to remove that from me! Please! Don't kill me!"

There was an awkward silence. Then, "I don't want to kill you. I don't win anything by killing you. We"–she moved her hand back and forth, signifying that she was referring to Ariel and herself–"know that we're safe and don't have any immediate need to kill you." She breathed out. "Your feet look like they're made of . . . rock dust . . . you can rest on my hands and not die, yeah?"

"They are, but I know you're going to kill me. I know you want to destroy me and–"

Ariel placed the critter in both of Tanya's hands, making sure that the only part that touched her was its little rock feet. Its feet pushed them away, doing anything it could to escape.

She then received a thought.

She didn't know where it came from, nor who gave it to her, but she had faith that it was the best thing to do.

She pulled the critter closer to her face, aligning the base of its wings with her mouth, and she blew gently on the creature.

As soon as she did, a fog of black came off the little critter. A piercing roar was heard from it, having never felt something so painful before.

She stopped, realizing that she was hurting it.

"Keep going. It's okay," the voice in her head said. It could feel a relief when she blew on it.

She closed her eyes and blew again.

It continued to yell, feeling its very reason for existence be stripped from itself. The black fog she made drifted away with the wind, never to be seen again.

The little critter resting on her hands underwent a phenomenal transformation. It was once a dark red.

Now it was a creamy white.

It had the exact same form as before, but she had breathed off every part of hate that made itself one with the little critter.

She talked with the little critter. "See, I didn't kill you."

The little critter was still breathing, but it was shaking violently, trying to process what just happened. Ariel looked in wonder at what her friend was capable of.

Tanya laughed. "Now, I've been very rude. I haven't asked for your name. Mine is Tanya. What's yours?"

The critter tried to slow its shivering, but was struggling. It tried to speak, but speaking proved itself to be a task requiring great strength.

"I . . . don't . . . have . . . a . . . name . . . we . . . sludge . . . don't . . . get . . . names."

Tanya breathed out through her nose, and the critter shivered and cowered into her hands. "Please don't . . . breathe on me . . . any more . . . I feel good . . . but . . . please . . . no more."

Tanya smiled, then spoke. Her words were not her own, and she had no knowledge of who was speaking into her, but she trusted that it was a good thing to do.

She had found everything this voice told her was good to do.

"I won't blow on you. I've blown all the hate and darkness you've held on to, and now there is nothing left to blow off. Now, you must determine who it is that you are. You are no longer made of sludge. You are made of white, and I have faith you will become a gentle character." She looked to Ariel. "I have a name for him: Laban."

Ariel nodded in agreement. "I like that. It's a cool name for a little . . . winged . . . creature." She slowly let go of Laban's wings, trusting that it wouldn't fly away.

Laban looked at Tanya. He rested his wings and sat in her hands, then spoke in her mind. "I have a name?"

Tanya smiled. "Yes, Laban. You have a name."

He looked to Ariel, then back to Tanya. "And . . . you're my . . . friends?"

"Yes. We are."

He paused. Then, facing Tanya, "My . . . 'master' . . . gave me the power of thought and movement. You . . . you showed me grace. You could have killed me, and you would have a lot of reasons to do so, but . . . you freed me."

Tanya laughed. "I apparently have this gift, and I really like using it."

Ariel was watching this little critter be given a name and a new life, and a thought came across her mind that she couldn't help but voice to Tanya and Laban.

"How closely did you serve under your master?"

Laban turned to Ariel. "We sludge"–he shook his body as a sign of disagreement–"his red sludge is vital to everything he does. The sludge and him are almost one. We as the sludge also communicate among ourselves."

"Perfect. Do you know where he operates from?"

"Yes. He has network. He connects key places all over the Earth. He can't fly, so he uses that to get around quickly."

"So, he can't think he's somewhere and be there? You just made that up?"

"I was informed of some of my old master's character and behavior. He has never told anyone how he does what he does. But if he did, it would have been beneficial for him to pass that on to me."

Ariel looked at Tanya. "Laban can help us! We know more about the creature that wrecked both our lives than anyone else–"

"Not quite . . . " Tanya said. She put Laban down and pressed her face into her hands. She rubbed her eyes in self-guilt. "I forgot about Boris. I got taken by these Hailers and he . . . I hope he's okay. We need to find him." She took a breath, then, "he had a friend that we saved today. His name was Patrick, and he wrote a book about this red sludge and where it comes from. I have a feeling it talks about events that happened before the red sludge was first created. He should have it by now. We need to find him."

Ariel replied. "I can fly you there. I'll fly closer to the ground this time. It should keep you warmer–"

Laban spoke. "You know Patrick?"

There was an awkward silence. Tanya answered, "Yeah?"

Laban paused, then spoke. "The sludge killed him."

Again, a pause.

Laban continued. "He was reaching for his things, and he contacted a drop of us . . . "

Again, an awkward silence.

Then Tanya kissed Laban on his front edge, defined by a wider edge of rock dust. "You're not sludge anymore," she said. "You're with us."

As an expression of appreciation, Laban rubbed his front end into Tanya's hands. He then turned to Ariel. "If I can fly on your back"–he stuttered Ariel's name, having not said an actual name before–"I can't fly as fast as you."

Ariel smiled and helped Laban rest on her pack, scratching his front edge on her hand as she did so. Laban pressed his little rock powder feet into anything that gave him traction. She made a harness knot for Tanya like before, gently rose from the ground, then gradually accelerated. She flew over the tips of the trees to stay out of the cold air higher up.

CHAPTER 9

"So, you're sure they're going to find the note you got me to write for them?" Boris asked Nehemiah.

"I assure you, Boris. They will find your note. Everything has been undertaken as I intended it to be."

"You aren't going to tell me what your plan is either, will you?"

"No, young Boris. I'm afraid not. There, good Boris, you will need to trust me. Do you trust me?"

"I do, yeah. I've got no real reason not to trust you. I'm annoyed with you sometimes, but I trust you."

"Excellent," he replied.

They were making their way to Ohlman's Tree, having given directions and updates to Tanya. The sun was peaking over the edge of the horizon when Boris finished writing the note, having rested well and satisfied his desire to eat and be clean. He was going with Nehemiah to read through Patrick's book.

It had not been given a unique name unto itself, but Boris thought best that the work of his friend be remembered through the name of its author.

Amongst all of this, he had started to understand that there was a reason behind Patrick's death. He found processing his death much easier once he realized this. He found that trusting Nehemiah also made his life easier, and it hurt less when he didn't try and understand.

They had arrived at Ohlman's Tree. Boris began making his way up the tree, wanting to distance himself as far as he could from anyone that might pass by and unintentionally distract him. He wanted as many branches surrounding him as he could find to help himself feel shielded and at peace. He climbed a decent height, though it dawned on him that a fall from that height would not end well.

Nehemiah felt this uneasiness and thought to be of service. "Young Boris, can you please place me in the large branch you're sitting on?"

Boris grabbed Nehemiah from his shirt pocket—a shirt that was clean and comfortable and not his uniform—and placed his stem in-between the cracks of the bark.

Nehemiah glowed on and off while he talked *into* the tree.

Boris saw how there were branches beginning to surround him and make a floor for him to rest his feet on. The wood creaked as it moved, but it was not done in pain. The wood never cracked or splintered—it felt okay doing what Nehemiah asked. The leaves rustled as they moved, providing a wonderful shade that kept him cool.

"Thank you, Nehemiah," Boris said as he felt the calm and safety surround him.

"You are most welcome, Boris."

Boris removed his backpack from his shoulders and undid the zips. He tipped the bag down and gently slid Patrick's book out, wanting to avoid touching it as best he could. Nehemiah established some smaller branches to grow from the round branch it found itself resting on to help balance the book. Boris picked a leaf, wanting to properly position Patrick's book on his new table. He could flip with the pages with it too.

Boris opened the cover with his newfound leaf and began to read.

"If you're reading this, it is my hope that two things have happened. The first: you have encountered a substance that is most closely described as a 'red sludge'. The second: you have encountered a white flower with a small yellow bud and a dark green stem who his named 'Nehemiah'. If this is so, it would then be my hope that you have encountered a tall creature with four-pointed legs, red and white eyes, a bald head, and multiple rows of curved and sharp teeth. You will find this creature to be called 'Raktaar', though this is a name he gave himself.

"To have read this far would state another fact; these three conditions must then support one more. That condition: you are a part of a small group of human beings. You might have, at one time or another in your life, realized that you aren't like everyone else. You walk one way when everyone else goes another. You think one thought when everyone else thinks another. What you've experienced is a part of human existence that very few are blessed to experience. You have been given a sense of uniqueness and greatness that would rival many others. You have a strength in some area that has wonderful potential to do good; though, I fear, that strength is what makes you a target."

Boris turned the page with his leaf and continued.

"Many centuries ago, there lived two brothers. They were close, and they were not like other children. The older brother was named Adam and the younger Nehemiah. They were born with a skill not known to any before them: they had a marvelous ability to communicate with any living creature. They were able to feel the terror of a chased prey and talk with what was around them. They discovered this when they could hear the chirps of birds and understand what they were saying to each other, each chirp an entirely different message.

"They lived in the Northern Woods of the world, where the temperature was almost always some translation of cold. They would explore the woods surrounding their small home with such delight, and make all manner of friends amongst the animals that lived there.

"Their younger years were splendid for them both, for they both appreciated the goodness of their gift and had a childlike enjoyment about it. Their teenage years saw them part ways in the use of their gift, for their gift was made stronger as the years passed.

"Adam had the shorter temper out of the two boys ever since they were little. This grew only worse as they aged. When he was older, he found himself capable of *controlling* the animal as opposed to simply communicating with it. Nehemiah was opposed to this power that Adam had found himself possessing. He could also see, in his brother, a look in his eyes that suggested he wasn't controlling the animals with its best interest in consideration. This was solidified on the final day they saw each other.

"They were enjoying the woods on a stormy night, their ears in awe of the awesome cracks of thunder. Their eyes witnessed the splendor of the vast flashes of lightning. They saw how the forest adopted an entirely new persona in a storm.

"In amongst this, Adam thought to capture and control a small fox, thinking it could go around and scare any small animals it could find. He smiled to himself while he saw the young fox scurry about and scare anything it found. Nehemiah told his brother that the gift they had shouldn't be used as he was using it, hearing in the fox's thoughts how it wanted to escape Adam's control. Adam resisted this, having a dear appreciation for this control. Nehemiah gave Adam a gentle shove, wanting to help him understand what he was really doing. In retaliation, Adam drove his fist through his brother's face and watched as he fell to the ground. Adam, in anger of his brother, and having listened intently to the carnal thoughts of predatory animals, forced his fox slave to eat what he could of his brother, not caring for how that would impact anyone else. Nehemiah tried to run, but a tree root made Nehemiah trip. Adam's anger saw him stand on top of his brother, not wanting him to escape. He twisted more foxes into being his slaves and forced each of them to eat a part of his brother. Nehemiah wanted to escape but despised the idea of hurting his brother. He looked up and saw the root of a smaller tree he could reach with his right hand. He brought it up, fighting foxes as he did, and touched the trunk of the small tree. It was a baby tree, but Nehemiah saw it as his escape. How Adam's gift grew into control of animals, Nehemiah's gift widened to communicating with plants. He asked the baby tree to talk with the larger tree he tripped on, for he could not talk with plants unless directly contacting them. He felt the baby tree talk with the larger tree as easily as he felt more and more of his muscles be chewed on by small, sharp mouths. The larger tree creaked as it moved, wrapping a root around Adam's ankles. It drew its roots closer to itself, and Adam fell. He commanded his foxes to start eating the large tree as best it could, and Nehemiah used this to escape. He ran as fast as he could, winding his way through trees. His body dripped with blood as he ran, almost having no skin on his body. Small bite marks covered what once held the form of a young man. His desire to evade his brother was being quickly matched with the unbearable pain of blood coming from his muscles. He collapsed and couldn't raise himself with his arms. He tried, but he winced loudly. All of his muscles had been damaged in some way, and it took more effort to move than he thought would be practical. He lied on the forest floor, feeling the twigs and leaves on what skin he had left, crying as he felt them also on his exposed flesh. He feared that he would die far from his home, and that the foxes would begin what they attempted not long ago. He could hear their footsteps approaching from a distance.

"As he felt this, he looked up. He saw a tree with a wide trunk, wider than he'd ever seen. Its branches were up higher than any other, save for one: there was one branch unusually low. It was within his line of sight on the ground, with some dark green leaves growing from its end. He tried to move towards the branch, but he couldn't move. He saw the last hope he had ahead of him, hearing again the crunching leaves of the running foxes. He couldn't draw the strength to take hold of the extended branch. He found the strength to keep his eyes open also leave him, and he closed his eyes just as he saw the dark green leaves glow gently.

"The tree that he saw was a Hololume Tree. Its small branch near its base had been grown specifically for this time: it had anticipated this moment since it planted itself. It's origins, like most things, are unknown. It was known, though, that this tree was not like a single other tree. It extended its small branch to him and grabbed him by the shoulders, extending further to uphold his midsection, not wanting to drag his body. It stood his body up and let his feet dangle, then cut itself open from the inside. It slid him inside and closed itself around him. He died that day, but he was reborn into something far greater.

"To understand how the Hololume Tree changed Nehemiah, you need only see what he has become now. Knowing the origins of the Hololume tree is entirely unknown and will forever be unknown. The tree no longer exists either—Nehemiah embodied the tree. As of present, and for the rest, he will be a continual source of information for you regarding his past. The rest of these pages are to inform you of what happened with Adam. That story is not known to anyone else, save you when you finish reading."

Boris looked to the next page.

He saw nothing.

"Hey Nehemiah?" Boris asked in confusion.

"Yes, Boris."

"What am I reading?"

"At the moment, nothing."

Boris paused and looked at him with sarcastic amazement. "What am I supposed to read?"

"At this current moment, with your current mindset, nothing."

Boris looked in confusion, not liking how literal Nehemiah was being but knowing that was his humor. "Well . . . how am I supposed to read everything that's after this? Patrick wouldn't leave all of this blank; there has to be more to read."

"There is, yes." Nehemiah paused. "To read it, you must experience anger. When this happens, the pages you see before you can then experience anger. One cannot truly understand when one hasn't truly experienced."

"So, I get angry, and I can read it?"

"True . . . the book also requires this emotion."

Boris gave a confused pause. "How am I supposed to make Patrick's book feel anger?"

"By hitting it."

Boris stared at Nehemiah. "By hitting it?!"

"Yes. You must express your anger into the pages you see before you for the text on it to make itself known."

"But . . . that's my friend's book! My *dead* friend's book! Patrick's book! This is the last thing he left me, and you want me to hurt it?!"

"Yes Boris. To understand anger, you must experience it. To under-stand Raktaar, you must delve into a part of yourself that you shy away from, for this is then a taste of what his life is like-"

"I'm not going to punch my friend's book, or do anything to harm it!" He tried to talk, but he didn't know which thought he wanted to project. His mouth moved, trying very hard to express the pain he was experiencing in his head. "Why can't you tell me?!"

Nehemiah breathed in Boris' head, having thought through that question regularly himself.

He then spoke.

"Good Boris, can you please explain to me what a spur gear is."

Boris' face twisted with confusion and frustration. "What?!"

"You trust me, Boris, yes?"

"Yeah, I trust you–"

"Good Boris, can you please explain to me what a spur gear is."

Boris breathed out; his face now relaxed. "A spur gear is a piece of material that has had cut out of its center a circle, with carefully designed teeth on its edge. These teeth mesh with other gears that have teeth of the *exact* same design." Boris' face twisted into confusion. "How is this relevant?"

"I know you are mechanically minded, Boris. I knew you would understand what I asked quite well. Now, say I was to explain what you said to me just then to a young boy who had not yet started school. The best I could do would be to say it's a circle with its edge lined with teeth. The young boy has a horrible idea in his head, for his concept of teeth is the white, hard things in his mouth. That is not what you told me. I then attempt to explain to him that a spur gear is a circle with things coming out of its side, but each thing coming out of its side must be *the same. Exactly.* He now believes, in his head, that he can make a spur gear out of his colored pencils and anything circular that he can find. Would this work, Boris?"

"The first is gross. The second kinda works, but not very well."

"Exactly Boris; but, his ability to communicate and understand through the English language limits him to such things. In my example, I am likening human concepts. Between you and me, I must tear into smaller pieces my concepts such to show you a *bleak* something of the original, so that you, in any language, could understand. You would then shabbily understand what actually is an incredibly powerful idea. I assure you, young Boris, more harm is done this way. Am I being understood?"

Boris breathed out in disappointment. "Yeah, you are . . . you're talking into a tree. You know more than me, but my lack of understanding would make me dangerous . . . it doesn't make it any easier though."

"I know Boris. I know."

Boris looked at the book that rested before him. "So . . . you're telling me . . . that if I hit this book, I can read about who Raktaar is and how he can be defeated?"

Nehemiah replied. "The first, yes. The second . . . that's for me to arrange. You will play a powerful role however Boris."

Boris paused. "I'm going to damage the last thing my friend gave me so I can save everyone I know and hold dear from what truly is a monster . . . " He hung his head and breathed deeply. "My life."

"Good Boris, you are experiencing a conflict of interests where you are required to experience a darker necessity within you. You balance the greater good with the morality in the smallest of choices. You fight your comfort with the work you have been tasked to do and a sweet, victorious end"–he paused before continuing–"good Boris, this is your welcome to the land of darkness. Stay not long here, for it will be the *real* end of you. But . . . it is my thought that you collide your fists with the book as hard as you can muscle. The pages will feel your anger and will show the writing on them as long as you feel the anger rise through you. To understand darkness–"

"You need to experience it. I get it . . . thank you." He breathed.

He then prepared his right fist, raising it above his head.

As he drove his fist into Patrick's book, he pulled with his left and twisted with his torso, wanting to hit as hard as he could.

It would mean fewer punches.

His face scrunched itself, contorting itself into disgust and dislike.

He felt the page on his skin.

When he contacted the book, everything he saw changed.

A quick flash of strange colors surrounded him when he touched the paper. He could not distinguish what he saw, but he knew it wasn't natural. Nehemiah had a strong glow; there were patches of white and dark grey trickling through distorted colors that looked off to the eye. He could tell that the leaves were green and the bark was a woody brown, but it didn't feel like the right color. There was also a ringing in his ears that elevated his alerted state, causing him to feel on edge with what was around him.

He didn't like it, and he was thankful he only needed to experience it briefly.

He looked down.

He could see some writing show itself.

He read as fast as he could, not wanting to punch more than he had to.

"If you are reading this, you are connecting with a component of the human experience that we humans don't *really* enjoy. Many of us despise and press it as deep as we can, some delight in it, and few decide to treat it and face it properly. If you are reading this, you have chosen the third. You have connected with your moral wrong such to understand the wrong you see around you and, most personally, the wrong you have experienced–"

The writing began to fade. Boris punched the page, saw his world show colors he wasn't expecting to be there, and continued.

"Spend not long here, trudging through the darkness as you pull from the light—your mind will suffer.

"When Adam felt himself be pulled into a tree by one of its roots, he saw that his foxes were unable to save him. They clawed and bit as much as they could, but it meant nothing against the hard wood of the tree. Adam did, however, see his escape. He watched as the fox's eyes and mouth bled as they bit and maimed the bark. Each drop singed the tree. He commanded all his foxes to bite the root that was holding him, watching as the bite marks worked with the drops of burning blood–"

Text faded.

Boris punched.

World flashed.

He read.

"He found himself free, and he stumbled away from the tree. He roared out of anger, knowing that his brother had escaped him. He knew he had hurt his brother considerably, and he was satisfied with this. He looked down and saw each of his foxes stand at his feet and convulse randomly. He could see clearly now that their ears were bleeding as well, and their drops of blood singed the leaves they stood on. He dropped to a squat, and his foxes lowered their heads. They shivered when he walked closer to them, bled more, and had blood that birthed more smoke when it hit the ground. He stood up in curiosity and saw as the bleeding slowed and the blood burnt with less heat. He realized that he could terrorize anything that pumped blood and create a substance that burns. He wanted to feel what this blood felt like, and so put his hand underneath the droplets of blood. As soon as the falling crimson landed on his hand, he collapsed in pain. His foxes could see that they had a chance to escape and did so, for they were freed from the cruel service of a horrible tyrant. They felt his anger in their heads. They had no control over themselves. They saw everything, but they could do nothing. When Adam was distracted, this control was removed. He could not understand the pain he was experiencing, for it felt like the drop that landed on his hand was burning his skin and tearing itself from himself. He concentrated on where he felt the pain, and connected with the blood using his gift. He could hear the wincing of foxes in his head, a remnant of their pain finding itself amongst the blood. He then found control of the living substance, and the substance found itself resting on his hand. He no longer felt his skin burn and be torn apart, and the winces of his foxes weren't as loud in his head. He moved the drop around his hand, and thought to understand more of what appeared to be a powerful resource–"

"He walked through the woods and thought as he went. He wanted to know whether it was the blood itself that did what it did or something *inside* the blood. He determined, through capturing small animals, scaring them, and working with their blood over a fire, that there was a gluggy part of their blood that did what he wanted. You have encountered this, and you have seen both its thick consistency and its dark red color. There is a good chance, while you were encountering this sludge, that you were the next opportunity Raktaar could take to make more sludge."

"He had found, when he went and explored for more opportunities to make this sludge, that you and I, human beings, yield the most. He went about and observed how terrified everyone was of even the smallest things. He saw how the tiniest occurrences could invoke the most startling of reactions. He thought to be subtle and not take more than two from each town he visited, finding that younger ones produce more of this sludge. He filled wooden barrels with his growing collection, travelling around on horse and cart as he went. He told everyone that he passed that he was carrying 'goods', for that was what it was to him."

Maintaining his anger towards Raktaar, and the pages apparently doing the same, he continued. "On his travels, he came across a cave. This cave had an incredibly deep hole not far from its entrance, and Adam had thought to make use of it. He poured the sludge from almost every barrel he had into this deep hole, making a pool of reduced blood. He put his entire hand into the sludge and felt the burn and tear as he usually felt. He focused and controlled the sludge, seeing how the surface of the sludge made itself smooth and flat. He thought through the sludge, and he made crests in some places and valleys in others. He could form anything he wanted, and he felt a connection grow between him and the red sludge before him. He had a smile on his face, seeing how incredible his find was. He turned to walk out of the cave, but his foot found itself on some moss. He lost contact with the ground, and fell into his large vat of red sludge. He began to sink. It was hard for him to move, and he didn't know how he could get up. He felt the tsunami of noise crash into his head. He felt his skin sear and his muscles be ripped from itself and the bone it held too. He opened his mouth, despite the difficulty it took to move, and tried to release his anguish as he yelled. Bubbles formed: they rose to the surface and released a small 'pop'. He felt small drops of sludge fall into his mouth, forcing him to yell even more. His mouth could feel in even greater detail what the sludge did to him. He felt his tongue be pulled from itself and be set alight, his teeth beginning to crack. He couldn't take control of the sludge around him: the searing pain was overwhelming. He found it impossible to focus. He realized that this was to be his death. He closed his eyes, keeping his mouth opened to make the death quicker. He relaxed everything, realizing the frivolity of resisting, and submitted to his impotence. He let more sludge fall into his mouth, and he swallowed–"

Being satisfied with this punishment, Boris and the book needed a resurge of anger. Another strike, and Boris kept reading. "He felt the sludge burn his insides. It ate everything that used to keep him alive, pulling himself apart and searing anything that it touched. What he didn't know was that it was putting himself back together. His muscles felt stronger, having hate and fear be its newfound reserve of superhuman strength. He felt, with truly unbearable clarity, how his legs were cut into a front and back half. His hips and knees were realigned, forming four separate limbs that stuck out then down. His feet dissolved into sludge, and his 'feet' were now exposed bone that the sludge hardened. He felt his fingertips experience something similar, the tips being burnt off and the bone underneath solid and black. He felt his torso fill with sludge and grow in length, his spine changing with it. His teeth slimmed and sharpened, his mouth now having two rows of sharp fangs. He felt his hair dissolve away, with his ears and nose feeling the same, though they weren't dissolved entirely. He then felt the sludge push his body to the surface and rest himself where he stood not long ago. His eyes were the last to change, the white remnants of his humanity mellowed with the red of his newfound power. He was granted a new sight, and his eyes opened."

"It took some time for Adam to learn how to walk again, and his sight took longer to understand. He developed a rhythm for his legs to move in, realizing that having a consistent rhythm helped him move with some speed. His eyes, he figured after much self-deliberation, allowed him to see humans that were gifted remarkably. The human's gift was two-fold: some advantage they had over their fellow humans, and their ability to resist fear. He saw them as a threat, for they were able to pass their resistance of fear to others. His new identity was vulnerable to these humans, feeling himself degrade the longer he went without bathing in his sludge. He set about destroying any that he could find. His new identity also saw the adoption of his new name: Raktaar."

"His technique improved with time, realizing as well that he was invisible to human eyes unless he directly contacted them. He realized that once a human eye saw him, he could never be *unseen* by them. He could originate a red glow over his head and redirect it wherever he chose. He has few abilities, but he is creative in his use of them. The most dramatic of these is how simple it is for him to now obtain his sludge—he has no more need of a fire. This sludge is a powerful part of him."

"As I close, I should explain this: I have the knowledge that I just shared with you because of two sources. The rivalry between Adam and Nehemiah was from Nehemiah, wanting these details to be recorded. The origin of Raktaar comes from a little bit of sludge Nehemiah was able to contain, such that he could let it rest on one of my pencils. I saw what the sludge saw, and did what I could to put it to words. With this said, you have now finished reading. Go and save the ones your heart beats for. Persist. Fight. Weigh the odds of battle beyond exaggeration such that you will rise as the victor. Go."

Nehemiah spoke, "Good Boris?"

"Yeah, Nehemiah?"

"I do believe, on that topic, we are to depart." He removed the branches surrounding Boris, showing how it was midday. "I must show you something." Nehemiah rose the table Patrick's book rested on, helping Boris put it into his backpack without touching it.

"What is it?" Boris asked.

"Lower yourself down the tree, and you will see in the distance."

Boris shrugged. "Alright then." He backtracked the path he used to get up, finding himself on the ground. He walked away from Ohlman's Tree, feeling the sun above him and the dry ground under his feet. It was nice to walk on this ground and not drag himself on it.

He also admired how Nehemiah—he assumed it was Nehemiah—undid his trench down the side of the hill and left this place like nothing happened.

He turned to his right to face where he remembered the sun started to set the day before, past many gentle and wavy hills. He remembered how hot the sun was on his back, and how he had to be careful of where he crawled.

He looked as far as he could see, but saw nothing that presented itself. He paused and looked. He panned left as far as the buildings of his town and saw nothing. He panned right as far as his school.

"I'm not seeing anything Nehemiah."

"I knew that would be so, for I must prepare you with the following knowledge. You will recall the dream you had the night before last?"

Boris looked down at Nehemiah, hating where this conversation was going. His voice was filled with nervousness and fear. "Yeah?"

Nehemiah intentionally paused before he replied, evidencing how he didn't want to say this. "Good Boris, that dream was not simply a dream. That dream . . . was a vision; though, there are some things that will be different."

Boris breathing quickened as he spoke.

"My good Boris, tonight will present itself with a thunderstorm. When the first clap of thunder is heard, I have strong reason to believe that my old brother will unleash an attack more overwhelming than anything he has ever constructed to kill you and your sister."

CHAPTER 10

THE SUN WAS RISING when Tanya, Ariel, and Laban arrived at Tanya's home. The Gollum and Hailer Facility was always placed a reasonable distance from the town or city they were tasked with protecting, being that it was *their* home. They wanted some separation from their working lives and their 'human' lives. This distance meant it took some time for the three of them to make their way back.

When they did make it back, Tanya spoke. "There it is, the one furthest from the road" Tanya pointed as she spoke. Ariel looked down to try and see where Tanya pointed as she swayed on the end of the S.M.A.R.T. rope. Laban rested on Ariel's back, turning around to also see where Tanya was pointing.

"Alright. Going down." Ariel dropped altitude to Tanya's house, though she curved up when she got closer to the ground. She went vertical and gently lowered Tanya to the ground, giving the rope time to undo itself. Laban flew off and flittered to Tanya, resting its four legs on her right shoulder. Ariel got to the ground, folded in her wings, and spoke to Tanya. "So, what next?"

"Go inside and read the note Boris left you, mighty Ariel."

The voice was audible to all three of them.

Ariel flicked her swords from both of her palms and stepped back, wanting to see who was there. Tanya and Laban found themselves confused, wondering where the voice came from.

"Show yourself!" Ariel commanded. She hated how there was something that she couldn't see. It was a threat she didn't know about.

"You'll find that I have. Look down, Ariel, for the white flower."

Ariel slowed her breathing and found the small flower amongst the grass.

Nehemiah spoke. "Hello mighty Ariel. My name is Nehemiah–"

Ariel grabbed both her swords, took a step forward, and stabbed into the flower as hard as she could. She wanted to destroy the flower, and knew her swords would do that quite effectively.

Her blades touched Nehemiah's petals.

She was forced back with a powerful shove no-one could see.

Ariel got up with haste, keeping herself ready. Her training told every part of her to destroy the flower that could speak to her but didn't have a mouth to move.

"You need not harm me, Ariel. I wish nothing but peace upon all of you, and many of your wishes are the same as mine concerning Raktaar."

"You know about my old master?" Laban asked.

"Yes, Laban. I knew him as Adam when he was my brother. I have no blood ties with Raktaar, but I have many fond memories with Adam." He then spoke to Tanya. "Laban is the craft of my old brother," he said like he already knew it was a fact.

Tanya replied, wondering why the flower's voice sounded familiar. "Yes. Yes, he was." She quickened her speech. "I had this thought to breathe on him when I first met him. I'm sorry. I didn't know it would be that close to you–"

"Good Tanya, who do you believe gave you the thought to blow on who you now call Laban?"

Tanya's face dropped into wonder. "You're also the one that told me to hug Ariel?"

"Yes, Tanya. That would be me."

Tanya lowered herself into a squat. "It's a pleasure to meet you Nehemiah." She reached to the flower and tried to pull it from the ground. She was surprised when she saw how it was simply resting on the ground. She put Nehemiah in her shirt pocket, letting him rest by his petals.

Ariel had slid her blades into her palms, but she was still hesitant of Nehemiah. "You . . . you're . . . a flower . . . "

"I have the form of a flower yes. What I really am, I have found, is too large for anything practical at this part of my plan. Something so small holds the attention of human eyes, so I am still noticeable, and I can go about my plan through you all and find good company amongst you. My larger form would be more intimidating. You *will* see my proper form tonight, though you should read your brother's note first. He will be some time."

"You know where my brother is?" Tanya asked.

"Yes, good Tanya. He is, right now, reading through a text he has dubbed 'Patrick's book'. That is the book mentioned in the note you read to him some time ago. Not being limited by matter, I am both here and with your brother."

"So, he's okay." She breathed out. "Thank you."

"You're most welcome–"

"How are you trusting this thing?!" Ariel interrupted. "You're holding a conversation with a talking flower!" She deployed a panel from the outside of her thighs. The panels pivoted at an angle such that the openings faced the top of her thighs, with the pivot for the panel being near her knees.

Tanya saw how Ariel's pants was actually skin, like her shirt, seeing a part of the long pants move neatly with the panel.

The panel exposed two hand grips with a button where her index finger would rest. She pulled and raised them, the hand grips a molded item with a thick thread extending perpendicular to the handle, almost an extension to her outstretched arms. It held a dark grey rectangular box underneath the thick thread.

She pointed her weapons at Nehemiah.

She spoke with volume and sternness towards Nehemiah. "If touching you doesn't work, I'll rain some Hailer Hail on you!" She looked to Tanya. "Please put the flower on the ground Tanya. I don't want to shoot you."

Tanya, alarmed at how frightened Ariel was, replied. "He's not a threat Ariel! He's okay."

"How do you know?!"

"Because the only other thing that can talk in our heads has four legs, a disgusting laugh, and has hurt the both of us more than we knew was possible! He"–she pointed to the flower–"hasn't made any attempts to hurt us–"

"He can't hurt us because he's a *flower!* I've stood on flowers and seen them crumple. He can't hurt us *physically!* He's been sent by you-know-who to bring *us* back to *him!* I can't let that happen. You turned that little thing"–she looked at Laban–"from a disgusting red into a *beautiful,* creamy white." She looked at Tanya. "If what he"–she nodded to Laban–"says is true, and his old master is strongly connected with what he used to be made of, he'll be terrified of you! You're our greatest weapon Tanya!" Her voice now spoke with heart and care. "I need to keep you safe."

Her tone changed. It became dark and cold. "I can't let . . . Nehemiah . . . *potentially* . . . mess that up. Please . . . " She paused, wanting the desperation in her voice to be heard. "Please. *Put. Him. Down.*"

Tanya looked at Ariel in shock, but knew she could do nothing. She breathed out and looked down at Nehemiah, who spoke to her in her mind and hers alone. She heard vividly the deepness of his voice. "It is quite okay, good Tanya. Do you trust me?"

She smiled and replied in a quiet whisper. "Yeah . . . I do." She pulled Nehemiah from her pocket and let him rest amongst the grass.

Ariel breathed out in relief, who kept her weapons pointed at Nehemiah during the move. "Thank you, Tanya." She looked to Nehemiah. "Anything you want to say, 'Nehemiah'?"

He intentionally stayed silent, then replied. "Yes. There is something I would like to say."

He stayed silent for a small moment.

He glowed.

Then a blast of air forced all three of them back, a powerful shove that made them all collapse on the grass and dirt.

The ground went unexpectedly soft on their landing.

They each slowly rose to their feet. Tanya and Ariel rubbed their eyes, feeling how the wind made them dry and how the dirt made it harder to see.

All three looked to where Nehemiah once was.

They saw two wooden boots so large that the leg that rose from them was twice as wide as the width of Tanya's shoulders.

They followed the wooden legs with their eyes. They saw how the ankle to the wooden boot had many smaller branches, each branch arching outwards. The gap inside the joint was as large as Tanya's forearm length.

They saw how the legs looked like human legs, with the knee joint twice as tall as the ankle joint. The calves and thighs were straight logs with a thick, dark brown bark coating it.

They saw the hip joints looking a little longer than the knee joints. The hip joints connected legs taller than Tanya's house with a wooden torso. Six smaller vertical logs, each the same, two columns by three rows, made its abdomen. Two larger logs resting on their sides made its chest. The left and right of its torso saw two longer logs standing vertically on both sides, its back made of vertical, smaller, thinner logs the entire way across, stopping short just before the waist logs. The waist logs were two horizontal logs that were the base of the entire torso, each the same thickness as the logs making the sides of his abdomen.

Ariel aimed both her weapons at the ginormous wooden man that stood before her. Every part of her training, and her life, yelled at her to pull the triggers. She wanted to activate her wings, fly at a decent height, and rain as much Hailer Hail as she could on what stood before her.

Then it spoke.

It was Nehemiah's voice.

"If I wanted to hurt you, I could have done that by now. I could have stomped on you. I could have grabbed you and painfully squeezed you. My size allows me to do many things to anything that's around me. But . . . " He lowered himself into a squat, resting his arms and hands on his knees. They were both proportional to the rest of his body and looked remarkably like human arms and hands. Every joint was made from smaller branches arching outwards, and every solid limb was made from a log of a proportional thickness.

Ariel could now see his face. It was on a log the same width as his legs where each facial feature—his facial features from when he died—carved from the wood. His eyelids could close, simply to be more personable, and his face made up the width of the head log, with a little excess on the top and bottom. His neck was exactly like his hip joint, and it allowed his head to directly face hers. "I've chosen not too."

He intentionally paused to reinforce his point. He breathed out with his mouth, and Ariel could feel the breeze against her face. It was gentle and cool, but still there.

He wanted to demonstrate how much stronger he was than her without any harm.

He continued. "I have been shown knowledge through a power greater, again, than myself. I have been taught the ways of the mighty Hololume Tree, and I know how to rid the world of what was once my brother Adam. I have determined that this is to be done through you, little Laban"–he motioned with his right hand. "Tanya"–he positioned to let Ariel see–"and Boris, who you haven't met yet." He reset himself, looked directly at Ariel for a moment, then sat cross-legged, resting his elbows on his knees. They could all feel the ground slightly shake as he sat, knowing it could have been much worse. He spoke to Ariel. "I wish to help you on your endeavor to save everyone from my once brother, but if you choose to help me with my endeavor to do the same, you will find success be brought to you."

Ariel continued to look at Nehemiah with a face of confusion, terror, and awe. She wondered whether to press the triggers simply to see if it would make any mark, but she thought against it. She slowly lowered her weapons, not knowing how to respond. She deployed her thigh weapon panel, slid her weapons in, then closed them inside.

Nehemiah smiled.

She slowly walked to him, not knowing what she was doing. He could have easily killed the three of them by now.

But he hadn't.

He had gently proven his power over the three of them, knowing he could best any of them and prove himself victor.

But he didn't.

This went against everything Ariel was taught.

Nehemiah saw this.

He could easily see the fear on her face, having never encountered something so large before. Tears slowly streamed down her cheeks, and her sobs slowly grew in volume.

"I'm scared," she said as she broke into tears.

Tanya ran to her side and hugged her. She cried with her friend, having felt this uncertainty all too much before.

Nehemiah felt the pain that was on display, and his face twisted into sadness. He didn't have eyes that could cry, but he had a face that showed how his heart was breaking. He thought to speak and bring certainty to her life. "Gentle Ariel?"

Tanya loosened her hug to let Ariel face him. He could see the face of a young woman, full of violence and control, longing for a life without it. She replied. "Yeah Nehemiah . . . ?"

"You have lived a life of much hate, young Ariel. You see me, and you see an enemy that you would be unable to defeat. Tanya sees me, and she sees a friend." He paused. "I am going to ask much of you, Ariel, for the task we are about to undertake is not one to be handled lightly. I am unable to express the reasons for my plan in human language, and much of what I say will need to be listened to with a basis of trust. I must then ask: do you trust me?"

She was wiping the tears from her face, and sniffled before she spoke. "I trust that you won't hurt me. I trust that you'll keep the three of us safe . . ." She paused, knowing this wouldn't be heard well. "But I don't trust you as a friend. I'm sorry." She cried as she finished.

"That is quite okay, Ariel. I can sense that a large part of you still wants to shoot me, for your training and life commands that you do." He reached his right hand and laid it flat on the ground. "If I may?"

Ariel nodded, still in tears, and walked on Nehemiah's large wooden hand. They saw how his palms were smaller logs, one log for each finger. They lay in the same direction as his arm logs when they were outstretched. His wrist was a branch joint, and it shaped itself from a circle on his forearm log to a rectangle at the base of his hand.

He cupped his right hand with his left, giving something for Ariel to hold on to. He raised her to his chest, letting her arms wrap around his neck. He supported her with his right hand and stroked her back with his right thumb. He closed his eyes and felt Ariel press her face into his shoulder. She felt how soft the bark was against her cheek.

"Let go of your pain, Ariel. Let me take that from you."

Ariel began to cry, her tears falling onto his shoulders, and her arms gripping his neck, wanting the pain to be out of her life. She sobbed and gasped, having never felt what she felt in that moment. Every tear that fell on the bark sent a small whiff of smoke that drifted away.

Then she spoke. "Please help me Nehemiah. Please help me . . . "

As soon as she spoke, Nehemiah closed his eyes, preparing for what he was to do next. He let his left hand rest a small distance away from her back, and he arched his fingers.

He breathed in and slowly moved his hand away.

He started to pull a black powder from her body.

Ariel yelled and shouted in pain, letting more of her tears fall onto his shoulder. She held his neck tighter and pressed herself onto him more, wanting to feel him as best she could, wanting the pain to be over with.

His hand was now in-line with his knees, and between his hand and Ariel floated a mass of black powder, more than what could have fitted in her human body. It was randomly shaped, with no real, recognizable form to it.

He guided it to be in-line with his abdomen, breathed in and out again, then drove the mass of black into his chest.

He winced, and Ariel heard.

Wiping the tears from her eyes, she spoke from concern. "You okay big guy?"

He nodded. "It's best you wait on the ground for now," he said like he was holding his breath. He put Ariel down, letting her walk off his hands.

He closed his eyes and let his hands rest on his knees.

He then set his chest ablaze.

His face showed that it hurt, and his hands gripped his knees harder.

Ariel looked concerned. "What's he doing?"

Tanya replied. "I don't know–"

"I do," Laban interjected.

Ariel objected. "What's he doing? He's hurting himself!"

"Yes, he is, but he got all the hurt out of you."

Ariel was taken back by this.

Laban nodded with his body, then spoke. "When he was pulling his hand back from you, he was pulling the hurt out of you."

Tanya now looked confused and anxious. "Why is he burning himself?"

Laban answered. "When you blew the hate out of me, and turned me from red to white, the hate you blew out of me was carried into the wind, never to be seen again." He turned to face Nehemiah. "When he pulls the hurt from you, he burns it."

A roaring flame was growing in Nehemiah, and his face showed the pain he was in.

Ariel felt horrible. "No! No! He can't do this! I could have carried it! How's it fair to force him to carry it for me?!" She paused. "That's so selfish of me . . . " She turned to Tanya and cried into her shoulder. Tanya wanted to say that she was wrong, but she didn't know if that was entirely true. She watched with Laban as the flame inside Nehemiah was the size of his entire midsection. She could feel the heat on her face, and she watched as the dark smoke drifted up and away.

Nehemiah took a large breath in, then closed his mouth and plugged his nose. He breathed out through his chest, and a massive gush of ash flew through the sides of his midsection.

The flames were instantly snuffed.

He breathed in through his nose and out through his mouth, then spoke. "It was not selfish of you to pass your hurt to me. You'll find I took it from you, for now your trepidation of me has been removed. It is now burnt, and no longer of any real power. Tanya can do some of what I do, but burning a great deal of your hurt is not a task to be taken easily. Someone of my size and experience is capable of such things. It was also not the hurt from my old brother's red sludge. It was a different hurt that was a part of you."

Ariel looked at Nehemiah's eyes. "So, I wasn't selfish?"

"No, good Ariel! You were *selfless* in recognizing that there are parts of you that you do not have a remedy for. That's where I come in." He smiled as he finished.

Ariel breathed in, and felt how light her chest now felt. She felt a little happier and less inclined to hurt anyone around her. She breathed out, feeling a sense of peace she had never experienced before. A smile found itself planted on her face, and she cried the most joyful tears she'd ever experienced. She sat on the ground, realizing she needed to adjust herself with a life of much less hate. Her brain wasn't forcing her to look everywhere as if anything could be a threat. She didn't need to be afraid of Laban or Tanya in the event of a betrayal. She could also know that Nehemiah was in front of her, but know she would be safe—safer than she had ever felt.

She held her head in her hands and breathed deeply, helping her brain to make connections it hadn't ever made.

Nehemiah spoke to Tanya and Laban. "It would be best if we left her to herself. She will need some time alone." He spoke to Tanya, "Can you please go and read your brother's note?"

"That I can."

He spoke to Laban. "Please keep her company, Laban."

"Following," he said as he flittered his wings and went to Tanya's side.

Nehemiah could see that Laban and Tanya were inside. He closed his eyes, and a smaller blast of wind was sent towards himself. He resumed the form of a flower and stood upright against the ground. He detached the head of the flower from its stem, angled his petals, and flew to Ariel, resting himself directly in front of her.

When she looked up and saw Nehemiah landing on the ground by her shins, she looked at it with an awe and uncertainty she had never felt before. She had a desire to hold Nehemiah in her hands, but she would never have had the confidence before to consciously do things peacefully. She slowly reached with her right hand and picked up Nehemiah, letting him lie on his side in her cupped hands. He saw him glow a gentle glow, and felt an undeniable sense of strength and satisfaction wash over her.

She cried some more and let her head hang.

She let herself feel happiness.

TANYA HAD A FEELING Boris would leave his note on his desk, considering that *he* wrote it. She went to her brother's room.

Before she continued, she noticed the blood patch on the carpet in the hallway.

She froze as she was about to walk through.

She walked gently over it, holding her breath, then continued.

She froze again when she looked down and saw the large break in the wall on her left.

She knew how that happened.

She remembered the bald man.

The anger.

His violence.

Her weakness.

His power.

Her helplessness.

She closed her eyes and dropped to the ground, falling through the doorway. Her eyes watered, and she began to sob.

The dam wall of her emotions and memories had just broken, now recollecting something to add to what was a terrible day.

She remembered the awkwardness of first meeting Ariel.

She remembered how she was beaten by someone that was once her friend.

She remembered The Day.

Each time she felt powerless: she had no way of escaping.

Each time, she got hurt.

She crawled on her hands and knees to Boris' bedside, ignoring how his door was on the floor. She grabbed the metal bedframe, gripped it as hard as she could, wanting the metal frame to feel the pain and fury burning her alive.

She screamed as loud as she could. Her ears could only hear the horror in her memories try and leave her. Tears streamed down her cheeks. Her palms hurt from how hard they gripped the metal. Her fingers were white with frustration. Her face showed how desperately she wanted those memories out of her head.

She let go of the bedframe, then, drawing back with the left and punching with her right, drove as much anger as she could into his brother's mattress. It went flying off the bed, colliding with the wall opposite her.

The memories returned.

Beringei's large fists pounding her face, the one thing that wasn't ruined by The Day save her back.

The bald man running his finger along her throat, and how she couldn't do anything to stop it.

Ariel's body against hers; the cold she felt, and how she felt a machine, not a teenage girl.

She got into a low crouch, grabbed the side of Boris' bed, and flipped it up, lifting as hard and fast and strong and angrily as she could. She wanted everything she felt out of her head and out of her chest.

The memories returned again.

She remembered how Boris bludgeoned the face of someone that was once her friend.

She remembered the terror she felt when the bald man dove over Boris' bed. He came from nowhere and overpowered her almost instantly.

She remembered seeing how twisted and broken Ariel was, knowing firsthand the pain Ariel would have felt when she got her scars.

Then she remembered her wall.

She jumped up and sprinted to her room. She saw her wall, and felt a small sense of relief flow through her. She put her hands on her wall, resting her forehead on it shortly after. She slowly dropped to her knees, and breathed deeply.

She felt some calm enter her. She felt the softness of the paint on her fingertips. She felt her breathing slow. She felt, in her chest, as the ensuing waves of emotion attempted to crumble her, the calmness bite a nip out of each wave. The more she focused on her wall, the more she felt at peace.

She took a larger breath and felt the air flow through her nose and fill her lungs with new air. She breathed out, and stood up.

She made her way to Boris' room, doing her best not to notice the large break in the wall or the bed she overturned. She saw the note on his desk, retrieved it, and exited the room. She walked with a slightly faster pace, promptly wanting to go outside, ignoring the wet footsteps through the blood stain.

When she walked through her front door, she felt the sun on her face and the warmth on her skin. She knew that she was now safe, and she felt much calmer now.

She looked down to see the note in her hands.

She also saw Laban flying behind her. She extended her arm to give him something to rest on. She felt how he was quite light, and how it was easy to hold him up. He walked across her arm, up her neck, and rested on the top of her head. She felt the small, round feet rest gently on her scalp, and she felt the shade of his wings when he let them fall to his sides.

She looked up and talked to Laban. "I'm sorry you had to see that."

"It's okay."

There was a silence between them.

"Hey Tanya?" Laban asked.

"Yeah Laban?"

"You okay?"

Tanya was silent for a little, looked aside, really not wanting to answer that question, and did not reply.

Laban heard the indecision in her head and knew he struck something personal. "Never mind. You don't need to answer that."

Tanya breathed relief. "Thank you, Laban. Maybe another time?"

"Yeah . . . that would be good."

She looked up at him for a little, scratched his rock dust edge, then looked down to Boris' note.

As she was about to read, Laban spoke in her head again. "Hey Tanya?"

"Yeah Laban?"

"Can I say something?"

She folded the note and put it in her dress pocket. "You can, yes."

A pause. "My old master . . . he . . . well . . . how do I say this . . . "

Tanya was confused. "You're old master?"

"My old master . . . he . . . " A pause. "Whatever you're holding inside . . . you'll *need* to get that out of you."

"I know I should. I don't *need* to though–"

"I'd really like it if you did."

Tanya smiled. "That's really kind of you Laban–"

He spoke quickly. "Thank you, but I'm saying this for you. You *need* to get that out–"

"Why do I *need* to get it out? It's not like it'll kill me . . . " She smiled as she finished, thinking to be humorous.

Laban remained perfectly still, looking down at Tanya.

She repeated. "It's not like it'll kill me . . . yeah?"

He remained perfectly still, looking down at her.

She grew concerned. "Laban . . . what aren't you telling me?"

He paused. "My old master . . . he . . . he . . . it's what he uses. He will use that to destroy you. He will use the pain you hold inside of you and harvest as much sludge as he can from it. He can . . . he can even use that to control you. If you don't get in control of whatever you have in your head . . . you'll become Beringei. That's how he snapped–"

Tanya continued to look up at Laban. "I'll become Beringei if I don't deal with what's in my head? Wait . . . you can see what's in my head? What are you doing looking around in my head–"

"I saw how you acted in your brother's room. I could hear and see a lot in your head. I could feel that it wasn't my place to know. I don't know what it is that hurts you so deeply, but I do know the power you let it have over you. You can't let that be Tanya . . . " She heard sobs in her head. "You saved me from being made from sludge—a thing whose existence is birthed from total fear—into something better. I can't lose the person that saved me when I can return it."

Tanya was silent for a moment, not realizing the heaviness of something she wanted to ignore entirely. "You're really sweet for caring for me like that." She smiled as she realized how Laban was trying to be a friend and was being good at it. "I don't think now is the right time though. I need to read my brother's note and work with Nehemiah. After that, how would you feel if you helped me out?"

Laban flapped his wings with excitement. "Amazing! Thank you."

Tanya looked at Laban in appreciation, then looked down to his brother's note after grabbing it from her pocket.

She read. "Hey Tanya. If you're reading this, it means you're safe. It is so good to know that. Crazy days, right? I was wondering if it was the best idea to let the Hailers take you, but I knew you needed someone to properly care for you.

"Now, the rest of this note is what Nehemiah wants me to write. He wants me to write that, as you read this, he and I are currently at Ohlman's Tree reading Patrick's book. We are safe, and his plan is being undertaken quite nicely. He wants to destroy the thing that made The Day more than we do. He will inform you on what you are to do for the rest of the day. Stay safe and well; we will meet again not long from now. Your brother, Boris."

Tanya nodded her head. "Alright then . . . " feeling ready to undertake whatever Nehemiah gave her. She yelled to Nehemiah, not knowing where he went. "Hey Nehemiah!"

"Yes, Tanya," he replied.

She was startled. "Oh . . . hi . . . so, what do you want us to do for the rest of the day?"

"Tanya, the first task I ask of you is that you discuss your past with Laban."

She didn't appreciate that response.

"You want me to talk with Laban for the rest of the day?" she asked.

"Not for the rest of the day. Simply until your brother arrives. Seeing where the sun is, that should only be a little while."

Tanya's face twisted into confusion. "Why do you want me to talk with Laban for a while? If we're going to destroy the thing that made The Day, we need to prepare! To train for a battle! Not talk about the pain I've had in my teenage years."

"Good Tanya, my task for you, until your brother arrives, is to talk with Laban. Are you saying that you are not capable of a simple and deep reciprocation of ideas?"

Tanya didn't know how to respond to that.

She looked to Laban with a smile saying how she was going to enjoy the company but not the conversation. "It looks like I'm having that talk you wanted to have with me."

Laban replied. "And I'm really keen for it."

"We'll go to my room. It's quiet there."

They both went to Tanya's room, ignoring again the large break in the wall, and closed the door. Laban flapped his wings and landed on her bed on his back. She lay on her back next to him.

She spoke first. "So . . . I'm supposed to talk with you until Boris arrives?"

"That's what Nehemiah wants us to do," Laban responded.

"What are we supposed to talk about? I've gotten to terms about The Day. It's not like there's much else to talk about . . . "

There was an awkward silence before Laban corrected. "You don't think you should talk about yesterday?"

She rubbed her eyes with her hands. "I really don't want too." She gave him a glare as she finished before letting her head rest and her eyes look to the ceiling.

"You really should though. I wasn't messing with you when I said that you could die because of it–"

Tanya looked at Laban. "How will I die because I don't want to talk about my miserable teenage years? Will I have my soul sucked from me for not being strong enough to handle everything? Oh, I know! I'll feel the literal weight of what I carry with me until I can't move anymore." She laughed and looked to the ceiling. "I could die by having it infect the rest of my body until all I am is hate and anger"–she laughed again, holding her stomach. "Wouldn't that be hilarious. Your entire existence is summed up into two small words: hate and anger–"

As she finished, she looked at Laban.

She stopped laughing, and her face dropped.

She paused as she processed her revelation. "Your . . . you . . . your entire existence was . . . " She retreated into her own head, the connections now putting themselves together. She didn't know how to verbalize the only deduction that presented itself to her. She sat against her bedhead and focused on Laban. "If I don't talk about what happened to me, I'll become what you used to be?"

"To some extent, yes. You will assist my old master in everything that he does, be left with no other choice, and the shouts of help and despair will be the only thing you hear." He paused. "I remember, when I first became sludge, I was made to rest on his abdomen. There was this young boy that he wanted to turn into more sludge. He . . . he scared the young boy until the slightest noise would send him into a wild panic. He would then get his index fingers and make this really long cut down his midsection. Then he . . . he . . . he . . . pulled . . . their blood . . . *through* the thin cut he made. It was thicker and darker than normal, and I could feel the fear in the young boy as he was absorbed into my old master's body. My old master grew as he absorbed the fear of the young boy. He then grabbed what remained of the young boy, not caring for how wrinkled and deflated it now became, and lifted it as high as his arms could reach, and sent a red glow through his hands, and threw the body into the ground, and turned a young boy into a thin splash of black dust . . . " his legs convulsed as he spoke. "If you don't deal with everything that you hold inside of you, you will be forced to live what I have experienced and be forced to watch from the perspective of a truly despicable creature. I don't want you to experience that."

Her eyes started to tear, feeling how much he cared for her. "Okay." She breathed deeply, only now grasping the heaviness of it all. "Wow . . . okay . . . okay." She repositioned herself on her bedhead, knowing that this conversation was going to last a while. "So . . . what do I do now?"

Laban flipped onto his legs and flapped his wings with excitement. "Talk to me."

She nodded her head, and she started from after The Day.

EVER SINCE THE DAY, she never felt how she used to feel. When she got treated for her multitude of cuts, and Boris' dishonesty to anyone that asked how they got there, her life was a consistent sense of normal with a large part *ripped* from it. She would wake up in the morning, rub her eyes with her hands, and notice, for the nth time, the scars that found themselves there. As she looked down, she would see the cuts on her legs for the nth time. She would run her finger down her midsection, feeling, for the nth time, the very large and very thick scar that found itself there. As she ran her finger down, she felt other smaller cuts around it, across her midsection. She would remember Raktaar chasing her, and diving into her, and scaring her, and hurting her.

She cried for the nth time.

There were some nights that were better than others. Raktaar would haunt her dreams some nights. Others would see a normal, teenage sleep, often quite peaceful. She never knew which was about to be which.

As time passed, the dreams didn't stop, nor did her painful flashbacks. She wanted to move on; to recognize that something horrible had happened but *without* the emotion coming with it.

She did this through her art.

Every time she painted there was a part of her darkness that went into her work. She would look at it, recognize that there was still hatred in it, then burn it, knowing she never needed to look at it again. Over time, this worked very well for her. She started processing what happened on The Day and how that affected her. She started to accept her scars, not feeling compelled to hide them even in ridiculous heat. She found a confidence in herself that she had never found before.

She was changed though, even after the inspiring confidence.

It occurred to her, after The Day, that she needed to be better; to be a more skillful and prepared young woman. She learned and practiced martial arts that catered for her smaller frame as a female. She sharpened her brain such to think quicker and have a wider, more practical knowledge base. What took most women decades to appreciate and understand, she forced into a few years.

This came at a steep price that she, too late, found about.

She realized, as she grew older, how other young women her age would be fools and do dangerous things simply because they didn't know better. She would know how to make what they were doing safer, always enjoying a fun time herself. But no-one appreciated her maturity.

Her teenage years were very lonely.

This, she realized, gave her time for Boris, who wasn't handling The Day as well as her.

She remembered how much Boris struggled with trying to process The Day. She remembered how reserved Boris was, how distant he could make himself be, and how, for a long while, he barely said anything.

She realized that, in his head, he was still trying to process what had happened, and his brain mostly concentrated on doing so. She remembered how she would randomly hug him, and how, every time, he would flinch at first, then learn to embrace it. She remembered how much longer it took him to process The Day, and she remembered how he, also, thought to be more prepared.

He felt a particularly strong motivation to do so, realizing that the one thing that saved her sister was his Mech-Ants.

He knew he could do better.

He sharpened his abilities to make machines, learned martial arts that worked for a male build, and prepared himself for the future. He was like his sister in that they both wanted to avoid being clueless should they face anything as powerful again. They didn't care for how incredibly unlikely that chance would be, nor the hard work required to be successfully ready, nor the strange looks as they tried so hard to prepare for something that, really, shouldn't happen again.

But when Raktaar exposed Beringei to his red sludge, which Tony first observed with curiosity, they both knew it had been for something.

TANYA CONTINUED TO TALK with Laban about yesterday's events, recalling everything she felt, crying when she remembered the pain and struggling to find anything to smile about.

When she finished, with her eyes red from how much they cried, her cheeks moist with her newly fallen tears. She asked, "is that what you're after?"

Laban replied. "It is actually. Do you feel any better?"

"I do, yes." She rubbed the smooth join between his wings. "Thank you little guy."

He flittered his wings, showing appreciation of Tanya's pat.

She looked up, through her window, and saw how much the sun had moved. It was nearly midday.

She talked to Laban. "Boris should be home soon."

She started to walk through her door, picking Laban up as she did and letting him rest on her back. She looked down to the large section of wall that was now missing.

She stared at it.

She breathed in.

She breathed out.

She smiled.

She had moved on.

They both made their way outside, seeing how Ariel had climbed a tree and thought to enjoy the sun, bringing a warmth to her face unlike anything it previously knew. Her eyes were closed, and she looked at peace.

It was a stunning sight.

It was one of the few times she looked like a normal teenage girl.

The sun struck her at an amazing angle too.

Tanya could see how Nehemiah was resting in Ariel's hands, though he talked in her head from such a far distance. "How did your talk go?"

Tanya replied. "Very well, thank you. I feel much better now."

Laban flittered his wings again, knowing he was the one that helped her be so.

"Most excellent."

Tanya saw something move to her left.

"Boris!" She yelled.

She ran to him and gave him the largest hug she'd ever given him. She had never felt so excited to see her brother.

Laban thought to drop off near the front door, knowing first introductions were going to be interesting.

Boris returned the hug, knowing he needed her more than ever.

"It's so good to see you Boris," Tanya said.

He pressed his face into her shoulder, knowing that Tanya couldn't begin to understand how desperately he needed her hugs.

He began to cry into her shoulder.

Tanya loosened her grip. "What's wrong Boris?"

He looked into her eyes, not knowing how to say the truthful answer. He tried to speak, but it proved to be an incredibly difficult task. He closed his eyes and drew on every of courage he could find. He opened them and, looking dead into her eyes, replied. "I'm going to die tonight."

He cracked as he finished.

He burst into tears and collapsed to the ground.

He slammed his hand into the dirt and grass as hard as his muscles would let him. He punched the ground, feeling the solidity of the brown beneath him.

He punched again.

And again.

And again.

And again.

He dropped to the ground, letting himself weep amongst the dirt.

Tanya picked up his head with both her hands, looking at him with confusion. "What?! How do you know?"

Nehemiah spoke in both their heads. "Yes Boris. How do you know?"

Boris sat up and looked into his shirt pocket. Tanya looked down with him, seeing how Nehemiah got into her brother's pocket. She turned, expecting him to be out of Ariel's hands.

He wasn't.

He was there *and* in Boris' pocket.

Nehemiah sensed her confusion and spoke in her head alone. "I must explain later Tanya."

He spoke in both Tanya's and Boris' heads. "Boris. How do you know that you will die tonight?"

Boris replied in anger. "Because you said that my dream yesterday was a vision! In that vision, I die!" He pressed his finger into his chest as he finished.

Nehemiah spoke. "Young Boris, can you please describe your vision to your sister and myself?"

Boris straightened his posture. "I was alone with a really cool sword in my right hand. It was dusk, and the horizon was filled with these . . . things . . . " She looked to Tanya. "Like Hailers but *so* much scarier." He looked down. "I had a strong connection with those hills. The whole place really. I don't know why, but I did. I fought as hard as I could, but I was overrun. I shouldn't have lasted so long either. It was my sword against a whole swarm of these things. I don't know how I did so well." He closed his eyes and drew a breath. "They started to eat me, and I woke up." He looked to his pocket. "I died Nehemiah!"

"In that vision, you did indeed die. But, Boris, could you please look up?"

He did so in confusion.

"What is in front of you?"

He looked. He saw Tanya. She was worried about him like always. She started looking to the house, then stared at a small critter with four legs and two wings that flittered when he looked at them.

Boris was too emotional to be surprised.

He panned left, realizing there was someone in the tree.

He looked to his pocket, wondering what he was seeing.

"Boris, the little critter you see is named Laban. The young woman in the tree goes by Ariel. You know Tanya"–he looked up, and Tanya gave a small wave– "and you know me."

He laughed as he looked at his pocket. "And you're supposed to become this epic beast that can save me from thousands of flying creatures?"

Tanya spoke up. "He's not a beast, but he's epic." She finished with a smile.

Boris looked at her with intrigue. "How epic are we talking?"

Her face showed a bigger smile. "So epic that none of these trees were taller than him."

"You've seen his actual form? The one that can actually do stuff?"

"Yeah! He's . . . ginormous!"

Boris processed that idea. He looked around and closely looked at the tallest trees he could find. The tallest he found was about twice his house size. He looked at his pocket with true admiration and curiosity.

"Boris," Nehemiah began, "I do assure you. On your own, tonight, you will die. With those that are currently around you . . . there is a greater chance for each of us."

Boris looked around again, seeing who he now knew as Laban and Ariel. He looked up at his sister, who was still smiling.

He looked down to Nehemiah. "So . . . I'm not going to die tonight?"

"No, my good Boris. There is every chance you might. Tonight will . . . it will not be simple or safe."

Boris breathed out, realizing the intensity of the events that were about to unfold. "Alright . . . what do you want us to do?"

CHAPTER 11

RAKTAAR WAS SUBMERGED IN his pool of sludge, wanting to recharge after chasing Nehemiah and Boris. While he rested in his sludge, he thought through what he could do to eliminate the very existence of them both.

It was not the first time he and Nehemiah caused each other problems. He remembered, very distinctly, how they would mess with each other when they were younger.

He remembered how juvenile they both were.

Their confrontations now were combating the reasons of their existence.

RAKTAAR REMEMBERED THE CONFUSION and shock when he first saw Nehemiah's gift of living on his plane of existence. He also remembered how much shorter he was next to Nehemiah's humungous form.

This first encounter took place a few centuries after he had become one with his sludge and got better at fear harvesting. The new moon bored a very black night, with very little light to shine the living face of the Earth. He was about to exit his cave and work under the cover of the black, but he was abruptly stopped by Nehemiah, who was hiding on top of the cave when night established itself.

He grabbed Raktaar, wanting to be as forceful as he could, and threw him into the air as high as he could. He saw the height he achieved with his throw, seeing him start to disappear into the sky. He then saw how his old brother was arching away from himself and gaining distance.

Distance that Raktaar could disappear in.

Nehemiah couldn't have that.

He ran, wanting to intersect his old brother's landing. He jumped as high as he could, made a fist around Raktaar, and made it face the ground. As Nehemiah landed, he opened his palm and forced it over the ground, sliding with it over the forest floor. He forced his way through trees and soft dirt, making sure Raktaar was always being pressed into the ground.

A Nehemiah sized trench was left behind him.

As always, no-one saw this.

Nehemiah lifted his hand to check the condition of his old brother.

Raktaar sent a red pulse from each arm, directing it at Nehemiah's face, knocking Nehemiah back with the unexpected blast.

Raktaar had established a field in front of himself to protect him from the ground and was incredibly furious that someone had tried to kill him.

He was, however, made uneasy about his opponent's height.

He was made even more uneasy by the face of his opponent.

He stopped and realized that the face he shot with his red pulse was the face of his brother Nehemiah.

"Nehemiah?!" He yelled.

He shook his head, realizing that it didn't matter.

It wasn't the first time he tried to kill his brother.

He ran towards Nehemiah and jumped when he got closer. He sent a blast through each of his legs as he jumped, allowing him to jump with great height.

He sent himself into Nehemiah's chest, grabbing with both his hands and cushioning the landing with his legs. He let go with his right, seeing how Nehemiah was still disoriented from his blast, and let a small blob of his sludge develop in his palm.

He knew it would infect him brilliantly well.

Nehemiah was regaining his senses though.

He saw his old brother on his chest.

He grabbed the red thing hanging from his chest and wrapped both hands around it, wanting to end this as efficiently as he could.

He wanted to break his old brother's spine and tear him in two.

Raktaar wouldn't let that happen.

Before the massive wooden man before him could wrap its large hands around him, he threw his blob of sludge. His eyes were covered before he saw what happened with the sludge.

He then heard Nehemiah groan in pain.

He felt as the large wooden hands loosened their grip and dropped him to the ground. He saw as the wooden face twisted in pain and clutched his chest.

Then its eyes opened.

They looked into his.

They were angry.

Raktaar realized the severity of what he had just done.

He bolted.

He turned around and went about escaping this giant wooden man. He heard the thundering footsteps follow him, and felt as the ground shook with every step. He felt as a wooden hand wrapped around his body.

He felt as he was lifted into the air.

He felt as he was thrown out of the forest.

Nehemiah could see his old brother disappear into the distance, trying to remove the sludge from his chest.

These confrontations took place over thousands of years, each time not much different from the last. Nehemiah would attempt to ambush his old brother, Raktaar would blast red pulses and launch blobs of his sludge, Nehemiah would need to treat the sludge before he became fatally wounded, and Raktaar would be thrown a far distance.

RAKTAAR REMAINED IN HIS sludge as he thought through every confrontation he and his 'brother' had. He knew he was a small flower when he went into hiding, but he could do nothing against it. He knew his 'brother' couldn't be versed directly, seeing that it hadn't work for centuries.

He had realized this a while ago, but each meeting confirmed it.

Now, he also realized, he has a teenage boy.

It was the same boy he wanted to ruin a few years ago.

It was the same boy that received his nightmare two nights ago.

He knew he needed to destroy the boy, for he proved to be a mighty foe that was successful in protecting his sister.

His sister, he realized.

She was the true enemy.

She threatened his very existence.

He had learned that she undid what he did to Laban, knowing that was the only way the sludge could be defeated.

She was immune to his sludge.

She was immune to him.

No-one had ever been immune to him.

He removed himself from his pool of sludge, desperately wanting a solution to an incredibly formidable foe.

He absorbed the dripping sludge and felt his size increase slightly. He wanted to keep as much sludge as he could on himself as a future reserve.

He tapped for Maargalla.

She approached on her ten sludge infected octopus-like legs, tapping in response. "You called Raktaar?"

Raktaar replied. "Hello Maargalla. Yes, I did. You were telling me just yesterday about a Gollum you were experimenting with?"

"Yes Raktaar. I'm so very pleased you asked. I believe I am near its completion."

He smiled. "Well done Maargalla. Might I see?"

"I would be delighted Raktaar." She retreated into the darkness of her workspace to retrieve her new creature.

Maargalla was only a recent creation for Raktaar; only a few centuries old. He originally just wanted some company, but he soon recognized that she could make more creatures. Maargalla had been practicing this for centuries, her specialty being Screams. She had created variants of the original Scream, but she soon learned that quantity over quality was more effective. She couldn't be terribly creative either: making living things out of borrowed parts is difficult.

This new creation, however, was far more formidable than any Scream she had ever produced.

When she came out of her dark workspace, she brought a giant creature with her; larger than Nehemiah. Its legs were two incredibly long tentacles with a form very similar to Maargalla's legs. Its arms and hands were large rocks, no rock being the same as the next, in the shape of a human arm and hand. Encased by a large, oddly shaped rock was the Gollum that controlled it all. It was porous; its holes about the size of a finger such that the Gollum inside could see its surroundings.

Maargalla had on her back a mound of sludge that she let fall to the floor when she entered with her new creation. She picked up a small amount with her right arm tentacle and slapped it with her left arm tentacle.

The giant creature looked down. It looked as if the front of the porous rock was the main eye of the creature.

Maargalla manipulated the sludge and slapped it such that it could communicate with its creature. She talked to it, though it could only understand simple instructions. She told the creature that the bald man with four legs in front of it was its new master. When she did, the creature dropped to where its knees would be.

Raktaar marveled at Maargalla's work. "It . . . is . . . simply . . . incredible Maargalla. Wonderful indeed."

"Thank you Raktaar," she replied. "I wanted to make him particularly large. It will be a challenge to defeat him."

"Do you have a name for this delightful creature?"

"Krawlaga, Raktaar. I thought to make its legs flexible tentacles for greater speed. The rocks of this cave are excellent building materials as well. Making the pores of the main rock into eyes for the creature were difficult but . . . it appears this is what you had in mind?"

"This will serve me most well, Maargalla. My thanks are with you for this new weapon. I hope to take proper care of it."

Maargalla disappeared into her dark workspace, and Raktaar had before him the mighty Krawlaga. He was astonished by its height, admiring its gargantuan size. He looked to the mound of sludge next to it and realized it could communicate with it better than Maargalla could, being the one in control of the sludge. He walked too it and grabbed its left hand with both of his. He thought through his hands and into its, a gentle red glow making its way down his arms.

When the glow reached its stone hand, Krawlaga's whole body convulsed. It looked at the ceiling of his cave with its arms and legs tensed, and a slow yell made its way out into the cave. The yell was in fact a roar that grew in volume as a mouth made itself appear on its porous face. It was only a mouth that showed, and the mouth went across the entire width of the porous face. It dripped with red sludge, as if it was saliva that it couldn't swallow.

When the mouth finished appearing, the roar in the cave was deafening to what was left of Raktaar's ears. It bent forward and puked up a mound of sludge, such to make a small opening for its mouth.

It was finally able to speak. It spoke to Raktaar with a voice of a young man. "You are my master?"

"I am, yes. I am *Raktaar*. You are *Krawlaga*–"

It picked up Raktaar with both its hands and drew him closer to its face.

He was not afraid, knowing his place *above* his creature.

"What makes you my master?!" The creature yelled. "I could crumple you in my hands!"

"You could . . . and I could do this–" As he finished, he glowed a bright and menacing red.

Krawlaga dropped him, pressing its face into the ground. "Shut up! Shut it all up!" It yelled and roared. It heard the shouts of pain in his head. The screams of terror and the weeps of hopelessness. It was all it could hear.

"Very well." He pulled a red field out of the scared creature. "Now, I am your master, *Raktaar*. You are *Krawlaga*. Is that understood Krawlaga?"

"Yes . . . 'master'."

"Now, Krawlaga. I'm going to give you a task, and it is critically important you undertake this task *well*. Am I being understood, Krawlaga?"

"*Critically important?* What, we'll die if I stuff up?"

Raktaar glared at Krawlaga, emphasizing the seriousness of the task and the stupidity in its question.

The red in his eyes were particularly terrifying.

Its mouth twisted into sad agreement. It nodded. "Understood. What do you want me to do?"

"There is a young woman that I need you to kill."

Krawlaga looked with its giant rock face in silence. "You want me to kill a young woman?" He started to laugh, but Raktaar interrupted.

"Do not think simply of this young woman, Krawlaga. You must understand that. She has a gift that, if used against you, will end you. She can remove the power that gives you life. Am I being understood Krawlaga?"

Its mouth twisted into anger. "She can kill *me*?! Look at *me*! I can wrap my legs around her and *squeeze* the life out of her–"

"She has a glow unlike anything I've ever seen, and a strength unlike any other! I had suspicions about her gift, and the lacking presence of a small critter I sent for her confirms that!" He drew a breath in and then out, wanting to say each word exactly as he wanted to say it. "I know not how she does it, but she can remove the hate and pain from you. Your existence is derived from hate and pain! If you give her the chance, she will remove from you the very essence, the very driving force, that makes you *you*!" He finished with a pause, wanting the heaviness of this conversation to take its full effect, adding to the intensity a wide-eyed stare.

Krawlaga nodded in understanding. "You speak of her as though she is a formidable foe . . . " It paused to process its thoughts: its ability to think was done through the Gollum that controlled it all. "I will do as you request."

"Thank you Krawlaga. Your service is a testament to your maker. It is dusk where the young woman and her younger brother find their places to rest. You are to follow me and assist in gathering my amassing army of Screams." He paused briefly and relished in how he could bring to existence what he thought of in his imagination, even if it was as wild as a horizon full of Screams. "I cannot delay the end of these two. We begin our work tonight. May the storm that brews empower us to fight for our survival."

Chapter 12

A LARGE STORM WAS covering the sky when Ariel, Tanya, Boris, Nehemiah, and Laban began their walk to Ohlman's Tree. Ariel knew that she could fly there, but Nehemiah insisted that they all walked together.

THEY HAD SPENT THE afternoon preparing at Boris' and Tanya's home, one way or another, for the night. As usual, no-one saw. Ariel spent most of it enjoying her new freedom, experiencing new emotions and interpretations of her physical senses that she never knew she could experience. The late afternoon saw her practice her flying skills and combat readiness, which, as always, she did masterfully.

Tanya and Boris had spent the afternoon preparing with their fists and their heads, both fueled by their hearts. They also got changed out of their clothes, realizing they should wear something more comfortable for the night's battle.

When Tanya told Boris about how destructive their past could prove to them both, they spent as long as they needed to unravelling everything they felt and experienced over the past two days.

They wanted no part in the life Laban used to have.

When they were finished with this, they got to work ensuring they could do *something* useful during the battle. After becoming his wooden self, Nehemiah knew he could be of help with this, cupping his hands together and causing a magnificent fire to build in-between them. He let the fire die and gave Boris a sword and Tanya a wooden staff.

Boris' manly strength was better suited for a sword, for he could hold it with greater ease and strike heavy blows with it. The sword itself was made from a light grey rock, about as long as his legs, and double-edged. It was a very sharp weapon with a blade that could slice through tree trunks. It had weight to it, yet it was gentle on the wrists. Its smooth wooden handle could be held by both his hands, and it connected to the sword through finely woven vines.

Tanya's staff was incredibly different. It was much lighter than Boris' sword and nearly a head taller than her. It was easy to grip, entirely smooth, evenly balanced, and worked well with her feminine flexibility.

They both spent the rest of the afternoon getting used to their new weapons, knowing there was a strong chance it would save their lives and the lives of those around them.

Laban spent his time very uniquely in comparison.

He was unlike anyone in the group, and therefore was different in how he prepared for the night to be. He realized, through Nehemiah's insight, that he was made from a substance that could be turned into anything. He was free to mold and shape himself into anything he desired. When he processed this, it took effort to hold his current form, now realizing he could form himself into *anything* he could imagine. He spent his afternoon wondering how creative he could be, having never felt such potential in himself before.

Nehemiah's afternoon was spent with much emotional turmoil.

He was of service to his newly made friends, assisting them and supporting them in their training. When he wasn't doing this, he was preparing himself for the night to be. If his plan was followed, as it had been since he started to execute it, tonight would be truly strenuous for them all. He determined that his old brother's new anger would suggest tonight's violent engagement. Both of their fascinations for storms added to the timing that he predicted.

When the sun began to set, they saw how the storm covered the stars that would otherwise have lit the night. Lightning could be seen in the clouds, but no thunder could be heard.

Nehemiah wanted the group to walk together, such to prepare themselves on their way. They could better divulge what fear they felt rise inside them, bond as a group, and feel ready for the battle ahead. Nehemiah was his flower self as they walked.

Boris threw up on occasion, still feeling the terror of potentially dying.

When they arrived at Ohlman's Tree, Nehemiah flew both his flowers together at a fair distance from the group. He let them both glow as they came together, and he changed into his larger self. Going back to stand with the group, they faced the setting sun in a line.

Only a small part peaked over the hills, but the sun's final goodbye for the day could be seen. The moon shone with an excitement that, when the sun finished setting, would provide the light for tonight's battle. It had the permission of the clouds to shine through unhindered.

The group waited as the storm brewed above them. They all knew that the battle against them would begin when the first thunderclap was heard.

They hadn't heard it yet.

More lightning struck overhead, lighting the ground with every flash. They felt the strong wind on their faces. They also felt the intense rain fall on them all.

They hadn't heard anything yet.

Then they heard a boom louder than anything they've ever heard.

The first thunderclap.

As the thunder roared across the hills, an almost blinding flash of lightning struck amongst the clouds and lit up the hills that would become the battlefield.

With the flash of lightning came a truly terrible view.

As far left as the houses, and as far right as the school wall, were Screams.

They were first seen, then, sometime later, heard.

The shrieks of the Screams eventually came to them.

It was a foul sound for their ears to hear.

Boris let himself rest on his knees, wanting to ready himself for what was to come. Tanya followed, thinking it would help her as well. Laban tipped his front to the ground. Ariel saw her friends find rest and peace on their knees and thought to try as well. Nehemiah saw what Ariel saw and thought the same as her.

They were all on their knees, controlling their breathing, and readying themselves for what was about to be. They all closed their eyes, and, separately, they breathed. They felt the air rush through their nose, the scents of the storm overhead and the moist ground beneath them, and they delighted in such amazing smells. They breathed out, feeling the air push against their teeth and the warmth on their lips.

The shrieks of the Screams grew louder.

Their eyes opened.

They showed that they were focused, that they were determined, and that they were justly angry.

They were ready.

Boris was the first to rise.

He jumped up, began walking forward, and tossed his sword into the air, regripping it as it landed. He spun it around, feeling its well-crafted weight spin with great ease.

Tanya rose next, also tossing her staff into the air and regripping it as she caught it. She also smiled, having waited for this day for years. She spun her staff around in excitement while being powered by passion.

Ariel walked next, grabbing her thigh weapons as she did. She tossed them into the air, letting them flip, then feeling their weight as she caught them.

Nehemiah rose next, his footsteps shaking the ground. He, more than anyone, wanted to destroy his old brother. He had tried for centuries, unsuccessfully, and this was his greatest chance to save the world. His face twisted in a pure anger that wanted, so desperately, to spare the world of Raktaar's hate.

Laban, being different than anyone there, rose uniquely. He dropped to the ground, contacting as much of the dirt as he could. He thought of his new form and went about grabbing as much dirt as he could. He released himself into a creamy liquid, letting himself spread as far as he could.

The Screams were getting closer to the group.

The group were making a slow approach to the impending armada.

The Screams twisted their heads to better see the human mortals they were tasked with destroying, their mouths opening to show the teeth designed to rip flesh from bone.

The group held firm their weapons.

The Screams centered their flight paths to the group.

Laban had finished making his form. He was now two larger wings with a slim center body, his wingspan as large as Ariel's. He flew up, wanting to be higher than his enemy. He spun as he flew, eager to get into the fight against his old master.

Boris roared, charging with sword.

Tanya roared, running with her staff.

Ariel roared, shooting herself into flight with her pack.

Nehemiah let out the loudest roar, his hands in fists and his chest out. His roar echoed through the hills, and he finished by hitting his chest with both his hands.

As he did, he set himself on fire.

Every part of him had a flame coming from it, providing a bright light and an immense heat.

The fight had begun.

BORIS RAN AS FAST as his legs would let him, wanting to approach the incoming Screams rapidly. When he could see their mangled faces, he pressed his heels into the ground. He looked at the first creature, seeing its dead black eyes look back at him. Boris saw as its head twisted to an angle, hoping to rip whatever it could from his body. He raised his sword, holding it with both hands, held firm, and smiled.

Every creature that he sliced found itself in two halves behind him.

Ariel reached some height from the ground and unleashed her storm of Hailer Hail onto the Screams, seeing how each explosion removed a Scream from the skies. She watched as small flashes of orange flame and black smoke killed some Screams and seriously hurt others.

Tanya was on the ground, seeing how many Screams were now falling to the ground. She watched as they fell to the ground and collided the dirt with much force. If she saw one of them move, she held her staff by its end and swung it into the Scream's face. The Scream would be knocked onto its back, where she realized that their chests weren't strong at all. She easily stabbed her blunt staff through it, seeing their red, sludge infected heart now with a large hole in it.

They had nearly the body of a person, and the Screams heart would be where hers would be—they were vulnerable in the same ways.

At this, she smiled.

Laban flew and sliced through Screams as he flew into them. He had used the stone dust from his original form and made from it a sharp blade on the front of his body where his wings were joined together. He would flap his wings to get more speed, aim his center, then slice directly through the Scream. He flew faster than them and he was more maneuverable than them. They were easy for him to kill.

Nehemiah, also on the ground, looked up at the sky. What proved to be the challenge of the night was the sheer quantity of Screams. He saw the flashes of lightning behind a thick crowd of Screams, seeing only small glimpses of lightning scrape through and reach his eyes. He looked to Tanya and Boris, knowing they couldn't survive against so many and seeing how many Screams were aimlessly determining what to do. He looked to Ariel and Laban, knowing they wouldn't be able to kill them fast enough.

He knew he needed to help.

He knew exactly how he would.

He had kept his hands as fists, and he now arched his back forward, bending towards the ground. He closed his eyes, and, while dropping his weight, punched the ground with both fists.

The ground shook violently, but Nehemiah didn't move his fists.

When he punched, he kept his fists on the ground. While he did this, a blinding mass of light accumulated in the clouds, almost covering the entire field of battle.

Then he got his hands and laid his right on his left. When Tanya and Boris and Ariel saw the lightning with their eyes, Nehemiah instantly spoke into their heads: *Get your ears in the ground! Now!*

Nehemiah stood up, then he dropped his weight, contacting the ground with his overlapping hands.

Everything shook.

The ground beneath him felt the strong push of his hands. Dust rose from the ground. Grass was blown onto its side. Ohlman's Tree even swayed.

Then the sky shook.

When he slammed his overlapped hands into the ground, he let loose the collection of lightning that he built.

Half the Screams were struck—they were the shield for the other half.

The lightning itself was *incredibly* blinding.

Tanya and Boris followed Nehemiah's directive and nearly dived into the ground.

Ariel had seen the beginnings of a powerful strike of lightning and knew to lower her altitude. She was close to the ground, so when she heard Nehemiah's instruction, she stopped her thrusters, kicked her legs so that they were flying ahead of her, and used them to cushion her landing. She too dropped her head into the ground.

As soon as their ears were in the dirt, they *felt* the thunderclap on their bodies. They felt it push against them, and they could hear the loud crack even in the ground.

It was *almost* louder than their ears could handle.

They each then heard Nehemiah's voice in their heads. *Rise fighters! The battle is ours!*

They pushed with their hands to get their heads out of the ground. Boris held his sword, seeing how there were still Screams wanting to maul him. They came only from his front, wanting to target the face they were inscribed to destroy and lacked the intelligence to think of any strategy.

Tanya held her staff in her hands and watched as the Screams around her attempted to rise to their feet. She tossed her staff gently into the air with her right, catching it with her left.

She smiled, knowing she would enjoy this.

She went to the closest Scream. She held her staff by its center, pushed the Scream onto its back, and stabbed its chest. A Scream approached her from behind her. She felt that it was approaching. She regripped her staff by its end with both hands and lifted her left knee, using it to spin around.

She kicked up with her right leg, feeling herself spin vertically around. She landed on the ball of her right foot, now facing the Scream. She let her momentum continue to spin her around, and when she faced the Scream again, she planted her left foot and continued to pivot with her torso.

Her staff collided with its head.

It dropped to the ground and failed to get up.

A Scream started to crawl to her from her left.

She realized that it was close. She gripped her staff from its center, raised her right knee, used it to spin to her right, having spun on the ball of her left foot, and drove her staff into its chest. She stepped on the exposed end of her staff, pressing it into the ground, and flipped the Scream up and over her. She forced its head to slam into the ground, watching its neck snap. She looked up and caught the movement of a Scream just getting up. She ran towards it, seeing with greater clarity how there was one that was trying to fly and three others that were just getting up. She went to the airborne Scream first, jumping first with her right foot only to bring them both together and jump with both feet. She got above the creature, and aimed in-between the Scream's wings.

She landed.

Her staff went through.

The Scream was dead.

ARIEL REMOVED HER HEAD from the dirt and *immediately* sent power to her thrusters. She flew with both her swords in hand, knowing that she would almost be out of Hailer Hail.

She was far from the ground and let loose the Hail from her wings. She aimed each shot before firing, waiting for her Hailer Eye to be *certain* that each shot would down a Scream. She watched as small explosions sent flying abominations to the ground.

Then a thought came to her, realizing how efficient this new thought of hers was.

She flew straight to the thick swarm of Screams.

She held her swords in front of her and overlapped them. She saw a line of Screams she could cut through in one sweep. She lined herself up.

She went through the first Scream.

She rolled to her right and pitched up.

Through the second Scream.

Through the third Scream.

Through the fourth Scream.

Through the fifth Scream.

Through the sixth Scream.

She was covered in their gluggy red blood and had fresh in her memory the feeling of their rotting skin on hers.

The rain helped to wash both away.

She regripped her swords, their blades now facing outwards, and went around slicing through as many Screams that she could. She felt as her blades went through the wings of some and the chests of others. She smiled with every Scream she downed.

She saw a long line of Screams she could cut, waving in and out in an awkward and tricky path that her Hailer Eye could observe.

She knew she could fly it though.

She followed the line and sliced through what she could.

A long line of Screams fell to the ground.

Another line showed itself through her Hailer Eye.

Another line of Screams fell.

More lines were shown, and more Screams fell to their deaths.

She was very happy.

LABAN WAS SIMILAR IN his approach. His lines were simpler in shape, but he was able to cut himself through many Screams with every one of his passes. His mostly dirt body held strong through his intense flying, where his wings flapped strongly and he regularly spiraled through a line of Screams. He was appreciative that the rain made his dirt mud. It allowed his sludge to marble with the soft brown mud, giving greater strength to his form.

When he went through Screams in his new form, he felt their skin and gluggy blood slide over him with ease. He could fly faster, cut harder, and be better for his friends.

NEHEMIAH WAS THE GREATEST threat to the Screams.

He could catch them like they were small, slow bugs and squish them in his hands. He could walk about and stomp on whatever Scream hadn't died yet.

He saw a large huddle try to fly. He dug his hand into the ground, feeling a solid handful of dirt.

He overarm threw it to the huddle.

The huddle dropped to the ground.

Any Scream that got close to him was burned by his flames.

THEY EACH THEN HEARD a loud scream make its way from *across* the battlefield.

The Screams joined.

Ariel, Tanya, Laban, and Boris were each made disorientated by the sheer noise that came from everywhere around them. Laban could feel the noise, and it made him lose focus. Ariel's, Tanya's, and Boris' ears found the noise incredibly piercing.

Nehemiah could hear the pain that filled the air, but he determined himself to remain alert.

Something drastic had happened, and he knew it.

He did his best to keep his eyes open, though it meant it was harder to block out the horrible sound. He panned the battlefield, having a strong desire to know what caused the change.

He saw it.

Directly in line with him.

He ran to it, knowing he had to destroy it. As he ran, he processed what he saw. Its legs were tentacles, and its top half was made of rocks, no rock being the same as the next. He had no clue what it was, nor did he care.

Then a flash of lightning arced between the clouds above him.

He then knew that the storm had enough in their clouds to bring down another strike. He knew a bolt of lightning would work faster than he could, so he stopped and drove his fists into the ground.

The volume of the scream quietened for a small moment.

He overlapped his hands, right over left, and brought it high.

He dropped his weight, slamming his hands into the ground.

The clouds let forth a strike of lightning on the tall creature before him.

He saw as the creature fell to the ground, holding itself up with its hands.

The main scream stopped.

The smaller screams did as well.

He continued to run to the large tentacled rock thing in front of him, knowing that his friends weren't ready to take it yet.

He got closer to the creature and saw its finer details. It had, on its main porous rock, a mouth, but nothing more. He saw how his arms and hands looked much like a human's. Its tentacles were very large octopus legs, nearly as tall as him.

When he got closer to the foe before him, he jumped with his right and swung his left knee up. His foe was still recovering from the lightning strike, its large, center, porous rock not far from the ground. He put his hands in front of him while he was in the air, making a triangle with his pointer fingers and thumbs, keeping his other fingers and his arms straight. He let himself fall forward, wanting to land with his hands first.

He landed.

The ground shook again.

Nehemiah pushed his foe's face into the ground, forcing it to slide along the mud. He felt the slimy brown across his own body and felt the small holes on his hands.

He pressed his opponent into the ground for a good distance, wanting to force its 'face' to grind against the ground as much as it could. When he stopped sliding, he got to his feet. He stepped on and over his foe's main rock, getting to the long tentacles. He grabbed the tentacles by their ends and started to flip his opponent over him. He felt his hands burn from the slimy stuff on the tentacles, but it wasn't as strong as his old brother's sludge.

He knew he could care for that later.

He watched as his foe slammed into the ground, a massive splash of mud sent out as he did. He kept holding his foe's tentacles, forcing its body over him and slamming into the ground again.

And again.

And again.

And again.

On his final slam, he lifted his foe like before but brought him down with both hands, dropping his weight as he did. He saw his foe lie on the ground, lacking the strength to get up. Nehemiah took that time to remove the burning pain from his hands. He held them closer to his fire and realized how it was his old brother's red sludge. He held them against his chest, letting his chest fire burn it all away. A thick, black smoke rose from him. He closed his eyes, wanting to make this process as fast as he could make it. He could feel his hands not hurt as much, and he could feel that he didn't have much more to burn away.

He opened his eyes.

A rock fist was approaching his face.

It connected, and Nehemiah felt the ground approach him quickly and unexpectedly. The rock thing approached him and wrapped its tentacles around his legs. It bent over Nehemiah.

Then it screamed.

A chorus of smaller screams joined.

The battlefield was filled with a *truly* deafening, *truly* violent sound.

As his opponent screamed, it punched.

Its first hit landed on his face. Its rock fist was incredibly hard, rough, and sharp. The second hit was on his face. The third hit was on his chest. The fourth also on the chest. The fifth, sixth, and seventh alternated between head and chest.

Nehemiah knew he couldn't burn the sludge on his foe's tentacles even though his legs were alight—only his chest could remove the sludge's potency.

He knew he could catch one of its arms though.

He grabbed its left arm with his right. He reached his left arm through, putting his left hand behind its left shoulder, and pinned his foe into the ground. He used the dirt underneath him to push himself up and over his opponent, also using his grip on the rock arm to get on top of the porous rock that was its body.

He then dropped his weight onto the amalgamated rocks that made an arm.

The left arm snapped from its main rock.

He threw it aside, knowing it meant nothing to either of them now.

He grabbed its right arm with his right hand. He brought it behind its main rock, holding its right shoulder with his left.

He raised himself, extending his arms.

He dropped his weight.

Its right arm snapped off.

He tossed it aside, knowing he, nor his foe, had no use for it anymore.

Knowing he was now in a place of control over his foe, he got to work on freeing himself from its legs. He grabbed the highest part of the tentacle that he could grab with his right, and put his left next to its socket.

He pulled with his right and pushed with his left.

Its right tentacle was pulled out.

He grabbed its left tentacle with his left and held its main rock with his right.

He pulled with his left and pushed with his right.

Its left tentacle was pulled out.

He grabbed both sides of the main, porous rock, seeing how it angled into a curved edge where its tentacles used to be. He picked it up and stabbed it into the ground, not wanting it to roll away. He freed himself from its tentacles and stayed in a low squat. He spun his opponent around to look at its mouth, which was yelling in pain, then looked at where its eyes should have gone. "End this now!"

It spat back at him, a large drop of thick sludge shooting through the air and landing on his chest. It laughed.

He lifted the main, porous rock and dropped his weight, hoping to spear it into the ground as much as he could. He stood, taking some steps back. He dropped his weight, driving his fists into the ground. He rose again, hands overlapped, and slammed them into the ground.

A bolt of lightning landed powerfully on what was left of his foe.

It yelled in pain.

He approached it, picking it up from the ground, and looking at it where its eyes should have been. "You can control all of these things with your scream. End this! Now!"

It knew it couldn't do anything against Nehemiah. He could burn the potency out of his spit, and he would send a strike of lightning anytime it resisted.

It spat at the ground. "You'll have to turn me."

Nehemiah did so.

It now faced the Screams. It roared, then spat a large blob of his dark red spit.

Across the battlefield, at that moment, Screams rose to the skies.

Nehemiah dug the main, porous rock of his foe into the ground.

"Wait! Wait! Don't! Please! I'm doing what you asked!"

Nehemiah picked it up. "Then why, good challenger, are they being told to fly?"

"Because Screams aren't very tough. I've told them to fly to the clouds, then to fly into the ground. They'll do *exactly* what I tell them to do."

Nehemiah looked to the clouds, seeing how the Screams were beginning to disappear. He looked to what was left of the rock creature, then, after a moment, angled it up. "If you're wrong . . . " He let go with one of his hands, holding it in front of where its eyes should have been. He held it open, then closed it. When he closed his fist, flashes of lightning shone from the clouds and thunder could be heard from it.

It spoke. "I'm promising you. I don't want that. I've done what you asked."

Nehemiah nodded. He held what left of his foe in his hands, walking slowly to his friends.

ARIEL AND LABAN WERE in better health than Boris and Tanya.

Ariel had experience with loud noises and wasn't too disoriented from the Screams. She was able to fly relatively well and didn't sustain too many injuries. Laban simply ignored his ability to hear things, having not been given physical ears.

Tanya and Boris were not in good health.

Their human ears reeled at the pain of the two screeching choruses of Screams. The first brought them to the ground and tears in their eyes, only *just* escaping from the Screams that surrounded them in their weakness.

The second saw an even narrower escape.

THE FOUR OF THEM watched as Nehemiah approached. They all saw that something was in his hands. He pressed it into the ground, then spoke. "Ariel, Tanya, Laban, Boris. We have another to add to our merry group." He tapped on the top of the porous rock.

It spat.

Ariel deployed her thigh panels and pulled from them her weapons, knowing there was ammunition in them. "I'm taking that as a sign of aggression."

Tanya nodded. "It is . . . but . . . something about this thing . . . " She approached the porous rock, raising her right arm as she approached.

It spat at her hand.

She stopped, feeling how cold and disgusting it felt on her skin. She raised her sludge covered hand and dropped it quickly, removing most of the sludge.

She wiped the rest on her pants.

Its mouth dropped into shock and terror.

She moved closer.

It spoke. "What . . . who . . . how . . . you . . . how?!"

She stopped and replied. "How what?"

It paused, its mouth showing the emotion of fear. "You . . . you aren't affected by . . . that should have killed you!"

"I've been told that a lot."

"My master told me that you could *kill* me. I didn't believe it, but . . . "

She rested her right hand on the porous rock.

It spoke quickly. "What will you do?"

She looked to Nehemiah, who replied with a nod.

It spoke again. "What's happening?!"

She rested her left hand on it and brought her face close.

She blew her breath on it.

A thick cloud of black came off it. It yelled and roared, pleading that Tanya stop whatever she was doing.

She had her eyes closed and concentrated on blowing on the porous rock before her. The more she blew, the more she felt the rock begin to crumble. She could feel the rock turn into powder and feel how its strength was being lost. She could also hear the shouts and roars of its sludge filled mouth continue to plead with her.

Then she felt a face.

She opened her eyes.

It was the face of a young man.

Ariel put her weapons into her thighs, closed the panel, and walked slowly to the face. She watched as Tanya blew more rock from the young man's face. She watched the eyes and the nose make itself known.

She knew that face.

She knew it very well.

She collapsed backwards, cushioning her landing with her hands. Her face showed surprise and overwhelming relief. She brought her hands to her face and sobbed, feeling her whole chest move and tears stream down her face.

"Boaz?" she asked.

Tanya had blown on his eyes and mouth, showing the rough skin of a Gollum.

The young man replied. "Ariel?" He broke into tears, having never seen a human face in years.

Ariel ran to Boaz, put her hands around his head, and hugged him as best she could.

"I could have shot you," she realized. "I could have killed you . . . " She hugged him tighter.

"Ariel . . . it's okay . . . it's okay . . . you didn't know," Boaz replied.

Tanya continued to blow, having removed almost all the rock around Boaz. She smiled when she saw the reunion between him and Ariel.

Boaz talked to Ariel. "It was really brave and stupid what you did when we last saw each other."

She laughed. "In this line of work there isn't much difference."

He laughed, knowing how true it was. He paused, then said, "Thank you for fighting for me." He kept crying when he said this.

"I didn't save you though–"

"But you got very close–"

"But it didn't save you from–"

"He is unlike anything we've ever versed. Ariel. Ariel!" She looked into his eyes. "It's okay. You did what you could. That's all a friend could ask for." He smiled as he finished.

She sobbed violently and held him tighter. "I missed you so much Boaz."

"I missed you too Ariel."

Tanya was nearly done with blowing off the rock. Her lips and lungs felt sore, and Nehemiah helped remove most of the rock. She was satisfied Ariel now had Boaz in her life again. She could understand why Ariel thought so highly of him as well. It would take both her hands to not even wrap around his arm, and his legs were like small trees. His hands were gloved, his abdomen was covered in his Gollum vest, and he had the same vibrant blue in his blood that Ariel did.

Boaz and Ariel had finished crying and were now smiling. Feeling his hands be freed from the rock, he put them behind Ariel's head and held it against his chest.

She lifted her head, and she smiled.

He then felt goosebumps grow along his left side.

He looked right and saw Nehemiah's legs.

He looked up and saw Nehemiah's face.

His face dropped in terror. "About earlier, I . . . that wasn't . . . " His mouth moved, but no sound was made.

Nehemiah replied. "You need not fear, Boaz. Tanya is blowing out what made you do that to me. It is quite okay."

Boaz laughed a nervous laugh, then it became genuine, feeling the gladness in not needing to fight Nehemiah again. He also felt how Tanya had freed him from the rock that encased him. He brushed off what rock powder remained, stood on his large feet, and looked around.

Boris approached first. "The name's Boris. A pleasure to meet you." He extended his right hand as an invitation for a handshake.

Boaz accepted the invitation, and extended his light grey gloved hand that was nearly twice the size of Boris' hand. "The name's Boaz. A pleasure," he said as he looked into Boris' eyes and gave a real smile.

Then Laban lifted his wings and rested himself on them.

Boaz, in instinct, saw Boris' sword on the ground, quickly tucked his right foot underneath it, tossed it to his right hand, dropped his right knee while the sword was in the air, spun on the ball of his left foot, and threw the sword at Laban.

Laban, having a delayed reaction, let himself melt over the sword and caught the flying blade.

Ariel ran in front of him. "It's okay. He's with us."

Boaz breathed heavily. "What . . . are you?"

Laban replied. "I was once what you were. Then Tanya did to you what she did to me. I felt everything you just felt. But . . . I'm now here."

He nodded. "You don't have a mouth, do you?"

"No, I don't. I just talk in your head."

Boaz rubbed his eyes.

Boris spoke. "Don't worry. It gets easier."

Boaz looked at him. "I'm hoping it does." He then looked at Tanya. "You must be Tanya then."

She replied with a smile. "That's me."

"So . . . you . . . you just breathed on me and . . . " He looked down, seeing the lack of rock surround him. "I'm here?"

"Yeah . . . that's how it works. Apparently."

Boaz walked quickly to her, putting his arms around her in appreciation. "I am grateful for what you've just done."

Tanya returned the embrace. "It's okay. It's good to meet you." She let go of him, and he understood to let go of her. "Ariel talks highly of you."

He turned around and saw Ariel, who was still smiling.

He smiled back.

Nehemiah laughed, then spoke. "What a delightful reunion! Though . . . it saddens me to say that we must bring an end to our warm greetings."

They all looked at him in confusion, each of them arching their back to see his face.

"My apologies. One moment please." He turned around, took two steps, jumped, then imploded into his flower self. They all watched as the flower glided back to them, landing in the center of the group. "Now, we have survived this assault. Respectfully done, I might add, though I'm noting the injuries you each have sustained. I do believe we should make use of Ohlman's Tree for the night. I will inform you all in the morning about what we are to do next."

They each agreed that some rest would be appreciated. They went to Ohlman's Tree and began climbing, each of them hoping to find a good branch to sleep in.

As they climbed, Screams started to fly into the ground.

They were quiet thuds, but the sheer quantity of Screams meant the thuds accumulated in volume. They all watched as Screams flew into the ground and a graveyard of the twice dead establish itself.

When they could see that no Scream was going to land in Ohlman's Tree, they rested.

CHAPTER 13

RAKTAAR SAW THE BATTLE take place during the storm.

He watched as hundreds of Screams versed three teenagers, a wooden giant, and his converted- sludge- mimic from before. He saw how closely Tanya and Boris had gotten to their demise. He saw how futile Maargalla's Screams were. He watched in anticipation when Krawlaga began to combat Nehemiah.

He watched in dread when he saw his hope, Maargalla's newest creature, have its limbs ripped from its sockets.

He watched as Nehemiah brought Krawlaga's main, porous rock to the group, and continued to watch in terror as Tanya removed the Gollum controlling Krawlaga from the large rock.

He raced to his closest network trapdoor.

AS HE WALKED THROUGH his network, he thought about how he could best combat Nehemiah. He knew he was the greatest threat amongst the group; hence, the creature devised for his protection must be made against Nehemiah *specifically*.

To do so, he required a creature that was gigantic in size.

Excessively gigantic.

He couldn't risk any more mistakes.

He walked his way into his throne room and tapped for Maargalla.

She approached from the darkness opposite him.

"Maargalla?" he asked.

"Yes, Raktaar," she replied.

"I bring hurtful news." He paused, then continued. "Krawlaga didn't work. It died, and the Gollum that controlled him has been taken."

She slapped her tentacle on the dark red cave floor. "I put much effort and resources into that creation!" She paused. "How did my Screams fair?"

Raktaar hesitated in replying, remembering the call Krawlaga made before Nehemiah moved what was left of Krawlaga to the group.

He knew that every Scream she had made was now flying a suicidal path into the ground.

"Raktaar"–she said sternly–"how did my Screams fair in battle?"

Raktaar reluctantly tapped. "None survived–"

Maargalla violently slapped the ground with her tentacles. Splatters of red sludge flew, and the cave echoed each slap. "You said they worked really well!"

"They do, Maargalla! You make *so* many of them that any other human mortal would have died tonight! But these aren't normal human mortals Maargalla! Nehemiah is their leader! One of my sludge critters is now working with them and can change into *anything* he pleases! Then those human mortals"–he hit the ground with his front right foot before continuing– "they are *unkillable*–"

She had walked over to Raktaar and used her tentacles to slam his face into the cave floor. She watched as he straightened himself.

She then slammed his face into the cave floor again.

And again.

And again.

He grabbed both her eye tentacles with his right hand and put his left on her body.

He pulled with his right and pushed with his left. "*What did you just do?!*"

Maargalla stabbed one of her hard points through his right forearm, forcing him to let go of her eye tentacles. While he was distracted by the sudden pain, she crawled onto him and wrapped her tentacles around him, holding everything tightly.

She pressed her hard point against his neck.

He attempted to retaliate by sending a glow of red through her.

"That won't do anything against me! My brain swims through *your* sludge! I've already got the shouts and yells of your victims in my head–"

"*What are you doing–*"

"*What do you mean they're unkillable?!*"

"I've done everything I can to work against them! I've versed them myself! I've sent your Screams against them–"

Maargalla pressed her point against his neck firmly.

Raktaar was silenced.

"Being the real creative one out of the both of us, might I talk now?"

Raktaar nodded in fear, hating how his creature was becoming more powerful than him.

"*You* have versed them. *My Screams* have versed them. *My Krawlaga* has versed them. *None of them have proven useful.* Now, we need something better than *any* of them–"

"I know that Maargalla–"

"*Then why are you panicking?!*"

He didn't have a response.

"We need something *big*–"

"*I know that Maargalla!* We need your creature to be *gigantic!* More humongous than anything you have *ever made!* We also need it to be made against Nehemiah *specifically.* We both know he is the greatest threat against our existence–"

"That girl you keep talking about is the greatest threat against our existence–"

"She comes *very* close. The only way she stays alive is if her head works. Her head connects her mind, who she is, with her body. *Her head* is what allows her breath to kill both of us. *Nehemiah's existence* flows through *every part of him!* His head is just as much a part of him as his hand, or his boot, *or any part of him!* To kill Nehemiah, you need to kill *all* of him."

Maargalla loosened her grip with her tentacles, seeing now that he was acting with reason.

She also had thoughts about how that could happen. "What if"–she said with excitement–"I make something that unleashes your sludge. Embodies it . . . yes . . . that will work very well . . . " She went quickly into her work space, only to quickly turn around. "The Screams that died today. Where are they?"

He replied. "Now, they're on the battlefield where I first sent them. Krawlaga's limbs are there as well. Why?"

"I need you to grab them. *All of them.*"

"Yes Maargalla." He turned to exit his cave, only to turn around. "Maargalla?"

She turned her eyes to face him.

"Do that to me again . . . " He laid his hand flat on the cave floor and talked into his pool of sludge. He told it to form human arms, tentacles, and arms with hands made from rocks, each slowly rising from the pool of sludge.

When the limbs were fully grown, the pool was densely populated by dark red limbs.

The tentacles slapped the sludge and violently splashed red glops. The human arms reached to Maargalla, but only went as far as the confines of the pool. The rock arms made themselves into fists and struck the sides of the pool, slowly chipping away at its borders.

He lifted his hand from the ground, and the pool returned to normal. He tapped, "I can create another creature maker."

She replied, "I can create a better master–"

He forced his hand to the ground and made the pool of limbs again, each performing their actions with greater ferocity.

She continued to walk to her work space, tapping as she went.

She was laughing.

He was furious.

He lifted both hands, and slammed them into the ground.

His pool of sludge exploded into the air, then returned to its rock container, knowing it was supposed to remain inside the confines of his pool.

He exited his throne room and went to collect her dead Screams.

CHAPTER 14

THE SUN WAS RISING when Ariel, Laban, Tanya, Boris, Boaz, and Nehemiah awoke. They saw the full moon set in the distance and the marvelous 'hello' of the sun opposite it.

As it rose, two emotions were strongly felt among the group.

The first was delight.

They each saw the wonderful colors fill the sky. An incredible pink melted with a bright orange, and touches of blue brought balance to the sun's artwork. The clouds' inherent white gave a unique diversity to the sun's piece. It was a remarkable sight, and they each enjoyed it thoroughly.

The second was fear.

A risen sun gives easy sight to the visual senses, and this sight showed each of them how empty the battlefield now was.

No Screams could be seen.

It was a muddy mess of lines the width of Screams and their wings—all the lines went somewhere.

Boaz was the first to notice the imprints of someone's work from the night before.

"Hey . . . that's . . . weird," he said. He made his way to the ground, wanting to see the muddy ground better.

They each saw him go down the tree, and they all followed him, wondering what he saw.

When they got down, they each looked with fear.

Boaz spoke first. "Look at this! He was here last night! You see that!" He ran to the edge of the tree's branches and pointed to the ground. "You see how close he got to us?! He could have killed us *while we slept!*"

Nehemiah spoke next. "He could have, but he didn't . . . how odd . . . " He paused. "I didn't think he would do it."

Ariel was the first to reply. "Going to do *what?*"

Nehemiah clicked his flowerhead, angled his petals, and flew a fair distance away. He changed into his wooden form and lowered himself to the ground, where he used his fingers to measure the distance between the trenches in the ground. "I hoped he wasn't so petrified. I hoped he was going to be like his usual arrogant self . . . but . . . he's become . . . desperate."

Tanya anxiously replied. "*Desperate?*"

Boris joined the conversation. "Yeah. How can *he* become desperate?"

Nehemiah answered. "He can become desperate when I become so determined to end his life. To exaggerate this, we have Tanya."

Tanya looked at Nehemiah in confusion. "He's *desperate* because of *me?*"

Nehemiah replied. "Oh yes! Tanya, he has good reason to be terrified of you!"

Tanya processed this, and her face showed the extent to her revelation. "He's *terrified* of me?"

"Yes Tanya."

Ariel continued. "Laban was first scared of you, remember? You make the thing made from fear *feel* fear. I told you he's scared of you!"

She began to tear when she realized this.

She heard Ariel say it the first time, but now it made sense.

She had a power over the thing that had a power over most of her life.

She had never experienced such supremacy before.

Ariel and Boris went to her and put their arms around her. She responded by putting her arms around them.

Nehemiah continued. "You are able to kill him, Tanya. You and I are the only ones that can truly end his existence. He's lived so long because of his sludge, hence any physical strike against him can be healed. But *we* can remove that power from him. He's tried regularly to kill me and failed, but he's failed *every time* he's tried to kill you. Next to your gift, that is why he is terrified of you."

Tanya broke into tears and held onto Ariel and Boris tightly.

Boaz smiled, enjoying the happiness Tanya had on her face. He then spoke to Nehemiah. "So, what do we do now?"

Laban replied. "What else is there to do? We kill our old master."

Nehemiah agreed, but added to the thought. "There is something else we are to kill as well."

They all looked nervously to Nehemiah.

He continued. "There is a reason this battlefield is barren and marked with these shallow trenches. He cleared this land, through desperation, against Tanya and myself." He paused, breathing in then out, then continued. "He cannot *really* create. None of us can. He is a master manipulator however, using what he can and mangling it into some abhorred abomination. Considering how much of his resources he's regathered . . . how he collected his Screams I mean . . . I am disheartened to say we will soon be facing a creature of towering size."

Boaz talked next, feeling his inexperience weigh against him. "Towering? What, more than you?"

"More than I, Boaz. More, even, than the creature you controlled last night. He intends to destroy me, being that I pose the greatest threat to him, hence . . . " He tapped the ground as he thought, wanting to be sure he was right. "He will twist something against me *specifically*. Yes . . . he must. He wouldn't exert unnecessary effort to collect *all* those Screams unless he needed them for something. All those Screams put together will be truly towering." He paused. "He has tried killing me himself, through his Screams, and through the rock creature from last night. He is only left with using as much of his resources as he can against me . . . but . . . this is easily countered. Trivially even." He smiled as he finished.

Boris spoke in curiosity. "What would that be?"

Nehemiah replied. "Well . . . he is making something to kill me specifically. He doesn't care about killing any of you with his latest manipulation . . . just me. I'm the one he's had centuries of struggles with. In his anger and haste, he'll want me gone before any of you. Hence . . . we don't make it verse me."

Ariel looked up in trepidation, hating the answer that cleared the confusion. "We're going to kill it, aren't we?"

Nehemiah replied. "For each of us to survive, yes."

Boris uneasily spoke. "How are we supposed to kill it?! We barely made it out of last night!"

Ariel answered Boris. "Last night was difficult because there were Screams *everywhere*. There won't be that when we kill whatever 'he' plans to create."

Laban joined the conversation anxiously. "How are we supposed to kill something so massive? Wait . . . are you sure *you*"–he turned to Nehemiah– "can't kill it?"

"I am sure, Laban."

Tanya then laughed. She had a smile grew on her face while she was thinking, and when the thoughts in her head connected well, she joyously laughed.

They each looked to her with dumbfounded looks, wondering what the cause of her laughter was.

She saw the looks and spoke. "This creature is made against *you specifically*." She looked to Nehemiah, then to the group. "This thing is made to kill Nehemiah and Nehemiah alone. *It won't be made to verse any of us.* It won't know how to kill any of us." She laughed again. "It'll be terrified of us."

Boris nodded in agreement. "Yeah . . . yeah it will!"

Ariel began to laugh. "I'm gonna enjoy killing this thing!"

Laban interrupted. "What is it that we're killing anyway?"

Nehemiah answered. "To be honest, I have no knowledge of the creature my old brother wants to create. I do know, however, that following these lines and finding where they lead would prove beneficial to us." He began to walk along them, seeing from his height how they all led somewhere. He turned back to the group. "Care to join me?"

They all walked behind Nehemiah, who led them along the scattered pattern of lines.

Boaz noticed an inconsistency. "If Laban's and my old master can 'make' what he makes, how was he so clueless to leave this?"

Laban answered. "Remember how driven he is by his emotions? You don't think clearly when you think through your heart, which he does all the time."

Nehemiah presented another thought. "You will find *we think* through our heads but are *pushed* by our hearts."

"Screams don't have that second bit," Boaz realized. "They only barely think; they have no heart."

Ariel, thinking tactically, asked a question. "Why hasn't he tried this before?"

Nehemiah answered. "It's an all-in of resources." He turned around, walked backward, and continued. "His success in besting us will leave him unstopped and unstoppable, knowing there will be nothing that can best him and his latest creation. His failure will leave most of his resources abolished—anything that can remove us at least—and leave him at his most vulnerable. His next move will the riskiest he's ever taken." He turned around and walked normally.

THEY ALL CONTINUED TO follow Nehemiah, who noticed the lines in the ground were beginning to join.

A track had been made, going some distance away from the school.

The track then disappeared into a small mound overgrown with grass.

Laban and Boaz stopped when they saw this.

Ariel, Tanya, Boris, and Nehemiah noticed this.

"Everything alright?" Boris asked them both.

Laban replied. "No."

Boaz continued. "We know what's under there."

Laban added. "We used to live down there."

"We died down there."

"I can't go down there!" Laban shouted as he tried to scurry away.

"I can't either!" Boaz shouted as he stepped back.

Nehemiah spoke up. "You won't need to go down there now. His creature will be too large to enter the world through there."

Laban spoke. "You make it sound like a giant!"

"Young Laban"–Nehemiah replied–"it will be."

Boaz talked next. "How are we supposed to kill a giant?!"

Nehemiah answered. "You don't need to kill the whole giant. You simply kill what controls it. See, you are not much different from a giant."

They all looked at him totally puzzled.

"What allows *you* to be *you* is not limited to your brain. Your mind is not limited to neural networks. What the brain *is*, however, is the channel between *you*—your mind—and your body. That is what makes the head so important to mankind. That's the only way you can do anything through your body. Giants are *the same*."

Boris understood. "We just need to kill the giant's head." He nodded. "That's doable."

Ariel nodded. "It is, but we aren't ready to verse it. Not yet. We need to *resupply* and *train* and *prepare*."

Nehemiah nodded. "It would be best if we stayed here, near Ohlman's Tree. It can serve each of our purposes quite well. Does anyone object?"

They all shook their heads.

Ariel spoke next. "I'll fly Boaz and myself to the Facility. We can resupply with what we need."

Nehemiah agreed. "Excellent thinking, Ariel."

Ariel deployed her wings and stood in-front of Boaz, letting a handle spring open from the bottom of her pack, well away from her pack's thrusters. Boaz grabbed it with his left hand and Ariel began to fly, making her way to the Facility with her oldest friend.

Nehemiah looked to Boris and Laban next. "I had a thought for you both. I remember your contributions to the battle last night were separate. I do feel that a synergy of your skills would be most mighty."

Laban replied, looking to Boris. "Yeah . . . that would be epic!"

Boris agreed. "We'll see what we can do," finishing with a smile. He made his way with Laban to open ground.

"What would you like me to do?" Tanya asked.

"Good Tanya, I wish to teach you something," Nehemiah replied.

"You want to *teach* me something?" Tanya said.

"I do. I remember when you saved Boaz from the rock last night, it took some time for you to blow the rock off him."

"It did . . . I'm sorry I wasn't faster."

"Oh Tanya!" He sat cross-legged on the ground. "You need not say 'sorry'. You saved strong Boaz from the capsule of my old brother's manipulation. That is respectable. I can, though, teach you to do what I did to mighty Ariel just yesterday."

She looked at him uneasily. "I can't light myself on fire. I can't pull the black stuff out of things like you can."

Nehemiah replied. "Not yet, no. But I can teach you."

"How do I do what you do?"

"Well . . . you'll note how you and I are the only ones that can remove my old brother's essence from something. You through your breath, and myself by pulling it out. You are close to doing what I do, however. I do believe we can start your practice with the sludge on your thigh."

She looked down. She remembered wiping the rock creature's spit on them after last night's battle. She looked up. "What do I do?"

"Tanya, you must first feel the pain in the sludge. You will want to sit though; there's no urgent need to stand."

Tanya sat with her legs extended, still looking at him.

"If you could please hover both your hands near the sludge."

She let her hands hover near the red sludge.

"Now simply feel yourself pulling the black dust from the sludge."

She closed her eyes.

She pulled.

As she pulled, she felt a searing heat on her hands. She opened her eyes and saw black dust on the sludge.

She laughed with excitement.

She lost focus.

The black dust shot into her leg.

She winced.

Nehemiah spoke. "Pull the black dust, good Tanya!"

She pulled, feeling how it took more effort the more she pulled. She tried to pull quickly, using her arms and core to do so, but the black powder resisted her. She felt the black powder weigh on her leg, a throbbing pain that caused it to swell a horrible color. She felt the powder sear her thigh from the inside, and she groaned.

She slowly pulled the black powder from her leg, seeing the dark stuff seep through her skin. She felt its warmth on her palms, and she felt the weight of what looked light to lift. She saw it slowly release from her leg, still feeling the pain that drove her to work with haste.

She saw the last of it leave her leg.

It was all out.

She breathed out, then laughed, still concentrating on the black powder in her hands. She looked to Nehemiah. "What now?"

He replied. "I will take that from you Tanya, until you set your chest alight."

She gladly held the mass of black powder at arm's length, where Nehemiah bent forward and took the mass from her, letting it hover a small distance from his palm.

Then she spoke in confusion. "I can't set myself on fire. We can't do that."

He replied. "Not *normally*, no. Remember, however, that much changes when you communicate either with myself or my old brother. There is more to life than what you can experience through your physical senses."

"So . . . " she tried to understand, though it proved to be a challenge. "How am I supposed to set myself on fire?"

"Not *yourself*, good Tanya. Simply your chest. See, when you look at the black powder in front of you, and you realize how much hurt it can bring, you rightly feel enraged. When you're holding this"–he gestured to the black powder– "that anger shows itself as a flame. With that flame, you burn this"–he gestured again to the oddly shaped black mass.

"So . . . I just feel angry while I'm holding that"–she gestured to the black near his palm– "and I'll—my chest—will be on fire?"

He smiled and nodded.

"Won't it hurt? I'll be *on fire.*"

"You will feel warm, but it will only feel painfully hot if you let it feel painfully hot. You will be quite okay, good Tanya."

She closed her eyes and breathed out, preparing herself for a truly different experience. She reached out her hands and took a small part of the randomly shifting black from his hands, feeling its heat on her hands and the effort required to hold it. She closed her eyes and thought of all that this blackness had done to her, to Boris, to Ariel, to Laban, and to Boaz.

She remembered.

She pictured.

The screams.

The shouts.

The cries for help.

The desperation to have it all over with.

Then the anger came.

Her chest was set ablaze.

She looked down, seeing the upper half of her torso, up to her shoulders, alight. She laughed, having never seen or felt something so unusually amazing.

Nehemiah joined her laughter. "I am glad you're enjoying yourself Tanya . . . ." He paused. Then, "This next step does bring with it great self-hurt, however . . . " He then made his chest be alight.

Tanya looked up, still concentrating on the black held by her hands and the fire covering her upper torso. She looked first in confusion, then in realization, remembering how he did this to Ariel yesterday, then in worry, remembering next how intense it was for him. "How bad will it be for me?"

He replied. "For something so small, only slightly. You will, though, feel great discomfort."

She nodded, then added. "If I can do what you did to Ariel yesterday . . . that *really* helped her . . . " She nodded fervently. "What do I do?"

Nehemiah smiled a warm smile. "Raktaar will be truly fearful of you, mighty Tanya. Simply push the blackness into your chest. It is best done in one execution, from what I have learned." He extended the black dust at arm's reach, then drove it into his chest. He closed his eyes, let the fire burn the black dust, then extinguished the flame by blowing through the sides of his midsection.

She nodded, now preparing herself for what was about to happen. The memory of Nehemiah in great self-affliction yesterday was fresh and intimidating. She breathed in, then out.

In, then out again.

She extended her arms as far as they could reach.

Then she plunged the blackness into her chest.

She yelled in pain.

She felt her chest burn from the inside; a scorching hot that she couldn't reach. She knew she needed to burn the black powder, but she questioned if she had the strength to do so. She knew the powder was in her chest and couldn't be removed. She knew this was something she was called to do. She knew this would be one of her greatest strengths.

She also knew how it made her lungs feel like they were melting.

She yelled in pain, her hands and knees pressing into her chest. She smelt the thick smoke rise from her, and she felt, inside her chest, strong walls of fire slowly squish the slowly shrinking black powder. She felt how she had to squish the black powder with the walls of flame in her chest, and she felt how strongly the black powder resisted. Yelling in pain, tears started to fall down her face. Her heart and mind battled against her deep desire to satisfy an amazing purpose, but it was so dramatically unusual and fierce.

Then it stopped.

She breathed heavily, thankful that it was done with, and relaxed. She lay on the ground, resting her hands on her head.

Nehemiah laughed. "Masterfully done, Tanya."

She was appreciative. "That's . . . kind . . . of you . . . to say . . . Nehe . . . miah." She breathed heavily. "I'm sure . . . my lungs . . . appreciate . . . being thrashed . . . with fierce . . . heat." She continued to breath heavily.

"Yes . . . I remember that vividly . . . you will find a way to tolerate its ferocity, good Tanya. It will come with practice."

"Everything . . . does." When her breathing slowed, she sat up and continued. "What do I do now?"

"Tanya, now you must remove yourself of the ash that sits inside you . . . " He paused, realizing the issue that now presented itself. "I have openings in my sides, such that I can blow the ash out of them. You . . . do not have . . . that gift."

She remembered yesterday that Nehemiah held his nose and mouth and breathed out *through* the sides of his midsection. She thought to try the same, knowing it wouldn't repeat what Nehemiah did.

She held her nose and mouth and breathed out, knowing that *something* would happen.

She felt the ash blow out of her upper back, and her midsection lighten.

She had successfully removed the power from the red sludge, proving herself better than Raktaar.

She roared with energy, feeling the satisfaction from her success.

Nehemiah smiled with warmth, like a father to his daughter.

Ariel and Boaz were approaching the boring, bland box that was the Facility.

"Here she is. Boring as always," Ariel said.

"It hasn't changed at all?" Boaz asked. "Not since . . . " He stopped himself when he realized too late how that sentence had to end.

"It's the Facility. It hasn't changed since it was built."

A silence was held between them.

Then Boaz spoke. "We grew up in there . . . what a horrible childhood . . . "

Ariel turned her head and continued. "What do you mean? I've got explosive rounds in my thighs, Brasher Blood in me, and a Hailer Eye. We turned out great!" She smiled as she looked ahead.

Boaz couldn't understand whether that was genuine or not, though he knew, for himself, that it as an awkward mix of both. "We can do some really amazing things Ariel."

She knew it was true.

She breathed out as the smile faded from her face. "I *love* to fly. I *love* to *protect* and *defend* and *guard*. I love having a meaning to my life that's *so important* to *so many*. It's just"–she shook her head– "on any day, the only times I smile a *real* smile is either when I fly—flying is *amazing*—and when I get to chill with you—you were my *only* friend for a *long* time. But"–she shouted, then continued. "When Nehemiah pulled this black powder from me yesterday, I've never felt so . . . good! Yesterday, I . . . I . . . I could . . . I could sit in a tree and simply *enjoy* it!"

Boaz looked at her with shock. He tried to speak, but his mouth simply moved without sound. "I've seen you sit in a tree. I've seen you on the roof of that thing"–he nodded to the Facility– "you can't stop looking around. It's a tactical awareness. You can't stop checking to see what might try to attack you. You can't stop . . . ever." He looked at her with amazement.

She smiled and laughed. "It was *so incredible!*"

Boaz laughed with her. "That's really great Ariel," he said with a smile. "I'd really like to experience that . . . " he drifted into silence. His face slowly dropped into sadness: it was a gradual transition from excitement to depression. He paused, then spoke. "We aren't okay, are we?"

She closed her eyes and hung her head, knowing too well the answer to that question.

She looked to Boaz. "We both love what we do. Flying is . . . it's something that's become *me*. You . . . you're *so strong!* You've saved lives because of your strength! We both love that . . . but . . . we . . . " She breathed out and yelled in frustration. "I've taken more souls from bodies than I would have ever liked to. You're the same. The dilemma is, we both have powerfully strong protective instincts. That's *in us*. No-one can take that . . . " She yelled a longer yell in frustration, then spoke quickly and with anger. "When some of your earliest memories involve being taught how best to kill a human being, and since then you're taught to watch and observe *everything* to notice if there's anything you *need* to kill . . . and you . . . " She closed her eyes with sadness, shook her head, then opened them. "And you watch kids not much different than you climb trees and run around with no real reason, and they're smiling and laughing and are actually happy . . . and you know . . . you *know* . . . that you're not much older than them . . . and you . . . and you're tasked with destroying a threat to their society . . . " She cried.

Boaz nodded and began to cry. "We aren't okay . . . cool . . . now I know . . . "

Ariel wiped her eyes with her hands. "Alright," she sniffed. "We can cry later. Let's resupply." They were very close to the Facility when she said this.

Boaz wiped his eyes to help him see. "Alright. Let's go."

She banked left, knowing the storage sector was on the other side of the Facility. She knew that no-one would care about either of them resupplying, knowing that whenever either of them went back to the town they were tasked with protecting, they did so with unrivalled effectiveness.

Nobody questioned any of what they did.

She flew beside the dark grey stone of the Facility, seeing how smooth it was and feeling how cold it was even without touching it. Windows broke the smoothness of the wall for patient rooms, a whole sector dedicated to doing so. It was covered in windows, and they had already replaced the wall next to the window that Ariel broke.

She flew past them, knowing it wouldn't be unusual for patients to see Hailers fly past.

They both saw the storage sector of the Facility.

It was windowless and a lighter grey than the other sectors. It had been strengthened with volcanic crystals and, when the sun struck it right, it was the only part of the Facility that was appealing to the eye.

The crystals made it nearly undestroyable.

There was only one entrance from the outside.

She pitched up and flew to it, watching not to scorch Boaz with her thrusters.

She saw the top of the Facility in all its emptiness. Yet another flat, boring side amongst many flat, boring sides. The roof could deploy hidden turrets should it need to, but no-one was so immensely stupid. She could make out the faint lines that marked the panels that would move when a turret rose. The whole roof was covered in them.

She saw the roof entrance to the storage sector, and she was pleased.

It was a break in the roof.

No-one guarded it.

There was nothing stopping her.

Nothing restricted her.

She knew that the only way anyone could get up here was either by walking through the Facility or flying to the roof, both of which would be lethal to the average human mortal.

She landed on the edge of the wide opening. Boaz dismounted as she cut power to her thrusters.

He investigated the darkness. A painful memory presented itself. "The last time we were here . . . " He looked to Ariel.

She continued. "We . . . I . . . " She had been primarily focused on resupplying.

She hadn't been through this entrance since she last saw him.

They both, vividly and hurtfully, remembered the day when they last saw each other.

SOME YEARS AGO, WHEN Boaz and Ariel were younger teens, their friendship was at their strongest. They found it frightfully challenging to get along with *anyone*: every Gollum was considerably older than Boaz, and Ariel was so unique from everyone that *no-one* was like her.

They were the first attempts of making orphans into effective combatants.

They were the only ones that survived anyways.

They found that Ariel couldn't enjoy the top of the Facility, and Boaz couldn't feel calm in the darkness of the Facility's under pipes. They found, though, that their personal sleeping sectors worked quite well. They would spend much of their spare time there, simply relaxing after stressful and strenuous operations. They would laugh. They would feel connection. They would feel goodness.

They would feel friendship.

As time passed, talk spread amongst the Gollums and Hailers about a creature that could make them powerful. It was always done secretly, but their improved performance was undeniable. It was said amongst them all that the 'guy' was called 'The Crawler', and that 'he' will give you a unique and remarkable improvement in some area. He had the facial features of a man, but wasn't anything like a man. The cost of the improvement would be to continually inform 'him' of human beings that were impressive in some way. Many Gollums and Hailers couldn't fault 'his' terms. The more scrutinous among them had questions, but they couldn't deny the improved performance they saw from the operatives that worked with 'him'.

Boaz heard about The Crawler and was very intrigued. He was told that his intrigue meant he would be approached by 'him' at some time when he was alone.

Certainly, 'he' did.

He was thought to be alone in the storage sector, under the light of the full moon from the roof entrance when 'he' approached him. He was first uncomfortable by 'his' outer look, but 'his' words and ideas were very appealing. He could receive strength unlike anyone before or after him; he could be the strongest Gollum to ever exist.

Then Ariel came out of the darkness.

She came to be the voice of reason to Boaz, also intrigued by The Crawler.

The Crawler, however, found difficulty in answering her questions: 'he' couldn't answer easily what 'he' did with the remarkable humans that 'he' was told about. 'He' also couldn't answer easily the consequences if a Gollum or Hailer failed to report regularly on remarkable humans.

When she heard this, she wanted to kill The Crawler.

Boaz wanted to join 'him'.

He was about to shake 'his' hand in agreement.

She drew her thigh weapons and shot at his hand, blasting it off.

'He' yelled in pain, then looked at her with ravenous fury.

'He' threw a blob of 'his' sludge at her. She watched it *narrowly* pass her. She shot more Hail at 'him', watching each shot explode on the red barrier 'he' held up with 'his' hand. She put her weapons in her thighs, flicked her forearms, and held both her swords. She jumped at The Crawler, extending her wings and engaging her thrusters as she did. She flew into The Crawler, wanting to take 'him' off 'his' feet. She pushed 'him' into the shelves behind 'him', seeing how 'his' back collided painfully against the solid metal. She stabbed her swords into 'him', seeing how they both went into 'his' chest. She continued to push, wanting to press them both in as much as she could. 'He' winced in pain, then grabbed her. 'He' pulled her to 'him', opening his mouth as 'he' did. She instantly pushed away from 'him', using her swords to do so.

She felt herself get closer to The Crawler.

She quickly put her left foot on 'his' stomach, trying desperately to get away. She did the same with her right foot, knowing she would need both feet to pull away. She pushed with both her legs, using every fiber of muscle to push away.

She felt herself get closer to The Crawler.

She engaged her thrusters and pushed with her swords and feet. She couldn't understand 'his' unescapable strength, and she was doing everything she could to escape 'his' grasp.

She felt herself get closer to The Crawler.

She slowly set the Hailer Hail turrets on her wings to aim at The Crawler's legs, wanting to keep 'his' attention on her, not on her wings.

She fired.

'He' let go of her.

Unable to slow herself fast enough, with a flight powered by her fully-engaged thrusters, she flew into the metal shelves behind her. She braced for impact with her arms, not wanting her head to be the first part of her that made contact with the metal.

She collapsed to the floor, knowing she couldn't physically get up for a while.

The Crawler leaped to her, crossing the large gap in a single bound.

When 'he' landed, 'he' grabbed her face with 'his' right. With 'his' core, and 'his' left, 'he' lifted her above 'him', only to powerfully slam her into the cold stone floor.

She lay on the floor, unable to defend herself.

Boaz, all the while, was unable to help.

When The Crawler extended his hand to shake Boaz's, 'he' had no interest in doing usual business with him.

'He', instead, wanted to capture him.

'He' let a small amount of sludge collect on 'his' hand, then let it discharge into his hand as they were about to shake. When 'he' did this, he felt it burn with ferocity and attempt to tear his skin from his flesh.

Ariel was too concentrated on The Crawler to notice this.

He watched as the dark red sludge sprawled over his hand. He fell to his left, losing the concentration to stand at all.

He watched as Ariel collided with the metal shelves.

Boaz then watched, with real and overwhelming hate, as 'he' slammed her into the floor.

He wanted to rise and fight for his only friend, slamming both his hands into the floor as he did.

He then watched as the sludge exploded along his arm.

It was now at his shoulder.

He thought to slow its spread, grabbing his right arm with his left.

He watched as his right arm grabbed his left hand.

He then felt as his right hand twisted his left wrist.

He could feel it almost snap.

He then heard four taps play in a unique rhythm.

The Crawler was approaching.

He looked up and saw 'him' with his right hand outstretched, seeing how 'he' was controlling his arm.

'He' then made a sweeping motion with his left hand.

The sludge spread through his entire body.

He was now trapped inside himself.

Ariel only found the consciousness to look up as Boaz was tossed to the roof. She remembered seeing a flower fly past as well, but she couldn't make out its colors. She used everything she could to try and get up, but it proved useless.

The last she saw of her only friend was his limp, distorted body be carried by 'him'.

ARIEL WENT TO BOAZ and hugged his side. "I really missed you Boaz." She started to cry.

He returned the hug. "I was stupid enough to think deeper about The Crawler. I'm sorry I hurt you."

They both stood there, arms around the other, reminiscing and crying, realizing how much they missed the other.

Boaz then let go. "We can go down. I'm back now." He laughed.

Ariel nodded her head in agreement. "Alright." She breathed in and out sharply. She looked down into the dark space beneath her, and nodded.

Boaz was the first to go down. He got his back to face the entrance, then he let his entire weight rest on the edge by the balls of his feet. He let himself drop, catching himself with his left hand, extending his right hand to Ariel. She slowly stepped over the edge holding onto his right hand with hers, knowing that he would catch her. She dangled under him before he released his Gollum grip on the edge, where they both fell to the floor.

She looked around and remembered this space.

She remembered the shelves that she pushed The Crawler into.

She remembered the shelves that she crashed into.

She looked to the floor and remembered where she was slammed into the ground.

Her breathing quickened.

Her fists tensed.

Then Boaz's hand rested on her shoulders. "Let's resupply Ariel. We have a chance to kill him. Let's make the most of it."

She nodded. "Let's go."

They both walked with haste to their personal areas of the storage sector. When they arrived, they went to work.

Ariel knew exactly what she needed.

She held in her hands her thigh weapons. She deployed the outer panel on her calves, exposing another magazine for her thigh weapons, and slid her weapons over them from the outside in. The new magazine clicked onto her thigh weapons, and she moved them away from her calves. Her old magazines slid onto an extended groove that had just held the new magazines. They retracted into her calves, and she felt at peace knowing her thigh weapons were now full of ammunition. She put her thigh weapons back into her thighs, then grabbed the old magazines from her calves, letting them rest on the floor. She grabbed the Hailer Hail dispenser from her set of shelves, feeling its immense weight, and placed it next to the closest vertical beam of her set of shelves. She sat on the cold stone beneath her, removed one Hailer Hail from the dispenser, and placed it in the magazine. She knew that, after filling her magazines like this, she would replenish the magazine in her pack, which she knew would also take some time. She would then sharpen her swords, refill her pack's Hailer Spit—volatile fuel for her thrusters—and remove her Hailer Eye to inspect its condition.

BOAZ HAD GREATER DIFFICULTY in finding his supplies.

When he arrived at where he remembered his personal sector to be, he was given a painful revelation.

For years, everyone thought he was dead.

He knew that, for the most part, they weren't wrong.

He then took a sharp breath in and out, knowing he would need to employ a different approach. He knew he couldn't take all his supplies from one Gollum's personal sector, knowing that would be cause for concern.

So, he rummaged from as many Gollums as he could.

He knew that, if he spread his collecting as wide as he could, his impact would barely be felt.

He looked at the set of Gollum shelves in front of him, seeing how amply supplied it was. He looked at the canister of Gollum Spheres—spheres covered in smooth bumps, each exactly like the next. He hit his chest with both his fists, and every opening on his body opened. Chutes and panels to internal compartments showed themselves. One chute just beside his neck allowed him to store the smooth bumped spheres *inside* himself, an internal compartment of throwable explosives that he accessed through a small tray just above either of his hips. He grabbed one Gollum Sphere and placed it in his neck chute. He grabbed a handful of Gollum Tears—very smooth balls of solid metal—and placed half in one thigh and half in the other.

He knew that would be enough from that Gollum, so he moved on to the next.

He went around grabbing no more than one Gollum Sphere and one handful of Gollum Tears from each personal Gollum sector that he could find. As he went around, he also connected his left shoulder to the cylinders of Hailer Spit, which filled the containers in his calves. The Hailer Spit allowed himself to fire his Gollum Tears with powerful speed.

When he fired his Gollum Tears, it was both marvelous to see and brutally effective.

He knew, after a very lengthy collection process, that he would need to find two spare Gollum Tooths: small, double-edged daggers with a smooth handgrip.

After he found these (being a simpler setup for a younger Gollum), he knew he would be ready for battle.

CHAPTER 15

"MAARGALLA?" RAKTAAR TAPPED.

"Yes Raktaar?" she replied.

"This thing . . . it's . . . beautiful . . . " he said as he looked up.

He had helped Maargalla construct their final creature. It took them the entire night and the morning of the following day, but they had created it.

WHEN THEY BEGAN CONSTRUCTING it, they knew they had to make it against Nehemiah: tall, made from wood, noble hearted, and able to control nature. Raktaar observed that lightning was one of Krawlaga's weaknesses, followed by detachable limbs.

They decided that the best use of their Scream conglomerate was a *total* collaboration: they would join to become one. They realized that they could free themselves from the rigidity of flesh and bones and extract as much sludge as they could.

This is what took the longest.

As they did this, Raktaar grew frustrated that he hadn't done this sooner. Maargalla then explained that, after working with the sludge and the resources Raktaar gave her, she had made the sludge stronger in the creatures. The sludge, after gaining experience in her Screams, was stronger, more potent, and more dangerous.

This new creation would be made from an improved sludge that had taken Raktaar centuries to accrue.

Anything smaller would also be countered by Nehemiah. It needed to be so stupidly tall that there couldn't be a chance against Nehemiah.

When they were complete, they were left with a remarkable pile of sludge with greater responsiveness and strength that could hold and grow on a command given by Raktaar. His previous, unexperienced sludge was only responsive, never adaptive.

The sludge could now have an independence under, and separate from, Raktaar.

The next challenge was to form it.

They decided that an imitation of Raktaar, as close as they could imitate, would prove most useful. He directed as much of his identity as he could collect into his left arm, letting it amass to a bright glow. He let the glow flow gently down his arm.

Then he blasted it at the pile of sludge.

The sludge began to take its form.

Once the red glow infected some of the sludge, the infection spread.

As some time passed, Raktaar could see himself in the sludge.

He could see himself with truly frightful height.

RAKTAAR LAUGHED, THEN TALKED with Maargalla. "Nehemiah won't survive this thing. What should we call it?"

Maargalla replied. "Haakaaka . . . my greatest work."

Raktaar continued. "It is your finest creation Maargalla. You've done well."

She responded. "It was a delight making it Raktaar."

"I can see you being a wonderful addition to it as well . . . "

She pointed her eyes at him with fear.

Before she could react, he jumped back a fair distance. When he landed, he faced his left palm to Haakaaka. With his right arm, he made the motion of reaching down, grabbing something, then plunging it into himself.

Haakaaka mimicked.

As it was reaching down, Maargalla was sprinting to Raktaar, wanting to kill him before she was a part of Haakaaka. She was getting close, launching all ten of her legs to close the distance.

He could see her tentacles get close to him.

Then he saw her in a sludge hand.

She was then plunged into its chest, never to be seen again.

He stopped controlling Haakaaka, forcing it to return to its resting position: arms straight down, looking ahead, legs equally distanced apart.

He spoke. "I birthed you out of sludge. Now you are amongst it." He laughed, knowing he was truly powerful.

He looked to Haakaaka's face. "What can I do with you I wonder . . . " He thought.

He then had a realization and laughed again. "I can do anything with you . . . " He laughed louder.

His whole chest moved.

His fists hit his chest with pride.

His front two legs stomped.
He had in his possession a powerful weapon.
With it, he would do everything he could to kill Nehemiah.

Chapter 16

Ariel and Boaz were flying to Ohlman's Tree, having supplied sufficiently for the expected battle. As they approached, they saw Ohlman's Tree and Nehemiah. They could only see Boris and Tanya as they got closer.

When they landed, Nehemiah spoke. "Good Ariel and Boaz. A pleasure seeing you again."

Ariel responded. "Same with you Nehemiah."

Boaz smiled, waving as they approached.

When they landed, Nehemiah spoke to them all. "Ariel, Tanya, Boaz, Boris, Laban, the time for combat is near. Are we each satisfied with our preparation?"

They each nodded with excitement, knowing the strenuous challenge they were tasked with completing was nearing its end.

Nehemiah continued to speak. "I know not how my old brother intends to kill me, though I know it is with a creature of remarkable size. It is my thought that, given we are in a suitable condition for battle, *we* start the fight before he does."

Boaz processed this thought, recognizing what that would entail. "We're going into his network, aren't we?"

Nehemiah replied. "Yes, Boaz. I see that as our best move against my old brother. Can anyone object?"

Nearly everyone shook their heads; Laban and Boaz were hesitant.

Laban voiced his concerns the loudest, holding Boris' sword to his back as he spoke. "There isn't anything better?! Boaz and I died down there! Neither of us want to go back there–"

Boris reached his right hand around, signaling to Laban to get on his hand. He did, and Boris caught his sword, stabbing it into the ground. Boris then pressed Laban into his chest, stroking him with his thumb. "It's okay buddy. It's okay. We'll be there with you. You'll never have to go down there again after this."

Nehemiah added to what Boris said. "I intended to destroy those tunnels once my old brother is killed. Not another creature will suffer in that abhorred labyrinth."

Laban paused, then spoke in a shaky voice. "Okay . . . " He started to shiver in Boris' hands.

Boris spoke to him. "It's okay buddy. It's okay." He started to lift Laban to his back when Laban spoke in his head alone. "Wait! Please, keep holding me."

Boris smiled. He put Laban on his chest, stroking the little guy with his thumb.

Boaz closed his eyes and breathed in, then out again. He felt his chest rise and fall, knowing how hard this would be. He looked to Nehemiah. "How are we going to get in there?"

He replied. "Strong Boaz, if you could please have in your hands the thick book in the backpack by Ohlman's Tree."

Boaz nodded and went over to the backpack resting in the shade of the Ohlman's Tree and undid its zippers.

As he was doing this, Boris remembered what happens when someone touched Patrick's book.

He turned to warn Boaz.

By then, Boaz was holding Patrick's book.

He was touching Patrick's book with his bare hands.

Boris looked to Nehemiah and was about to speak, but Nehemiah answered his question before it was asked. "Now is the time when you are each to experience physical contact with Patrick's book. I feel, Boaz, that this sight is not new to you?"

Boaz answered. "It . . . it's . . . when I was . . . " He looked around, wanting to be sure. "This is what I saw when I was that thing . . . "

All around him was the same world that he saw, but it was slightly darker. He saw everything he expected to see through human eyes, but the faintest tinge of black changed all that he saw. When he looked to Nehemiah, he saw him be slightly brighter.

He saw the same effect on Tanya.

In the distance, he saw something he never saw before.

He saw, on a small undulation, a bumpy circle shaped patch of dark, rotten wood.

When he saw this, he dropped Patrick's book.

Boris was watching Boaz's hands carefully and saw Boaz's fingers gently release. He threw Laban at the dropping book when he saw fear grow on Boaz's face, knowing he would cushion its impact and keep it clean.

Laban flew with brilliant speed, making himself into a form that cut through the air as best he could.

When he got close, he grabbed the book and the ground. He let himself pool on the ground, contacting as much as he could, and holding the book by its large cover.

After a few moments, he started to shiver.

Then he threw Patrick's book into the air.

Boris instantly ran underneath it, wanting to catch it and protect the last gift Patrick gave him.

He did his best to be under the book's falling path, watching it fall to him.

When he caught Patrick's book, he did his best not to let go of it.

He saw, with greater clarity, what Patrick's book allowed him to see.

He didn't like it, and now he knew why.

None of it looked right.

It felt overwhelmingly terrifying. There was a rustling in his ears and over his skin that couldn't be shut out. He couldn't explain how or why, but everything in him shouted to let the book go.

He ran as fast as he could to his backpack, wanting to put it down safely.

He tripped on a hole in the ground, just large enough to catch his right foot.

He collided with the ground, feeling his neck jolt violently and his shoulder painfully cushion his trip.

He used his left hand to get up, knowing he would be tempted to let go of Patrick's book if he used his right.

He sprinted to his backpack.

He hated holding this book.

He also hated letting anything happen to it.

When he got to his backpack, he opened its largest pocket with his left and shoved Patrick's book into it as hard as he could.

When he did, everything around him went to normal.

He let his hands rest against Ohlman's Tree, breathing heavily as he did.

Then he yelled in pain.

As he yelled, he released into the air everything he had fighting within himself. He let loose the pain of his lost friend and the pain of caring for himself.

He then looked to Laban. "Hey Laban?" he asked.

Laban replied. "Yeah Boris?"

"You knew what I was thinking when I threw you, yeah?" Boris asked.

Laban answered. "I did–"

"*Then why did you throw my dead friend's book into the air?!*"

As he said this, he ran to Laban.

Laban melted into the dirt.

Boris yelled in anger. "Come back!"

Laban responded in his head alone. "I can see what you're thinking Boris–"

Boris yelled again. "*Then you know–*"

"I know you want to hurt me–"

"*Let me hurt you–*"

"I'm sorry–"

"You're sorry! That was *my friend's* book Laban! That was *my brother's* book–"

"I know what it was Boris–"

"*Then why did you throw it in the air like you were scared of it?!*"

"Because I was–"

"*You were what?! Scared like always?!*"

As Boris shouted at Laban, Tanya and Ariel looked to Nehemiah, silently asking whether they should intervene.

Nehemiah shook his head, lowering himself gently to sit on the ground as he did.

He spoke in their heads. "They need to settle this without external assistance. They will heal that way."

Nehemiah could see that Boris hadn't talked to Boaz yet.

He knew that, after that, they would all be ready to enter his old brother's labyrinth.

At that time, Boaz talked to Boris. "I'm sorry I dropped it–"

Until Boaz spoke, Boris hadn't realized that Boaz dropped his dead friend's book.

When he did, his attention turned to Boaz. "*You're sorry?!*"

Boaz answered. "I am! Touching that thing made me see a side of life I don't want to see–"

Boris yelled at Boaz. "*I saw too!* I saw how weird *everything* looked, but I held it–"

"Congratulations! You have enough of you to spare!"

Boris was taken off-guard. "What's that supposed to mean?!"

"We aren't supposed to see what that book lets us see! The white spheres in our heads weren't made for that–"

Boris froze.

As he did, all humanity drained from his face.

Then he yelled as loud as his lungs would let him. *"Those are Patrick's words! You can't quote my dead friend!"*

When he finished, he took large strides and walked to his sword, removing it from the ground.

As he did, Tanya and Ariel looked to Nehemiah, desperately wanting to help Boris.

Nehemiah shook his head.

Ariel thought to ignore Nehemiah.

She was about to take a step, but Nehemiah spoke in her head. "No, good Ariel," he said. "Not yet."

As he said this, he saw Boris with his sword in his right hand, spinning it around.

Boris shouted at Boaz, fast-walking to him as he did. "Laban is too weak to face me, and you can't disappear."

Boaz shouted back. "You don't want to do this Boris–"

Boris roared.

He raised his sword, bringing it down across Boaz's chest.

Boaz let his weight rest on his right foot, pivoted on it, and swept his left leg in an arc away from Boris' sword.

He then quickly brought up his left knee, bringing it as high as his muscles would let him. He used the momentum of his left knee to lead into a jump, kicking his right leg up as he did. He got his right leg above Boris' head, allowing his calf and thigh to squeeze Boris' neck. He pushed down on Boris to get his left foot anchored to his right.

With his arms overlapped on his chest, he swung backwards around Boris' neck, up and around his body, then slammed Boris to the ground.

When he landed, his grip tightened.

Boris had let go of his sword when Boaz was swinging around him, leaving him with only his hands to fight. He hit Boaz's legs with the hard lower-half of his palm, knowing the angles were entirely wrong for a punch. He struck Boaz's grey thighs as hard as he could muscle, using his arms and his core to strike Boaz's legs.

As he did, he only felt Boaz make it harder for him to breathe.

He stopped, wanting to save his energy and breath.

He then had a realization.

As fast as he could, as to avoid Boaz's attention, he made his right hand into a fist and quickly contacted a spot just above Boaz's waist.

When he did, he felt a metal panel abruptly push his hand away.

He then heard a Gollum Sphere gently roll onto the ground.

As it did, Boaz looked to his waist. He then watched as Boris grabbed the Gollum Sphere and pushed the fuse bump, a single bump slightly darker than the others.

They both knew, after three seconds, it would explode.

Boris held it for one second.

Laban came from the ground and uncurled Boris' fingers. He surrounded the Gollum Sphere with himself, took it from Boris, and dug a skinny hole into the ground as far as he could reach.

Two seconds.

Laban then placed the Gollum Sphere at the bottom of the hole he had dug, burying it with the dirt he was holding up.

Three seconds.

Dirt and twigs shot from the ground, showering Boris and Boaz with a spatter of earthy brown. A bump of dirt rose from the ground before falling again under its own weight, and Nehemiah used the dirt to keep Boaz, Boris, and Laban alive.

As dirt was falling on them, Boaz loosened his grip on Boris' neck. Boris shoved Boaz's leg off him, got up, and raced to his sword. Boaz got to his feet when he saw Boris on his.

Holding the sword's grip in his hands, Boris raced back to Boaz.

Boaz went to grab his Gollum Tooths from his lower back, preparing to undertake lethal safety measures. He stood in a fighting stance with his weight evenly split over his feet. He held his Gollum Tooths with their blades away from his thumbs, his left hand a small distance from his shoulder and his right by his neck. He watched as Boris jumped to him, seeing the sword above his head with both hands holding it tight.

He then watched as Laban burst from the ground as a sticky strand, grabbing Boris' foot, and bringing him to the ground. He continued to watch as Boris lay on the hardened brown, stunned by the sudden meeting with the dirt. He noticed the directionally-sprawling Laban climb over Boris to get the sword that now rested by Boris' head.

When Laban got under the sword, he carried it back to Nehemiah, Ariel, and Tanya, crawling over the rough ground as he did.

Boris started putting his weight on his hands and feet, now able to process his surroundings. The sudden meeting with the ground forced him to better process what he was doing and thinking. He placed his weight on his knees and insteps, knowing he wasn't acting rationally.

With painful vivacity, he realized why.

He remembered that everything he felt and thought in that moment was what he felt with Beringei. He remembered the unjustified aura of supremacy, the unconquerable wave of emotion, and the beautifully clear opportunistic drive.

With this remembrance, he was debilitated by the guilt and shame, whose sheer power was unfightable.

He looked up, seeing Boaz's height be greater than his, noting also the iconic daggers in both of his hands. Their blades were slightly curved, double edged, famously sharp, and well known to the common man, as was the fighting stance.

It then occurred to him that, at any point throughout his incapacitation, Boaz could have ended the physical confrontation with remarkable proficiency.

He also knew that Boaz had the choice, simply in his technique, between a blissfully painless or a blindingly painful death.

He looked into his cold and distant Gollum eyes, taking a breath in then out, then nodded. "You could have killed me now," the look said. He watched as Boaz nodded in response, understanding that the message was successfully received, placing his Gollum Tooths in his lower back.

Boris rose to his feet, his eyes filling with tears, and his mind struggling to process the violence he brought himself to.

He lunged to Boaz with his arms outstretched, wrapping them around Boaz's broad Gollum shoulders.

He then cried on Boaz's shoulder, sobbing intensely.

Boaz responded with his shoulders around Boris' smaller teenage shoulders.

Boris whispered to Boaz. "I'm sorry. I'm sorry. I'm sorry. I'm sorry–"

Boaz interrupted. "You were emotional–"

Boris interrupted. "I wanted to *kill* you–"

Boaz interrupted. "You were emotional–"

Boris tried to talk, but Boaz continued. "You didn't really want to kill me. You wanted to get the anger out of you, and you did. You should thank me for not killing you."

Boris didn't talk for a small while before he squeezed Boaz as hard as he could, pressing his face into Boaz's shoulder. "Thank you," he whispered.

Boaz tapped Boris' shoulder with his right hand. "Any time," the gesture said. He then let go of Boris. Boris let go of Boaz, tapping Boaz's right shoulder with his left hand, smiling as he did.

Tanya looked to Nehemiah as Boaz and Boris were reconciling. Nehemiah looked at her and nodded. Having understood why she couldn't intervene, she smiled.

Ariel looked to Nehemiah with confusion.

Nehemiah nodded at her.

Ariel understood why she couldn't intervene, but she thought poorly of the reasoning.

She shrugged and breathed out.

Nehemiah spoke aloud. "Boris, could you please obtain Patrick's book."

Boris wiped his tears with his shirt, smiled, nodded, then gently jogged to his backpack.

He was about to grab Patrick's book directly, but he caught himself before his right hand got too close to the text of his murdered friend. He zipped his backpack shut and put the straps on his shoulder. He gently jogged back to the group, where he unzipped the backpack and placed it on the ground.

He then stepped back, getting distance between himself and Patrick's book.

Nehemiah spoke to the group. "Patrick's book is the way you each can access my old brother's network. To do so, you must physically contact the text. It can be observed that, when you do, it is not a pleasant experience. You three can attest to this."

Boris, Boaz, and Laban nodded in agreement, stepping slightly further away from the text.

Nehemiah continued. "You each need only contact Patrick's book whilst you pass through my old brother's trapdoor. After doing so, you have no need to hold the text."

There was a quiet agreement, followed by a short silence, when Boaz spoke. "Can I go in last?"

Nehemiah turned to Ariel, who was about to speak. She stopped herself, then looked to Nehemiah, wondering how he did that.

He laughed with amusement, then motioned for her to answer Boaz's question.

She shook her head with annoyance, then spoke. "That's not the best approach to this Boaz."

Boaz replied with confusion and concern. "How is that 'not the best approach'?"

She smiled. "Two words: Directive Seven."

He looked at her with continued confusion, then clarity washed over his face. He held his head in his hands, despising and bitterly accepting the truth in her words.

He groaned, then spoke. "Why did you have to say that?"

She answered. "Because it's right and because you know how much we live by it. You know how right it is too–"

Boaz groaned into his hands again. "You're right." He lifted his head. "Why do you have to be right?"

She laughed pleasantly to herself.

Tanya was curious. "What's Directive Seven?"

Boaz answered. "When faced with overpowering fear, know your reason for continuing, draw your weapons, and run with overwhelming strength at what stops you."

Ariel clarified. "The best way for this to go is if Boaz leads us in."

Boaz breathed in, then sharply out, hating how right Ariel was. He walked with haste towards Patrick's book.

He stopped, closed his eyes, breathed in slowly, then out sharply, then stood straight. He did what he could to push every memory of that network into the past where it belonged.

He then grabbed the book, breathed in again when he saw what he saw, and walked with greater haste towards the trapdoor to Raktaar's network.

As he walked, he held Patrick's book firmly with his left hand. He flicked his right arm violently down, revealing a small metal pole that came out of his right palm. He grabbed the small metal pole with his right hand and pulled it to himself, letting the pole rest in between his thumb and pointer finger, shoving his forearm away from himself as he did.

From his forearm came a cylinder similar in size to what Hailer's have on their wings.

When Boaz got closer to Raktaar's network trapdoor, the rest of the group learned quickly that their battle against Nehemiah's old brother was about to take place. Boris and Tanya found and held their weapons, Ariel held her thigh weapons in her hands, Laban attached himself to Boris' back while holding the backpack, and Nehemiah jumped into the small white flower he liked being.

When Boaz reached the edge of the trapdoor, he stopped and turned to see if everyone else was ready.

When he saw everyone with weapons in hand, he turned to the trap-door, aimed his right arm, and prepared his thumb to push the button on the small metal pole's top. He knew, when he did, that he would feel the power of Gollum Tears leaving his arm with merciless speed and hear its brilliantly loud and unique sound.

When he realized this, he froze.

He bent his right elbow, pointed the cylinder in his right arm to the sky, and turned around. He spoke. "When I start shooting, it won't be subtle."

Ariel nodded in agreement. "Once you start, we start."

Tanya nodded her head and continued. "When we start, we don't stop until we win the fight we have *always* lost."

Boris clarified. "When we start, we can only stop when we kill that thing, or . . . when . . . we . . . die."

There was an awkward silence among the group.

Boaz broke it. "Are we ready to do this?"

Another silence fell upon the group.

Then Boris answered. "No. We aren't." He then rubbed his head with his left hand with his sword in his right, remembering the horrible vision he had two nights ago. He looked to Tanya, recalling a horrible and bloody flashback where she was barely being held together. He continued. "I . . . " He looked to Tanya. "You . . . " He looked to Ariel, Boaz, Laban, and Nehemiah. "We . . . " He stopped, found his words, then spoke. "We all have felt what Nehemiah's old brother can do to each of us . . . " He looked up, seeing the houses in the distance. He looked to his sword, remembering how he cut up many Screams the night before. He closed his eyes, breathed slowly in, then breathed slowly out and continued. "Even if we don't kill that thing, we will have done our best to stop him." He paused for a big breath, then continued. "We could, quite easily, walk away and try and live normal lives, but it says in that book"–he motioned to Patrick's book–"that once he's been seen by someone, he can never be unseen by that someone. We *can*, and *always will*, see what he is doing to everyone he messes with . . . " He gripped his sword tighter and took another big breath. "I can't live and know I could have done something to stop him, and didn't. If I'm going to die so that another little boy doesn't have to watch his sister almost break apart in his arms . . ." Another deep breath in and out. "Then let me die."

Tanya closed her eyes, breathed in, then out, and continued. "We're all going to die at some point . . . " She twirled her staff gently in her right hand. "Let's die with honor."

Ariel looked to Tanya and Boris, agreeing with them both, feeling ecstatic that she had made friends with valor.

Boaz smiled. "It's confirmed. Let's kill this thing . . . or die with honor." He turned around, lowered his right arm, and aimed at the trapdoor. He brought his left hand behind his back, still holding Patrick's book with his pinkie finger and thumb, and extended the rest of his fingers, having an awkward comfort with the sight it provided.

Three, the gesture said.

Nehemiah flew and placed himself on Ariel's pack. Tanya and Boris readied their stance.

Boaz dropped his ring finger.

Two, the gesture said.

Tanya turned to Boris and whispered, "For Patrick."

Boaz dropped his middle finger.

One, the gesture said.

Boris was taken back to every memory he had with Patrick. He recalled all the enjoyment he had with Patrick. The brotherhood they had. The bond they shared.

The anger when he died.

He whispered back as his skin crawled with passion. "For Patrick."

He felt unrivalled, uncontrollable anger flood his blood, his eyes screamed for justice, and goosebumps covered his skin.

Boaz dropped his pointer finger.

Zero, the gesture said.

He pressed the button on the small metal pole's top.

The moment he did, a bright orange was seen from the cylinder's tip. A loud and unique popping sound populated the air.

Gollum Tears entered the world with violence, anger, and destruction.

As the Tears struck the old, rotten, wooden trapdoor, small holes quickly littered the surface. Wood dust rose gently into the air, and the trapdoor lost the strength to hold itself together.

Only a small time later, the wood caved into the tunnel underneath.

The fight had begun.

Boaz leapt in, cushioned the landing with his legs, then extended the book to Ariel. She ran forward, grabbed the book, jumped into the tunnel, then passed it up to Tanya. She did the same to Boris, who gave it to Laban to put into his backpack. Boaz ran ahead, deploying a cylinder in his left arm exactly like his right arm. Having been through this tunnel before, he remembered the way to his old master's main room.

As he was running, he recognized the spacious walls made from dark red rock. He recalled using his tentacle legs to crawl through these tunnels to reach the surface.

This recollection was broken by the echoing of footsteps behind him.

They were sprinting footsteps.

Boris and Tanya ran with all their strength, weapons in hand, knowing Boaz was their guide. Ariel knew she could fly faster than Boaz could run, but she too needed him for guidance.

Boaz did his best to navigate at speed, knowing that time was not a friend. When the tunnel broke into more tunnels, he looked at each option no more than he needed to, then committed with his final decision. He remembered that the tunnels grew darker the further he was from the main room. When he started to see the tunnels glow a brighter orange and red, he knew his decisions were correct and he ran even faster. As he ran more, every decision presented to him had a tunnel that was slightly brighter. As he ran further, that specific tunnel grew brighter and brighter.

Then he saw the main room.

His old master's throne room.

Empty and without any motion.

Boaz yelled as he ran.

Then a cool sticky feeling came across his back.

He then felt his arms, legs, and head continue forward while his midsection was held back.

Ariel and Tanya tried to run around Boaz, feeling also the passion to slay an old foe.

They also felt their arms, legs, and head continue forward while their midsections were held back.

The three of them found themselves sitting abruptly on the cold tunnel floor.

Laban had attached himself to each of their backs and to the tunnel's floor. He then crawled back to Boris, who was slowly walking towards them.

"What are you doing?" Boaz asked angrily.

"Saving your lives," Boris answered.

Boaz pointed his arm cylinders at Boris and yelled, almost pressing the button with his thumb.

Then Ariel touched his arm.

He looked at her, utterly confused and entirely angered.

She motioned that he should wait a moment, then looked to the throne room in front of her.

Tanya looked to the throne room, then thought to run. She took a step, then was stopped by Ariel's arm.

Ariel, looking through her Hailer Eye, noticed that the ceiling of the throne room was remarkably cold. She reached out to Laban, who, having read her thoughts, attached himself to the ceiling of the tunnel, her left foot, and her left hand. He brought her closer to the tunnel ceiling, then crawled closer to the tunnel's opening. She looked to the ceiling and confirmed her concern.

For a room with side walls of fire, the roof was scarily cold.

No gradient of heat.

No orange or red at all.

It was then that what color was left in Ariel's face was removed.

Laban saw Ariel's thoughts and lowered her to the ground.

She slowly turned to face Boris, failing to comprehend how she didn't see something so obvious yet so stealthy.

"Thank you, Boris," she said. "You did just save our lives."

Boaz and Tanya, their blood reeking with malice and vengeance, stared at Ariel.

Ariel spoke to Boaz. "When I last saw you, what did I do to try and save you?"

"You!" He started with his voice raised. "You . . . " He realized what she was saying. He looked to the throne room, then to Ariel. "He's–"

Ariel nodded.

What color was left in Boaz's face was removed.

He turned to Boris with burdening humility. "Sorry."

Tanya was still confused and enraged. "Why are we stopping?!" she yelled.

Boris answered. "When we first met that thing that ruined our child-hoods . . . Raktaar . . . we didn't know he was there. As we were running, I saw how empty the room was. There's *no-one* in there. When Boaz broke that trapdoor with his Gollum Tears, you would expect either someone, or something, to come out and investigate, or be *deafened* by an already ear-piercing noise that's exaggerated in a tunnel. I don't see anything. That . . . doesn't . . . make . . . sense. Either that room"–he pointed with his sword–"is empty, or Nehemiah's old brother heard us and is hiding."

Ariel spoke next. "The ceiling is scary cold too. You'd expect some of the heat from the walls of fire on the sides to show on the ceiling, but there's nothing. Something is up there"–she said as she tried to look up at its roof without entering the room.

Tanya sighed, rubbed her eyes, then spoke. "So, what do we do? We know there's a trap on, or in, the ceiling. We know that *he's* hiding in there, somewhere, or returning at *some* time. What do we do?"

Boaz reversed the motions to bring his right cylinder back into his right forearm and the small metal pole into his right palm, made a fist with his right hand, and struck his right hip, opening the Gollum Sphere canister tray.

"We say hello," he said.

He precariously and skillfully held four Gollum Spheres in his right hand, then turned to face the throne room. "You'll want to cover your ears," he then said. Ariel, Tanya, and Boris, knelt to the ground, pinned their weapons under knee and foot, and did their best to block the incoming noise. They balanced themselves so that they faced the incoming blast. Boaz then extended his left arm for additional power, held it for a moment, then pulled it back, twisting his shoulders as he did, side-arm throwing the Gol-lum Spheres into the center of the pool of sludge.

Just before they contacted the surface of the sludge, he mentally commanded them to explode.

Boom.

The Spheres forced sludge into the air, flying as high as the throne room ceiling. Their shockwave was felt by the group, who found it an abrupt and powerful shove.

With it, Raktaar's trap was activated.

Sludge began to crawl rapidly down from the ceilings, a concentrated effort directed at the tunnel.

It hastily trickled down the sides of the throne room, knowing its entire being was to be used against the five opponents it was presented with. Its size stopped it from being terrifyingly fast, but it could move with a speed that caused trembling concern.

When the group saw the sludge approaching the tunnel, they began to retreat into the network, knowing they couldn't immediately do anything against it. Ariel then shot some Hailer Hail at the tunnel exit, wanting it to collapse and stop the encroaching sludge.

Large and small dark red rocks fell to the tunnel floor, an oddly shaped wall now keeping the tunnel closed.

They all looked at the wall, hoping with all their capacity that it would keep them safe.

Its odd shape, though, left small gaps.

Through these small gaps, the sludge seeped through.

As the group watched the sludge seep through, they heard a sound they wanted very much to forget.

Four rhythmic taps on a hard surface.

The sludge on the opposite side of the wall of rock amplified the footsteps, dislodging loose rocks from the wall. When they all heard the noise, they gripped their weapons as hard as they could.

It was this moment, at this time, that their fate would be chosen.

Raktaar's death, or their own.

Tanya placed her staff on her back, knowing that Laban would hold it there, and approached the wall. The anger she felt centered in her chest, a flame enveloping her upper midsection. With hands outstretched, she pulled as much black dust from the sludge as she could. She watched as the little trickles of sludge subsided as the mass of black dust grew. She watched the black dust grow larger and larger; its weight almost unbearable. She forced the black dust into her chest, letting the fire inside her prove to be more powerful than the sludge could ever be, then dropped to the ground under the burden she now held. She was on her knees, her hands on her chest, and her mind doing everything to burn the black dust and defeat her enemy.

As she was on the ground, the sludge directed its attention to her. It collected in front of her, growing larger in size, then reached out to her, forming a Raktaar hand.

Boris ran forward and severed the arm from its source, watched it fall to the ground, then stabbed it and threw the severed arm into the wall of rocks.

As he did, another arm began to grow.

Again, he severed it, stabbed it, then discarded it.

As he did, another arm began to grow.

Again, he severed it, stabbed it, then discarded it.

Then he looked around and saw the wall of rock be covered in sludge arms reaching out to Tanya, each one wanting to kill the only human mortal that could threaten it.

Then he felt himself be pulled violently from the wall of rock in front of him.

Tanya, having only just burnt the black dust, looked up, and felt herself also be pulled violently away.

It was Boaz.

When they got a safe distance away, Ariel fired her Hailer Hail into the wall of rock, waited for it to collapse, put her thigh weapons back into her thighs, then flew into the throne room. She fired Hailer Hail from her wings as she flew, leaving a narrow tunnel through the beast of sludge for her.

Small drops of sludge landed on her.

When she found herself in the throne room, she saw Raktaar standing in line with the tunnel. She flew as fast as her thrusters could, grabbed one of his legs, flew him to the opposite side of the throne room, and let her S.M.A.R.T. rope unwind from her pack and wrap itself around him, keeping him restrained. She started flying back to the tunnel, firing more Hailer Hail through the beast of sludge, wanting to bring Raktaar to the surface.

More small drops of sludge landed on her.

When she was in the tunnel, she stopped her thrusters, kicked her legs, landed on her feet, put her right arm around Boris, ran a few steps, then resumed flight. He had the backpack containing Patrick's book on his shoulders, and it was what Ariel needed to leave the network. She knew that to fight where Raktaar was familiar would prove disastrous for her and her friends.

She also knew that the drops of sludge that landed on her were slowly burning her skin.

Raktaar saw this.

He had spent until then resisting the S.M.A.R.T. rope and doing everything he could to escape it. Without the freedom of his limbs, however, he could do nothing but hate Ariel even more.

When he saw the sludge on Ariel, he laughed a deep, maniacal laugh.

He forced the sludge droplets into sharp pins that, on Ariel's thin frame, reached bone.

Ariel dove into the tunnel floor, grinded against it for a fair distance, then yelled in pain. Her wings automatically retracted into her pack, but she lost conscious control of the S.M.A.R.T. rope, and Raktaar released himself from it. Standing on his four spear-like feet, he forced the sludge to expand inside her skin, tiny spheres of agony that kept Ariel to the ground.

Boris was getting to his feet after yet another forceful meeting with the ground. Grounding himself, he remembered with fury and passion why he was in this tunnel. He saw Ariel on the ground, noticing how she couldn't rise to fight for herself. He gripped his sword, his knuckles going whiter than they ever had.

Raktaar saw Boris rise to his feet and look at Ariel. Boris then looked at him, and he returned the stare into Boris' natural eyes.

Raktaar launched ferociously towards Boris with arms outstretched.

Boris raised his sword, holding it with both hands, aiming for Raktaar's chest.

Contact.

Boris' back slapped the tunnel floor, taking most of the force quite painfully, with the back of his head bleeding gently.

Raktaar balanced uncomfortably on his front two knees and hands with a sword through his chest. He groaned in pain, but he knew he could mend the injury later. He tightly held Boris' right shoulder with his left hand, using it to keep balance, and thrusted his right hand onto Boris' neck. He wanted to squeeze all the life out of Boris and satisfy a long, deep grudge.

Boris felt his airways rapidly close, his lungs unable to outmuscle the grip that resisted the air he needed. He looked directly into the eyes of Raktaar, the vile creature that corrupted any chance of him having a simple, normal, teenage upbringing. He watched a mouth with many spiked teeth roar in satisfied anger. He let go of his sword, knowing it didn't help him now, hoping to retaliate against Raktaar's peeling flesh through other means. When his hands found themselves by his sides, he then felt Raktaar's right front foot press into his left hand and his right arm be held down by Raktaar's left hand. He tried to resist, pushing and pulling with full strength, trying to gain movement of his arms, but Raktaar pressed harder.

Then Raktaar was caught off-balance.

His legs were brought abruptly together, and he collapsed to the ground. He lost his grip on Boris' neck, and Boris went to his feet with dramatic speed. Boris looked to see what had saved him.

It was Laban.

He had gripped Raktaar's legs together.

In the distance, Tanya was sprinting with her staff in hand. Boaz, having just thrown Laban at Raktaar's legs, quickly followed.

Laban crawled with haste to Raktaar's chest, removed the sword, gently tossing it to the tunnel floor, then kept holding Raktaar's legs together. Boris grabbed his sword with his left, then, wanting to continue what had been started, went to grab Laban and dragged Raktaar across the dark red tunnel floor to the tunnel entrance. After running a fair distance, Boaz caught up to Boris and assisted dragging Raktaar. They then moved with much greater speed.

It was here that Raktaar scooped some sludge dripping from his chest, sent a quick glow through both his arms, then dropped it on the tunnel floor.

Tanya knelt beside Ariel, seeing the harsh swelling that the little dots of red caused on Ariel's cold skin. She hovered her hand over each little pebble of sheer hurt, removed the black dust, and watched with joy as Ariel started rising to her feet. She then plunged the black dust into her chest; something she was growing accustomed to.

Ariel slowed her breathing, processed her surroundings, then launched into flight, flying directly to Raktaar, Boaz, and Boris, who saw her approach. She powered off her thrusters, kicked her legs, and ran in-between Boaz and Boris, who both made way for Ariel. Having heard Ariel's thrusters from a fair distance, Boris quickly took off his backpack and let Laban hold onto it. Laban could also sense what Ariel would want and formed accordingly, letting Ariel land behind him before jumping over him and latching onto her feet, knowing she couldn't lift Raktaar at such a speed so quickly.

She flew with remarkable speed through the tunnels, knowing she could make Raktaar weakest when they reached the surface. As she flew, she let her S.M.A.R.T. rope extend (she retracted it before her painful landing) and let it find its way to Patrick's book. It undid the zippers and reached inside, grabbing Patrick's book, then gently brought it to Ariel's chest, not wanting to grab the book until she absolutely needed to.

As she flew, her Hailer Eye observed the opening to be a patch of blue with sporadic patches of darker blue.

It was raining.

She held the book with both hands, watched as her surroundings took on a glaringly scary red, and approached the trapdoor opening.

She went through, instantly feeling the sky's intense gift of cool drop-lets all over her. She gained elevation and felt the water fall on her face, hearing the roar of the rain against the Earth.

It was cheering her.

"Do what you need to do," it said. "I'll remind you of your fight, and I'll clean you after you rise as the victor."

Its cheer was loud.

She smiled.

She gave the book back to Laban, lent back in a large arc, letting herself fly towards the sky then down to the ground. Nehemiah detached himself and floated to the ground. She then changed direction sharply, letting go of Raktaar as she did and continuing her hold on Laban

Raktaar collided with the soft brown with his arms bracing for impact.

Ariel circled around in a wide circle horizontal with the ground, let-ting Raktaar rise to his four feet and dropping Laban on the ground with Patrick's book. Raktaar felt his four spear-like feet dig into the mushy dirt beneath him, then looked around for Ariel.

She was approaching at a shallow angle with great speed.

Contact.

Raktaar grinded against mud, sticks, leaves, and rocks, and Ariel pushed him with full intensity. As she pushed, she forced all the embers of hate she held against him into his decaying body, forcing him to grind into the ground. She yelled with unstoppable anger, her eyes roaring for fierce justice, and her hands ignoring how they were slowly being burnt by the sludge on his body.

She thought the thought to let him stand, but she thought to grind him against the ground a little longer.

Then a little longer.

Then a little longer.

She then let the rain wash the sludge off her hands, grabbed two of his feet with her S.M.A.R.T. rope, and brought herself to a higher altitude. She felt that she had flown high enough, but thought to fly a little higher.

Raktaar, at such speed, couldn't throw anything at her to free himself, and found difficulty in freeing himself from the S.M.A.R.T. rope that held his legs.

She then swung herself around, started directly to the ground, and prepared to squish Raktaar into the brown mud below. She cut power to her thrusters, told her S.M.A.R.T. rope to squeeze Raktaar's neck, reached around such that her hands rested on his chest, then activated her thrusters. Her S.M.A.R.T. rope didn't have the strength to pull Raktaar down to her hands at such a speed, so she went up to it.

With full speed, arms tensed, hands on Raktaar's chest, she dived.

Raktaar felt his head go light. It was slower than normal, but he managed to accumulate a red glow in his head that he would send to his chest.

It was going down his neck, nearly reaching Ariel's hands, wanting to inflict and hurt them with his sludge, then–

Boom!

Contact.

Mud exploded from the impact. It flew up to the skies and scattered well away from them both.

A crater was left from the impact.

In it, Raktaar found himself a terribly broken puzzle of bones held together by century-old muscle. Ariel found herself with sore arms and much less fuel in her pack—she had lost her 'L.I.F.E.' in the collision.

When Ariel collided with the ground, she used what would be half her pack's reserve in fuel in the smallest of moments to fire two thrusters over the top of her pack angled in line with her shoulders. They were designed—at their greatest—to bring a Hailer to an instant stop from a direct collision to the ground—like now. This feature was called a 'L.I.F.E.'—Limited Inverted Force Engine—and every Hailer only got one. After that, the L.I.F.E. was inoperable and needed complete reconstruction. When she slammed Raktaar into the ground she activated her L.I.F.E. just as her arms began to bend.

She fell to her feet, slowly rose, letting her back arch then straighten, feeling the compression of the impact all through what was left of her natural spine. The rain again washed the sludge off her hands, helping her to stay operable during the fight, though tiny spots remained on her palms.

She looked up and saw how Ohlman's Tree was as large as her thumbprint.

Almost directly next to Ohlman's Tree was a wide trench slowly filling with the rain, leading almost to where she now stood. She looked down to Raktaar, saw how broken every one of his bones were, and thought to end the vile beast that took from her the only friend she knew. As she went to grab her thigh weapons, she felt her palms begin to sear. She looked down and realized the sludge was starting to work. She went into flight, knowing she would need Tanya to remove the sludge. She had hoped Laban went to the tunnel and released the rest of the group from the tunnel, though this was only a hope.

Raktaar remained in the crater while Ariel flew away.

He couldn't move anything, for his muscles would usually hold onto the century old bones when they moved; but, those bones were now in pieces. Knowing he was now safe from Ariel, he did his best to disconnect from the cyclone of pain and brokenness he was feeling.

He knew this wasn't going to be his death.

He planted the little blob of glow-powered sludge in his tunnel for this very moment.

He knew he had to get one of his pulses of red into the ground for the little blob of glow-powered sludge to become a moving blob of glow-powered sludge. He looked at his hands, only able to move his eyes, and saw how they were facing the skies. *Nope,* he thought. He looked down to his legs, seeing the groan-worthy angles they were making, and found one leg aimed almost directly into the ground. In his head, he laughed a maniacal laugh and smiled a maniacal smile, knowing he couldn't embody those actions with his nearly broken skull. A glow radiated first from his head, then travelled down to the leg that pointed almost directly into the ground. It took great effort to navigate the glow between the broken bones, but he was well familiar with continuing forward with intolerable agony. When the glow reached his leg, he let it become dense in its size to increase its intensity.

With every bit of will to live he could scrape from his century dead existence, he sent the glow from his leg into the ground and felt all the bones in his body grind against each other.

With the pulse of red, he also let go a tiny bit of sludge he could gently release. The bit of sludge was superpowered from the density of the red pulse, and it buzzed quickly to the network entrance.

When the little bit of sludge met the blob of sludge in Raktaar's network, the little blob of glow-powered sludge glowed again.

Its glow was a dim light in a dark tunnel, but the glow gave it unconscious life. It went to the closest side wall of the tunnel, climbed up it, then made itself stick to the roof of the tunnel. It let itself go, made itself into a glider that found stable flight, and gently glided through the tunnel. When it did this, it then made for itself a fin on the center of its rear and gave itself propelled flight, like it was swimming through the air. It made its slow way to the throne room, gently navigating the tunnels of its master. When it reached the throne room, it gave itself as much height from the ground as it could, flying in a spiral motion to reach the roof of the throne room.

It then grabbed the roof of the throne room, pushed violently away from it directly towards the ground, made itself into the fastest shape that it could make, and landed in the massive landscape of sludge sprawled through the throne room tunnel.

It was slow at first, but the glow from the little blob of glow-powered sludge spread.

The more it spread, the faster it spread.

Then a small sea of red sludge came to unconscious life.

It went through the tunnel with the greatest speed that it could exert, swamping the tunnel with its existence, navigating itself to the trapdoor opening that would lead to its master.

It wanted to save him, and it wanted to swallow the group.

It slopped about the dark tunnels of its master's network until it sensed that it was close to the network opening that its master was brought through. When it reached the network opening, it knew it couldn't splurge with a wild, powerful entrance into battle. It knew, given what it could do, and with directions from the pulse that Raktaar sent, that it must enter the battlefield quietly. It seeped through the trapdoor entrance, instantly making itself sink through the soft mud and into the ground. It displaced the ground around itself, raising the mud above it only slightly, and made haste to where it sensed its master to be.

ARIEL WAS FLYING TOWARDS Ohlman's Tree and saw Tanya, Boaz, and Boris run beside the long trench she had made with Raktaar. She landed next to Tanya, wanting to rid herself of the sludge on her hands, feeling it burn and pull at her skin. Boris ran to where he saw the end of the trench lead. Boaz, with his mightier Gollum strength, ran faster still.

Boaz saw Ariel land next to Tanya.

The sludge on her hands fired him to anger.

He saw the most powerful weapon of his old master infecting and hurting his friend. He remembered being overwhelmed by the sloppy red years ago. For years, he was physically restrained and mentally chained because of the stuff.

For years, he was the victim.

For years, he was forced to hate everyone and everything.

Today, he would end that.

He stomped the ground harder with every footstep, extended every stride, and fueled himself with a just hatred of the evil his old master caused.

This fuel nearly burst from his skin in hot anger when he saw his old master mangled in a crater at the end of the trench. He ran with as much intensity as his muscles could output. He wanted – more than anything he ever wanted – to rip the life out of the old wreck of a creature he was once forced to serve. When he saw the crater be in jumping distance, he jumped off his left foot, scissor-kicked his legs to twist himself around, then landed on his feet and hands, using everything to slow down with speed. He pushed his feet into the sloppy brown and gripped the wet soil with his lightly grey fingers, his Gollum strength making many smaller trenches along the ground. When he came to a stop, he ran to Raktaar with every reserve his muscles could find, grabbed his daggers from his lower back, jumped, and aimed for Raktaar's chest.

As he jumped, he observed Raktaar's skin ooze sludge only just before landing.

He narrowly missed touching any sludge. A *splash* of mud flew away from where he landed, and his landing made a sloppy *thud*. His daggers mercilessly stabbed the almost liquid dirt.

When he landed, he found his eyes to be directly in-front of Raktaar's.

He had grown painfully familiar with those eyes.

He had looked into those eyes when a disgusting tentacled creature poked, slapped, and played with him.

He had looked into those eyes as the sludge overcame him.

He let go of his right dagger and shaped his thumb and fingers around Raktaar's neck. He felt some warmth, but it was much cooler than what a human neck should feel like. He held his hands there for a few moments, but he didn't choke Raktaar—he couldn't touch the sludge. He roared into Raktaar's face, grabbed his right dagger, got up, and found some distance between him and the dark red half-a-man. He let the rain wash off most of the mud on his daggers, wiped off the rest with his hands, then let them sit nicely in his lower back. He prepared his forearms to fire Gollum Tears, but he refrained from doing so.

He knew it wouldn't do anything to a creature that could heal itself.

As he prepared his forearms, Boris made his way to the crater.

Like Boaz, he made a leap to Raktaar.

Boaz stepped towards Boris, and, lacking the reach to do anything gentler, slammed Boris into the ground with the cylinder protruding from his right forearm. He slotted his forearm cylinders back into his forearms, knowing the retaliation he would now receive.

Boris rose from the ground after a few moments of confusion, lacking the awareness to see that he dropped his sword, and saw Boaz. He knew that Boaz was the one that stopped him from ripping to limbs the abomination that ruined his childhood and left her sister almost falling apart. He got up and sprinted towards Boaz's legs, aiming to lift Boaz up and slam his large Gollum chest into the wet and sloppy ground.

Anticipating this, Boaz lowered himself and braced for Boris' impact. When Boris collided, he reached his arms underneath Boris' to prevent any of Boris' punches. "The sludge," he said in Boris' right ear. "The sludge. The sludge." Over and over, in a gentle voice, wanting to remind Boris of what could have happened.

After a few moments, it worked.

Boris slowed his anger, began to turn, and noticed also how Raktaar's skin oozed the red sludge that he had felt before. He saw in his head what could have happened if Boaz hadn't redirected him into the ground.

He didn't have the resistance to contact the sloppy red.

He would have been eaten alive by the sludge.

Literally.

Still breathing quickly, he ran his fingers through his hair in frustration of himself. This was the second time Boaz had saved him. He couldn't bring himself to look at him, but he did express his gratitude. "Thank you . . . again."

Boaz nodded, smiled, then saw Ariel flying to where he stood with Tanya in Ariel's S.M.A.R.T. rope harness, which wasn't operating as well as it could.

Raktaar didn't break through it, but he did damage it.

They both landed, and Ariel rewound her S.M.A.R.T. rope. She turned to face Raktaar, knowing she couldn't touch him but also knowing where she could fire her Hailer Hail to watch him explode.

Tanya stood with a strength unlike anyone present.

With her, Raktaar's eyes opened wide.

She smiled a powerful smile, shouted her supremacy through her eyes, and stood with a posture that demanded respect from Raktaar.

Boris approached behind his sister, wanting to back her on this triumphant execution. He then reached down to grab his sword with his right. Raktaar did his best to spit at Boris, knowing Boris couldn't do anything lasting against him. The attempted spit landed just at the edge of the crater.

When it landed, Tanya crouched down, extracted the black dust from the small drop of spit, then plunged it into her chest and caused it to go fantastically ablaze. She brought herself close to Raktaar, seeing how broken his limbs were, and forced him to watch the intensity of her flames.

He moved some sludge to his jaw and neck so that he could speak. "Kill me then," Raktaar said. "Why don't you start already?" He would have shouted, but his lungs pressed against his many broken ribs.

"I can't hold all the black dust I would get from you. My chest isn't that big–"

Raktaar spat on her. Being near his face, it made contact. Just below her eyes.

Tanya was, for a moment, hushed. She then removed the black dust from the drop of spit on her face and plunged that into her chest, moving herself closer to Raktaar. When she felt she sufficiently intimidated the broken mess of bones and flesh beneath her, she stood straight, held her nose, and blew the ash out. She watched as a cloud of ash filled the crater and covered Raktaar.

She wanted to prove who was better, but she didn't want to hurt Raktaar. Mercy wasn't something Raktaar knew, but it was something Tanya knew very well.

She knew that would always make her greater.

She stepped back, calmed herself, then turned around. She looked first to Ariel's pack, remembering that was where she last saw Nehemiah. She was confused. She looked to each member of the group, but Nehemiah wasn't on any of them. "Anyone see Nehemiah?" she asked inquisitively and nervously.

They all shook their heads and began to agree with her nervousness.

A moment later, there was a fade-in of massive footsteps heard from the direction of Ohlman's Tree. They all turned and saw Nehemiah running full sprint towards them all.

He looked scared.

While he was sprinting, he slightly extended his right arm. He turned and did two side-steps leading with his left, twisted on his left foot, threw something small from his right hand, then continued his sprint. The ground shook as he approached.

The object Nehemiah threw became clearer when it got closer.

It was a very fast-shaped Laban.

His voice got louder in each of their heads as he approached. It was hard to hear at first, though they each attempted to listen. They could hear that he was shouting something. They could hear he was afraid of something.

After a few moments, as Laban got closer, his message was clearly heard. "*Step back!*"

As he got closer, the fear in his voice was undeniable. "*Step back!*" he yelled. "*Step back!*"

The group began to share his fear, and they grew nervous.

"*Step back!*"

Then they ran.

They sprinted with whatever strength was left in their legs, though they couldn't understand what was the cause of Nehemiah and Laban's uneasiness.

Then they heard Raktaar's laughter and instantly froze.

They turned hastily, and felt every strength they previously had over Raktaar surrender in shame.

They watched, with horror, as Raktaar rose from the crater. Under him was a pillar of red sludge. When he rose to nearly twice Nehemiah's height, the rest of the sludge came from the ground and grew its form.

It became a Raktaar made entirely of red sludge, its head gigantically high and surrounding where the original Raktaar was now kept, working through it and feeling all that it felt.

It then roared a *deafening* roar. They each felt the wind push against them as it roared, and they each felt how freezing it was. The roar pushed against the rain, sending a thick onslaught of water with the freezing rush of wind.

Ariel was about to launch into flight, but caught sight of her fuel gauge in her Hailer Eye. She knew she would need to ration it, and she knew flying the entire group would not be for far. Flight wasn't something she could use this time.

For the first time since Boaz was taken from Raktaar, she felt hopeless.

"Any thoughts?" she asked the group. Her gaze was intent on tracking their new massive opponent.

Tanya thought to run, and she was about to turn, when she felt Nehemiah's footsteps through the ground. She was reminded of a revelation she had: *it will be terrified of us.* She spoke to the group. "This thing was made to fight Nehemiah, remember? Not us."

Boaz responded. *"Do you see it!"*

She responded, though she said nothing. She looked to her chest and remembered The Day with unrivalled vivacity—the long scar always reminded her of that. She then laid her hands on her chest, as if she was plunging some black dust into it, and remembered the amazing gift she was shown. She looked up, and knew, within the sludge head that rose twice Nehemiah's height, was the man controlling the massive sludge beast. She then looked past the giant sludge creature, still establishing its outer layer to mimic Raktaar's skin, and noticed Nehemiah growing very close. She smiled. "Do you see this?" she asked.

A moment after she asked, Nehemiah launched from his right foot, and jumped at the sludge beast's back. It stuttered forward slightly, having not braced for him to jump on its back, and felt him climb onto its head.

He then straightened his fingers, kept his thumb to his palm, and speared his hand through the sludge, wanting to directly hit the original Raktaar. The sludge beast collapsed to the ground, holding its head in pain. He jumped off, covered in sludge, and ran as far as he reasonably could, wanting to heal himself before he struck again.

The group watched in amazement at what was a massive beast fall to the ground and now look much, much shorter.

In each of them, bravery grew through their chests into their arms and legs. They each smiled, knowing they could defeat Raktaar.

They only had to figure out how.

Boris spoke first. "If we hit its head, we sort-of hit him."

Tanya agreed and added, "When you hit it, you'll be infected with sludge. I'll have to remove it for you." She dropped her staff to the ground, knowing she only needed it for the Screams from the night before.

Boaz was quiet for a moment, looked at Ariel, then to the sludge beast. He laughed. "Only if you need to touch it." He flicked his forearms, extending the metal poles from his hands, then pulled to deploy the metal cylinders from his forearms. He turned and gained distance from the group, knowing how loud his Gollum Tears would be. He twisted the metal pole that extended from his hands, increasing the Hailer Spit that would be used to fire the Gollum Tears.

It was going to be very, very loud, and very, very deadly.

Then, with the happiest and most blissful smile his Gollum face had ever shown, he pushed the buttons on the metal poles within his right and left hands.

Click.

Boom-boom-boom-boom-boom-boom-boom-boom-boom-boom-boom-boom.

Out of the cylinders came little puffs of orange that flashed almost as fast as the human eye could tell. Each puff, after a small delay, sent a truly deep and quick *boom* that each of the group felt. The group looked to the sludge beast and saw its face instantly littered with many little ripples. It moved to cover its face, then felt on the back of its hands the sting of these little beads of Gollum-class hate. It tried to move away from it as it rose to its feet, but Boaz kept firing onto it. Its large size forced it to be slow, making it too slow to escape Boaz's Gollum Tears easily.

Ariel thought to bring its head closer to the ground. She first saw its knees, removed both her thigh weapons, and aimed at its front right knee. Every shot she fired saw another chunk of sludge be blasted away until there was no more knee left to destroy. The calf of the sludge leg was left to stand by itself, slowly toppling to the sludge beast's right. The sludge beast was distracted still by the incessant stinging peppering of the Gollum Tears, and couldn't remake its broken leg before it toppled to its front right. The fall was felt by the group in their feet through the ground, watching very thankfully as a massive splash of mud was sent into the air.

They then watched with fear as the sludge beast melted into the ground with a speed that surprised each of them.

Raktaar stood where the sludge beast's head used to be. His arms were extended, fingers curled, and back hunched. He breathed heavily. His eyes were wide. His teeth were exposed.

He was enraged.

Boris and Tanya knew, while he was exposed, that they could be useful. Tanya bent down, held her staff in her right hand, then followed Boris as they ran to Raktaar. Boaz ran to their left, then fired his Gollum Tears at the now vulnerable Raktaar, knowing Boris and Tanya would be safe from the little spheres that could pierce nearly anything.

His Gollum Tears were met with a solid wall of sludge.

He continued to fire, hoping and wishing that his old master would feel the stinging pain like he did only a few moments ago.

The wall stayed strong.

It was then that Raktaar saw Boris and Tanya pass the wall. Keeping the wall of sludge against Boaz up with his right hand, Raktaar used his left hand to send a surge of sludge against Boris and Tanya. A wave of sludge overcame them both, covering them both with the dark sloppy red.

Every muscle seared, and they felt every part of themselves slowly being pulled apart from the other.

Boaz saw this.

He breathed angrily through his nose.

He looked back to the wall of sludge, having a new urgency to disorient his old master. Seeing how short the wall was, he kept firing with his left hand, let the cylinder and metal pole on his right arm find themselves in the inside of his right arm, grabbed for a Gollum Sphere, and, while firing at the wall with his left, threw a Gollum Sphere over the strong dark red wall. He threw it as high as he could, keeping it out of Raktaar's sight as best he could

A few moments passed.

Boom.

As always, Boaz's timing and range was near perfect.

The Gollum Sphere exploded a short distance from Raktaar, forcing him backwards and sliding across the very wet mud behind him.

Tanya and Boris felt most of the sludge quickly disappear from them, but large patches remained. Tanya got up, put a hand over Boris and herself, and went about getting black dust to burn in her chest. When she had cleaned them both, she passed him his sword, helped him up, grabbed her staff, then ran to Raktaar.

Unsure what else to do, Ariel joined them with her thigh weapons holstered and her forearm blades in hand.

Boaz stopped firing his Gollum Tears but prepared his right forearm to fire if he needed to. He knew he needed to conserve his Gollum Tears, but he also knew that whenever he had a chance to blast his old master to pieces, he would.

RAKTAAR REMAINED LYING ON the ground, letting the sludge heal his burned skin and muscle. He made his legs as flat to the ground as his four leg joints could, wanting to avoid any pestering Gollum Tears and knowing being flat made it hard to be shot at.

Then he had a thought.

He smiled and quietly laughed to himself.

He commanded his sludge to bury himself under the wet dirt.

Then he waited.

ARIEL, TANYA, BORIS, AND Boaz were running towards Raktaar with every part of them wanting to end this fight. As they ran, they felt, then heard, the mighty footsteps of Nehemiah.

As he was running, he was looking near them and around himself.

He couldn't see his old brother.

He sprinted faster.

When he found himself approaching the group, he reached down and let Laban climb up his finger. Laban was then thrown to the group while Nehemiah kept running, getting closer to the group.

When Laban landed just next to the group, he reached up and grabbed the backs of Ariel, Boaz, and Boris. He then held himself up as high as he could reach, where Nehemiah ran past and, with Laban's assistance, held the three of them in cupped hands. Laban dropped to the ground after doing so and returned to Tanya.

Tanya remained entirely confused and scared.

It was then when reality flooded her thoughts and senses.

She was wetter than she knew she could be, colder than she'd ever felt before, dirty with wet and cold mud, and had little energy left in her. She stood there, started to shiver, and dropped her staff.

She looked to Laban with a look that shouted of confusion and anger.

Laban came from the ground and made the face of Nehemiah. He spoke with Nehemiah's voice, "We're built differently. Don't fight like me. Fight like you."

Tanya looked at Laban with increased intensity, lacking the energy to scream in desperation and knowing that kneeling in defeat would make her colder and dirtier. As sharply as she had the strength to show, she asked, "What does that mean?!"

Laban, not knowing when Raktaar would appear, was quick with his answer after a moment to think how else he could say the message Nehemiah had passed on to him. He made himself into as large a Nehemiah as he could mimic, went through the motions of removing the black dust, plunging it into his chest, then expelling the ash from his sides, using little drops of himself to mimic the dust and ash. He did this twice before returning to the form of Nehemiah's face, shaking his head in disapproval. He then mimicked Tanya removing black dust with both her arms and her chest, with the dust going straight to her chest, using little drops of himself to mimic the dust and the ash, with the ash falling to the ground from her back.

After doing that twice, the sound of falling sludge was heard behind Tanya.

She turned and saw a sludge Raktaar rise from the ground. It rose quickly, and when it was fully formed it looked around. It tried to see anyone else present, but it only saw Laban and Tanya. When it couldn't see anyone else, it smiled a slimy smile and roared with delight.

It then made its right hand into a fist, grabbed it with its left, and slammed them both to where Tanya was standing.

Tanya took a few steps forward, then dove, narrowly escaping the mass of deadly sludge. She was now covered in mud and felt the cold more intensely now. She was hesitant to rise, wondering if there was any way or reason to continue fighting by herself.

When she thought this, she felt Laban turning her over.

She then saw a left-handed sludge fist making its approach.

When it got close, Laban made a spike aimed at the valley between the fist's two middle knuckles. It speared exactly where Laban wanted the sludge fist to hurt, and the sludge beast reeled back in pain. Laban threw off the sludge to avoid contamination. The sludge beast brought down its fist again and again, both times stopped by the stabbing pain of Laban.

When it realized that punches wouldn't work, it went about smothering Tanya and Laban.

It brought its right fist down as if to punch, expecting Laban to make a spike again, and let its fist absorb Laban's spike, surrounding Laban's white form with a corrosive dark red.

It wanted to remove one opponent at a time.

Laban felt himself be surrounded and pushed against the dark red, wanting to escape. He felt the burning red pull and stretch him thinner than he liked. He pushed through to where he remembered seeing Tanya, feeling how strongly the red sludge wanted to stop him, wanting to save a small bit of himself. He felt the surrounding red sludge grab wherever it could, ripping small pieces of himself and converting it into its own.

He pierced through the dark red surface with barely any of himself left and dropped to Tanya, unable to save the rest of his contaminated self.

Tanya watched as Laban was enveloped by the red sludge. She watched as a fight between the sludge and Laban almost killed the little guy.

She remembered holding a little winged critter in her hands, blowing away its hate, and making it into a wonderfully white little critter. She remembered and felt the bond she had grown with Laban.

As she watched him nearly die, she felt an empowering anger.

She recalled Laban's demonstration of Nehemiah's message, remembering how he used both arms and chest. She got her palms to face the sludge, and, driven by her just anger, sucked the black dust from the sludge. She felt as the black dust went through her arms, into her chest, be burned to grey ashes, and fall through her back. She watched as the sludge was dissolved away at a considerable pace, smiled with satisfaction, then yelled with passion.

It was then that the sludge beast made its fist contact the ground, swallowing Tanya in one motion.

Initially slowed by the imminent death, she kept sucking black dust through her arms and now through her chest, forcing her chest to create remarkable pressure and heat. When she felt sludge break into her skin, she felt the black dust come through her skin and into her chest—she absorbed and burned the sludge till its power was destroyed. She felt in control, knowing the sludge beast couldn't hurt her anymore. When she felt the beast's fist rise from the ground, feeling itself be killed, she kept herself to the ground and stood on what was now a thick layer of ash. When she looked at the sludge beast, she saw its fist back by its side.

When she looked at its face, she saw the greatest sight she had ever seen.

It was scared.

It was terrified of her.

She had the power now.

She sprinted to the leg closest to her and climbed it, feeling the sludge break into black dust that she burned in her chest. When she reached its upper leg and was running to its hip, it tried to stay solid and squish what was now its greatest enemy. It made a fist with its right hand and brought it down where Tanya was running. She burned her way through its leg, finding herself inside its leg. When the fist hit its leg, the sludge beast let its right arm fall away and surround Tanya, wanting to overwhelm her with sludge.

Tanya felt every part of her be pulled and burnt by the sludge, then felt the black dust make its way from every part of her to her chest. She felt the strain of concentrating for so long and so intensely, but she knew she could continue.

She knew she was winning.

Raktaar felt his sludge be destroyed by Tanya.

RAKTAAR WATCHED AS THE mass of sludge around Tanya decreased in size. He was slowly losing his most powerful weapon. He lowered himself down to the ground as far as his sludge would let him, wanting to control the sludge externally. When he was on his own four feet, he let go of Tanya and made a sludge arm with a fist on its end. He swung it to Tanya's side, hoping she couldn't burn through the sludge moving at such speed.

He was wrong.

He felt as Tanya went through the sludge.

He watched as his fist reformed itself to a smaller size.

He was angry.

He then looked to the ground and saw the mud.

He then smiled.

He got his sludge under some mud, picked it up, and went to smash it on Tanya.

TANYA SAW THE MUD rise from the ground and aim itself at her. She ran and jumped just as the mud clump was landing where she just was. She kept running, running straight to Raktaar, knowing that he wouldn't pile anything on himself. When she was getting closer to Raktaar, he brought from the ground a wave of mud between them both. She ran left, wanting to run around the wave. Raktaar moved the wave around, letting the wave fall just after she had run past it.

He then sent a wave to land ahead of Tanya.

His timing was perfect.

She was forced to the ground and covered in mud. When she tried to get up, she felt a wave of mud land on her and stay on her. She was pinned to the ground under a mass of mud, and she couldn't burn her way through something that wasn't sludge.

She drew in a large breath and closed her eyes before she felt the mud press on her. She couldn't move anything, though she tried with great effort. She felt the extreme urge to breathe that she couldn't satisfy. Her body wanted to shiver from the cold of the mud, but it couldn't. She found herself reaching a new level of cold she hadn't experienced before, where movement couldn't provide heat. The mud stopped all sound and light from getting in.

Then her body chose to remove warmth from her limbs to keep her organs alive.

She could feel control of her hands, arms, legs, and feet stop. She felt a wonderful warmth begin to radiate from her midsection, but the cold mud on her limbs was terrifying.

Then her lungs couldn't offer any air.

Her brain went foggy.

Her heartbeat slowed.

She started to die.

RAKTAAR STOOD OUTSIDE THE mass of mud, pressing his hands together to force the mud onto Tanya. He knew she couldn't survive much longer under the pressure and without breath.

He knew he was winning.

He smiled, and he laughed. His laughter was roaring, sickening, and filled with a disturbed happiness. He knew, after he killed Tanya, that there couldn't be anything left to stop him.

Then he had the feeling to look up.

When he did, he saw Nehemiah falling from the sky with his right wrist held by his left hand, and a fist facing directly downwards.

It was lined up perfectly to where he was standing.

An epic *boom* resonated over the muddy plains as Raktaar was squished under a mighty wooden fist.

It was joined by a *crack* and *snap* as Nehemiah's right arm broke off from the impact.

Nehemiah was shaken by the landing, but he found his feet as he saw some of Raktaar's sludge redirect itself to his head and prevent the intense hit from killing him. He then saw some of the sludge go from the mass of mud to his body, wanting to restore the rest of him. Before any more could reach his body, Nehemiah scooped up Raktaar's body and some mud with his left hand, and ran to where Boris and Boaz would be running from.

He looked up and saw Ariel flying near the clouds, having brought him to an excellent drop height.

AS HE WATCHED THE fight from a distance as a flower, he wanted to be ready if Tanya was faced with something unexpected—like being buried in mud. He knew, with Ariel's speed, that help could be provided rapidly.

It was her speed that he needed again.

He looked behind him and saw a layer of red sludge crawl with haste over the mud. He looked up and saw Ariel bring herself down from the clouds, knowing she started her rapid descent when he landed. She knew Raktaar needed to be far from his sludge to be killed, so she undid her S.M.A.R.T. rope and made a slipknot at its end, using her Hailer Eye to align the knot with Raktaar's neck.

When she got close, Nehemiah threw Raktaar into the air as high as he could, and the knot landed around Raktaar's neck.

When it was tight, she flew.

She started to fly the same way Nehemiah was running, preparing to meet Boris and Boaz and knowing they would be needed to finish this.

When Nehemiah saw Ariel catch Raktaar, he dug his feet into the sloppy mud, rolled out of the sludge's path, knowing it was after Raktaar, not him, and ran back to Tanya. When he was beside the mound of mud, he scooped up what he could and let the mud sift through his hand. He felt his joints go stiff under the cool of the mud, and only imagined how cold Tanya would be.

He then saw her limp body lie covered in mud and lying on his hand.

He cupped his hand and blew into it, knowing most of the mud would be blown off. When it was just her mud-covered body that remained, he set his chest ablaze and held her body at a safe distance.

He felt his joints become looser under the flame's soothing heat, and he saw Tanya's whole-body shiver violently. She was breathing and getting warm, but she needed to recover. He let the rain extinguish the flame inside his chest, got onto his feet, and ran to the rest of the group with Tanya in his left hand.

ARIEL COULD SEE BORIS and Boaz sprinting harder than they've ever sprinted. When she got closer, she pitched up and released Raktaar, letting him fly up before falling. She then turned, grabbed a thigh weapon for each hand, prepared her wings' Hailer Hail, and fired up the red sludge wanting to re-meet with its master. Boaz saw the mass of dark red make its approach and let the Gollum Tears fly forth. The Hailer Hail caused explosions of mud and the Gollum Tears slowed down the sludge.

As Raktaar was falling, Boris saw his chance to be involved.

Not wanting to waste a strike, he waited until he knew where Raktaar would land, then ran with his sword in hand.

Before Raktaar could get on his feet and heal the bones broken from the impact, Boris ran and jumped with his sword held sideways, severing Raktaar's head from his body.

Surviving only on the sludge, Raktaar's head was still alive, but now he had no body to work with.

The mass of sludge following his head continued pursuing its master's head.

Before the sludge in his body could reconnect the head, Boris stabbed it with his sword, spun, and let Raktaar's head fly off his sword and away from the sludge. It flew a nice distance away from where he was standing. He ran after it, wanting to increase that distance however he could.

Raktaar's head collided harshly with the ground. It hurt, but his head didn't weigh much, and the ground was saturated. It continued to roll, balanced on his sort-of nose, then toppled to one side, finally landing with his eyes faced towards the fight. He saw Ariel and Boaz slowing down his main mass of sludge, and he saw Boris running towards him.

He then saw Nehemiah run from behind it all, holding Tanya in his left hand.

He took control of the main mass of sludge and forced it to seep into the mud, making it disappear. He then forced any spare sludge he could find in his head to tilt his head upward, preparing to spit at Boris.

When Boris got within a close distance, Raktaar spat, sending a pulse with it for extra velocity.

The small drop of sludge connected with Boris' chest, sending him to the ground in agony.

When Raktaar could see Nehemiah with greater clarity, he commanded the mass of sludge to rise from the ground. It enveloped his legs, and forced him to fall, forcing Tanya out of his hand, who was beginning to find her warmth and alertness. The sludge pinned Nehemiah's arm to his body, stopping the only way he could combat it.

After Nehemiah's fall, Tanya found her feet on the sloppy mud.

She walked a few steps away before turning around and seeing everything that was happening.

Nehemiah was pinned to the ground, being burned and pulled apart by the sludge. Boaz and Ariel continued their fire on the sludge, but they couldn't destroy it. Boris lay on the ground with a blob of sludge on his chest, the small mass of dark red getting close to his organs. Raktaar's body slid across the ground above a layer of sludge that carried it, allowing the body and head to re-unite. He stood on four feet and, with greater strength, made the sludge around Nehemiah be more intense, the shouts and groans of pain being easier to hear.

What she saw saddened her, for she was seeing the demise of her brother and friend, with the most powerful humans she knew unable to stop it.

That was her job.

That was her part.

She scowled with anger.

"Enough!" she shouted.

She started running to Raktaar, who was distracted with the demise of his brother. He had waited centuries to watch his brother be eaten like the foxes that first killed him, and this sight was delightful for him.

Until he saw Tanya running to him.

His face changed to shock and fear. He withdrew the sludge from around Nehemiah and from Boris' chest and forced it to create a wave of mud behind Tanya. The little bit of sludge that immobilized Boris could do nothing meaningful by itself, so it returned to the large mass of sludge to increase its intensity.

She could feel the wave of mud grow behind her as she saw Raktaar grow larger and larger. His hands controlled the wave, and they were gently rising as the wave got closer. She could feel the wet mud slop under her feet as she ran, feeling her feet sink into the mud and provide the only traction she could find. Raktaar's feet were speared into the ground and stood strong, but they did something they've never done before.

They were shaking with fear.

Tanya was getting close with the wave almost directly behind her, but there was still a useful distance between them both.

He externalized a drop of sludge from his reserves, removing direct control of the mud wave that could continue with a directive without being intentionally commanded. Knowing the small drop of sludge couldn't hold her with mud—knowing too that she could kill the small reserve of sludge quite easily—he attempted a different approach. Knowing the mud beneath him creates a defense for the red sludge, he knelt and scooped a handful of the sloppy brown. The small reserve of sludge marbled with the wet mud, then it held itself on his chest directly between his shoulders. He made an intense glow of red come from his head, and he directed it down to his shoulders.

Then he used the red glow to shoot the reserve of sludge with frightful power, aiming at Tanya's forehead.

Tanya saw that Raktaar was doing something, but she figured she could treat it like the fist he had used earlier, not seeing the mud marbled with the sludge reserve.

Laban, having held onto Tanya since he nearly died, read Raktaar's thoughts. He raced to her forehead and braced for impact.

When the sludge-mud projectile came closer to Tanya's head at painful speeds—enough to force Raktaar's shoulders back—Laban extended himself on her forehead. The projectile drove itself into Laban, who used Tanya as a foundation and absorbed all the impact from the projectile. The projectile collapsed to the floor, and Tanya took no notice of it.

She was focused on killing Raktaar.

In taking the impact, Laban had used all his strength. He couldn't physically keep himself together, and broke into small drops that fell to the wet ground.

When Raktaar saw this, he lowered his hands.

In the next few moments, Tanya would reach him, burn the immortality out of him, and he would die.

Knowing he could only live on through his sludge beast, he made another red glow come from his head, through his feet, and be released with a tiny dot of sludge that connected with the giant mass of sludge, stopping it.

Just after the tiny dot was released, Tanya jumped towards Raktaar.

The moment Tanya felt her hands touch Raktaar's centuries dead midsection, she started killing him.

She watched as the muscle and skin receded to black bones. He went to spear his fingers through her flesh, but she burnt through the sludge and let the black finger bones fall. She saw how much more black dust there was to burn, feeling how this took longer to do than it was for normal sludge. She grabbed his arms by the shoulders and burnt the sludge away, leaving his arm bones lying in the mud. He kicked with his feet, but she put her hands on his waist and watched as his leg bones fell away.

She kneeled on top of him, waiting for the rest of the group to arrive.

Boris crawled over, recovering from the nasty burn left on his chest that bled more than he liked. Nehemiah got onto his feet, and walked over. Ariel, having run out of fuel, glided back to the ground next to Boaz, who was walking over to the execution as well.

When they all gathered around Raktaar and Tanya, there was a solemn silence. They had won, and that reality was grappled with some effort. For years, they each had hated Raktaar for all that he had done. For years, they wanted to kill the four-legged creature that proved almost impossible to kill.

Now, the impossible had become possible.

Tanya looked around at the group and saw the wonderful friends she had made over this endeavor. The reason was sour, but the fruit was sweet. She looked back to Raktaar, smiling and crying tears of happiness.

Wanting to free himself, Raktaar spat as far as he could, wanting it to land on anyone. Tanya saw him ready himself for the spit and caught the little blob of sludge, letting it burn away and the ash fall to the wet ground.

Then she heard a drop of mud fall behind her.

A wall of mud was rising from the ground—Raktaar's only hope for killing the one that could kill him.

Before the wall of mud could reach a threatening height, she reached down and burnt the last of the sludge in Raktaar's head.

The wall of mud continued to grow.

Still in a frenzy of wanting to kill Raktaar, she made quick work on his midsection, removing all the sludge from it.

The wall of mud then collapsed on to the group.

Nehemiah shrunk down into his flower form, preparing for when he needed to explode into his giant self again. Boaz ran away from the sludge-mud wall and continued firing his Gollum Tears, knowing he was nearly empty. Ariel did the same with her Hailer Hail, blasting away what mud the sludge could use.

Tanya and Boris felt themselves be buried alive by the living sludge pressing down this brown slop on top of them.

Nehemiah flew to Tanya before the mud wall fell and exploded into his giant wooden self. Tanya felt this freedom and gained some distance from her and the living sludge, knowing she couldn't verse the mud. Nehemiah then went to free Boris, shoveling away the mud and the dirt off his friend.

During this, Laban found himself in the wet mud that got wetter with the rain.

He felt how small he was, even after gaining the strength to piece himself together.

This gave him a thought.

He swam through the mud to Tanya, who was still determining how she could be of use.

"Tanya!" Laban yelled.

She replied. "Yeah?"

Laban had surfaced now. "How can you make more of me?"

She went back to when she first made Laban. "I need to blow on some sludge. Actual sludge. If I do it through you, white sludge that has its own identity, it will add to you. Being you, it isn't like normal sludge that goes into black dust."

Laban crawled up Tanya's leg to her right hand. Seeing this, Tanya started running to the living sludge.

When she got close, she saw Boaz and Ariel distracting the living sludge.

She appreciated this.

She saw an exposed patch of living sludge. Holding Laban in her cupped hands, she got close to it and blew. She watched Laban glow a stunning white glow, and the living sludge before her go white.

The living sludge didn't like this.

Following to the instructions from its dead master, it swallowed Tanya in mud. It could handle Boaz, Ariel, and Tanya all at once.

Tanya, feeling how she couldn't breathe, thought to be creative. She let Laban stretch while she held him, bringing him to her chest.

She then set herself ablaze and watched as Laban glowed stronger than before.

She could either blow the black dust away or add to the sludge anomaly that was Laban. She could do this better with the fire in her chest.

Boris, seeing Tanya be swallowed in mud, used his sword to cut away at the mud, such that she could breathe.

When some mud fell away to show Tanya's face, she breathed, looked at Boris with a smile, then closed her eyes and fueled Laban as much as she could.

Boris then looked to his left and saw a wave of mud crash over him and bury him alive.

He closed his eyes, having faith that Tanya would save them all.

Tanya felt the mud bury her again.

She drew a big breath before she was buried, then hoped that Laban would save them all.

Laban had never felt so alive before.

He connected with Tanya's purifying fire, and he used it to add to himself.

The more sludge he added to himself, the smaller his opponent became.

His opponent, however, had the mud as his defense, slowing Laban down.

Laban, being an independent living organism, made a powerful observation: the mud can only be held up. It cannot be an independent barrier.

This meant that the defense wasn't hard to penetrate.

He pierced his way through the mud, making random spikes through the living sludge's barrier, and expanded himself in small bursts.

He sensed Tanya's strain to power him, and Boris' struggle to stay alive, and he knew he could alleviate that.

Shrinking back to behind them both, still keeping a forward attack, he broke through the mud that confined them both, connected himself to their faces, and created an open connection between their faces and a break in the mud.

He helped them both to breathe.

Upon feeling the living sludge make an attack on the only way Boris and Tanya could breathe, he simply expanded himself and made it a chance to expand himself.

So long as Tanya kept her chest ablaze, Laban couldn't be overcome by the living sludge.

So long as Tanya kept her chest ablaze, they would win.

BOAZ, ARIEL, AND NEHEMIAH observed that Laban was taking over what was Raktaar's most effective weapon. They saw Tanya and Boris be pressed under the sludge, but also saw that Laban was working to protect them both.

Despite this, they felt torn.

Feeling how light his legs were, Boaz spoke first. "There's not much more we can do." That statement made his throat sore.

Ariel, knowing she could no longer fly and having half a magazine in each of her thigh weapons left, agreed. "We can't do anything." She made and relaxed her fists to try and feel okay while she said that.

It didn't work.

Nehemiah too felt a tension within himself. His rigidity spoke of it. His words only added to it. "The sludge will tear us apart. The mud will inhibit any resistance . . . " He shook his head with malice. "What a terrible weapon my old brother made."

Ariel, being the feistiest of the group, tightened her thigh weapon grip. "Let's help kill it then." She yelled a tired yell, then resumed fire. The mud broke away, and it gave Laban less resistance.

Boaz, knowing he would need to resupply anyways, did the same. He also broke away what gave Laban resistance, watching his white presence spread faster.

Nehemiah, being the second most-important next to Tanya, knew he could help Tanya. He went around behind her, cut away from the mud that limited her movement beyond comparison, and breathed through the fire in Tanya's chest.

LABAN FELT THIS.

He was unstoppable.

He pierced through the mud with little resistance and expanded himself further with each burst.

He couldn't be stopped.

The smaller mound of mud and living sludge showed that. More of Laban's white presence was beginning to show itself, and less mud was being held up.

Then it reached a pivotal point: Laban grew larger in size than the living sludge holding up its dynamic mud wall. It was then that he pushed away the mud surrounding Boris and Tanya and surrounded the mound of sludge and mud entirely. Then he squeezed. Hard. Any mud he found, he let go of.

Any living sludge he found, he conquered and added to himself.

The mound grew smaller and smaller, with boring mud piling around him.

The pile became smaller.

And smaller.

And smaller.

And smaller.

Then it stopped.

It stopped shrinking.

No more mud gushing out.

No more living sludge to kill.

No more enemies on the sopping wet battlefield.

No more current threats to take down.

After everything that happened, they all turned to what was left, besides an unusual pile of mud.

A skeleton of black bones.

The skeleton of the terrible creature that brought too much misery.

The skeleton that was without mercy and knew no goodness.

It was over.

Years of hatred had been brought to an end.

After nearly dying, the intensity was over.

It was all over.

They had won.

TANYA BURST INTO TEARS of relief when she saw the bones of Raktaar. Boris came beside her and hugged her, his eyes also watering. Boaz went to Ariel and hugged her, having now found a peace they never knew before.

Nehemiah stood tall, one arm less than when he started, and looked on the bones of his dead old brother.

He remembered when they used to play as kids with their gift, smiling and laughing when they could hear the conversations between the birds in the morning. They were amazed at how each little animal had within it a personality: some were hilarious and comedic, others serious—some sad, some full of life.

But no more harm would be brought by Raktaar's hands.

At his, he smiled.

They all knew something had to be done with Raktaar's skeleton. Knowing it was easiest for him to carry, Laban crawled under the black bones and went to his old master's network. The group followed behind with Boris still holding his sword. Nehemiah went to where Tanya dropped her staff and went to obtain it, knowing he could quickly re-join the group. While he was there, he also got his right arm.

As they were walking, Boris noticed the bleeding from his chest worsen. Laban, reading Boris' thoughts, severed a bit of himself and blocked the hole in Boris' chest. Boris smiled and stroked the little bit of Laban with his thumb. As they kept walking, they looked around and saw how wet everything was. It was still raining as they were walking back, and the mess they had made from their fight was extensive.

With Nehemiah there, no-one besides them could see it.

Like everything else that had happened that day.

WHEN THEY GOT CLOSER to the network's entrance, they found that it worked as Raktaar did with their sight: once looked upon, never removed from their sight. They saw the backpack containing Patrick's book near the entrance, and Ariel, having done the least running out of the entire group, went to get it. Boris wondered whether he should keep the book, remembering that was his friend's last work.

He then remembered the emblem he found on the envelope.

He smiled, knowing that's what he would remember Patrick with.

Laban first let his old master's bones rest inside the network as far as he could reach. Ariel followed and threw the backpack with Patrick's book as hard as she could. Tanya and Boris tossed their weapons inside, now having no use for them. Having no way to reconnect his arm, Nehemiah thought to get it destroyed as well, letting Laban navigate the wooden limb through the opening.

They then looked at the opening a little longer.

After this, Laban disappeared into the network, navigating his way back to Raktaar's throne room. When he reached it, he connected himself to the floor and roof, then contracted himself as abruptly as he could, forcing the throne room to collapse. This forced the walls of the throne room to go down, then cascaded into a collapse through all the tunnels in the network. He navigated his way back to the trapdoor closest to all the group, exiting the network just as the dark red rubble crashed and crumbled into ruins.

The network, Nehemiah's right arm, Boris' sword and backpack, Tanya's staff, Raktaar's skeleton, and Patrick's book were buried under enormous weight, never to be found again.

After a few moments of silence, brought from both total exhaustion and a storm of emotions felt by them all, Nehemiah walked forward and paid respect to a brother he once had.

For centuries, they had been equally matched, both undoing the work of the other.

With the assistance of valiant friends, the fight shifted.

With this shift, Nehemiah watched his old brother die.

He knelt in front of the opening, laid his hand beside it, then let his forehead rest on the opening.

"Goodbye Adam," he said quietly to the ground.

He had no tears to cry, but his hand tensed on the dirt.

He straightened himself, made his left hand a fist, made another magnificent fire in his fist, then let the seed that he made rest on the trapdoor opening. He buried this seed under some mud and blew on it, letting the little seed grow into a small sprout that he knew would one day be an epic tree that everyone could see. He rose, knowing he shouldn't stay long.

Wanting to get warm, dry, and clean, they all began to walk away from the fight. As they walked, the rain stopped. The clouds were dark overhead, but for the first time since they got out, they felt dry air.

As they walked, they had smiles on their faces.

It was over.

They had won.

CHAPTER 17

BORIS SAT ON THE chair in his room, looking at Patrick's emblem: two arrows with their heads facing up and the quill facing downwards with a feather of fire. He had pressed the emblem onto a small metal disk. At the top of the metal disk, he let a metal chain no thicker than the thin disk hang from it. He knew he could change its length as he grew.

He looked down and delighted in this little piece.

He thought to not let this one be buried with Patrick. He wanted to bury the original wax seal with his friend.

Tanya walked by and lent on Boris' doorframe. "That looks really nice," she said. She walked in, wiping her hands on her apron as she walked, wanting to remove whatever wet pain was left on her hands and fingers. "May I?" she asked. Her hands were outstretched outstretched, motioning to put the necklace on for him. He nodded, feeling the cool of the metal touch his neck. He felt the small disk rest on his chest. It was a feeling that made him smile. He looked down and stroked the little emblem. He then remembered that Raktaar's sludge made a nasty hole there that Laban held together.

A few weeks later, it was healing nicely.

Boris happened to see Tanya's hands. "May I?" He motioned to her hands, indirectly asking if he could see her artwork. She responded with a happy smile, knowing this was her greatest work.

They both walked to her room.

THERE WAS A SMALL easel on her desk with a canvas resting on it. It had space to paint a colorful display of decent size, but the finer details of the work were not lost in its size. There was a good balance.

Boris looked at the painting, seeing the field of flowers. In the field of flowers, he saw a young woman walking through them with a staff on her back and a white flower in her hair. To her right was a thick, strong tree with dark brown bark.

He tried to look for anything particularly special about the piece, but he couldn't find anything. He liked his sister's works, but this one left her more gleeful than usual.

He couldn't determine why.

She saw his appreciation and confusion. She pointed to the woman at the painting's center. "That's me," she said.

Boris looked, and he saw how the woman's build and features matched Tanya's.

"She's free," she then added.

Boris was starting to understand, though still felt clueless.

He then looked at her face.

Then he understood.

Ever since The Day, Tanya had a sadness about her. She was never as bubbly as she used to be. There was a look in her eyes that hinted at a past hurt, and her movement suggested that anything she did was held back by a weight, something she had to fight to move.

The woman in the painting was graceful and free.

Tanya's smile and eyes gave Boris a little life, as if they breathed an energy into Boris that he lacked before.

They hugged and cried with happiness.

Since The Day, they had never felt this peace.

The pain. The flashbacks. The continual sluggishness. The battles. The stretch of what they could do. It was over.

It was all over.

They had won.

"YOU SURE YOU WANT it that large?" Ariel said. She was looking at the four sticks Boaz used to make the two opposite corners of a rectangle. "We'll need a lot of wood for that."

This was the floor plan for their home.

Boaz replied. "Yeah. We can still make it cozy, but there'll be places where you want some space."

Ariel slowly nodded in agreeance, understanding that decent space is also nice. She heard the chirps of birds behind her and a rustle of branches in the wind to her left. The orange of the leaves brought a fantastic peace over the area.

The forest was the most peaceful environment she had found herself in.

It was also cool to her skin. More than she expected.

She knew the tree sap she found would work well enough for her pack, knowing also that it wasn't Hailer Spit. The sap did allow her to fly, much slower than she normally could, and stay warm in the cooler surroundings, so she didn't mind.

With the cool, she was brought back to her memories of their fight against Raktaar.

"How do you think they're all doing?" she asked.

"The group?" he replied.

"Yeah," she clarified.

"Well . . . without Raktaar . . . probably really nice."

She nodded in agreement. "But . . . us all staying together . . . "

He nodded.

He walked up to her, grabbed her hands, and let his fingers slide between hers, a tight bond made with their hands. "We're at our freest like this. We get to share a life together"–he stroked her hair back behind her ears. She smiled, blushed, and looked away. "Boris and Tanya get to live their lives with a youth—we didn't get that." He breathed in and out deeply, still feeling that loss. "Then Nehemiah and Laban . . . how do you hide either of them? With what they can do, hiding them would be a waste. They can hide themselves, and, when they don't need to hide, they can do things we could never do. They got a different sight, remember?"

She nodded, still looking and feeling a little sad that they all had to split into their pairs. She really liked having a friend like Tanya, a young woman she could get along with. Boris was young, Nehemiah was the closest she had to a dad, and Laban was just amazing.

Then she felt Boaz's lips meet hers for the shortest and sweetest of moments, and she remembered why they chose to live in a cold, northern forest.

Boaz was her love.

After reuniting those few weeks ago, their strong friendship grew into something deeper.

She looked into his eyes and smiled, her face showing more color and feeling warmer than she'd ever felt before. She let out a giggle of happiness. She didn't normally giggle, and it still felt awkward. She felt embarrassed every time she did, with a snort sometimes showing that. Boaz joined with a smile, his face also going a bit more colorful than he knew it could. He was using new muscles when he smiled. It felt a little sore sometimes.

Then Ariel saw a light flashing in her Hailer Eye. She'd need to find some rogue Hailers of her own to scavenge some of her special supplies, but for now her equipment was working.

Through the receiver in Ariel's pack, her Hailer Eye showed her a distress beacon somewhere not far from her. She knew she would need a new interest when not enjoying a home with her love, and she knew her skills worked nicely with search and rescue.

Boaz saw her eyes move like they were reading something. "You're going?"

She nodded slowly, still determining where the beacon was coming from.

He nodded in response. "Love you," he said, ending with a kiss, loving her for the work she did.

"Love you too," she replied with a smile.

She flew above the trees, feeling how slower her flight was with a less volatile fuel. She watched on her Hailer Eye where the distress was coming from. She banked left, then levelled out, flying directly towards her destination.

When she got closer, she landed and walked, wanting to be stealthier.

When she walked closer, she saw a young man with a backpack of hiking and camping supplies. While wearing his backpack, he was holding his ankle. She saw how the young man's ankle didn't look in place, and she deduced it was broken. She walked around in a large circle, wanting to keep her distance, and walked directly towards him from behind him. When she knew she was close enough, she laid on the ground on her stomach and let a tiny turret deploy from her pack. On the turret was a tiny glider that was exactly like a Hailer's black disk. She let the turret aim and launch the little glider, where it flew in a nice arc and landed just above the young man before zapping him with enough electricity to force unconsciousness but not death. The glider landed at the young man's legs, and she grabbed the little glider before letting her S.M.A.R.T. rope put the glider back on the turret in her pack. The turret then folded itself back into her pack. She found the young man's distress beacon and switched it off, letting the emergency crew go somewhere more important. She let the S.M.A.R.T. rope tie itself into a harness and secure the young man before she took off and flew to the nearest town, knowing she could hide him in the outskirts. She would let him find help for himself when he came too, knowing he could do that for himself.

As she flew, she realized that she had saved the young man's life. The young man couldn't get anywhere with any speed, and his broken ankle would cause more issues than he could handle with his limited supplies.

At this, Ariel smiled.

She saved a life.

Out of the thousands she had taken, this is one of the firsts that she saved.

This made her smile a big smile, laugh a big laugh, and let her find a life she wanted.

BOAZ WATCHED AS ARIEL flew away, still getting used to her pack's thrusters burning a different color than what he remembered. He turned around and thought to get to the work he did for himself—more accurately, for the village he helped.

Not far from where they chose to build their home was a village. Boaz knew his skillset would be very helpful to the village, so he thought to make use of them.

He started by using his Gollum strength and uprooted a fully grown tree near where he and Ariel wanted to have their house, giving them more space to help the home feel relaxed and not press against the surrounding trees. He cut the main roots with his Gollum Tooths and carried the trunk to the village, letting the village use it as they please. He put it near the entrance of the village—to the side so it wouldn't look out of place—also letting them roll it in when they wanted it.

Then he looked up and saw a hunter in the distance.

Camo under a fluorescent pink singlet told the eyes he was an experienced hunter, with the long rifle slung over his shoulder. The rifle hung on a hiking backpack that was done up like he was a serious hunter. It was not a slack, sloppy amateur that was walking to the village.

He also had no business going near the village.

If he was injured, Boaz knew he would run and provide aid.

But the man walked quite well.

He held his rifle easily too.

He could even hold his aim well enough to aim at Boaz.

Boaz dived behind the trunk, knowing a hunter could trace a moving target. He heard the gunshot and the wood splinter, but he couldn't see an exit hole for the bullet.

He didn't want to kill the hunter—he had done more killing than he wanted in his lifetime—but he had to stop the guy.

Like Ariel, he wanted to stay anonymous.

Like Ariel, his equipment needed resupply.

While tree sap worked in Ariel's thrusters, it wasn't volatile enough to launch Gollum Tears, and his Gollum Spheres were too deadly to throw at the guy.

Throwing his Gollum Spheres *in front* of the guy and showering him in dirt was something he could do.

He peaked his head over just enough to let him see where the hunter was. He got a Gollum Sphere in his right hand, lobbed it, then hid behind the log just as a bullet skimmed the top of the trunk.

Boom.

Boaz jumped over the log and sprinted at the hunter, knowing this was his time to seize the hunter. The ground was wetter than he planned, seeing a lack of dirt cloud between him and the hunter.

But the hunter was still on the ground recovering from the explosion.

Boaz went beside the hunter, pulled the magazine from his rifle, unchambered the loaded bullet, then snapped the rifle over his knee. He put his hand around the hunter's throat, wanting to make the individual go unconscious. He used his fingers to press the hunter's mouth into the ground after turning him over, wanting to keep this part quiet. He put his entire weight on the hunter's limbs and, seeing the hunter's knife on his right hip, positioned his left leg to block all access to the knife.

He then watched the hunter's body relax onto the ground after a few moments of flailing limbs and desperate attempts to fight.

The hunter was controlled.

The village was safe.

He threw the hunter over his right shoulder, keeping him there with his right hand, held the pieces of the hunter's rifle with his left hand and walked to the village, letting them choose what to do with the trespasser.

The entrance to the village wasn't *close* to the village. The entrance was more an entrance to the people's land, where the people lived more at its center. It wasn't the first gunshot the village would have heard either—this was popular hunting ground.

When he got to the village, he used the rope the hunter had on his pack to tie the hunter to one of the large rocks the village children liked to play on. He tied the hunter's hands behind his back, then slid the rope underneath the hunter and tied the hunter's feet and hands together. He put the hunter's supplies a short distance from his feet.

Then he stood up.

He turned around and saw a young boy running towards the village fire.

He had just run out the front door of a log home—a home that, with a few dimension changes, was like every other home in the village—and was running to get some more autumn leaves, which he would carry in a large stick nest he also ran with.

Boaz determined the boy was using the leaves for the village festivities.

He didn't know the details, but he observed the night before a great bonfire with much eating and music and singing and dancing and laughing.

Everyone had used tree sap—a resource the village used remarkably—to stick leaves onto themselves, clothes and all. Boaz didn't know why the village folk did this ceremony, but he saw how joyous it was.

He then saw the young boy look at him and freeze.

He wasn't unfamiliar with outsiders though.

There was a radio tower that a nearby city woman gave to the village should they need anything from the outside world. She had a heart for the local people. The villagers knew the team that maintained it. Any random hiker or camper—even hunters removing pests from the forest—that strolled into the village thinking it was a small town was taken in, cared for, then sent on their way with help from the villagers, knowing these forests with amazing skill. The villagers could recognize the lost and confused, and got excited at the new faces they could bring to the community. The village also received supplies from an organization that gave them resources to fix problems they had no capacity to solve. That team made their drop a few days ago, and the villagers knew them well, knowing when they needed to ask for help.

The young boy, however, hadn't met a Gollum—a big, grey skinned man.

His attention then froze on the hunter behind Boaz.

Boaz saw from the young boy's face that this wasn't the first time they've faced hunters like this.

Boaz didn't know how to handle the young boy.

Then the hunter started to wake up.

Boaz turned around and drove his fist into the hunter's jaw. It sat unevenly, but the hunter was quiet again.

He turned back to the boy. He looked less scared now, seeing how Boaz didn't like hunters like this either.

The boy still looked scared.

Boaz, after a moment of stress and confusion, found his solution.

He slowly walked forward. When he saw the young boy tense, Boaz dropped to his knees and showed the young boy his hands. After a short moment, the boy relaxed. Boaz slowly rose again and continued, eventually sitting down in front of the boy but at a distance.

He then put his forearms together and cupped his hands, as if he were giving the boy a bowl but holding it with both hands. He also looked into the boy's eyes

"Hello," the gesture said. This was the greeting he observed from the ceremony last night. The villagers did this to other villagers.

The young boy put his large nest aside and did the same to Boaz, knowing this was the greeting of his people. "Hello," the gesture said back.

Boaz then picked a flower he saw to his right—small and purple—and laid it in his hands. He put his arms like he did for 'hello', but hung his head and lifted his hands to the boy. He observed last night that, after a heated disagreement, they would give each other a flower in the same way they said 'hello'. "Peace," the gesture said.

The young boy, understanding and acknowledging this greeting, received the flower and put it in his nest. He then did the same to Boaz. "Peace," he agreed.

Boaz looked at the flower, seeing how it was a yellow flower, and took it from the boy. He looked at the boy and smiled.

The boy smiled back and giggled with so much uncontained joy he didn't know how to release it.

Boaz then handed the young boy his large nest. A wave of realization washed over the young boy's face, and he went running to get some leaves by the village fire. Boaz made his stealthy and speedy exit from the village, knowing he had been there long enough. He disappeared into the forest, flower in hand, with a smile wider than he knew he could smile.

He had just made a friend without saying a word.

He laughed and sighed with relief.

This was the life he wanted.

"So, how do you want to do this?" Laban asked.

Nehemiah replied, "I'll throw you, you contain him, then we'll heal him."

Nehemiah and Laban had sighted a Hailer making his approach to a house. Normally, they wouldn't bother, knowing Hailers and Gollums had their own business to attend to.

Nehemiah and Laban, however, could see something different.

They saw an aura of red come from this Hailer.

This Hailer had used Raktaar's sludge, and he had it inside him still.

"Ready?" Nehemiah asked.

"Yeah. I'll remember to let them breathe this time," Laban replied.

Nehemiah chuckled, looked at the approaching Hailer, and launched Laban, who shaped himself into something that could fly with speed.

Laban banked to align with the Hailer, then–

Contact.

The Hailer was swallowed by Laban, who changed into a form that allowed for a slower flight. He glided back down to Nehemiah. When he was within Nehemiah's arm reach, he kept the Hailer surrounded but let Nehemiah access the Hailer's chest, holding on to Nehemiah by his right shoulder.

Then Nehemiah sucked the black dust out of the Hailer and burned it in his chest.

While Nehemiah did this, Laban lowered the Hailer to the ground and gently choked the Hailer out. He then let the Hailer rest on the ground.

Nehemiah had finished burning the black dust, so Laban attached himself to Nehemiah's right shoulder and formed into a right arm, looking like a white mirror of Nehemiah's left arm.

Nehemiah walked gently through the town, knowing there would be many more Hailers and Gollums and normal humans that needed healing from his old brother's sludge.

Until then, they enjoyed the quiet.

Laban had a thought. "What do you want to do after all of this?"

Nehemiah was confused. "After what?"

Laban explained. "Well . . . there's only so much healing to do. Once the sludge is gone, it's gone. There'll be a point where we don't need to do this anymore. What do you want to do then?"

Nehemiah exhaled, having asked himself that question already and wondering the same. He told Laban his answer. "How would you feel if we cared for a forest? A mighty oak forest."

"You want to look after a forest?" Laban wasn't expecting that response.

"I do." At this, Nehemiah smiled. He then grew sad. "I'm a wooden giant that can either walk around with one arm or fly around as a flower. You're a . . . I'm not sure what to call you good Laban." He exhaled again. "Neither of us can live the lives of those down there"–he motioned to the houses by his feet. "We're not normal, and we don't fit in anywhere."

Laban agreed. "Yeah . . . we're like Boaz and Ariel but . . . "

A silence was held between them. Nehemiah was brought back to his memories of Ariel and Boaz, recalling how they both couldn't be detected by Project Solace anymore.

Next to their disappearance and the removal of resources over the past few days, they were cleared as deceased. A faked death brought a new life.

Nehemiah then smiled, remembering his future idea. "How great would it be then to care and sustain an epic oak forest. Small animals roaming about. So many living things. Our little project, good Laban."

"Yeah . . . that could be alright." His tone was unconvincing.

"You could fly really high and really far," Nehemiah whispered. "It will only be us. It can be our nature home."

Laban laughed in agreement. "I get to fly? All the time?! Easy!"

Nehemiah joined in his laughter.

He then caught sight of a Gollum with a red aura around it not far from them.

Laban launched himself from Nehemiah, surrounded the Gollum, let Nehemiah remove the black dust and burn it while he choked the Gollum, then they both moved on.

They kept walking. Then healed a Hailer. Then walked again. Then healed another Hailer. Then walked again. Then healed a Gollum.

This was their life for now.

This was what Nehemiah knew he needed to do. His life after Raktaar wasn't as appeasing as the others, but after this there would be nothing left of his old brother, save the black bones that were buried under a tree.

After this, he would enjoy a whole space to himself to be himself and delight in the thing he essentially was: nature.

When he did this, he would be joined by a youthful friend of wild possibilities: his friend Laban.

They would be happy. They would smile. They would feel peace.

They would know that it was all over, and they would know that they had won.

www.ingramcontent.com/pod-product-compliance
Lightning Source LLC
Chambersburg PA
CBHW070222030726
47505CB00006B/1776